CW01337156

THE WOLF HE FEEDS

ALSO BY BRANDON HUGHES

The Hero Rule

Barclay Griffith Book 1

The 4th Prisoner

Barclay Griffith Book 2

The Red Room: A Dark Web Thriller

THE WOLF HE FEEDS

BARCLAY GRIFFITH
BOOK 3

BRANDON HUGHES

TENSION
BOOKS

TENSION
BOOKS

Copyright © 2025 by Brandon Hughes

All rights reserved.

No part of this book may be reproduced in any form or by any electronic or mechanical means, including information storage and retrieval systems, without written permission from the author, except for the use of brief quotations in a book review.

For my sister Morgan

Nobody on this earth is perfect. Everybody has their flaws; everybody has their dark secrets and vices.

JUICE WRLD

A Cherokee Indian chief was teaching his grandson about life.

"A fight is going on inside me," he told the young boy. "It's a terrible fight between two wolves. The Dark one is evil - he is anger, envy, sorrow, regret, greed, arrogance, self-pity, guilt, resentment, inferiority, lies, false pride, superiority, and ego."

The chief continued, "The Light Wolf is good - he is joy, peace, love, hope, serenity, humility, kindness, benevolence, empathy, generosity, truth, compassion, and faith. The same fight is going on inside you, grandson...and inside of every other person on the face of this earth."

The grandson pondered this for a moment and then asked, "Grandfather, which wolf will win?"

The old Cherokee replied, "The one you feed."

THE TALE OF TWO WOLVES - A
CHEROKEE PROVERB

ONE

The house was shrouded in near-total darkness. There were no exterior lights because the homeowner was not concerned with security, and the windows were black as pitch because the home's lone occupant had long since gone to bed.

It was dark. The moon's phase was a slim fingernail amid the heavy cloud cover. This was not a part of my plan as I hadn't even considered such a thing; I chalked it up to beginner's luck. Initially, I considered it divine intervention, but that somehow felt...dangerous. I'm not an overtly religious person, but I wasn't about to jab my finger in God's eye...assuming there was a God.

It was almost 1:00 AM, and traffic on this particular county road was non-existent. That *was* by design. I couldn't very well execute my plan—rudimentary as it may be—with traffic to worry about. In fact, I had chosen this house and this victim almost entirely because of the home's secluded location. Nestled amid mature pines and hardwoods on a seldom-used road, it was the perfect location.

When devising my plan, the first task was to identify a victim.

In addition to privacy, my ideal victim would be someone I could control. I knocked on several doors and scouted three potential targets before settling on Jed Burlington.

The second task was to scout the place out. In the days of video doorbells and easy-to-install surveillance cameras, it was imperative I choose a house without such accouterments.

A few weeks ago, I knocked on Jed's door under the guise of a lost dog—mine, not his.

"I live a mile or so from here," I had told the man, who I put somewhere in his upper sixties, "and during the recent thunderstorm, my dog got spooked and ran away. I haven't had him long —picked him up from a shelter, actually—and I was worried the poor thing wouldn't be able to find his way back to his new home." The man told me he hadn't seen any stray dogs as of late but that he would keep an eye out. I gave him a fake phone number, knowing he would never call.

I took full advantage of this encounter. The first thing I noticed was the absence of a video doorbell, which was promising. I then asked permission to walk around his property to look for my dog so I could ensure there were no exterior cameras. I didn't expect any, but I couldn't take the chance. Not with what I was planning.

The gentleman seemed to buy my story but asked about my car. Or rather, the absence of a car. I told him that I was on foot because I was making my way through the woods, and, after all, it wasn't that far. It was Alabama in mid-April, and the weather was beginning to warm, so getting in some exercise on a nice day was another excuse. He seemed to like that answer as we spoke about the weather for the next three minutes, as old folks are wont to do.

I watched the house over the next few weeks, primarily at night, observing any patterns. No one ever visited the small, dingy house that had an equally grimy detached garage, and the last light was always extinguished by 10:30 PM, but sometimes earlier than that. In the more than a dozen trips I'd made, I hadn't seen him leave, nor had I seen him take in a visitor. I had no clue if the man still worked, and, quite frankly, it didn't seem all that important to what I was planning other than knowing that past a particular hour, he was going to be home. Alone.

I leaned against a tall, skinny pine as I gathered myself and mentally ran through my plan one more time. The plan itself was simple: get in, kill the man, and get out.

———

I'M NOT A BAD PERSON. I recycle, I've never eaten the last slice of pizza, I call my mother once a week. I'm a regular guy—a co-worker, a neighbor, someone who stands next to you in line at the grocery store.

No, I'm no monster. I just wanted to commit a murder.

TWO

The thought of committing a random murder and being the only person who truly knew what happened always stuck with me. It was the biggest possible secret I could imagine. I believed there would be power in that.

I remember the first time the idea crept into my mind. It was fleeting, dismissed as quickly as it came. But it lingered, growing roots deep within my psyche. The notion of taking a life and holding that dark knowledge alone became intoxicating. It was a perverse fantasy that set me apart from everyone else, granting me a unique and untouchable superiority.

The reality was even more powerful than I had imagined. From the moment I began planning, I felt I crossed a line. I felt a surge of control over my world that I had never experienced before. This dark knowledge made me feel invincible, a master of my own fate and a silent puppet master of those around me. In their ignorance, they were mere players on the stage I commanded from the shadows.

The duality of my hidden nature was both thrilling and empowering. I could navigate society with a mask of normalcy, exchanging pleasantries and maintaining relationships while harboring a sinister truth that could shatter everything. The secret became my personal weapon, feeding my ego and reinforcing my belief in my own cunning and invincibility. Every smile I gave, every handshake I offered, was a testament to my deceitful brilliance.

No one could suspect that beneath my calm exterior lay the mind of a murderer.

———

It was time.

I pushed off the pine tree, steeled myself, and walked through the woods fronting the house—the pine straw and other debris deadening the sound of my steps. The dark sky brightened with a flash of lightning, and the trees rustled with a cool, almost cold breeze. I checked the forecast half a dozen times in the last twenty-four hours, and there was never more than a fifteen percent chance of rain, but April showers and all, I guess. I pushed the weather to the back of my mind and moved forward.

I rounded to the rear of the house and took three deliberate steps up to the backdoor. I tried the knob with a gloved hand, and, as I hoped, it was unlocked. The lack of so much as an exterior light told me this man was of a time and place where locking your door wasn't routine; he did not worry about anyone with ill intentions finding their way to him.

He was wrong, and it would cost him his life.

The door to the old house stuck a little and made a dull wood-on-wood scraping noise as I shouldered it open. I paused, ready to run if the noise had awakened the homeowner. I waited a full minute and heard nothing but the hum of the refrigerator. I entered and pushed the door to, but not closed.

I paused again. Listened. Nothing.

I made my way slowly across the linoleum kitchen floor—through the smell of fried onions—onto the worn carpet of the small living room and into the hallway. I had four doors to choose from, two on the left and two on the right—the two closest to me were open while the furthest two were closed. I peered into the first room on my right and found a half-bathroom.

I eased down the hall, eyes on the closed door to the right, on the softest steps possible, left hand out in front of me and my trailing right hand lightly moving down the wall of the darkened space, feeling wallpaper seams as I moved. I grasped the cheap doorknob and twisted it slowly, not pushing on the door. When the knob was turned to its maximum, I pushed the hollow wood door open silently and without any resistance.

The bedroom was cool and bathed in a soft green glow, owed to the faux-wood digital bedside clock, which had to be at least forty years old if it were a day. The digital numerals read 1:18. The nighttime silence was sporadically punctured by the soft, uneven snores of the person fast asleep in the bed.

Lightning flashed, illuminating the room just enough to catch sight of myself in a wall mirror at my periphery, startling me. A low rumble of thunder followed the flash, maybe five seconds later, indicating the storm was only about a mile away.

I eased toward the right side of the bed, positioning myself between the bed and the adjoining bathroom, the door of which was partially open. I quietly shouldered off the backpack and laid it at my feet. The main compartment was already open because I did not want to risk the sound of the zipper waking my soon-to-be victim. I removed the 9 mm Glock 19 with an attached suppressor. Unlike in the movies, a silencer on this caliber handgun did not reduce the noise to a mere spit; however, it did quiet the noise enough not to be heard at the roadway or by the nearest neighbor. It would also not leave my ears ringing after firing a gun in such a small space.

I brought the gun up and took the stance I had practiced so often at the range. Feet shoulder-width apart, my left foot slightly out in front of my right. My right hand wrapped around the grip with my index finger on the trigger while my left hand cupped the base of the pistol's grip, adding stability. I fixed the lump in the tritium fiber optic night sight.

Another flash outside, another rumble—quicker this time.

I was sweating now, and a bead was snaking its way down from my hairline into my eyebrow and threatening to cascade into my right eye. I lowered the gun and wiped the sweat away with the sleeve of my right arm. I raised the gun again and edged forward until I was less than two feet away from where the man's head appeared to be. He lay on his right side facing away from me, covered up almost to the top of his shoulder. In the low luminescence, the head appeared bald, but I've seen him in the daylight, and he has hair. It's light and cut very short, but it's there.

I lowered the gun a few inches, staying in my shooting stance. I gathered myself and raised the pistol once more. I aimed for more than five seconds, willing myself to pull the trigger before lowering it slightly. I'm a little embarrassed to say that it proved more difficult than I imagined.

Coming to a decision, I raised the pistol, lined up the green dots that make up the sights, and, before I could think about it any longer, I pulled the trigger. The head rocked forward only slightly as the bullet entered just behind and above his left ear. The snoring stopped.

I had shot the gun with this same suppressor many times in preparation, but the bang was still much louder than anticipated. My hands began to shake a little as I lowered the gun while still maintaining my stance. It hit me what I had done—what I could not undo—and what I had to do next. I dropped the gun in the backpack and zipped it up, no longer having any reason to be quiet. I pulled a flashlight from my pocket and pointed it to my right, moving the beam in an arc, attempting to locate the ejected shell casing. I ran the light over the top of the dresser and along the carpeted floor where I expected the shell casing should be, but the dresser top was awash in mail, receipts, and other personal items. I didn't immediately see the casing on the floor, and as I stepped to the dresser for closer examination, I heard something. A door opened, and footsteps shuffled across the carpet.

I clicked off the flashlight, grabbed the backpack from the floor, and stepped into the bathroom, squeezing through the slim opening, not wanting to risk opening the door any wider. The footsteps grew only marginally louder on the carpet, and I knew this person was now in the bedroom. I slowly—so slowly—unzipped the backpack an inch at a time, and it sounded to my ears like a chainsaw in the quiet house. When I believed the opening was large enough, I slipped the handgun out and brought it up beside my face as I peered out of the bathroom and onto the bed where my victim lay. A figure eased over to the side of the bed and toward the top.

"Dad?" I heard a man say in a not-particularly-deep voice. "Dad," the voice said again, leaning over the lump in the bed. He straightened as another flash of lightning illuminated the room. His attention went to the standing mirror, which sat directly across the room from the bathroom door, and, for an ephemeral moment, we made eye contact.

He whirled around, perhaps questioning his own vision, and before he had time to reconcile what he had seen, I pulled the trigger once, and he went down.

I came to this place with a plan to commit a solitary murder, but now I have killed twice. I stood there in the bathroom's doorway, thinking. Wondering, first, where the hell this person had come from and, second, how this was going to impact my plan.

Suddenly, a third involuntary thought entered my mind: I had just murdered two people...and I liked it.

THREE

"Hey, Rita."

Deputy Hunter Stanton of the Towne County Sheriff's Office was on his dinner break, which he usually took around midnight, depending on his workload. Tonight's shift had been particularly busy, especially for a Wednesday, so it was after 12:30 AM when he stopped at Walter's Gas and Grub for his customary Conecuh sausage dog, onion rings, and Monster energy drink.

Walter's is located at an interstate exit and is the last diesel fuel for seventy-seven miles, so it stayed open twenty-four hours. It was warm inside and smelled of coffee and fry grease that needed changing.

"Hey, Hunter," said Rita Glisson, the overnight clerk.

Stanton is average height and weight, but he has thick arms and a barrel chest owed to the Kevlar under his tan uniform shirt. His copper-colored hair is shaved close on the sides and longer on the top, swept back off his head with hair product. Rita appreciates the deputy stopping in every night, both for security and personal reasons.

Stanton figures Rita for a couple of years younger than him—maybe twenty-three—unsure why he doesn't ask. She stands nearly his height, perhaps just an inch shorter, with black hair that hits at the middle of her back. Her light brown eyes, vibrant and expressive, combine with her ski slope nose to add a unique charm to her face. She wears too much eye makeup—clumps of mascara clinging stubbornly to her long eyelashes—yet it only enhances her spirited presence. As usual, he flirts with her, and she with him when their discussion turns to a paper she has due in her criminal justice class at the online university where she is enrolled. She aspires to have a career in law enforcement, preferably working with children.

Rita said, "My professor wants us to write about systemic racism in the criminal justice system and steps we can take to end it." She is sitting across the table from Stanton, leaning on her elbows and resting her chin in her hands.

"Buncha liberal bullshit, Rita. I hope you realize that."

She shrugged, not so sure it was bullshit but also not wanting to debate it. She knows where Stanton's politics lie, and though not too different from hers, they are different enough not to discuss.

"Gotta do what the prof asks," she says simply.

"I bet he tells you his pronouns."

"Oh, come on, Hunter. He does not." Her deep drawl becomes more pronounced when she's surly.

Stanton shrugged, unconvinced, as he pushed the last bite of his sausage dog into his mouth.

She makes a face but lets it pass before saying, "You're late tonight. Been busy?"

"Yeah," he said after swallowing his food. He sits back in the plastic booth and takes a long drink from his tall can of Monster. He burps and says, "Had some peckerwood standing in the middle of the road buck naked playing traffic cop over on Fourteen. Got tied up with that one for a minute. Gotta be drugs or some such."

"Maybe he's crazy, Hunter. Maybe he just needs some help."

"Ah, Jesus, Rita. That school of yours is really doing a number on you."

"What? Mental health is a real important issue, particularly in the criminal justice system. I've read articles about it."

"Articles given to you by that teacher of yours?" He gave her a look like his point was an obvious one.

"That's enough, Hunter. This is something I have to do to get somewhere in life." She looked around the small truck stop and said, "To get outta here." He took in the truck stop's interior as he dragged his onion rings through ketchup. It was her turn to lean back in her seat. She liked him, but he could be a lot sometimes.

"I hate when these liberal teachers try to teach about law enforcement and the criminal justice system, about how we're supposed to do our job, when they've never been in our shoes for so much as a minute. Let them strap on a gun and ride around one night. Let 'em make traffic stops by themselves or go to a DV call. They'd change their tune real quick." He inhaled through his nose and then said, "It really pisses me off," before going back to eating.

"I know it does, baby," she said as she reached over and placed her hand on his. That being the first time she called him *baby* and also the first time she touched his hand, he flicked his eyes up from his bowed head and smiled as he continued chewing.

"Just promise me something, Rita."

"Anything, baby."

He smiled that scamp's smile. "Don't forget about me when you graduate and get a good-paying job."

"Oh, stop it," she said just as a two-toned electronic bell signaled a customer.

Deputy Stanton cleaned off his table and stood over the trash can as he finished off his Monster drink and dropped it in. He burped again and called out, "Later, babe," with a wave as he walked past the counter.

"Wait," she called out as she finished the transaction.

Stanton stopped at the door and opened it for the customer, who was walking out with two Red Bulls and a Payday candy bar; the customer and deputy nodded at one another. Rita walked out from behind the counter and placed a warm fried pie wrapped in cling wrap in his hand.

He leaned in, kissed her on the cheek, and winked as he backed out the glass door. She watched him as he got into his brown Tahoe and threw a hand out the window as he left the parking lot.

FOUR

Deputy Stanton turned left onto the two-lane county road, traveling away from the interstate, and was getting comfortable in his seat as he accelerated. He unwrapped the warm pie and bit into it; the gooey middle dripped down his chin. Peach—his favorite. He looked around for a napkin, finding one in the console. When he looked up, he saw a pair of headlights crest a slight hill a couple hundred yards away.

As the vehicle drew closer, he noticed it begin to drift into his lane. He backed off the gas, expecting the person to correct, but the other driver remained oblivious.

"Shit!" Stanton shouted as he swerved onto the unpaved shoulder just as the other driver, illuminated now in the deputy's headlights, lifted his head up. The oncoming vehicle—a red Ford pickup truck—swerved back into its lane.

Stanton skidded to a stop and watched in his side mirror as the truck flashed brake lights before continuing on. Spitting a curse through gritted teeth, he spun the wheel and pressed the gas pedal to the floor, throwing up gravel in his wake. When the rear tires gained purchase on the pavement, the big SUV leaped forward, and Stanton was in pursuit. When he got the car in sight, he hit his blue lights and kept the gas pedal floored, the sound of the Tahoe's big engine filling the cab.

After maybe ten seconds, he saw the speeder's brake lights brighten, and the truck pulled into Walter's parking lot. Stanton closed the distance and pulled into the Gas and Grub with lights but no siren and came to a stop a few feet behind the older model red Ford. He called in the stop to dispatch and communicated the vehicle description and tag number. Not waiting for the dispatcher to respond, he rocked himself out of the SUV and carefully approached the driver's side of the vehicle, running his right hand down the length of the pickup and eyeing the bed of the truck for any contraband.

"Evening," he began as he came to the open driver's side window. Just then, he noticed Rita walking outside the gas station and threw her a smirk and wink. Smiling to himself, he returned his focus to the driver, and that's when he saw the flash of a gun.

The gun fired three times, but Stanton only heard the first shot because, after that, he was as good as dead.

———

RITA WAS MOPPING the floor behind the food counter when the blue lights caught her attention. She smiled and leaned the mop against the counter. She had never seen Hunter in action before and half walked, half skipped to the door to watch. She opened the door and straddled the threshold when Stanton noticed her and gave a wink and that smile again. She was about to wave, and that's when her world exploded.

Falling to the ground and landing on her left hip, she scrambled behind a concrete trash can and made herself as flat as possible. She was on the passenger side of the truck, so all she could see were the soles of Deputy Hunter Stanton's black boots as he lay sprawled spread eagle on his back. When the gunshots stopped— she registered three—she saw a pair of boots step down from the truck, the driver bend over, and appear to snatch something off Stanton's chest before getting back into the vehicle and driving off in what she would later describe to police as a casual manner.

In the din of silence that followed, the white noise of the nearby interstate was present, as was the squawk of Stanton's police radio, both on his person and coming from the open door of his brown cruiser. She pushed herself off the ground on unsteady arms and legs and bolted for the fallen police officer. She crashed into him as if her legs could carry her no further. She immediately saw the blood. She then noticed the lower half of his face was all but gone.

"Oh, baby, oh, baby, oh, baby," she repeated, holding her shaking hands on either side of his head but not touching him as if she didn't know quite where to place them. She had been a life-guard at the municipal swimming pool during high school, so she knew how to check his pulse. It was faint, but it was there.

She then noticed the radio mic clipped to his right shoulder. After failing to unclip it with shaking hands, she pressed the button on the side of the mic, leaned down within an inch of the black plastic square, and said, "P...p...please help me. Hu...Hu... Hunter's been shot...he's down...officer down!" Her voice, weak at first, grew in strength and belied the tears streaming down her face.

A voice chirped back through the radio: "Please repeat. Who is this, and where are you?"

"This is Rita at Walter's by the interstate. Hunter Stanton just got shot by someone in a red pickup truck. Send an ambulance... Please!"

Despite being located at the northwestern edge of the county, the first law enforcement arrived in seven minutes, and by twelve minutes, a dozen police units and two ambulances had descended on the truck stop, red and blue LED lights ricocheting off the nearby woods and the glass and steel gas station.

FIVE

Towne County District Attorney Barclay Griffith's phone rang at 1:42 AM.

The ringing first materialized as a sound in a dream he was having, but by the third ring, he was yanked from a deep sleep as if pulled by the sharp tug of a rope. His heart hammering, he realized it was his cell phone. He grabbed it off the nightstand and, seeing the caller ID, knew it wasn't good.

"Hey, Chief, what's happened?" he asked with no evidence of sleep in his voice. He could hear a siren wailing in the background and the roar of the vehicle's engine; the police chief was driving somewhere with great urgency.

"I'm headed to Walter's Gas and Grub. One of Sally's deputies was shot tonight on a traffic stop—Hunter Stanton. He's still alive, but barely. I told her I would call you—one less thing for her to worry about."

Barclay had two feet on the floor before Towne Police Chief Adam Greenhaw was done talking. "I'm on my way."

The district attorney arrived just as Chief Greenhaw was exiting his vehicle. Barclay looked like he had just stepped out of the casual section of a men's outdoor fashion magazine. He wore a plaid button-down, dark-washed jeans, and Wellington boots. The chief marched ahead wearing khakis, a navy blue TPD fleece zipped all the way up, and silver bedhead. Barclay jogged to catch up, wanting to talk before they met the sheriff, who was buzzing about the scene, yelling about setting the perimeter and collecting evidence.

Sally Ramos—a sturdy woman whose Cuban heritage showed in her olive skin, dark hair, and vibrant eyes—was appointed sheriff just over a year ago when her predecessor was removed from office for improprieties involving missing evidence and inmate safety. It had not been easy, but she had thus far succeeded in rebuilding the reputation of the sheriff's office. As a woman in a leadership position in a male-dominated field, she commanded the respect of her peers by the way she went about her job. In spite of all of that, she had been around long enough in her eighteen-year career to know that she would ultimately be judged on how she handled one of her own being seriously wounded in the line of duty.

After a brief discussion, Barclay and the chief took Ramos aside. Wearing her uniform and sidearm, Ramos looked the most official of the three, which didn't surprise either man.

Suggesting the police department be the investigating agency, Greenhaw said, "Sally, you don't need to be investigating one of your own being shot. If he dies, this becomes a capital case, and the death penalty is in play. You don't want to give the shooter any opportunity to say there was anything done improperly."

"Adam, you know I do everything by the book."

"Of course you do, Sheriff," Barclay interjected, drawing Ramos' attention. "Everyone knows that, but if this guy gets the death penalty, you don't need some Ivy League lawyer from New York or Boston or wherever coming down here twenty years from now trying to free him. Because at that point, they don't care he killed a cop; they just want to free someone from death row. And the fact that you investigated the case just gives them a toe hold... something to argue."

Sheriff Ramos weighed all of this. She knew they were right. "Okay," she said. "You take the lead, but I'm going to be there the whole way."

Greenhaw: "Of course, Sally. This is the right call."

She nodded. "But first, I'm going to interview Rita Glisson." Seeing both the chief and the DA about to object, she said, "That isn't up for debate. The scene is fresh. She's our only witness. I talk to her, then I step aside."

Chief Greenhaw looked at Barclay, who nodded. The chief said, "Alright," but his tone said he wasn't so sure.

———

ASHEN-FACED AND TREMBLING, Rita sat in a booth across from Towne County Sheriff Sally Ramos and Towne Police Chief Adam Greenhaw. District Attorney Barclay Griffith had grabbed a chair and pulled it to the end of the table, where he sat with his arms crossed, listening intently.

Rita, growing agitated, interrupted the questioning and asked, "How is he? Why won't y'all tell me anything?"

"Rita," said the sheriff, taking her hand. "I'm sorry, but you're not family, so until we are able to notify his parents, we can't tell you that." Rita opened her mouth to argue when Ramos said, "Rita, listen to me. I need you to help us find who did this. You're the only witness, so what you tell us could be very important." Rita nodded as she wiped at her eyes with a balled-up tissue.

Rita told what she saw.

Despite the DA, the DA's chief investigator, half a dozen investigators from the sheriff's office, and detectives from the PD now crowding around the table, she concentrated only on Ramos and Greenhaw seated in front of her. She told them that Stanton had been there earlier in the night for his regular dinner stop, and then he left. She skipped the contents of their conversation because she wasn't asked about it.

She told them Stanton hadn't been gone more than a few minutes when he pulled into the parking lot behind a red truck. "I was cleaning up and noticed the blue lights." She cast her eyes to the worn laminate tabletop, a little embarrassed. "I'd never seen him actually doing his job, you know, so I went outside to watch."

She was clearly upset, but she was holding it together, and Sally told her so. "Like a champ," the sheriff said.

"I went outside, and right before he gets to the truck's window, he looks at me, and he winks and gives me this smile." She pressed her lips together as a tear rolled down her cheek. "That's when I heard the first shot. Then another, then another. I went to the ground and tried to hide." Tears were coming more abundantly now, but her clinical speech betrayed none of it. No one dared to interrupt her.

"I saw the driver get out of his car, bend over Hunter and mess with his shirt, get back in his car, and drive off, calm as you please." She paused here, and, believing she was finished, the sheriff began to ask a question when Rita said, "After I was sure he was gone, I ran over to Hunter to check on him. That's when I called everything in." Now she was finished, and as if signaling so, she raised her eyes from the table and swiped a hand across her face, wiping away the tears.

Chief Greenhaw said, "That's great, Rita. Really good stuff. Did you get a good look at the driver?"

She shook her head. "I was on the ground. I only saw his boots as he stepped from the truck."

"You keep referring to the shooter as 'he,'" said Barclay, sitting back, arms crossed. "Why do you believe it was a man?"

Rita faced the DA and said, "I guess I just assumed...plus the boots, you know."

Barclay nodded as he leaned forward, elbows on his knees. He rubbed his hands together and asked, "What kind of boots were they?" Seeing the look on Rita's face, he said, "Were they cowboy boots, work boots, duck boots..."

Nodding her understanding, Rita said, "Hunting boots, I think. They were dark brown and had a buckle on them. I recognized them because my daddy has a pair like them that he hunts in." She looked up at the water-stained drop ceiling as she seemed to be trying to grab something in her mind. After a long moment, she said, "Russell Moccasin, I believe." She looked at Barclay and said, "That's the brand. Pretty sure they're kind of expensive." She smiled, "When my daddy retired from the box plant, the owner bought them for him as a retirement gift. He was so excited." A beat later, she shook her head. "I'm sorry. I don't know why I said that."

"You're doing just fine, Rita," Ramos interjected.

A male voice said, "Were they dirty?" Seeing Rita's confusion, Ramos said, "I think he means the boots. Were they dirty?"

It took Rita a beat to locate the source of the question. She then looked back at the tabletop before closing her eyes, running it through her mind, thinking. She said, "Actually, no. They were clean. Now that I think about it, I remember my mind going to that because my daddy's stay pretty dirty. Like caked with mud." She looked to her left at Barclay, then to Ramos and Greenhaw across from her. "Does that help?"

Ramos reached and placed her hands over both of Rita's, which were in a ball on the table. "Everything you're telling us helps. I assure you. Now, is there anything else, anything at all, no matter how small or insignificant, that you can think of?"

Rita thought about that, concentrating on the middle of the

table for about a minute before shaking her head. "Not right now. Like I said, I didn't see much. I just..." And she began to cry.

"It's okay, Rita. You did great," said Ramos, flicking a look to Greenhaw, who nodded back.

Chief Greenhaw arranged for one of his officers to drive Rita home, and then he, Ramos, and Barclay huddled at the back of the store.

"Where do we stand with the investigation?" asked Barclay.

"We were able to get the truck's tag number from dispatch," said Ramos. "The tag came back to a guy by the name of Ross Burlington—white male, twenty-eight, with an address in Eufaula. Captain Story called Eufaula PD to have them ride by the address. See what they could find out."

"What about video?" Barclay asked.

Sheriff Ramos said, "Remember Rita saying she saw the shooter mess with Stanton's shirt? He snatched his body camera."

"What about in-car?"

Ramos shook her head. "Sheriff Gillespie bought a bunch of liquidation stock three years ago, and it was all crap. I've been working on replacing all the busted units, but the budget's tight... Stanton's car hadn't been upgraded." She cursed silently with a snap of her head.

"Hey, Sally, none of that, alright," said Chief Greenhaw. "Gillespie left you a pile of shit in more ways than I can count. Nothing you could have done."

"Yeah? Try telling that to Hunter's parents."

"Chief's right," said Barclay. "Now's not the time. We've got to focus on finding this motherfucker." To Greenhaw: "Any cameras on the building?"

"Two, but just eyeballing their locations, it looks like they only cover the pumps for drive-offs. We have a store manager on the way to give us access to the video, but I don't believe the area of the shooting is going to be covered."

A mustachioed Captain Ricky Story of the Towne police department approached the trio with a wad of tobacco in his cheek. He spit in a mop bucket holding dirty water and said, "Excuse me, sir, but I just heard back from Eufaula PD. They went to Burlington's house, and no one was home. One of their cops knows a sister, though, and paid her a visit. She told them he was up here visiting their father, Jed Burlington." That energized the group. "Apparently, her father was a real sonofabitch. He was estranged from them but recently reached out. She didn't want anything to do with him, but her brother decided to give his old man a chance. He's been staying there since Monday."

"What do we know about the father?" asked Ramos.

"Lives two minutes from here on twenty-nine," Story replied.

"That fits," said Ramos. "Rita said Hunter turned left out of here, which would put Burlington driving toward the gas station headlong into Hunter. It's how you would get here from twenty-nine." Ramos looked at a wall of stacked twelve-packs of Coke next to a fountain drink machine as if she could see through it into the parking lot. She said, "That's the only way a traffic stop in the parking lot here makes any sense, given how the vehicles were positioned."

Captain Story said, "Do we know which direction the truck went when it drove off? The interstate is right there, so he could have jumped on, and, hell, he could be almost to Atlanta by now. I know I wouldn't hang around if I'd just shot a cop."

Greenhaw shook his head. "Rita thought maybe left, but couldn't be certain on that."

"Well, it's something," said Ramos. "I'll send a couple of units to ride by their old man's place; see what they can determine from the road."

Barclay said, "Better let the PD take it from here, Sheriff."

Sally Ramos crossed her arms and seemed to weigh a response

before giving a curt nod. She locked eyes with Greenhaw, the silent message sent and received.

Barclay said, "After the ride by, have someone sit on the house."

"Good idea," said Greenhaw before he walked off.

"Chief," Barclay called after him before he made it to the exit. "Call in Tina Crump. We're going to need her ASAP."

"But she's with the sheriff's office now. I thought—"

Barclay nodded and said, "I know, but she's the best there is around here with cell phones and computers, maybe even the best in the state. If it has an on/off switch or any type of memory, she can coax a story out of it. We need her." He shrugged. "And fuck 'em if someone wants to make a big deal about it. We'll deal with that later." Greenhaw nodded and walked outside.

To Captain Story, Barclay said, "Get with the sister and get Burlington's cell number and his service provider if she knows it." Story nodded and walked off, lifting the phone to his ear.

To Ramos, Barclay said, "I'll get with a judge and get a search warrant for his cell. We can reach out to the service provider and get real-time pings on his location. Go ahead and assemble the SWAT team and get the Marshall's task force here."

"You sure, Barclay? About me being involved? Even making those calls—"

"Sally," Barclay said, giving her a look.

A smile tugged at one corner of her mouth. "Right, fuck 'em."

Barclay gave her a wink and walked toward the exit.

Sheriff Sally Ramos steeled herself. This was her first encounter with an officer shot in the line of duty in her extensive law enforcement career. It was unlike anything she had ever investigated from an emotional and mental point of view. She was grateful for the help, even if she wouldn't say that out loud.

"Hey, Sheriff." Barclay's raised voice from across the store brought her back. She locked eyes with the DA, who said, "We're going to get this guy. Believe that."

SIX

Twenty minutes later, Tina Crump was inside the gas station turned command center dressed casually in dark jeans, a gray v-neck sweater, and fashion sneakers. Her longish blonde hair was up in her typical messy twist, and she carried a silver MacBook Pro under her right arm.

Things were progressing...

Members of the SWAT team and the Marshall's task force were trickling onto the site, the rear of the gas station serving as the staging ground for any potential assault. The sheriff from the neighboring county to the west had also shown up with four deputies along with a number of agents and supervisors from the State Bureau of Investigations (SBI) ready to assist however they were needed.

Given the vast acreage of dense woodlands, Ramos spoke to a captain with the SBI about the possibility of deploying a helicopter equipped with FLIR (Forward-Looking Infrared) technology. This advanced equipment would enable them to conduct thermographic imaging and detect heat sources from the air, greatly aiding their search efforts for a cop shooter on the run. The captain told her it was already handled, and a pilot was on standby, ready to lift off.

Barclay introduced Tina Crump to those who didn't know her, and he told her they were still waiting on the search warrant from Judge Arnett. Six minutes later, Barclay's phone rang. After the brief conversation, he said, "Paper's in hand. Let's do this."

While waiting for Crump and the warrant, they received word that Jed Burlington's house had a single light on inside. However, they saw no movement or a red truck at the property. A TPD patrol officer reported that there appeared to be a detached garage at the rear of the house, and they reasoned the truck could be stashed inside.

Now, with the judge's signature on the warrant, Tina went to work. She called her contact at Verizon, the service provider for Burlington's cell phone. After explaining the urgency of her phone call at such an ungodly hour, she was granted access to his current location.

Though not an exact GPS location, it got them close enough for everyone to believe the shooter, or at least his cell phone, was at his father's house.

SWAT formed a plan.

———

LAW ENFORCEMENT NEEDED to know if the red truck was in the garage. They reviewed a satellite image of the property—which encompassed a decent-sized wooded lot—and determined an approach could be made while remaining out of sight from the main house.

It took several minutes, but an officer made it to the garage and confirmed that a red Ford pickup truck was inside. The decision was made to attempt to contact Burlington. The SWAT team moved in and set up a perimeter.

Phone calls to the father's house phone and the suspect's cell phone went unanswered. After numerous calls to each line and waiting fifteen minutes for any type of response, they texted the cell phone. After eight minutes, a return text message was received. At about the same time, a figure appeared in a window. The sheer curtain was pulled aside, only slightly, before it was released and fell back to its original closed position.

The text message from Ross Burlington was two words: *I'm sorry.*

If police were looking for proof that this man was their shooter, it appeared they had it. They texted back, asking for him to come outside, backward, and with hands in the air. After not getting a response, they sent another message saying this was his last opportunity to give up before they came in for him. Still not receiving a response, the decision was made to make entry.

Typical protocol would have been to deploy flash-bang grenades upon breaching the door, but they were dealing with someone who had little left to lose, so they wanted to take all possible steps to ensure safe entry into the house. SWAT opted to fire off three canisters of tear gas through the same picture window the figure had appeared in minutes earlier and wait.

When the canisters exploded, one of the curtains caught fire, causing everyone to stand down. A Towne Fire Department ladder truck was on standby at the gas station and was called in along with an ambulance.

By the time the truck and ambulance arrived, the small fire had quickly transformed into a full-on blaze. As the firefighters worked unfurling hoses, hooking them to the truck's internal water supply, and manning the top-mounted water cannon, a single gunshot rang out over the din of the growing inferno. Instinctively, firefighters found cover behind their truck, and the SWAT team returned the gunshot with a barrage of firepower. Everyone then waited for a response that never came.

Ramos and Greenhaw spoke with the fire chief, and the decision was made to let the house burn. Fire Chief Jack Nolin squinted at the engulfed structure, his face slick with sweat, and said, "We'll keep the fire contained, but it's too dangerous for my team to go in there now. Not with a shooter inside." He then jutted his chin at the raging inferno in front of them, sparks and embers flying into the night sky, and said, "Probably nothing we can do to save the house, anyway. Not at this point."

"Be nice if the garage doesn't burn," said Greenhaw. "There may be some evidence in there, and we definitely want to save the truck."

"We won't let it burn." With that, Nolin began barking orders and waving his arms, pointing this way and that, and the firefighters went to work.

SEVEN

The phones of Ramos, Greenhaw, and Barclay Griffith were beginning to blow up with calls from media members as word of the shooting started to make its rounds. As the official head of the investigation, Chief Greenhaw arranged for a press conference offsite, and the three department heads stood before bright lights, a dozen cameras, and a cluster of microphones. One reporter, local newshound Wendy Wade of the ABC affiliate, was holding her cell phone broadcasting via Facebook Live.

Since it was a sheriff's deputy who was shot, it was agreed that Sheriff Ramos would make the opening remarks and then cede the press conference to the police chief to discuss the particulars.

Ramos, with her hair scraped back into a ponytail, was waiting for all of the reporters to signal they were ready for her to begin. Seeing nods all around, she opened her mouth to speak when Wendy Wade—a former Miss Something-or-other brunette who maintained her pageant presence—said, "Sheriff Ramos, what can you tell us about the events overnight? I understand one of your officers was shot."

That question drew daggers from her fellow reporters and a not-so-subtle eye-roll from both Barclay and Greenhaw.

Ramos set her lips in a terse line before speaking. "At approximately 1:42 this morning, Deputy Hunter Stanton was shot during a traffic stop."

Wendy Wade opened her mouth to speak, and Ramos held up a finger and shook her head once. The sheriff may only have been five-two, but she had an outsized personality and could be commanding when she needed to be, which was almost always. She said, "Deputy Stanton was transported by helicopter to Grady Memorial Hospital in Atlanta. We are not going to provide an update on his status at this time. Through the course of the investigation, which is being headed by Towne Police Chief Adam Greenhaw, we developed a suspect whom we are currently working to take into custody. I want to thank the countless number of law enforcement officers and agencies who have assisted in what you can imagine has been a very difficult investigation given the nature of the crime.

"Now, we will take questions...*But*," she said over the cacophony of voices that erupted at once, "it is an active investigation, so we are limited on what we can say." She then pointed around Wendy Wade to a reporter she knew to be from the *Towne Tribune*.

The *Trib's* beat writer was a copper-colored redhead with vintage oversized eyeglasses. Her hair fell just below her shoulder blades and was cut straight across to match her bangs, giving her eyebrows ample clearance. She looked barely old enough to drive, but she had been a solid addition to the paper. She asked, "What can you tell us about the suspect?"

Ramos looked up to the taller, but not tall, police chief who stepped forward—his silver bed head covered now in a TPD baseball cap for the cameras. He spoke with the cool detachment of a veteran cop and said, "We are withholding the suspect's name for the time being. We identified this person as a suspect by the tag number Deputy Stanton called in upon making the traffic stop. We have been unable to confirm the identity of the vehicle's driver, so until then, we won't be releasing the name. That said, we are confident the person who shot Deputy Stanton is holed up in a local residence where we are currently staged. Out of an abundance of caution, however, residents are encouraged to stay in their homes and to call 911 if they see something or someone suspicious." Knowing it would have the most live viewers at this hour, he found Wendy Wade's cell phone and looked right at it, saying, "Under no circumstances should you answer your door for anyone you do not absolutely know."

The newspaper reporter followed up: "Is it true the residence is on fire, and if so, is the suspect inside?"

"Gunfire was exchanged between law enforcement and someone in the house. Subsequent to that gunfire, a fire started inside the house, yes. We had the fire department on standby, and they responded quickly. They are currently working to contain the blaze. We believe our suspect remains inside the home, and when it is safe to do so, we will go inside and search the premises for any casualties and survivors." Greenhaw took a deep breath, held both hands up, and said, "Now, folks, that really is all we have to report at this time. We need to get back to the scene, but we will update you as soon as we have more information."

The group of reporters seemed to accept that, but as the three officials turned away, one reporter shouted, "I have a question."

They all turned around, and with exasperation creeping into his voice, Greenhaw said, "Yes, Ms. Wade."

"Where did the shooting occur?"

"Walter's Gas and Grub by the interstate."

"Barclay," she yelled, "Do you plan to seek the death penalty in this case?"

Barclay stepped back to the bank of microphones. "Wendy..."

Barclay measured his words. "I will reiterate that no announcement has been made regarding Hunter Stanton's condition. That said, murdering a police officer is a capital offense, and folks need to know that if you come to Towne, Alabama, and kill a police officer, my office will seek the absolute highest form of punishment allowed under the law. Right now, that's the death penalty. If we get something more harsh than that, then that's what I will ask for."

None of the reporters knew how to react to that, but after a beat, Wendy Wade attempted to ask a follow-up question, and Greenhaw said, "We have to go. Thank you."

———

THE SKY WAS a royal purple as night evolved into day, and the hum of generators powering light stands echoed throughout the wooded property. Almost two hours after the fire started, firefighters prepared to enter the smoldering husk. Free from danger, the garage was accessed earlier after securing a search warrant, and the red Ford was towed to the police impound lot for examination.

It took a while, but firefighters emerged carrying two black body bags. They were placed on the ground and unzipped at the direction of the fire chief. The bodies were charred, blistered, split open in parts, and smelled—Barclay thought of a pork shoulder left too long on the grill.

"Both bodies were recovered in what appears to be the master bedroom," Fire Chief Nolin said, squatting over the bodies. "This one"—he pointed his radio's antenna at the body bag with a slash of red spray paint on the outside—"was laying in a bed while the other was found on the floor." He looked at one of the firefighters, who nodded confirmation.

"I don't suppose a cause of death jumps out at you," said Barclay.

Nolin stood up on popping knees. "Too difficult to say just by eyeballing it. There appears to be skeletal damage, but it will take an autopsy to determine what damage may have been caused by the fire and what damage may have been caused by something else."

"What about how the bodies appear?" asked Barclay. "Is there any significance that they both have their elbows and knees flexed and their fists clenched in front of their chests?"

Nolin shook his head. "No. That's referred to as a pugilistic attitude because of its similarity to a boxer's defensive stance, and it's pretty common in burn cases. Basically, the soft tissue burns away, and the exposed tissue and muscle dehydrates from the heat, causing the extremities to draw up and posture."

"Any preliminaries on the fire?" Greenhaw asked.

"Based solely on what I was told about how everything went down, I'm guessing when the tear gas canisters exploded in the house, they caught something on fire—most likely the curtains. Of course, we will have to wait for a full arson investigation to know for certain." He paused, then said, "But I expect that's going to be the conclusion."

A uniformed deputy approached and pulled up short when he glanced at the open body bags. He was staring at the charred remains as he said, "Sheriff, the coroner is at the tape. Wants to know if you're ready for her to retrieve the bodies." Sally Ramos looked between the chief and the district attorney. They weighed it out and agreed they could release the bodies from the scene.

"Tell the coroner the bodies will be brought to her," Ramos said to the uniform, who nodded—finally taking his eyes off the blackened corpses—before hustling out. To Nolin: "Can your guys take the bodies up there?" Nolin nodded first at Ramos and then to the firemen who had brought the bodies from the house. They bent over, zipped up the body bags, and carried them off.

EIGHT

The killer emerged from the bathroom and shined his flashlight on the man dead on the floor. *This was not good.* Granted, the killer had not watched the homeowner twenty-four hours a day, but he had watched him enough, he thought, to not only believe that a visitor was highly unlikely but that an overnight guest was a near impossibility. He'd been wrong.

The killer wandered back to the kitchen, thinking. He knew he had not seen another vehicle on the property, so he exited the backdoor and went to the garage. He shined his light through the window of a door on the side of the garage and saw two vehicles inside: the homeowner's older model black Dodge Ram 1500 single cab and an older model red Ford F-150 Supercab.

"Shit," the killer hissed.

He went back into the house and back to the bedroom. As he stood over the body on the bedroom floor, he recalled hearing the man call out, "Dad," when he walked into the bedroom. He had no idea the homeowner had children, but when he thought about it, what did he really know about his target outside of what he observed from a distance? He only knew enough to believe the man did not ordinarily receive visitors, so he felt the body would not be discovered for quite a while. This was an essential part of his plan because the more time he could put between himself and the murder, the better.

But someone would probably come looking for this other man, and if he told anyone where he was staying—and that was likely—someone could be at the house as early as today if no one could get a hold of him or if he missed an appointment or something.

That's when he got an idea.

He picked up the dead man, who was gangly but not particularly heavy, and hoisted him over his shoulder and carried him through the darkened house and to the garage, where he dumped him on the ground. He tried the door he'd just looked through and found it unlocked.

He entered the garage and first tried to walk around the front of the Dodge. Then, seeing it parked too close to the cabinetry, he walked around the rear of the truck and to the driver's side door of the Ford. Also unlocked.

The truck's dome light came on, and the killer leaned in and saw the keys in the cupholder. There wasn't enough room in the garage to do what he needed to do, so he shone his flashlight around the garage's interior until he saw the door opening mechanism. He approached the white square button and, reaching around a stack of coolers and a cardboard box, he pressed the button, opening the roll-up door and activating the garage's overhead light.

The killer backed the truck out of the garage and, leaving the truck running, retrieved the body by sliding his arms under the knees and behind the man's back and lifting. He placed the body onto the front passenger seat, and the body fell over, the head toward the driver's seat. The killer then closed the garage's roll-up door.

He jogged back inside the house, down the hall, and into the bedroom to retrieve his backpack before heading back outside to the running truck. His plan was to drive the truck to the gas station by the interstate and park it behind the building. That was his planned escape route, so he had previously scouted it looking for any cameras that may cover the roadway and saw none; he discovered that its only cameras monitored the front of the business.

Someone would see the pickup truck sooner rather than later and discover the dead man inside. He hoped the police wouldn't track the body back to the murder house or, at least, that it would take a while.

The killer was now driving, careful not to exceed the speed limit lest he get stopped with a dead body lying beside him, when he thought about possible identification. He glanced down at the body, and that was when he realized the man was wearing only boxer shorts and a white T-shirt.

You idiot, he thought as he stared at the body. No one is going to believe the dead man was driving in just his underwear and a T-shirt. He was considering turning around and going back to the house and dressing his dead passenger when he sensed more than he saw the car coming toward him. As he was staring at the body, he had drifted into the oncoming lane and was about to collide head-on with a vehicle when he swerved back into his lane at the last minute, reflexively tapping the brakes to maintain control of the truck.

He glanced back in his rearview mirror, relieved he didn't strike the car, when he noticed the car making an aggressive u-turn.

"Fuck me," he said aloud. The last thing he needed was a run-in with a hot-headed road rager.

Make that the second to last thing he needed, he thought, when he saw the blue LED light bar atop the car behind him explode into the inky night. "Fuck me," he said again, louder this time. There was no way he would outrun this cop—not in this truck.

He glanced at the backpack sitting beside him on the bench seat and made a decision.

NINE

The gas station was ahead on his right, so he pulled in, careful to stop out of camera view. He put the truck into park and kept his right hand on the wheel at the two o'clock position. Not taking his eye off the rearview mirror, he sneaked his left hand under his right arm and into the backpack, retrieving the gun from inside and laying it on his lap. He put his left hand on the wheel, slowly lowered his right hand, and grabbed the pistol, sliding his finger into the curve of the trigger. He did all of this without taking his eyes off the mirror and the cop behind him, who was now exiting the vehicle.

He watched the officer approach in his side mirror, and just before he got to the window, he noticed the officer looking into the bed of the truck. When the officer got to the driver-side window—which was already down—he said, "Evening," and then looked over the top of the vehicle. The officer smiled, winked, and was just bringing his eyes to the driver when the killer brought the gun up and fired.

———

THINKING QUICKLY, the killer stepped out of the truck, reached down, and snatched the black rectangular body camera from the middle of the cop's chest. He sat back in the truck, closed the door, put it in gear, and drove away. His mind was working at ten times speed, but no ideas came forward. He opted to drive back to the house and put the truck back into the garage. Getting the red pickup out of sight seemed to make the most sense.

Once at the house, he stopped in front of the closed garage door and stepped out of the truck. He grabbed the prone figure and dragged him across the bench seat, out the driver's door, and onto the ground. He then ran through the garage's side door, opened the roll-up door, and drove the truck inside. He then closed the garage door, ran out the side door, and dragged the man into the house and back into the bedroom as if he needed to keep an eye on both corpses at the same time.

He paced, and he thought.

Had the cop called in the tag number when he was stopped? He must have. Surely, that was standard procedure on traffic stops. If so, what did that mean for him? It would mean they'd have the truck owner's name, which would almost certainly lead them to this location at some point. Or would it? He assumed it would but allowed that it would take a while.

Then it hit him: *It was the dead man's car tag. It was the dead man's truck. It was the dead man they would be after—not him.* He relaxed a bit and tried to settle his nerves. There was still a way out; he just had to figure it out.

Sirens.

The killer ran to the picture window at the front of the house and peered out between the sheer curtains. He could hear sirens. Not close, but a lot of them. He saw nothing. Not so much as the hint of a stray red or blue light. He backed away from the window and thought. He knew he needed to move but now wasn't the time. Too many police; they'd be everywhere.

He considered where he had stashed his car and felt good about it. He was parked maybe a mile away and walked in on foot. He had planned to go out the same way once the murder was carried out. He decided it wouldn't be a good idea to get caught out on foot right now—no way to explain it. And it certainly wasn't a good time to be in a car in the area—he guessed they'd have roadblocks set up. Sure, they'd be looking for a red Ford truck, but they would stop and question everyone. As much as he didn't want to, he decided to wait.

The killer perused the old man's cabinets looking for coffee and found a large, quarter-full jar of Sanka. He made a face and pulled it down. He heated a mug of water in the filthy, food-stained microwave, which filled the kitchen with the smell of fish sticks and burnt popcorn when he ran it.

He passed the time by drinking terrible coffee with loads of sugar and non-dairy creamer and staring at the cop's body camera. It was heavier and more solid than it looked. He turned it over in his hands, trying to determine how he could access the storage and watch the video of him shooting that cop. He turned on the twenty-four-inch Insignia flatscreen sitting on the cluttered kitchen counter and found the local television stations filming live near the scene. It was chaos where the reporters were stationed, and he almost convinced himself there was no getting away.

He choked down his second cup of instant coffee, as much out of boredom as anything, and figured he'd let enough time pass for it to be as safe to leave as it would get. He'd left his telephone at home, what with all the cell tracking capability nowadays, so he was growing excruciatingly bored and was forced to keep up with the time via an old cuckoo clock (that no longer cuckooed) in the den, unsure of the chipped and worn wooden clock's accuracy. He was trying to balance leaving too early and risking getting caught leaving the area with staying too long and risking getting caught in the house...which is exactly what happened.

TEN

The killer was going through the compact house, wiping down anywhere he thought he may have touched to erase his fingerprints, DNA, and any evidence that he was ever there, when he heard a ringing telephone—the house phone. He eyed the cuckoo clock and knew something was wrong. No one received calls this time of the night—make that morning—especially not this guy.

After a few seconds of silence, the phone rang again and again he did not answer. He stood frozen as the phone's incessant ringing echoed through the quiet house, each ring causing his heart to pound faster. Finally, after what felt like an eternity, the ringing stopped. This time, after the phone quit ringing, he heard the electronic ringtone of a cell phone that eventually quit ringing. After about a minute, the phone rang again, and the killer tracked it to the rear bedroom across the hall from the one containing the bodies. It was a flip phone plugged into its charger. He unplugged it and carried it to the front of the house. He stared at the phone for what seemed like hours, waiting for it to ring again, but it did not. He guessed it was the police, given the fact that both phones rang in such proximity to one another.

Had they given up? Moved on? As he held the phone and stared at the caller ID, a text message pinged. He flipped it open and read it.

It *was* the police.

How should he handle this? The killer thought back through what he knew, particularly the conclusion he came to about all the information they had coming back to the owner of the pickup truck. Then, as if through divine circumstances, he had his answer. He considered it twice, then a third time, and then thumbed out a text message. *I'm sorry.*

He made his way to the front window and stared out. There were police everywhere out front now. He lifted the phone's tiny screen to his face and considered the message one last time, then sent it. He received a text message response almost immediately, which he ignored as he made his way to the rear of the house and looked out the window to the backyard. Nothing.

Was it a trap? Either they had made themselves visible in the front yard in order to flush him out the back of the house and into the waiting arms of police hidden in the dark, wooded lot...or they weren't covering the rear of the property at all. They had him, the killer knew. He could choose to stay inside the house where he would surely be caught, or he could attempt an escape out the back. Slip out the back and hope for the best. He liked his plan, and he put it into motion.

He gathered his things and shrugged into his backpack, but not before withdrawing the gun. He removed the silencer because, whereas he valued silence before, his plan now required the loud report of his pistol.

He entered the hallway when he heard a huge crash followed by a *thwump*. The killer's first thought was that he'd pushed his luck and the police were making entry, but he saw—and smelled—

the tear gas and knew he had to hurry. He traversed the short hallway from the rear of the house, and through the haze, he saw flames crawling up the curtains covering the living room window he'd stood at only minutes before. He strode back to the bedroom and, after visualizing his plan one last time, fired a single shot into the corner of the room.

What happened next shook the killer more than anything that had occurred to this point.

At the echo of the gunshot, the house erupted in a cacophony of gunfire and broken glass, sending him to the floor and covering his head with his hands. Moments later, everything went silent, and the killer had one thought: *Move!*

He scrambled to his feet and bolted for the back door but was brought up short by the front of the house consumed by fire. He didn't have time to resolve what he was seeing and kept moving. He crashed through the back door and didn't look back, arms and legs pumping, certain he was going to be shot or tackled at any moment.

———

THE KILLER MADE it home without incident. Dawn was in full bloom when he pulled into his garage, and when the garage door closed, he turned off his car and allowed himself a moment's peace. He entered his kitchen from the garage and dropped his backpack on the kitchen table on the way to his bedroom. He picked up his cell phone off the nightstand and opened the Facebook app to check Wendy Wade's page, knowing she would have the most up-to-date information on the cop he had shot.

The last update of note was the impromptu press conference by the sheriff, police chief, and the DA, and it was clear to him they believed the truck's owner was the shooter. He was disappointed they didn't give an update on the health of the officer.

The last thing the killer needed was to get this far only to have the officer recover and announce that the true owner of the vehicle was, in fact, not his shooter.

The comment by the DA shook him a bit as the reality of killing a cop set in. What had started as a lark, so to speak, had ended...unexpectedly.

He dropped the phone on his bed and took a shower.

———

OUT OF THE SHOWER, he fixed himself a cup of coffee, happy to have the memory of the watery, flavorless, freeze-dried instant coffee replaced with his strong, bold brew made from fresh ground beans. The killer had checked the day's calendar the previous night before going out and knew his day was clear, so he was not in any hurry to get to work.

He scrolled the local news sites, fishing for information on the bodies at the house and the shooting of the deputy sheriff. He was on his third cup of coffee when a Facebook notification popped up on his iPhone. He had set up his account to send him a notification any time Wendy Wade broadcasted live, and she was getting ready to cover a press conference on the events overnight.

ELEVEN

The Towne police department was a veritable hive of activity. The shooting of Hunter Stanton, followed by the fire that resulted in the discovery of the two burned bodies, had every police detective working only on those two cases. Every other case they were working on was relegated to the back burner. The investigators from the sheriff's office were also doing what they could to assist at arm's length.

Chief Greenhaw was presiding over a meeting in the department's conference room. Sheriff Ramos, DA Barclay Griffith, the DA's chief investigator Winston Fitzsimmons, TPD captain Tony Jones, and TPD detectives Beck Lawson and Wayne Drummond were present. The police chief said, "Let's go through what we know and what we believe. TJ?"

Captain Tony "TJ" Jones loomed over his team in the cramped conference room, a towering figure at six-foot-seven, built like a modern-day G.I. Joe with the presence to match. The recessed lighting caught the sheen of his smooth, bald head, casting a sharp reflection that only added to his imposing aura. His salt-and-pepper beard, meticulously groomed, framed his square jaw like granite. Every inch of him spoke of discipline—his back ramrod straight, shoulders broad, his movements precise, as if he were still in uniform. It was no wonder he was the obvious choice to lead the high-stakes investigation into the shooting.

In a silky baritone, he began, "Deputy Stanton was at Walter's Gas and Grub on his dinner break. He went code seven at 00:41 and was 10-8 at 01:38."

Barclay translated on his legal pad: *12:41 AM dinner break. 1:38 AM back in service.*

TJ continued: "Stanton turned left out of the parking lot before making contact with the red Ford pickup. We don't know what caused him to initiate the traffic stop, but he called in a 10-39 at 01:46 on a red Ford pickup truck, tag number," he consulted his notes and read off the number, "The witness," he again consulted his notes, "Rita Glisson, stated that Stanton approached the driver's side of the vehicle and was shot almost immediately." His eyes panned the room before continuing. "That's what we know. Now, what we *believe* is that the bodies found inside the house are going to be Ross Burlington and his father, Jed. We also believe Ross is going to be the driver of the red pickup Stanton stopped. The vehicle is registered in his name. We learned that he was estranged from his father, so we suspect that, for whatever reason, he kills his father, and it's when he is fleeing the murder scene that he gets pulled over by Stanton. Knowing what he's just done, he panics, not wanting to get caught, and shoots Stanton. He then drives back to his father's house, and when the tear gas goes off and he knows we are coming in, he shoots himself, which accounts for the gunshot we heard."

"That definitely plays," said Barclay. "Where are we on identifying the bodies?"

At this point, Ramos' phone rang, and all eyes went to her. She checked the caller ID and bolted from the room.

TJ cleared his throat and said, "You were asking about identifying the bodies?" Barclay nodded. TJ inclined his head toward the mustachioed man to his right, rocked back in his chair, and said, "Drummond?" Detective Drummond then looked at Detective Lawson to his right, and she said, "The sister is on her way." While Wayne Drummond was brought in as the senior-most detective at TPD, Lawson was the first choice of both the sheriff and the district attorney, and they successfully lobbied the police chief for the assignment.

Lawson—a round-faced woman with a fair complexion, ice-blue eyes, and a white-blonde ponytail—unclipped the phone on her belt and looked at the screen. "She actually may be here by now. We will ask her to provide a cheek swab for DNA comparison. The bodies are too damaged for any other method of identification."

"Make sure we know immediately when she arrives. I'd like to send the swab along with the bodies. Streamline this thing as much as possible," TJ said.

The detective nodded and stood. "I'll go check now." She made for the door and almost collided with Ramos, who was coming back into the conference room.

"That was Ricky Story calling from the hospital," Ramos said. "Stanton didn't make it."

The effect of the news was immediate; a pall of grief fell over the room like a dense fog.

DA Chief Investigator Winston Fitzsimmons pounded his fist once on the pressboard and veneer conference table, causing a fracture.

Greenhaw stood slowly, walked to the bank of windows, and stared out. He said, "God help us."

———

A PRESS CONFERENCE was held on the steps of the Arnold Gillespie Municipal Complex, which housed the police department. Again, the chief, the sheriff, and the district attorney stood before the media.

A bereaved Sheriff Ramos announced the passing of Hunter Stanton. Following an appropriate moment of silence, Chief Greenhaw announced that two bodies were recovered from the burned house that was the sight of the standoff mentioned at the prior press conference, and he reiterated that no suspect's name would be released until they had a forensic identification.

Wendy Wade shouted a question as the three turned to leave. Neither so much as flinched as they disappeared into the building.

———

BARCLAY SPENT two more hours at the police department going through everything they had—and didn't have. The examination of the Ford truck was ongoing at the off-site impound yard, and two points of interest had arisen thus far. The first item of note from evidence tech Angie Presley was blood on the bench seat. A square containing the blood had been cut out of the cloth seat and would be submitted to forensics. The second thing that stood out to her was the lack of fingerprint evidence.

"The steering wheel appears to have been wiped down," she told the task force over speaker phone. "The same for the inside of the driver-side door and the exterior door handles on both the driver and passenger doors."

"We have cases all the time where fingerprints aren't recovered or aren't in a condition for comparison," said Barclay. "What makes this so different or even suspicious?"

"We found prints everywhere else you'd expect to find them, but none in the places we know had to have been touched by human hands. We didn't find so much as a ghost of a fingerprint in places where there should be smudges, overlaps, something. Again, we recovered prints elsewhere in and around the truck, but nothing in the obvious places. May not be anything, but I do find it unusual. I mean, did this guy take the time to wipe everything down before going back into the house?" When no one said anything, she said, "Look, I'm just trying to come up with anything right now."

"Sorry, Angie," said Ramos. "We're all just turning it over in our heads. Good work." Then, to the room, Ramos said, "Any other questions while we have her on the line?" Receiving no reply and seeing a couple of headshakes, she said, "That's it for now, Angie. Appreciate the update. Let us know if you find anything else."

"Will do. We'll swab for touch DNA, which is about all we have left to do. If you think of anything specific you want us to look into, let me know."

The consensus among the group was that they had their shooter, and there wasn't much left to do until they got a report from forensics. The autopsies, they were told, would be completed by close of business. They were hopeful for a preliminary report the same day even though they knew the final, official report would take weeks if not months. Barclay volunteered his chief investigator, Winston Fitzsimmons, to travel to Montgomery to observe the autopsies, saving the PD from having to send someone actively engaged in the investigation.

Greenhaw made the decision to wait for Stanton's body to arrive from Atlanta so they could transport all three at the same time. Someone would have to follow the coroner to the lab in Montgomery to maintain the chain of custody of the bodies, and multiple trips didn't make much sense. Georgia Highway Patrol was handling the escort from Atlanta to the state line, where Ramos sent a deputy to pick up the escort from there. "He's our guy, Chief," she said to the chief's objection.

Greenhaw held up a hand and nodded. "At least allow one of our guys to ride with, okay? We just don't need a fellow deputy to be alone in the chain of custody, Sally." She acquiesced, and the escorts were dispatched to the state line.

As soon as Stanton arrived, the body was loaded into the coroner's van alongside the Burlingtons and took off for Montgomery, followed by Fitzsimmons.

It was lunchtime, and everyone's lack of sleep was beginning to catch up. The adrenaline spike of the last several hours was fading, leaving them all dragging. Ollies, a local pizza place, delivered two dozen pizzas to the PD, and the unsolicited offering was a boon to the weary group and promptly devoured.

TWELVE

After leaving the police department, Barclay went home to shower and change clothes, but the day's emotions fell upon him like a hammer while in the steamy shower. It wasn't until he slowed down and the penetrating heat of the water and steam from the shower relaxed his tense muscles that he realized how mentally and physically exhausted he was. He laid down, ostensibly for a quick nap to recharge, but he had been asleep for almost four hours when the call came in.

The call was from Fitz, letting Barclay know that he was leaving the medical examiner's office and that a meeting was planned for 5:30 PM at the police department. When he hung up, he checked the time and saw he had just under an hour until the meeting. He got up and padded to the kitchen, where he sat with his laptop open, answering the numerous emails that had come in from reporters both local and statewide, along with two emails from national news media. They were all seeking a statement about the shooting of Hunter Stanton.

He crafted a response that stated how incredibly saddened he was by the officer's murder, that Deputy Stanton was a dedicated public servant simply doing his job when he was senselessly gunned down. He let them know the investigation was still ongoing, and he and his office were providing any and all assistance they could to catch the person responsible. He closed the statement by saying that he would provide an update as soon as he had something to give them, including the identity of the persons who died in the house fire.

He reviewed it twice, made a couple of minor changes, read it again, and then copied and pasted it into the nearly two dozen emails about the case. That done, he dressed in khakis and a white dress shirt. He stepped into a pair of Martin Dingman loafers and grabbed a navy windowpane blazer as he left his bedroom. On the way out the door, he kissed his wife, Brittany, and his young daughter, Macy, goodbye.

————

THE SAME GROUP from the morning was once again seated around the conference table, and Barclay observed that he appeared to be the only one who left and cleaned up, leaving him to feel guilty at having rested while others had pushed through their fatigue. The crack in the tabletop left by Fitz earlier served as a tangible reminder to everyone in the room of exactly why they were there.

Fitz had the floor. "Dr. Bev performed all three autopsies, beginning with Stanton. He was shot twice—once in the throat and once in the upper chest about halfway between his throat and the shoulder, slightly lower than the first shot." Fitz pointed out the second entry wound on himself. "She said the shot to the throat was not survivable. In her words, he could have been shot in the hospital parking lot, and he wouldn't have made it."

Everyone in the room was an experienced professional, so as difficult as this was to hear, they could compartmentalize. Time, even less than sixteen hours since the shooting, had focused them on the task at hand, moving them from grief to action.

Fitz continued his report: "As for the two crispy critters, the body found in the bed had a single gunshot wound entering just above and behind the left ear and exiting below the right eye. The second individual had a single gunshot wound right about here." Again, he pointed out the location on himself. He was pointing approximately two inches above his right eye at about the outer edge of his eyebrow. "There was a corresponding exit wound on the rear of the skull traversing from one side to the other." Fitz looked at Barclay and said, "I spoke directly with Ken Pevey, as you asked, and he is going to rush the DNA comparisons with the sister's swab. He said he would do what he could with the blood from the Ford but wouldn't make any promises. I told him the priority was ID'ing the bodies."

TJ spoke next, informing the group that Angie Presley had completed the examination of the truck and found nothing of value other than what she had mentioned earlier. He also summarized the interview of Burlington's sister, Jan Gamble: "Their father was an alcoholic's alcoholic. Her breaking point came eight years ago when he showed up drunk at the hospital for the birth of her first child. After that, he moved to Towne to sober up. Despite past relapses, he recently claimed to have been sober for over a year. She was too exhausted to care, but Ross, the baby of the family, felt he owed it to their dad. Mrs. Gamble said she spoke with her brother last night, and things seemed good. He told her their dad was committed to sobriety, unlike before. Ross even urged her to visit. She was insistent her brother would never shoot a cop and didn't even know him to own a handgun. He was an avid hunter—deer and turkey—so he owned rifles and shotguns, but no handguns to her knowledge."

That last statement brought Barclay up short. "Was a gun found...I'm sorry, TJ. Were you done?" TJ nodded, and Barclay continued, "Did the arson investigators find a gun at the scene?" That hit the rest of the group as it had Barclay. He wasn't the only one who hadn't considered that.

"I haven't spoken to them since they went inside the house. Just too many other things to focus on," said Greenhaw. Then, to Detective Drummond: "Reach out to Nolin, find out who the lead is on the fire investigation, and check on that. I expect they would've called if they'd found a gun."

Fitz: "They probably don't realize they need to be looking for one. I haven't spoken to anyone outside this room about the cause of death being gunshot on our two bodies."

"Fair point," said Greenhaw.

"But they know Stanton was shot," said Ramos. "Surely they're looking for a murder weapon."

"You're right, Sally," said Greenhaw with a sigh. "We may need to call it for the night. We're all running on fumes here, and I don't want to miss anything because of fatigue."

Barclay again felt a pang of guilt for falling asleep at home. "Before we all get out of here," he said, "am I the only one who isn't so sure this is as cut and dried as it seems?"

"How do you mean?" asked Drummond.

"The gunshot wound to Ross Burlington?" TJ asked.

"That's part of it, but yes, the location of the entry wound."

"Are we assuming the body recovered from the bed was the old man?" asked Fitz.

After a beat, TJ said, "That would seem to make the most sense, right?" Nods all around. "At least that's what makes sense under our working theory. The location of the entry wound behind the ear and lying in bed would indicate he didn't see the shot coming. In fact, it points to him being shot in his sleep. If it is a murder-suicide, the body on the floor has to be the doer." More nods.

"I believe I know where you're going with the entry wound, but what else are you thinking, Barclay?" Ramos asked.

Barclay stood up, needing to move around. "So we agree on the entry wound being in an odd place?"

TJ: "It is a very strange place for someone to shoot themselves. It's almost always a temple or a mouth shot, maybe even under the chin. I've seen a lot of self-inflicted gunshot wounds in my career, and I have never seen a person shoot themselves there."

"Me neither," said Barclay. "And because of the fire destroying all the skin and tissue on the head, we don't have any way of knowing if it were a close contact wound. It just seems...odd."

"I agree," said TJ. "It sounds like you've got something else?"

"The gun is obviously important. I mean, it should be there if Ross is the guy."

"*If?*" asked Drummond. "What are you saying? That Ross Burlington didn't do this?"

"I'm not there yet, Wayne. It's just...odd is all."

"Yeah, you said that already."

"What is it, Barclay?" Sheriff Ramos asked.

"Well, the gunshot, of course, and the possible missing gun—"

"Missing gun?" interrupted Drummond. "Jesus, Barclay, we haven't even spoken to the arson guys yet—"

"Detective," Ramos admonished. She glanced at Greenhaw. It was, after all, his detective she had snapped at, but, to his credit, he nodded his assent to her authority. She continued, "We all need to feel free to say whatever it is we're thinking. I know emotions are running high, but this case is too damned important to keep anything to ourselves." Then Ramos gave Barclay a look that told him to go on.

Barclay nodded at the sheriff. "As I was saying, the entry wound is atypical of a suicide, and we haven't found the gun. Yet," he added quickly when he saw Drummond open his mouth. "But the gun should be there if Burlington is our guy. And another thing: the guy drives an eighteen-year-old truck with over two hundred thousand miles on it and uses a flip phone but owns a pair of eight hundred dollar boots?"

"Eight hundred dollars? For boots?" said TJ.

"Yeah, they're custom made. Every pair."

Lawson perked up. "I bet that boot company keeps a customer list, and I can't imagine there are that many names from around here."

Greenhaw looked at Lawson and said, "Will you follow up on that?"

Lawson nodded and made a note in her reporter's notebook.

"Anything else?" Greenhaw asked, his eyes going around the table. "From anyone?"

"What about the fact that, according to the sister, things seemed okay between father and son? Why shoot him?" asked Barclay.

Drummond said, "Murder cases are ugly and often leave us with more questions than answers. You know that. Look, the sister says they spoke on Tuesday. The shooting occurred late Tuesday night/early Wednesday morning. Maybe the old man tied one on good sometime after the phone call. Maybe the stress of it all was too much, and he figured he'd have one drink, which turned into ten. Maybe Ross thought of his sister and everything their father had put them through, and it just became too much. The old man being passed out in bed would certainly explain his son being able to get the drop on him and shoot him where he lay." Drummond paused, searching Barclay's eyes. "I mean, what's the alternative?"

Barclay considered the question. "Since we're doing hypotheticals, maybe someone steals the truck and runs into Stanton. The driver has warrants, or he's on probation or parole, you know the drill, and he doesn't want to go to jail or back to prison, so he shoots a cop."

Lawson said, "That could work, but why go back to the house? He has to know we'd be out in force looking for the truck involved in the shooting of a cop. He could have jumped on I-85 and been in the wind. Atlanta's only an hour and a half away; he gets there and dumps the truck, and we'd never find him. Hell, leave it in the right spot, and the truck probably gets stolen within the hour and stripped for parts in half a day." Barclay knew she had a point. The detective continued: "Even if he chooses to return to the house, why hang around? Instead of getting the hell out of there, he goes inside the house and shoots two people— ostensibly with a single shot because that's all we heard—and texts police on Burlington's phone. Then, he somehow manages to escape before the place burns to the ground and gets by an entire battalion of law enforcement. How does he accomplish that?"

A shrug. "Maybe he slipped out the back. Was anyone covering the rear of the house?" Barclay looked around the table.

"Ah, jeez," said Greenhaw, face going sour. "I don't even—"

Drummond interrupted. "Barclay, man, you're always asking the question, 'What makes the most sense?' Well, what makes the most sense?"

Barclay said, "Look, I just want to be right, that's all. Same as each of you."

Drummond responded, "I hear you, man, but sometimes a cigar is just a cigar."

THIRTEEN

The funeral for Deputy Hunter Stanton was held the following Monday. A church large enough to accommodate what was expected to be a well-attended service wasn't available, so it was held at the Towne Civic Center, which usually hosts concerts and home and garden shows. The funeral was also broadcast live on one of the local network stations and on Facebook and Twitter.

The day following the announcement of Stanton's death, an officer with the NYPD reached out to Sheriff Ramos. The NYPD, the officer had said, had officers who traveled around the country to the funerals of fallen officers. They assisted in organizing the funerals and participated in the pageantry that was laying a fallen peace officer to rest. Stanton was the first law enforcement officer killed in the line of duty in Towne County history, so assistance from the NYPD was welcomed and appreciated.

The requisite city and county dignitaries attended the funeral, as did every city and county law enforcement officer not currently on duty. A number of state officials were also present, as were nearly four dozen law enforcement officers from around the country. Seeing the national support for their fallen brother made an already emotional day even more so.

The hour-long ceremony was led by Jim Rhodes, Stanton's preacher from the local Baptist church, and included words from Sally Ramos and Deputy Peter Morgan—Stanton's best friend. A bagpiper played Amazing Grace as the casket was carried out of the civic center and loaded into a hearse for the procession to the graveside.

The procession to the cemetery was approximately two and a half miles long, and the entire route was lined with Towne citizens showing their support for their fallen hero. American flags were held aloft, hats were removed, and hands were placed over hearts. Not a word was spoken, and many tear-streaked faces were observed as the near mile-long trail of vehicles snaked its way through the city.

Reverend Rhodes gave the final words at the graveside, and the service was concluded by playing the End of Watch call, which was gut-wrenching to all in attendance.

———

THREE AND A HALF hours after the funeral, a number of the attendees were milling about The Crafty Lefty, a local craft beer bar and grill owned by Barclay's brother, who went by Ivey owing to the Roman numerals in his name: Grover Griffith, IV. The melancholy from the funeral and the overall weight of the day were lifting, thanks in large part to the flow of alcohol.

At the bar was a large contingent of out-of-state cops who showed up in support of the Thin Blue Line. They were getting the most attention, as the local law enforcement officers could not stop gushing over the fact that so many had traveled so far on their own dime to support their brother. The out-of-towners had yet to pay for a drink.

Barclay's thoughts drifted to a similar scene almost three years prior when he was here with a large group celebrating the life of his best friend and colleague, Duncan Pheiffer, who was also murdered. He and Brittany had commandeered a couple of seats at the end of the bar when his thoughts were broken up by someone approaching from behind.

"Hey, you guys."

Barclay looked over his left shoulder and, seeing who it was, turned around on his bar stool until he was facing the visitor. Brittany did the same. It was ADA Stacy Steen dressed smartly in a navy skirt and soft blue button-down, with a simple gold necklace peeking out. Her gold-blonde hair was in a blunt bob that looked messy yet stylish.

He said, "Hey, Stacy. Buy you a beer?"

"I'm good right now," she said, holding up a freshly poured pint. "Have you met Franklin Masterson? He's a local lawyer."

Barclay eyed the pale, dark-haired, dark-eyed, and dark-suited figure looming over the prosecutor, thought *Dracula's accountant*, and said, "I have not."

Masterson awkwardly reached around Stacy and offered his slender, bony hand to Barclay. "It's nice to meet you." The lawyer's voice was quick, clipped, and earnest.

"Good to meet you, Frank."

"It's Franklin," he said as he squinted and pushed a pair of clubmaster-style frames higher on his blade of a nose.

"Right. Franklin. Sorry about that." Barclay expected him to wave off the apology, but he didn't. Instead, he nodded as if accepting it. "What type of law do you practice?"

"Tax law mainly." *Bingo*, thought Barclay. "I also handle estate law. Wills, trusts, that sort of thing."

Barclay nodded, then reached back for his beer and said, "I left all of that behind in my second year of law school." He tipped his glass in a *cheers* gesture and took a drink. Then he said,

"I don't suppose you could explain the *Rule Against Perpetuities*."

"Well...yes," said the lawyer. "You see, it really is quite simple—"

"I was kidding, Franklin. I've lost enough sleep dealing with this case. I don't need unsolvable law school problems slithering back into my brain." Sensing he offended the attorney, he said, "My apologies. It was a bad joke." Looking to extricate himself, he turned further to his left, almost making a complete circle, and said, "This is my wife, Brittany."

Brittany smiled, the freckles across her nose bunching in the way Barclay adored, and said, "Nice to meet you," as she tucked a strand of reddish-brown hair behind her ear. Masterson nodded and looked down and away.

"So, you bring a date to a funeral, Stacy?" Barclay asked.

She was taking a drink and almost spit it out. "What? No. I mean, we—"

"Relax, Stacy, I was only kidding."

"Oh, yeah." An embarrassed laugh. "Well, we, uh, have actually been going out for a couple of months now."

Barclay did a double take, which he hoped they didn't notice. The pair was a study of opposites, both in personality and appearance.

"How nice," Brittany said.

Stacy looked up at the pale attorney and said, "He knew this was going to be a tough day for me, so he offered to come with me."

"That was very sweet of you, Franklin. This is a tough day for all of us," Brittany said. "Makes me sick, to be honest. That poor deputy was just doing his job, and someone took his life like it was nothing."

Franklin ignored that and said, "I'm fascinated by the work you all get to do...as prosecutors."

"We're fortunate to be able to do what we do, especially where we get to do it," said Barclay. "I never forget that."

Franklin nodded, the conversation getting more awkward by the moment.

"You ought to come join us. We are always looking for good lawyers," Barclay said to be polite more than because he meant it.

"Oh no," the lawyer said, again looking down. "I'm afraid I'd be terrible in the courtroom. I like my office just fine."

"Of course you do. Probably make a much better living than working for the government anyway." Polite laughter was exchanged. Barclay continued, "None of us are performing brain surgery, my man. If you ever think you may want to dip your toe in, let me know. I'd be happy to discuss it with you."

Another nod, then, as if a switch was flipped, he looked Barclay in the eye and said, "You think one of those two bodies from the house was the person who shot the officer?"

"Franklin," Stacy admonished. "I don't think now is the time."

"It's okay, Stacy. That *is* the burning question—no pun intended, of course." More polite laughter, the smile on Masterson looking strained.

"That's terrible," said Brittany, lightly punching Barclay's arm.

"I can't speak about that right now. None of us can," Barclay said, eyeing Stacy, who got the point. "It's still an ongoing investigation. I'm sure you understand."

"I do. And believe me, Stacy here hasn't said a word about it. In fact, I haven't even asked her. I didn't even think she'd know anything about it. I'm sure you're handling this case personally, right?"

"I am, yes. But don't sell Stacy here short. She's a damned fine prosecutor, solid in the courtroom. We're lucky to have her."

Stacy looked down with an embarrassed smile. "Well, we'll leave you two alone."

Brittany said, "Pull up a seat—" A burst of laughter cut off her statement.

Barclay said, "I'm going to stretch my legs for a minute...go say hello to our visitors." Then he asked Brittany, "Do you have any challenge coins?"

She unhooked her purse from below the bar and set it on the bar top. "Of course I do," she said as she reached into her purse. "You know I always have you covered." She placed several of the heavy, silver dollar-sized coins emblazoned with the DA badge on one side and the office seal on the other into his hand and said, "I've got more if you need them."

He put them into his suit coat pocket and said, "What would I do without you?"

She raised her eyebrows, which was answer enough. He smiled back and winked at Stacy and Franklin before making his way to the source of the laughter.

FOURTEEN

The buzz was felt first from the inside pocket of his tan sport coat, then on his wrist. Barclay looked at his Apple watch and saw it was Chief Greenhaw calling. He took out his phone and texted the chief that he was at his weekly Rotary lunch and asked if he could call him back when the meeting was over or if he needed to step out and talk now. The chief texted back that it could wait.

Barclay was in his Tahoe headed to the office when he returned the call.

"Hey, Chief, what's up?"

"We got the report back from forensics, and they positively identified the bodies pulled from the fire. One of the bodies was that of Ross Burlington, and the other was his father, Jed—Jed being the one found in the bed."

There was silence on the line as Barclay considered this.

"Okay," Barclay began, "well, that was what we expected, so... where do we go from here?"

"I had our PIO," Barclay knew that to mean Public Information Officer, "type up a press release, and I want you to review it before we send it out. I will email it to you right now, so if you can go ahead and look at it and get back to me, I'd appreciate it."

"Will do. I should be at the office in about three minutes. Give me about twenty minutes to get back to you. That work?"

"That's fine. I want to push something out before word leaks."

"Are you going to do a press conference on this?"

"No. The statement contains all the information I would say, and I'd rather not have to repeat 'I can't discuss that at this time' ad nauseam to Wendy Wade as she asks the same question ten different ways. It'd just piss me off."

———

BARCLAY WAS at his desk and reading the release on his computer.

For Immediate Release

Towne, Alabama - Towne Police Chief Adam Greenhaw announced today the identification of the two bodies recovered from the house that burned down in the early morning hours of Thursday, April 14. The investigation into the shooting death of Towne County Deputy Hunter Stanton at approximately 1:48 on the morning of the 14th led police to the house in question. Attempts were made to communicate with the occupants for a peaceful surrender; however, after those attempts failed, police prepared to make entry into the home. Prior to entering the home, gunfire was exchanged, and the house subsequently caught fire. The Towne Fire Department successfully contained the blaze and subsequently removed two bodies from the burned home.

DNA testing conducted by the Alabama Department of Forensic Sciences identified the bodies as 38-year-old Ross Burlington of Eufaula, Alabama, and 72-year-old Jed Burlington of Towne, Alabama. The vehicle identified as being involved in the shooting of Deputy Stanton was owned by Ross Burlington. The investigation into the murder of Hunter Stanton is now concluded and will be presented to a Towne County Grand Jury.

Anyone with information on this case, please call the Towne police department's non-emergency number.

Barclay read and re-read the release. There were a couple of changes he would make if the release were his, but it wasn't, and they weren't major issues. He emailed the chief his okay, then received the email blast two minutes later.

Two minutes after that, his phone rang.

"Hey, Wendy."

"What the hell, Barclay? No press conference?" the reporter asked.

Barclay shrugged and said, "It's the chief's case, Wendy. Not my call."

"What am I supposed to do with this? I need video."

"I don't know what to tell you."

A beat of silence, then Wendy said, "Give me an interview."

"Me?"

"Yes, you. I need something to go to air with that isn't just me and a graphic of the release."

"There isn't much I can add."

"You let me worry about that. I can be at your office in half an hour. You available?"

"Sure, Wendy. I can make time for you."

"You're the best. See you then."

After he hung up, Barclay wondered if he hadn't agreed too soon. He really didn't have much to add, but she was right. That was for her to deal with.

———

THIRTY MINUTES LATER, Wendy was in his office setting up her camera. She wore a gray dress that hugged her figure as she balanced precariously yet deftly on black stilettos. Barclay had moved a chair in front of the camera and was clipping the wireless mic to the lapel of his coat. They made small talk about the shooting, and she was unusually demure when speaking about it.

Everything set, she flicked on the small light mounted to the top of the camera and asked Barclay to say and spell his name and title. Barclay rolled his eyes and did as he was asked. "I know," she said, " but I have to have that on record."

Barclay nodded and said, "Yeah, yeah."

She said, "Alright, Towne Police Chief Adam Greenhaw issued a press release today regarding the murder of Towne County Deputy Hunter Stanton. What can you tell us about that investigation?"

Looking at Wendy, who was just to his right of the camera's lens, he said, "I first want to thank and commend each and every law enforcement officer who showed up the night Hunter Stanton was shot. The response was immediate and overwhelming and served to advance the investigation much quicker than we otherwise would have been able to on our own. We worked with numerous agencies, both here locally and across the state. The FBI also assisted with technology support.

"As for the investigation itself, I am limited on what I can say, but thanks to the assistance of Eufaula PD, we were able to gather information on a potential suspect, which led us to the house on County Road 29. Unfortunately, during the standoff, it burned down, and two lives were lost."

"What was the source of the fire?"

"We have a preliminary opinion from the fire chief, but until he submits his official report, I won't have any comment."

"What about the cause of death on the bodies pulled from the fire?"

"I'm not going to comment on that at this point."

"What are the next steps in the investigation?"

"The next step is to present the case to a Towne County Grand Jury, which won't be for several months. The police have to complete their case file, and that can't be done until forensics concludes their investigation. This is a case with two potential crime scenes, a fire, and numerous pieces of firearms evidence, which takes the longest of all the forensic disciplines to complete. This investigation will not be rushed."

"But the chief said that the investigation has been concluded. Do you agree with that?" Wendy pressed.

Personally, that was one of the issues he had with the release, but he also knew he had to measure his words carefully. "I have the utmost trust in Chief Greenhaw leading this investigation. It's been handled swiftly and with tremendous professionalism thus far, and my office stands by to help in any way we can."

"Is there anything else you'd like to add that I haven't asked you about?"

Barclay shook his head *No,* and Wendy reached over and turned off the camera as Barclay removed the mic from his lapel. He stood and removed the mic's receiver from his pocket, wrapped the cord around the receiver, and handed the bundle to the veteran reporter.

Taking the mic set, she said, "You think you got the person who killed Deputy Stanton?" Barclay's dealings with Wendy Wade went back years, and this after-interview off-camera banter was routine with her—two friends talking, and always off the record.

Barclay considered the question and said, "I don't necessarily agree with the chief, but his reasoning is sound. Nothing really left for us to do except present it to a grand jury, and with the evidence we have right now, they are probably just going to no bill it because our suspect is dead, which is probably for the best. No reason to let this thing fester. The family needs closure."

"But what if you don't have the shooter? What then? The police department won't investigate it further, you know that."

"I know," he said with a sigh. "God help us if we're wrong on this, Wendy."

———

THE KILLER SAT on the edge of his bed after a long, busy day at work. He had been in the process of changing clothes and was currently barefooted and in his work pants and white undershirt. His hectic work schedule kept his mind off the murders in the days since the funeral for the dead cop, but he now was on his iPad scanning Wendy Wade's Facebook news feed for any updates on the investigation. That is when he saw the latest statement from the police chief, which he read multiple times. He also watched the accompanying news report by Ms. Wade, which included a video of the district attorney. After re-reading the statement once more and watching the news story—more specifically, the video of the DA—twice more, the killer had mixed feelings. On the one hand, he couldn't believe his good fortune reading that the investigation into the cop's murder was closed, but he had a nagging feeling about the district attorney. The DA didn't seem to share the belief that the case was closed and that this Burlington person was the shooter of both the old man and the dead cop.

Although he was not well-versed in the workings of a criminal investigation, he felt confident that if the police considered the case closed, then it was effectively closed. He tossed the iPad onto the bed and laid back, legs still hanging off the side. He closed his eyes and allowed himself to believe that he had murdered three people and gotten away with all of them.

FIFTEEN

It was time. Again.

The thrill of having committed the ultimate crime and getting away with it was beyond exhilarating. It was a silent testament to my brilliance and dominance over those around me. I reveled in this twisted sense of power, knowing that I could end a life and walk away unnoticed, blending back into the mundane flow of everyday life.

As I sat at my desk, attempting to work, the memories of my actions played in my mind like a private movie only I could watch. Each detail, each calculated step, was etched into my consciousness, reminding me of the power I held. It was a secret that strengthened me, made me feel alive in a way nothing else ever could.

Every day, I lived with the knowledge that I held the ultimate control. And every day, I felt more invincible, more untouchable. The world around me remained oblivious while I thrived in the shadows, a silent predator among the unsuspecting prey.

I had bided my time since my plan to take a single person's life, which in actuality turned into a three-person murder spree. If I'm being honest, I spent the first few days terrified I would be caught. Not because I wasn't confident in my method and procedure for killing the old man, but because I did not plan for things going so off schedule. I could scarcely concentrate on anything else for the amount of time I spent going over my every movement, every possible way I could have left the police evidentiary breadcrumbs that would lead them to my front door.

The fire was a stroke of good fortune that I did not readily dismiss; it certainly would have destroyed any possible evidence in the house. The truck, however, was a different story. Before leaving the truck in the garage, I wiped down every surface I remembered touching, even overcompensating by wiping those surfaces I don't recall coming in contact with but were common enough to be touched out of habit or muscle memory; such things I could have touched without thought and without recollection.

I was satisfied that I had not been captured on video—well, no video, that is, except for the cop's body camera, which I made sure to grab. It didn't dawn on me until the next day that the video recorded from the body cam could have been stored somewhere other than on the camera itself. I was greatly relieved when I checked and found a SIM card in the camera. I downloaded software online that allowed me to view the video from the SIM card, and I've watched it I don't know how many times.

Each time I hit play, I felt the adrenaline surge coming back. The high-definition footage starts with the officer's routine movements, the camera bobbing slightly with his steps. I hear his calm breathing and then the encounter. My face doesn't appear, just the edge of my sleeve, my hand, the gun. The confrontation happens fast. The camera catches the flash, the sharp crack of the gunshots, and the officer's fall.

During the first few viewings, I felt a rush of power, a sense of control. But as I kept watching, I began to notice details I had previously missed: the realization in the cop's sharp intake of breath, how he instinctively reached out as he fell, and the silence that immediately followed before registering the deputy's ragged breathing. I also discovered something about myself: a distinct lack of guilt...of feeling anything. It was as if this happened to someone else, and I was merely a spectator no different from a theatergoer.

I couldn't bring myself to delete the video or destroy the SIM card. It became a twisted form of penance, a constant reminder of the line I crossed, the life I took. I thought it would make me feel invincible, untouchable. Instead, it chained me to that moment, dragging me deeper into a guilt I couldn't escape. The detached feeling soon gave way to another, more visceral internal response: I was a killer.

My grandfather once told me that every man has within him two wolves: a dark wolf and a light wolf. The Dark Wolf represents evil, while the Light Wolf embodies good—they are in constant battle with one another. He finished the story by telling me that the wolf who wins is the one that gets fed. In murdering three people, I gave a taste to the Dark Wolf, and it seemed a taste was all it needed. Now, the Dark Wolf is growing an appetite I find harder and harder to ignore.

I have never taken an illegal narcotic, never so much as smoked weed. I drink alcohol socially, but my desire to always remain in control of myself overrides any desire for such excesses. I have surprised myself with the urge to kill again. What I don't understand is why. I wonder if this *urge* is what addiction feels like. The craving for something you know is bad for you and can only lead to harmful consequences; however, you do it anyway...with complete and utter surrender to the desire.

To feed the Dark Wolf.

The news last month that the grand jury voted to end the case against Ross Burlington due to his death and the announcement the case had been "exceptionally closed" only served to heighten my desire for another victim. I don't consider this a blood lust, though. I view it more as a challenge. *Can I get away with it?* Candidly, I already have once...three times, really.

The itch began to grow not long after the murders, but I scratched it by simply telling myself that I was *not* a killer. Sure, I did it once, okay, three times, but that was just because I wanted to know what it felt like to take a life. To be the only person who knew exactly what happened. To be the holder of the secret of secrets.

It was exhilarating, but I have been granted favor. The unexpected good fortune of this Ross Burlington person interceding and so wonderfully taking the blame was miraculous. I do not need to risk another killing; I accomplished my goal.

But I *did* get away with it. Can that be overlooked? And the urge—the craving, which I don't understand—is very, very real.

So, being the intentional and practical person I am, I began my research.

If I *was* going to kill again, and that was far from decided, I would need to prepare. I initially believed that the best path to getting away with murder was simply not getting caught. But the fallacy in such a belief is that the unsolved crime is the worst crime because there will always be someone searching for answers. No, after everything that happened, after so much contemplation, I concluded that the perfect murder is not the one that goes unsolved—it's the one where someone else gets the blame.

That's what worked last time, but that was owed entirely to happenstance—circumstances beyond my planning and control. Yet still...

As I have made clear before, I am not a religious person, nor do I believe in fate. Things happen to us—you and me—and it can neither be explained nor accounted for...it just is. *However,* perhaps I am wrong...about all of it. Why? Because the answer to my conundrum presented itself to me, at least the germ of an idea, quite by coincidence. Or was it something more than that?

A little over a year and a half ago, a sixty-year-old cold case was solved involving the murder of a young woman and a local politician. From that, the district attorney's office officially formed a cold case unit and hired a cold case investigator—some old retired state cop. Anyway, ever the politician, DA Barclay Griffith got the word out about this cold case unit, and the *Towne Tribune* did a story on it. The article included interviews with the DA and his investigator, AJ Murphy. In that article, in what was almost a throwaway line, the DA mentioned applying for a federal grant to help fund the investigation of cold cases—specifically, money for DNA and genealogy DNA testing. Things would have ended there if not for the go-getter reporter from the local newspaper.

Let me explain: in a city the size of Towne, there are lulls in crime reporting, which is bad for newspaper circulation numbers and local television news ratings (*If it bleeds, it leads* is a long-held aphorism for a reason). In such instances, news organizations need to get creative, which this cub reporter did.

Following my triple murder, the local media was downright orgasmic at the fount of available material, keeping reporters, readers, and viewers satiated for weeks. Still, all news stories have a life cycle. It's after one of these sensational moments that the lulls hit even harder.

It was in this very lull that Rebecca Kirby, the eager young reporter from the *Towne Tribune* with her distinctive red hair and retro glasses, saw the potential of a story and made a Freedom of Information request to obtain the grant application submitted by the district attorney's office. In that application, the DA included a list of all the unsolved homicide cases in Towne, which the reporter, in turn, published. At first, I couldn't believe what I was seeing. Several of the names listed in black and white were known to me, and that is where my seed of an idea germinated into a plan.

Seeing the list accompanying the news article sent me to the Internet and, due to the age of the cases, the local library on a research mission. I felt there was an opportunity here, and I turned out to be correct. A seemingly disconnected series of murders throughout the nineties remained unsolved, but connected they were.

And there it was. The perfect cover. A long-dormant serial killer back with a bullet—or rather a knife in this case—because, as luck would have it, I know what connected those murders to one another. When this next body shows up, neither the media nor the public will understand its significance, but the police definitely will.

I will make certain of it.

SIXTEEN

Now that I had a blueprint of sorts, I was limited by geography when choosing a victim. I did not like being confined to the city limits because the population density is so much greater than out in the county, and, if I were being blunt, the investigators were better at the PD. However, that decision was made for me by the original killer, so I was obligated to those boundaries for the sake of authenticity. It had to be authentic for it to be convincing, and it had to be convincing for all of this to work.

As with my first murder, I parked my car some distance from my target's house. I didn't want my vehicle spotted near the scene of the crime, but I had to balance that against the ability to quickly flee the area should things not go as planned. I also needed to make certain I chose an area where a person out walking at night would not stand out or be cause for alarm. I chose my next victim after great deliberation—the how or why is unimportant aside from the obvious victim demographic I inherited.

It was almost 7:30. Late enough for the neighbors to be inside and settled in their homes for the night, probably engrossed in their favorite television show, but not so late for my victim to be alarmed by the knock at the door. The elderly homeowner answered the knock by calling out, "Yes? Who is it?" To which I replied with my name.

Confusion tinted her voice as she replied, "Oh dear, okay. Give me a minute, please."

I heard the chain scraping along its track, followed by the click of the deadbolt retreating into the door and the dull tink of the lock on the doorknob being turned. She opened hesitantly yet deliberately, as if unsure I was who I said I was. Once the door was open enough, she peered up at me through her large, thick glasses, and, recognition dawning, she smiled and opened the door wider. That act alone almost made me call it off.

She invited me in, and the house was heavy with heat on this unseasonably cool September evening and smelled of beef stew with an undertone of carpet deodorizer. She offered me coffee or tea, which I declined; DNA and fingerprints were at the forefront of my mind, and used porcelain mugs are excellent receptacles for both. She nodded, turned, and walked through the short foyer into a den that I expect has changed very little over the decades. The lack of family pictures adorning the walls and shelves is at odds with the grandmotherly figure shuffling before me in a quilted, pilly housecoat. I knew she had no family to speak of, which is one reason I chose her. She is a widow and never had any children, so there won't be anyone pushing an investigation from the victim's side and pressuring investigators for answers when none would come.

She got to her blue-clothed Barcalounger and dropped into the seat, rocking back as she did. When she came forward, her eyes fell on me and the knife in my hand. "What is this?" she said. Then, "What, what are you doing here?"

"I'm sorry, Ms. Nelson," I said, and I meant it. She's lived her life, I rationalize. A damned good life. As I said before, she won't be leaving any family behind, so outside of a friend or two, and on that I'm just guessing, who will miss her?

But Freida Nelson is a tough old bird. She retired from the now-defunct tire plant, which took so many jobs with it when the company moved manufacturing to Mexico in the mid-nineties. She retired as the first and only female plant foreman when the plant closed shop. She and her late husband, who also retired from the tire manufacturer, acted as union busters when rumors of attempted unionization arose within the facility, so she was not easily intimidated.

She stood, pushing herself out of her overstuffed recliner, face turning hard. "I don't know what the fuck you think you're doing, but it ain't funny."

That shocked me. I'd never heard an old woman speak like that, and for a moment, it threw me. If I had felt some emotional reservation before, I was definitely reconsidering my selection now. I wasn't worried about taking this octogenarian, but I hoped for a more subservient response. My task was going to be hard enough, and I had no desire to get physical with this old woman outside of the final murderous act, strange as that sounds.

"Now, Ms. Nelson...," I said, unsure what else to say.

She began to shake her head slowly before turning toward the kitchen, her Deerfoams sliding silently across the worn carpet. I took a couple of tentative steps, my knife out in front, about waist height.

She made it to the kitchen and, with her left hand, grabbed an unseen telephone from the kitchen wall. Standing in the doorless entryway, she pulled the phone's butter-yellow receiver to her ear, the coiled phone cord of the same color stretching taught as she stood where I could see her.

"I'm about to call the police if you don't leave right this instant. You leave now and I'll forget about all of this so long as you never contact me again, hear?"

A flurry of thoughts ran through my head all at once. As I assessed my options, she mistook my hesitation as an answer to her proposition and moved to dial 911. At that moment, I launched at her, covering the ground between us in a blink, and I exploded onto her, knocking her sideways and to the floor; she took the phone with her as the cord ripped from the body of the telephone. I immediately depressed the switch hook, terminating any possible call, although I was sure she hadn't had time to complete even a three-digit dial on the bygone rotary telephone.

That act revealed something black inside me. For some strange reason, violently knocking this old woman to the floor seemed worse than the murder itself, yet it didn't bother me. Like diving into a pool of cold water, the thought, the anticipation of it, was almost incapacitating. Still, once the decision was made and you were in, after the initial shock, it was tolerable, and you knew the next time, the decision would be easier.

I took two steps toward Ms. Nelson and bent at the waist, examining her. She wasn't moving and didn't appear to be breathing. I noticed blood pooling and running out from under her head across the linoleum floor. My gaze went up the knotted red-brown oak cabinet to the hard edge of the yellow Formica countertop, and I saw the spray of blood where she must have hit the side of her head.

I stepped over the prone figure and squatted down, taking her pulse at her throat. Nothing. I removed the phone from her hand, hung it up on the receiver, and tried to plug the cord back in, but the plastic tab on the connector had broken, so I was forced to let the cord dangle, and I silently cursed. Like the first murder, this had not gone according to plan. Something that would have to be fixed next time...if there was a next time...but even in that moment, indeed before the task was completed, I knew there would be.

I pushed all thoughts out of my mind that had nothing to do

with what I was there to do. I scooped up the dead woman, careful to avoid getting her blood on my clothes, struck by just how light she was. I walked her back to her bedroom and lay her face up on what is obviously her side of the small double bed.

———

I STOOD over the dead woman, her neck now a gaping crimson maw.

I dipped the first two fingers of my latex-gloved right hand into the deep, wide, raw, and ragged wound, running them around inside. I then leaned in and made my mark on the headboard.

I removed the gloves, dropped them in the Ziplock bag I brought, and placed them in my back pocket for disposal. I wiped my knife clean of blood on the sheets, and then I rinsed the blade and handle in the bathroom.

As I passed through the bedroom to leave, I stopped at the foot of the bed, pulled a Polaroid from my back pocket, and compared it to the scene before me. I'd studied the pictures for so long that I didn't have to check, but I did so anyway. It wasn't perfect, but it was close enough. The police would understand, and that's what mattered.

In the kitchen, I removed another Ziplock from my front right pocket. Reaching in and grasping the item in such a way to avoid leaving fingerprints—not mine anyway—I left a second "calling card," which is much less conspicuous than what I'd left on the headboard above the body. Maybe I'm making it too easy on them, but I can't leave it to chance.

When I reached the back door to leave, I took a final look back at the home's interior, going through one last mental checklist to make sure I had not missed anything.

As I did, my chest swelled as I felt something unexpected. Pride.

SEVENTEEN

The September morning was verging on crisp with a high, blue, cloudless sky as Barclay approached two black and white Ford Police Interceptor SUVs—blue lights on and parked nose to nose at an angle blocking the roadway—and came to a stop. He flashed his blue lights, and an officer from the vehicle to his right exited the driver's side and approached Barclay's open window, where he held his badge up for the officer to see.

He didn't recognize the officer, which wasn't unusual. He did not often deal with patrol officers unless they assisted in a felony investigation he would prosecute. The newest officers typically pulled the short straw of monitoring ingress to the crime scene, which meant Barclay had probably never come in contact with him.

The officer looked at the badge, stepped back, looked toward the patrol vehicles, and nodded. Based on the reaction, Barclay didn't believe the officer knew who he was either. The vehicle on the left backed up, creating a gap for Barclay to drive through. He nodded, said, "Thanks," and drove through the roadblock.

He wound his way another half mile through the residential

street until he saw a bevy of police activity ahead. He pulled to the curb and got out. It was midmorning on a Thursday, and this neighborhood was full of working people, so the looky-loos were minimal. He grabbed his suit coat from the backseat and slipped into it as he walked. The phone in his pocket buzzed, and he saw the caller ID.

"That was quick."

"Hey, Barclay," said reporter Wendy Wade, "I'm on the way out there. What can you tell me?"

"Nothing yet. Just got here myself."

"Okay. I'll be set up as close as they'll let me. Come see me when you're done? Maybe do an interview?"

"Sure thing. I'll text you when I'm leaving."

He hung up as he reached the crime scene tape. "I got you down, Mr. Griffith," said the uniform keeping the crime scene log.

Barclay nodded and stepped under the tape while simultaneously stepping over the curb and onto the front lawn. He walked over to Chief Greenhaw. The two shook hands as they both looked at the house.

"What's got you out on a routine homicide, Chief?" Greenhaw wore khakis with a knife-edge crease, a starched white dress shirt with a TPD badge embroidered over the left chest above the shirt pocket containing reading glasses and a gold Cross pen. He also wore the burgundy, navy, and gold striped clip-on necktie he kept in his glove compartment for just such a last-minute necessity.

"Unfortunately, I'm not sure just how routine this is."

Barclay was about to inquire further when the chief's phone rang. He unclipped it from his belt, looked at the screen, and said, "I've got to take this. TJ'll be out in a minute to walk you through the scene." Barclay nodded and eased toward the house as Greenhaw walked in the opposite direction.

When there was a homicide in Towne, all detectives were

called in. A case agent was assigned to oversee the investigation, and everything went through them. The remaining detectives looked for evidence, questioned witnesses, and did anything that was asked of them. Barclay made small talk with two detectives standing idle in the front yard. Neither had been inside and were awaiting instructions on what to do.

After a few minutes, the unmistakable form of Captain Tony Jones ducked out of the house and strode easily toward Barclay. The two shook hands, and Barclay followed him toward the house. As they made their way to the concrete stoop, TJ said, "Our victim is Freida Nelson, aged sixty-four. She was supposed to meet up with her walking club at seven this morning, and her fellow walkers got worried when she didn't show." They walked up the three steps to the door, which was standing open, and entered the house. "One of the ladies called her when they finished their walk and grew more alarmed when she didn't answer. She and another of the walkers drove over here to check on her and saw her car under the carport."

The home wasn't small, but it wasn't large either, and the detectives and crime scene techs moving about made for a cramped interior. TJ stopped talking as he and Barclay had to maneuver through and around camera flashes, making sure not to be caught in any photographs of the scene.

The interior looked like a grandmother's cozy home. The den was neat and oddly barren, with a beige carpet and slightly darker brown walls.

They got to the hallway, and TJ continued. "Ms. Nelson's friends knocked on the door, rang the doorbell, and called again. Getting no response, they called us. By the time we'd gotten here, a neighbor had walked over. She's a stay-at-home mom, and she and her husband kept an eye on Ms. Nelson. She had a key to the house in case of emergencies and let our officer in who found her."

TJ and Barclay reached the bedroom at the end of the hallway and stood at the door. The headboard was against the wall the bedroom shared with the hallway, so from the doorway, the only visible portion of the victim was the hem of her housecoat and her bare, liver-spotted legs from just below the knee down to her feet. Nothing looked out of place from his current viewpoint except that one foot bore a slipper while the other did not.

"Excuse me," Angie Presley said, and the crime scene tech squeezed between the two men into the bedroom and began photographing the body.

"It's pretty messed up, what with her being an old lady and all," said TJ.

Barclay's phone buzzed again. "Hey, Fitz, you here?"

"Just pulled up, Boss," replied Barclay's chief investigator.

"I'm in the house with Captain Jones. We'll be out in a minute. In the meantime, check with...hold on." Barclay pulled the phone away and asked TJ, "Who's the case agent?" TJ replied, "Drummond," and Barclay raised an eyebrow before speaking into the phone. "Find Drummond and ask him what he needs from us."

"You got it. I'll also check with Presley. See if they need any help with evidence collection."

"She's in here taking photographs right now, so give her a few minutes."

Barclay hung up and slid the phone back into his pocket. He paused for a moment, then said, "Chief said this wasn't a routine homicide. Now you tell me you put Drummond on it. I take it this isn't a home invasion gone bad?"

"You about done in here, Angie?" TJ said in response to Barclay's inquiry.

"Almost."

TJ said, "Officer Wyatt found Ms. Nelson and called it in. He didn't go all the way into the bedroom. Took about a step inside and saw what you're about to see. He knew she was dead, so instead of risking contaminating the scene, he walked back outside and called it in. Detective Newman was next up in the assignment queue, so I sent him out here to secure the scene and get things started as we got everything together. I called him as I was leaving the station to head this way to get an assessment, and when he explained the scene to me, I knew this was going to be more than just some plain ol' murder."

Barclay was about to ask what made it so when Angie exited the bedroom, squeezing by again, and said, "All yours, gentlemen."

TJ walked into the bedroom, and Barclay followed. The big man turned toward the head of the bed and nodded. Barclay stepped around him to the foot of the bed. He could now see what he couldn't from the doorway.

"Jesus," Barclay muttered. He had seen his share of dead bodies, but it never ceased to cause a bit of a jolt—the starkness of it. The mere sight of a corpse wasn't what had caused his visceral reaction this time, though. Barclay observed someone's grand-mother lying on her back on top of the bedcovers. Her head lulled to her right, and on the left side of her neck was a gaping wound that gave the impression of a mouth in a silent scream. Something was off about the scene, but before he could grasp it, he observed the tall, wide, white headboard. On it, in what Barclay presumed to be the victim's blood, was a large capital *N*.

He pointed to the headboard and looked at the police captain.

"Yeah," said TJ, "I'll let the chief explain that in a bit."

Barclay nodded and went back to scanning the body when he finally realized the incongruity of the scene. "There's no blood spray. No real blood at all in here," he said as he scanned the area around the old lady's head as if he was merely overlooking it. "A throat slash like that should have caused massive blood loss." He slowly moved up the left side of the bed and saw where blood had wicked its way onto the pillowcase outward from under her head.

He bent down to within inches of the dead woman's face and open mouth. He tilted his head, trying to peer underneath the right side of her head, which lay flush with the pillow. He flicked his eyes to TJ, then raised up. "The killer clearly didn't clean up. Was her throat cut postmortem?"

"Appears so. Obviously, we'll have to wait until the autopsy, but...if you're finished here, there is something else I'd like to show you."

Barclay bent back down and allowed himself one last look at the neck wound. Then his eyes flashed on the bloody letter. He slowly nodded. He was still looking at the body as he rounded the foot of the bed to exit the bedroom when his eyes were drawn to the painting hanging above the headboard. It was a print of Monet's Garden at Giverny, the serenity in the painting at odds with the chaos on the bed.

Barclay was following TJ down the narrow hallway when he heard raised voices ahead. TJ said, "Ah, shit."

When Barclay caught up, there was a mass of bodies in the small foyer just inside the front door.

"You have to let me in. I'm the coroner!"

"What seems to be the problem, Curtis?"

Curtis Hammond was the Towne County coroner's top assistant and heir apparent and he was constantly at odds with law enforcement over access to the crime scene. At the Nelson crime scene, Chief Greenhaw had ordered the coroner not be allowed access to the body until the police were done with their work at the scene, and that was the cause of the current dust-up.

The beefy Hammond said, "Listen here, Captain, you need to tell your little minion to let me through. I'm the damn coroner."

TJ said, "We're almost done here, Curtis. Officer Andrews is simply following the orders of the chief. There's no need to get upset with him." He stepped into the coroner's space and said,

"Besides, you're not the coroner, Curtis. Not yet. So, you want to get mad at someone, get mad at me."

Barclay thought Captain Jones showed far more composure than he would have in the situation. He also had to acknowledge that Jones' size alone was enough to shut up the babbling man, which is exactly what happened as an angry Hammond tried to turn around in the tight space so he could leave. It reminded Barclay of an eighteen-wheeler trying to do a three-point turn in an alley.

TJ turned and exhaled a breath. "Now, Barclay, follow me."

They stood in the entryway to the kitchen where the blood Barclay expected to see in the bedroom was splashed about. "You saw the blood on the pillow," the captain began, and Barclay nodded, although TJ wasn't looking at him. "We believe the attack started in here. We suspect she either fell running from him—" he pointed at the single slipper in the middle of the linoleum floor that matched the slipper on the woman's foot in the bedroom— "or he pushed her down in a struggle. Either way, it appears she hit her head there." TJ carefully stepped around drops of blood on the floor and a myriad of numbered yellow evidence markers and pointed to the leading edge of the counter. "Hairs matted with blood were stuck in this joint. She hits her head, which probably incapacitates her, if not kills her. He then scoops her up and takes her to the bedroom, and slits her throat there after she's already dead. That would explain the lack of blood where we found the body."

"But why do all of that? Why not just leave her where she fell here in the kitchen?"

"Again, that's for the chief to explain."

Barclay nodded as he took in the scene. He had more questions, but he would wait for the chief to answer them.

EIGHTEEN

Barclay flashed his blue lights once again at the same two Towne Police vehicles blocking the roadway to and from the crime scene. He slowed almost to a stop when the vehicle to his right backed up and let him through. Fifty feet or so on the other side, he pulled over, got out, and walked to where Wendy Wade was set up with her news camera on a tripod.

"Thank you for agreeing to speak with me, Barclay. Are you good if I do Facebook Live for this interview?"

"Sure."

With a flip of her head, the reporter tossed her long dark hair of loose, bouncy curls and raised the phone in landscape mode. "Hey everybody, I've got District Attorney Barclay Griffith with me here on the scene of...well, Barclay, what can you tell us about what's going on?"

"I can tell you that we have a deceased female in her home, and police are working to determine what happened."

"Can you share with us how she died? Was she murdered? Was it natural causes...?"

"I'm not going to comment on that right now. The police

were called to the scene by some concerned friends, and when an officer arrived for a welfare check, the body was found, and detectives were called in."

"Detectives," Wendy said as if she had something. "So you do suspect foul play."

"It would be irresponsible to approach the discovery of a dead body with anything short of a full investigation from the outset. We never assume anything and will continue as we normally would whenever a body is found. We certainly have some ideas as to the cause of death, but I will wait for the medical examiner to render her findings before commenting on that; we are still very early in the process. I am headed to the PD now to meet with detectives to discuss this further."

Wendy seemed to be thinking of more questions before finally saying, "Is there anything the citizens should be made aware of?"

"We would just ask that anyone who believes they may have knowledge as to what happened here, if they saw something or heard something in the area, no matter how insignificant you believe it to be, please call the Towne police department or the district attorney's office."

"Thank you for the update."

"You bet."

As Barclay walked off, he looked back at the reporter, who was recapping the events as she knew them. Without missing a beat, she nodded and winked her thanks to him.

———

CHIEF GREENHAW SAT behind the desk in his spacious office. Barclay and TJ were seated across from him.

"So," Barclay said, "What's the deal with this case? Why did we wait to get back here to discuss it?"

"Back in the mid-to late-nineties, we had a string of murders spread out over four or five years—a serial," said the police chief.

Barclay took a moment to process this. Then, "How have I never heard of a serial killer in Towne?"

"Well," TJ said, "*we* knew it was a serial, and by *we*, I mean the police. But the public never did. We were able to keep that quiet. Didn't want to freak out the whole town and send everyone into a panic."

"Whoa," said Barclay.

"Yeah, *whoa* is right," said Greenhaw

"How did you know the cases were connected?"

TJ said, "He left us a calling card. This guy—we assume it's a guy based on statistical probability—he kills people then writes the last initial of the victim above their bed in blood—the victim's blood."

Barclay's mind flashed to the *N* on the headboard.

Greenhaw saw it click into place for Barclay. "Now you see? That call I took at the scene was the old sheriff—" Seeing the look on Barclay's face, he said, "Not Gillespie. The guy before him: Dawson. Before Dawson ran for sheriff, he was a detective here and headed up the task force assigned to investigate the murders. I needed this looked into quietly, so I phoned him and had him check his files."

Barclay nodded. "This killer have a name? All serials get a name, right?"

Greenhaw cleared his throat and flicked a glance at TJ, then back to Barclay. "The Alphabet Killer."

Barclay took a few seconds to consider the name, then said, "That may be the dumbest thing I've ever heard."

TJ said, "Dumb? It's fucking stupid, is what it is."

Greenhaw, taking a more diplomatic approach, said, "The police chief back then, Buddy Shaw, bless his heart, was so excited when he learned it was possibly a serial, he insisted on giving him a name, and that's what he came up with."

"But...The Alphabet Killer?" Barclay asked, pulling a face.

Chief Greenhaw held up a hand and said, "Shaw was a hell of a cop in his day. In fact, he's the one who put it together before anyone else; saw the connection when no one else did, so credit where it's due there."

"I guess," said Barclay. "But leaving a big bloody letter behind isn't exactly subtle."

TJ chuckled. Greenhaw did not.

Barclay: "Other than the letter, was there anything else that connected this murder to...to The Alphabet case?" Before anyone could answer, he said, "Ah, jeez, that sounded even dumber than I thought it would."

"Enough about the name," Greenhaw said testily. He cleared his throat more to calm down than because his throat needed clearing. "As for additional connections, we'll need to get back up to speed on these old cases, but as best as I can remember, yes. There was no forced entry, the murderer used a knife, and all the victims were older to elderly females who lived alone. One difference here is the scene in the kitchen. Correct me if I'm wrong, Captain, but there was no evidence of a struggle in any of the old homicides." As he said this, he leaned back in his chair before flailing his arms, catching himself from tipping all the way over. "Whoa..."

TJ stifled a laugh and said, "No signs of a struggle, sir."

"How were you able to keep this a secret for this long? How did this never get out?" Barclay asked.

"Different time," answered TJ. "No cell phones and no social media back then made disseminating information much more difficult. Plus, there was just more respect for the sanctity of an investigation. Nowadays, these young officers want everyone to know that they know something. It's an overshare culture, and investigative leaks are a byproduct of that."

"You also have to understand that the murders were spread out over time. We had, what"—Chief Greenhaw counted on his fingers—"seven cases over five or six years? Individually, they were just run-of-the-mill homicides as far as the media and the public were concerned. The killer's calling card, if you will, stayed quiet, so there was nothing to raise any alarm bells."

"Makes sense," said Barclay. "How do we keep a lid on this as we look into a connection."

Greenhaw said, "No one in the PD is still around from then, so there shouldn't be any immediate connections made. TJ and I were in patrol back then." To TJ, he said, "I don't believe you were even here for the first couple of killings, were you?"

A shake of his head. "No, I wasn't."

"We may not ultimately keep the details of this case quiet for as long as we need to, but I don't believe we have to worry about the possible connection to the previous cases getting out for a while. As the case agent, we need to go ahead and bring Drummond in on this." A pause as the chief thought. "Assign Lawson to the case as well and call in Tina Crump—get her on the electronics. Let's keep it at that for now. Gotta keep this circle tight."

Greenhaw continued, "The first thing we need to do is determine if these cases are all connected."

"I agree. Any leads at all in those old cases? Anything we may can use?" Barclay asked.

Greenhaw said, "None. We thought we had something with victim number three. She was found alive but unconscious. We held out hope as she lived for a few hours, but she never regained consciousness."

TJ said, "Do we honestly believe that this guy has sat dormant for twenty-some-odd years and up and decided to start killing again?"

"Well, BTK went silent for about that long before he resumed writing letters to the news and police," said Barclay. "Maybe your guy just got bored."

"Maybe he's been locked up and recently got released," Greenhaw said. "Probably want to check with the Department of Corrections for prisoners released in the last twelve months or so. Maybe a name'll jump out."

TJ considered that, nodded, and jotted down a note to do just that.

Greenhaw shook his head slowly. "If this case isn't connected, it'd be one hell of a coincidence."

NINETEEN

"You're shittin' me."

"I wish we were, but no. We believe this is connected to seven prior homicides—the last of which was in 1999," said Chief Greenhaw.

Detective Wayne Drummond could only throw his head back in exasperation at what the chief had just told him. He stood up and paced the room. Greenhaw leaned on his forearms resting on his ink blotter and watched his most experienced detective move about while Detective Beck Lawson sat back and absorbed everything she was hearing. Her placid temperament offset Drummond's fiery nature well. While Drummond was all emotion in an investigation, Lawson was measured and meticulous.

Drummond was a cop's cop who had turned down multiple promotions to sergeant because that would have meant leaving the detective division. He had thick, dark hair flecked with the first signs of age and a matching mustache. His blue and white striped oxford shirt was unbuttoned at the throat, and the tie knot of his threadbare navy and red striped tie was tugged loose. He was thick, bordering on fat, owed to the detective's declining immunity to the influences of quick and convenient fast food and the all-too-often need to eat on the run and at odd hours. The losing battle showed up in the midsection of the shirt that once fit perfectly.

Beck Lawson had an unassuming look about her: white blonde hair always worn in a ponytail with a few perpetually loose strands, light makeup, and gray or navy slacks paired with a long-sleeved dress shirt for a splash of color. Her round face, blue eyes, and fair skin gave her an innocent appearance that caused the bad guys to underestimate her, which she invariably used to their detriment. Her career was on a similar, if not slightly steeper, trajectory than Drummond's. She made no secret of her desire for advancement, and when asked about the possibility of her career path taking her out of detectives, at least temporarily, she always responded, "We'll see about that."

TJ broke the silence: "Wayne, this stays in this office until we say otherwise, okay?"

That stopped the detective, who turned to face his captain first, then his chief, then his partner on the case. He made his way back to his chair and sat. He said, "How am I...are *we* supposed to investigate this case without speaking about the other...seven?"

The chief nodded. "Look, you will have access to everything on the previous murders. We just need you not to mention these prior cases to anyone...not yet, anyway. We've talked through it some already, and while it is becoming increasingly clear they're connected, we don't want to stir up a shit storm until we have to... and this *will* be a shit storm."

"And there are the families of the previous victims to consider," Lawson said.

Greenhaw leaned back and said, "I didn't even consider that." Then, as more of an exhale, "Jesus Christ."

Tina Crump slipped into the room and took up a spot against the wall in the corner as Drummond clicked into detective mode and said, "Alright, let's talk this through. It seems we have two possibilities. The first is that this is the same guy who, for whatever reason, took a break from killing for two decades, and now he's back at it. *Or*," he began with emphasis, "it's a copycat. If that's the case, how did this copycat know about the letter thing?"

"There is a third option," said TJ. Three pairs of eyes flipped to him before he said, "It's not related at all."

"Yeah, but come on, Cap," said Drummond. "He wrote the letter on the headboard in blood. Granted, that isn't necessarily novel—I mean, Charles Manson and his folks wrote in blood on the wall."

"I agree it's the least likely scenario, but at this point, we can't take anything off the table. We definitely explore the other two options first, but until we get something definitive, it has to stay an option to explore."

"I guess," said the detective, unconvinced.

The chief spoke up, ending that line of discussion: "I've got the case files being dug up and brought over. Go through them and get back to me. Anything, and I do mean anything that looks the least bit odd, off, or connected—no matter how tenuous— you let me know. I'd suggest you start with the most recent homicide. That will make spotting potential links in the older cases easier."

Drummond almost remarked that he didn't need the chief telling him how to do his job but thought better of it. The chief was a passionate and thorough lawman and was still probably the best detective on the force. He couldn't begrudge the input.

Greenhaw nodded to TJ and said, "TJ and I will be your best resources from back then if you need to talk through something."

Tina raised a tentative hand. Greenhaw nodded for her to speak, and she said, "These older cases aren't likely to have any electronic evidence; you still want me involved?"

"Hell, yes. I'd bet my pension this murder is connected to all the others, and while the old cases probably won't have anything for you to work on, this new one almost certainly will, and through that case, we may find the connection we need." He waived a hand at Drummond. "He's certainly not going to recognize potentially valuable digital evidence, which is where you come in. You know what to look for. Besides, you're still a detective even when you're not working with those electronic gizmos... and a damned good one."

Tina looked down, a little embarrassed. She was aware of what the chief's opinion had been of her in the past, and she knew it was evolving—in a positive way. His last statement was the first affirming statement she'd gotten from him that he respected her work not just in her specialized field of digital forensics but also as an investigator. She wanted to tell him that had he said something like that before, she never would have left the PD, but now was not the time for such conversations. They had a homicide or eight to solve.

TWENTY

Detective Drummond was joined in the PD's conference room by DA chief investigator Winston Fitzsimmons. Near-empty banker's boxes sat on the blue industrial carpet as the reams of paper and crime scene photos they contained were scattered across the sizeable polished conference table in a messy yet organized manner.

Tina Crump and Beck Lawson had pressing work on a case involving human trafficking and a child porn ring that had to be completed by the end of the week. Time was of the essence, with a bond hearing quickly approaching on the suspects. For that reason, Lawson told Drummond to go through the old cases without her until she and Tina had completed the examinations and locked down the defendants, but also to let her know the moment he thought they needed her.

Cops have egos, and Drummond was no exception; however, he had long ago accepted the idiom that discretion was the better part of valor. Two heads were better than one. He knew full well the stress this was putting on the chief, and he wasn't going to let personal pride interfere, possibly missing the one thing that would tie it all together...if, in fact, there was a connection. With Beck Lawson on the shelf for at least one more day, he turned to Winston Fitzsimmons of the DA's office.

He knew that Fitz had been read in on the current murder as well as the seven potentially connected homicides, so he could include him without violating the chief's edict on compartmentalizing the investigation. Fitz was a top-notch investigator in his own right, so Drummond welcomed his assistance.

For the last few hours, they had read and re-read the seven unsolved homicide case files as well as what there was of the most recent murder. They had wordlessly passed the files back and forth and examined pictures, each man taking their respective notes. It was nearing 8:00 in the evening when Drummond leaned back in the reclining leather conference chair and stretched, making a groaning noise that pulled Fitz from the file he was reading. Fitz looked at Drummond and made a face.

"What?" asked Drummond.

"That little stretch of yours," he said, motioning with his head.

Drummond looked down to see that his movement had pulled his shirttail out, exposing his pale, hairy stomach. He laughed. "Shit, we aren't all blessed like you, my brother. You look like you could still lace 'em up." He was referring to Fitz's college football career as a tight end at the Division I level.

It was Fitz's turn to laugh. "Those days are long gone. And genes don't have anything to do with it. I bust my ass at the gym to stay looking like this."

Drummond made a noise with his mouth. "That cushy DA job allows you all that free time to workout, huh." The running joke between the two unclogged what had been a stale atmosphere the last few hours.

Fitz said, "I know you're hungry. Let's go grab a bite and talk through this. My treat."

"Free time *and* high pay. Let me know when one of those jobs opens up."

Fitz stood and made his way to the door. As he passed Drummond, he said, "These jobs don't open up, *my brother*. Too damn cushy."

"Asshole," Drummond said to Fitz's back.

————

The Downtowner was near empty, unsurprising for this late on a weeknight. Fitz and Drummond had secured their regular spot in the back, though, with the paucity of patrons, privacy didn't guide them to the booth so much as habit. Naomi Tyner was the only waitress on duty and had greeted them with a glance at the antique Coca-Cola clock above the door, reminding them that the restaurant closed in less than an hour. The diner smelled perpetually like coffee, grease, and syrup—an olfactory triumvirate that has kept The Downtowner in business longer than any other restaurant in the city.

Naomi approached the table, her silver bob held back by a plastic headband matching her red t-shirt. As she set two glasses of water on the table, a tired Wayne Drummond said, "Coffee, please, Naomi."

She eyed the big detective over her glasses and said, "Now, Wayne, you sure you need all that caffeine? It's late." Fitz turned toward the wall, trying but failing to suppress a grin.

"Aw, come on," he whined.

"'Aw, come on,' nothing, Wayne. What about your high blood pressure?"

"High blood pressure?" asked Fitz.

Drummond shot a look at Fitz, then at Naomi. "Look, I'm tired. We're working on a case, and we still have a lot of work to do." She was unmoved. "Please," he pleaded. She clicked her tongue and walked away.

Seeing Fitz about to speak, Drummond held up a hand and said, "Not now, huh? Everything's fine. Just stress from the job, that's all. I'm going to outlive you, just so you know."

"I didn't say anything."

"Yeah."

A thick brown mug landed hard on the tabletop, sloshing the steaming brown liquid within the cup, but miraculously, not a single drop escaped. She dropped three pods of half and half beside the cup. "Sugar's on the table," she said with a flick of her wrist, and she was gone as quickly as she appeared.

They sat in silence for a few minutes, decompressing. Fitz finished his glass of water when Naomi appeared with a refill and took their order. Drummond ordered a double cheeseburger with onion rings, which drew an unintelligible grumble from the waitress. Fitz ordered a chicken salad sandwich with a side of pasta salad.

When Naomi was out of earshot, Drummond said, "Why's she gotta be like that?"

"Who? Naomi? Man, she's just looking out for her customers. Something she's been doing for the last forty years or however long she's been working here." Drummond was stuffing an empty sugar packet into an empty creamer pod, pouting, when Fitz said, "I've closed this place down more than twice, so she and I have had some good conversations through the years. She never married and doesn't have kids, so her customers—particularly the regulars—are her family. She cares about you, that's all. Just let her have that."

Drummond thumped the paper-stuffed pod toward the wall and sighed. "You're right."

They discussed the old cases for the next several minutes,

comparing notes and thoughts without needing to consult anything they'd written down.

Drummond said, "Each of the victims are older white women living alone, either widowed or divorced…"

Fitz yawned.

"See. You should order a coffee."

"And have Miss Naomi upset with me? I don't think so."

"Anyway," Drummond said, "they were found on their bed, throats slashed, and the initial of their last name written either on the headboard or the wall above in their blood. That about cover it?"

"That's about it. Nothing too earth-shattering."

"There really wasn't a lot in those case files, was there?" Fitz shook his head as he grabbed a sugar packet to fiddle with. "Each case generated a lot of paper but not much substance."

Fitz slid the sugar packet toward the plastic holder against the wall with a snap of his wrist. "Nope."

Naomi arrived with their food, first serving Fitz, then dropping Drummond's plate in front of him before refilling his coffee without looking at him.

"What the heck is this?" He lifted the bun, then looked up at Naomi. "I ordered a double cheeseburger."

"I know what you ordered. I ain't deaf."

"Well, I only see one patty and no cheese."

"Executive decision," she replied as if she'd turned that phrase over in her head numerous times and had been waiting for the perfect time to use it.

Drummond shook his head and reached for the ketchup. Naomi looked at Fitz and winked. Drummond saw Fitz smiling back and said, "Wait a minute. This isn't one of those damned fake meat hamburger things, is it? I heard Ralph's been running his mouth about serving that mess here." Ralph was the diner's owner.

Naomi shrugged, said, "I don't know *what* you're talking about," and spun on her toes and walked away.

Drummond's shoulders dropped. "I can't eat this."

Fitz barked a laugh. "Why?"

"Because I don't know what it is. I can't eat that veggie crap."

"It's a hamburger. Real beef. You know Ralph isn't bringing that fake stuff within a hundred miles of this place."

Drummond seemed to contemplate it as Fitz took a bite of his sandwich. Finally, hunger won out.

"What did I tell ya?" Fitz said after Drummond had taken a bite.

Drummond looked back toward the counter and saw Naomi sitting on a barstool, staring at him. He held up the burger in a *cheers* gesture and smiled. She smiled back, slid off the stool, and disappeared through the double doors leading to the kitchen.

As they ate, they discussed more about the cases. It did not take them long to conclude that the cases were related by the killer's calling card alone if nothing else. They surmised further that if they were related by method, it only stood to reason that they were committed by the same person, but why the two-decade layoff? They spent more than a few minutes trying to make sense of that without reaching a consensus.

They talked through the possibility of a second killer. They agreed that if they were dealing with two different killers, the second, current killer must have intimate knowledge of the previous seven. They also concluded that such knowledge seemed almost impossible to have unless he (they never considered the prospect of a woman being the killer either then or now) was involved in the first seven.

Feeling like they were going in circles on this point, Fitz changed gears. "Let's go back to what we know for certain, and that is the fact that, demographically, these women are more or less the same."

Drummond nodded, following the DA investigator's logic. "He knew these women."

Fitz pointed at the detective with a fork stacked with rotini.

"But how?" said Drummond, looking off as if the answer were hanging in the air. After a few beats, as Fitz ate more of his pasta salad, Drummond said, "No Facebook back then, no social media of any kind. So how could one person have known each of these ladies and known them well enough to know they were living alone."

"Maybe he didn't know they were living alone," Fitz said, playing devil's advocate.

"So he accidentally chose seven victims living alone? No way."

"I agree. But since they were all older, if not elderly, it wouldn't be a stretch for someone to believe they were living by themselves."

"Maybe not, but does this guy strike you as leaving that to chance?"

Fitz shrugged, "But what would he be chancing? An old man also living there? Surely, that wouldn't be something he couldn't handle."

Drummond, chewing on an onion ring, began to shake his head. He took a sip of coffee and said, "You ever hear of the George Booker case?"

Fitz shook his head.

"When I was a rookie, there was a home invasion capital murder—huge case for this area. George Booker was eighty-six and home asleep with his wife Cindy when three big, strong young men decided to go into their home at three o'clock in the morning. Ol' George wakes up and surprises the pieces of shit and shoots two of them in his living room before the third intruder shoots George and kills him."

"Oh, damn."

"Yeah. This is Alabama, Fitz. Homeowners have guns here." Drummond sipped more lukewarm coffee. "Our guy knew these women."

"Wait," Fitz said, remembering. "Something that did stand out in the crime scene photos—outside of the bedrooms, the homes were pristine inside."

"I don't follow," Drummond said over the rim of the coffee cup.

"How often do you see a murder scene where not so much as a throw pillow is out of place?"

Drummond considered it. "True. But not this last homicide, right? The kitchen was bloody and more in line with what we're used to seeing at a murder scene."

"So maybe that's the difference. Maybe that tells us we're looking at a second suspect."

"That or after a two-decade vacation from killing, our guy got rusty.

"Maybe," Fitz said. "But back to the point, at least in the previous seven homicides, no mess; none whatsoever. That's gotta be significant, right?"

"Again, these women are elderly. Wouldn't be hard to subdue them before they could kick up a fuss."

Fitz shook his head. "You're right, but it doesn't feel that way. To your point, our guy isn't a risk-taker. And keep in mind that none of these houses appeared to be broken into. So unless he happened to choose seven women who kept their doors unlocked at night, then combined with the lack of a struggle inside, I'd say you're dead on about our guy being a known acquaintance."

"I'd like these cases better if it were just some doper breaking into a house to try and score their next fix. To have a person intent on killing little old ladies for the hell of it..." Drummond's voice trailed off into a heavy reticence.

Fitz was finishing the last of his meal when he stopped and said, "I don't recall seeing any financials in the files. You see anything?"

Drummond shook his head as he swirled the coffee around in his mug.

"Let's see what we can find on that," said Fitz, then: "The connection has got to be in those files somewhere."

"And let's ride by the houses where the murders occurred," said Drummond, setting his empty mug on the table. "Be good to lay eyes on the crime scenes. Maybe seeing them will shed some light."

"Good idea," said Fitz, moving food around his plate.

The pair fell into a contemplative silence.

It was Drummond who finally spoke. He said, "Still doesn't answer the question of this new case. I mean, who the hell could know so much about these old cases? Nothing about them was ever made public?" They considered this, sipping, chewing, thinking.

Finally, it was Fitz who tossed out what seemed to be drifting along the undercurrent at this point: "A cop would have access to these old case files. He'd have photographs and everything. What better way to learn a killer's methods?"

Drummond shook his head. "Man, I don't even..."

"Me neither, but..."

"I know. I know." Drummond laid his head back, resting his neck along the top edge of the booth bench.

Naomi dropped the check on the table, and Drummond leaned forward and placed his hand on hers. "I'm sorry, Naomi. I know you're just looking out for me, and I appreciate that. I really do."

Naomi looked down at his hand, then flicked a look at Fitz, who was peeling through folded cash and dropping it on the table.

Drummond patted her hand twice and drained his cup of coffee. She nonchalantly took the cash and said, "Well, I guess I can go ahead and tell you that I served you decaf."

A beat, then: "What?" Drummond yelled, but Naomi was already walking through the swinging door into the kitchen.

TWENTY-ONE

Barclay was behind schedule this morning owing to his class at All In CrossFit running long. Seven rounds of fifteen thrusters, twelve burpees over the bar, nine box jumps, and a four-hundred-meter run trended him to the upper edge in terms of time and exhaustion. As a result of the grueling workout, he was moving at a slower pace, showering, dressing, and leaving for the office. He was in his Tahoe and still in his neighborhood when Fitz called to catch him up on the murder investigation.

The update didn't take long because there wasn't a lot of information to give. He let his boss know that he had spoken to Beck Lawson about tracking down the financials for the most recent victim, Freida Nelson, as well as the previous seven presumably connected dead women. After a brief discussion of the difficulty and the merits of tracking down decades-old financial data, they agreed that if anyone could do it, it was Lawson. She wasn't on Tina Crump's level breaking down computer hardware and software, but she could more than hold her own tracking down information and records.

When Fitz mentioned that he and Drummond planned to visit the seven older crime scenes, Barclay told him he wanted to join them and asked Fitz to research the current property owners.

"I know you would rather just do a ride by at this point, but I think we go ahead and jump right in; see if we can make some contact. We need to generate some movement, and we aren't going to do that sitting in a car."

They agreed to meet when Fitz's research was done and devise a plan for approaching the site visits.

————

AT 10:15, detectives Drummond and Lawson sat before Barclay's paper-strewn desk, discussing how they would undertake the site visits. Drummond and Barclay debated whether to contact the homeowners or stick to the investigators' original thought of keeping it to a visual inspection only. Drummond was adamantly opposed to knocking on doors with what little information they had.

Barclay brought up the same points he had with Fitz; however, Drummond remained unmoved, while Beck stated she saw the merit in both arguments, which caused her grief from both her partner and the DA. She just shrugged as both men stared at her. Drummond and Barclay were two strong personalities used to getting their way, and they were at loggerheads on this issue. Barclay ultimately capitulated. It was, after all, Drummond's case, and he trusted the wiley detective implicitly. Barclay had made his case but respected Drummond's position.

Fitz was tabbed to take photographs because Drummond stated he couldn't effectively operate anything more complex than a cell phone camera, and, as the potential prosecutor, Barclay didn't want to generate potential evidence by taking the photos himself. Lawson was pressed for time since Tina's forensic report on the electronics from the human trafficking and child porn cases was imminent, but she volunteered nonetheless. Barclay waived her off. "We've put you behind schedule enough with this meeting. Go ahead and finish up that other stuff. We don't need those guys getting a bond, so make sure the judge has a complete picture of their depravity. Besides, picture duty is what Fitz gets for not being here on time. Drummond will report back to you anything we find, right?"

Drummond nodded, then said. "But when you get done with that case, be ready to hit the ground running."

Lawson returned the nod and got up to leave, passing Fitz in the doorway.

Fitz began talking before he made it to the recently vacated chair. "So, I did what you asked and looked into each of the seven murder houses. I printed off an overhead satellite view of each location and wrote the current owner's name and contact info on the back of each one."

"Good work. That'll be helpful," Barclay said as he slid his chair back, ready to stand.

Fitz looked at the printouts as he shuffled through them. He heard Barclay move to stand and said, "Hang on." He found the page he was looking for, flipped it over to read the back, and then placed it face up on Barclay's desk.

"That's victim number three's house. Inez Cooper." Barclay slid his chair forward and took the paper. "That's why I was late to the meeting. I was on the phone with the homeowner verifying that she was Ms. Cooper's daughter."

Barclay: "So, our victim's daughter lives in the house where her mother was murdered?"

"That's interesting," said Drummond.

Fitz nodded. "I didn't give her much. I just told her that we are looking into some unsolved cases and asked if she would be willing to speak with us, and she said she would. We can go over there now if you'd like."

"So, not just a simple ride by after all," said Drummond.

Barclay shrugged. "I guess not."

TWENTY-TWO

The home of Shirley Cooper Bates was a moderately sized single-level rancher on a main road with a carport in front of the far left side. Fitz pulled his Tahoe to the curb and turned the truck off. After a few seconds, Drummond said, "No way someone randomly chooses this house to enter for the purposes of a homicide."

Fitz and Barclay both agreed this was a decidedly poor choice as a place to commit a murder owing to its lack of privacy and semi-steady traffic. Fitz said, "It doesn't make any sense unless Inez Cooper was specifically targeted." He then told Barclay of his and Drummond's theory of the killer knowing each of his victims and why they believed that to be the case. Seeing the house in person only bolstered their summation. They exited the SUV and approached the front door.

Prior to leaving the district attorney's office, it was decided that Barclay would take the lead in speaking with Mrs. Bates. Their goal was to present this as an informal discussion, and a detective asking questions gave the distinctly opposite impression.

A tall, angular man neatly dressed in a flannel shirt buttoned at the collar and creased blue jeans answered the faded yellow door. "Mr. Bates?" said Barclay when it didn't seem as if the man was going to speak. The homeowner's eyes bounced between the three men squeezed onto the small porch.

"Are you with the police?"

"My name is Barclay Griffith. I'm the District Attorney." Barclay grabbed for his ID as he continued speaking. "My chief investigator spoke with your wife just a little bit ago, and she said now would be a good time to come by." He held up his badge.

The man leaned in, squinted, then nodded and stepped back, opening the door wide, welcoming the trio into his home. Each man nodded at Mr. Bates as they filed through the door. Unsure where to go, Barclay stopped far enough in for Drummond and Fitz to step inside and waited for Mr. Bates to take the lead. The space was cramped, so Bates was unable to make his way to the front and he told Barclay they would be meeting in the den, which was to the right at the end of the short hallway.

Barclay entered the cozy, low-ceilinged den, and having reviewed the crime scene photos beforehand, he recognized instantly that the room had been updated. What was brown on brown on brown twenty-six years ago was now awash in lighter tans and beiges, giving the room a more open feel. The slight burning odor of a recently used vacuum cleaner hung in the air, and Barclay noted the vacuum marks on the carpet. He heard the squeak of an oven door from the other side of the wall and noted the scent of freshly baked cookies wafting in from the kitchen.

Shirley Bates entered the den wearing a light green apron with *Mimi* stitched across the chest and carrying a plate of cookies. Tall and thin like her husband, with short gray hair, she looked at Barclay, and recognition bloomed on her face. "I've seen you on TV," she said with a big smile. Barclay nodded, slightly embarrassed. She held up the plate. "Cookies?"

"Ooh," said Barclay. "I'm a sucker for homemade chocolate

chip cookies. Thank you." Her smile grew wider as he took two before she offered cookies to Fitz and Drummond.

Introductions were made, and they learned Mr. Bates' first name was Hal. After introductions, they accepted the Bates' offer to sit. Hal and Shirley sat on a khaki-colored couch, the movement of which stirred the Yorkshire terrier that was napping on the far left cushion. The dog raised its head, eyed the strangers, yawned, and fell back asleep, causing Mrs. Bates to remark, "She's not much of a watchdog," to polite laughter. Then, seeing only a single recliner left to sit in, she said, "You can grab a couple of chairs from the kitchen."

Fitz volunteered to retrieve the chairs, and they all sat.

"I'm sorry," Mrs. Bates said. "Where are my manners? May I offer you gentlemen anything to drink with your cookies? Some milk, perhaps?"

"No, thank you," Barclay said with a smile. "We don't mean to intrude and only want a few minutes of your time."

She nodded, smiling, and Hal Bates said, "Can you tell us what this is about? From my wife's conversation with Mr. Fitzsimmons"—his eyes bounced between Drummond and Fitz, not having caught who was who—"and she got the impression this was about her mother's death?"

"Yes, sir," said Barclay, chewing the last of his second cookie.

Before he could continue, Shirley Bates said excitedly, "Are you looking into Mother's murder? As I'm sitting here, I remember your office solving a cold case last year, right?" Barclay nodded. "I remember you saying that you had started a cold case division or something like that. Is that what this is? Are y'all looking into Mother's case?" She had unconsciously removed a tea towel from her shoulder and was now twisting it in her hands. Hal Bates reached over and placed a hand over hers; a sad, pitied look on his face made Barclay feel awful about the subterfuge. He had not expected this reaction.

"You know, Mr. Griffith, I'm the same age my mother was when she was killed."

This realization stunned Barclay, and he didn't know how to respond. "Mr. and Mrs. Bates—"

"Hal and Shirley, please," she said.

Barclay nodded, thankful for the interruption, for an added moment to think about what to say. So far, the meeting had not gone as anticipated.

"Let me first say that no decisions have been made, and this is a very preliminary discussion." He cleared his throat, reminding himself to tread lightly, careful not to give false hope. "Before choosing an unsolved case to look into, we do some research on the front end. Because we generally only investigate one cold case at a time, it's important we choose the best case to get the most out of the resources we have. One of the things we examine is the solvability of the case—"

"So," Hal Bates said, "you only work on cases you think will be easy to solve, is that it?"

"Hal," Shirley scolded.

"No, Mrs. Bates—Shirley—that's a fair question. Hal, we aren't looking for easy. What we *are* looking for is something, anything, to work with. For example, a few years ago, we had a young man get shot inside his trailer while playing his X-Box. One minute, he and his buddies are playing a video game, and the next minute, the kid just falls over dead. Turns out a bullet entered the trailer and struck him in the neck, killing him almost instantly; no one in the trailer heard a gunshot. As best as we could surmise, someone fired a gun outside in the trailer park, and the bullet just happened to find this kid. Now, I absolutely believe someone knows something that could solve the case pretty easily, but without that person or persons coming forward, that case will never be solved. That is a case we likely won't investigate because there is nothing further for us to look at or look into.

"So, no, we aren't looking for the easy cases. On the contrary, cases go cold largely because they are difficult to solve. But we do need to know that there is something we can offer the case."

"So what about my wife's mother?"

"That's what we're here to discuss." Mr. Bates eased back into the sofa, seemingly placated for the moment, so Barclay continued. "Admittedly, none of the three of us were around when your mother was murdered, which I believe is a good thing. We aren't bringing in any preconceived ideas. Everything is new to us. Sometimes a fresh set of eyes is all it takes." He paused here, allowing the opportunity for questions. None came, so he continued, "I want to go back to when your mother was killed. Was there anything of significance going on then? Was it just a normal day? What can you tell us about that?"

Without hesitation and as if she'd been waiting for someone to ask her about this, Shirley Bates said, "My father had died just about six weeks prior to my mother being murdered."

Barclay was careful not to react, but he saw movement in his periphery—Fitz and Drummond exchanging a furtive glance. He wasn't certain, but he believed Hal Bates noticed them as well. *Now we know why she was alone*, he thought. Barclay said, "Oh my goodness, that's awful. How did he die, if you don't mind my asking."

"Aneurysm. The healthiest man I'd ever known. Can't remember him ever missing a day of work, then one day...The doctor said he was probably dead before he hit the floor."

"It's my understanding your mother was living alone when she was killed?"

A nod. "Yes." Shirley looked at her husband and said, "She moved in with us for a couple of weeks, but that was more than she could stand." She looked back to Barclay and smiled. "Like my father, Mother was a strong-willed lady, and she wasn't going to be kept from her home very long. It was shortly after she moved back in that she was murdered." There was no sadness in her voice so much as resignation.

"Had she ever had issues with a break-in? Anything like that?"

"No. Never. This is a very safe neighborhood, Mr. Griffith." After a beat: "At least we always thought so."

"Anything since then?"

"Nothing at all."

"Who would have known your mother was living alone?"

Barclay saw Hal's eyes narrow. *This man was sharp*, he thought. Shirley puffed out her cheeks and blew air out her mouth. "I guess anyone who knew her and knew my father had died." She leaned forward, elbows on knees. "Do you think that's significant?"

"No way to know at this point. Just asking questions."

"Strange thing, what with the killer drawing the letter *C* on the headboard," said Hal Bates, almost accusingly. "You'd think something like that would stand out; make it easier to catch the person who did this."

"You'd think so, Mr. Bates, but unfortunately, that doesn't appear to be the case." Barclay was skirting a line right now, and he hated it.

Barclay asked a few more questions and got innocuous answers. He looked to Fitz and Drummond, asking if they had any questions, and both shook their heads *No*. He then asked the homeowners if they would mind Fitz taking a few photographs of the property. He explained they had plenty of pictures of the inside of the home, but there were very few of the outside, and they wanted all the information they could get.

"Fine, fine. Go ahead if you think it will help," said Hal.

"I must ask that you keep this meeting between us—at least for the time being. We still have the element of surprise on whoever did this. If we do choose to investigate this case, we don't need to alert the bad guy we're coming for him." The Bateses nodded and stated they understood and wouldn't speak of it to anyone.

Barclay stood, followed by everyone else. He shook Mrs. Bates' hand, and she said, "Ooh, wait right here," and moved to the kitchen.

A minute later, she returned with a paper plate of cookies covered in plastic wrap. "For the road," she said.

Barclay accepted them with a smile and a thank you. He said he would be in touch, and Hal Bates offered to walk them out.

As they made their way to the front door, Barclay noticed a picture hanging on the foyer's wall. He pointed to it and asked, "Is this Shirley and her parents?"

"That's them. Standing in front of this house right after they bought the place. Guessing this was taken in the mid-sixties, maybe." Barclay stared at it for a few more seconds before walking outside.

Fitz led the way down the walkway and to the SUV, Drummond off his right shoulder. Barclay was trailing when Hal called his name. Barclay stopped and turned.

Hal said, "Back there, when my wife mentioned her father dying, your two detectives looked at each other. It wasn't much, but I noticed it."

"I don't believe you miss much, Mr. Bates," Barclay replied with a slight smile. The squeaky hinge of a mailbox opening a few houses down caught the attention of both men, and they saw a battered gray Ford Taurus with the driver sitting in the passenger seat putting mail in the box before closing it with a dull metallic clang.

Hal looked back at Barclay and said, "You're right, Mr. Griffith. I don't miss much." He smiled back, but there was little humor in it.

"Mr. Bates, there are just some things I am unable to discuss at this time. I hope you can understand that." Hal seemed to be weighing that and deciding how to respond. "One thing I can promise you is that I will never lie to you. I may not be able to tell you everything, but I won't ever lie to you." The old man nodded and looked down. Barclay glanced over the man's bowed head, and it clicked.

"That right there," he said, causing Hal Bates to look up, then behind him at what Barclay was staring at. "The house is different from the photograph in the foyer. The carport once stood where the end of the house now sits."

"Good eye," said Bates. "Yes, that was the original carport. Her parents had it bricked in as a solarium with a hot tub. They'd always talked about doing that: enclosing the carport and putting in a hot tub, and damn if they never got to use it. Life just ain't fair, Mr. Griffith."

"What do you mean they never got to use it?"

"They died before it was completed."

Barclay looked back at the SUV and then to Hal Bates. "When did construction begin?"

Bates put his hands on his hips and looked skyward. "Oh goodness, I have no idea. It was almost finished when they died, though. I think it was completed within a few weeks of Mrs. Cooper's passing."

"Do you know who the contractor was?"

"You think that's relevant?"

"I don't know. Probably not, but I've seen cases turn on less. Cases are often about exclusion as much as they are inclusion, if that makes sense."

"It does. As for the contractor, Tommy Cooper was a pretty meticulous record keeper, so I imagine the paperwork is around somewhere. But can't you go back and look at building permits?"

"We'll look into it."

Barclay turned to leave when Hal cleared his throat and said,

"One more thing, Mr. Griffith. The letter over the bed." He fixed Barclay with a stare.

"What about it?"

"As I said in the house, surely that has to help. I mean, that's got to be like a signature or whatever it is they call it."

"That would definitely be considered a signature, yes."

"So, are there any other cases out there where that has been done? Kill someone and write something, say, a letter, over the bed?"

Barclay looked at the SUV once again, then back to Mr. Bates. He meant what he said about never lying to him. It was a promise he made to all the victims he dealt with. There were ways he could answer the question without lying while also protecting the integrity of the investigation, but there was also something about Hal Bates. He felt he owed him...something.

He made a sound with his mouth and said, "Mr. Bates, that falls into the category of *unable to discuss at this time.* But like I said, you don't miss much."

Hal Bates considered that response, drew a deep breath, exhaled, and extended his hand, which Barclay shook. "I look forward to hearing from you soon."

TWENTY-THREE

The Royal Rooster served chicken fingers. Throw in french fries, cole slaw, garlic toast, and their special sauce, and, like similar restaurants in so many southern cities, that was the entirety of the menu. Barclay, Fitz, and Drummond sat at a table inside the busy restaurant.

Following the meeting with Hal and Shirley Bates, they decided to grab lunch before visiting other sites. They discussed the meeting over their chicken finger plates and sweet teas, not worried about being heard over the din of conversation and the *cha-ching* of the old cash register that was getting plenty of work in this cash-only business.

"What are the big takeaways from that meeting?" asked Barclay before dipping a chicken finger in the sauce and taking a bite.

Drummond drank some tea and said, "The fact that the murder occurred so soon after the death of Mrs. Bates' father seems significant. Can't put my finger on why, but it does."

"I agree," said Fitz, and Barclay nodded his agreement as he chewed.

Barclay pulled six Heinz ketchup packets from his jacket pocket and dropped them on the table. Drummond pointed and said, "What the hell is this?"

Fitz almost spit his tea. He wiped his mouth with a napkin and said, "They serve something here called *Fancy Catsup*, and my man ain't having it."

Barclay tore open a packet and squirted it on the side of the black styrofoam plate. He said, "Heinz has been making ketchup for a hundred and twenty-five years for a reason," as if that explained everything. He was emptying his second packet when he told them about the addition to the house, and that construction was going on during the time of the murder. "The portion of the house in front of the carport was added to the original home. Mr. Bates said the addition was under construction but practically completed when Mrs. Cooper was killed. I asked him to see what he had in the way of records. I'd like to know who the contractor was."

Drummond said, "Well, that's an interesting development. We believed the killer knew the victim because they seemed to be aware that she lived alone, though we couldn't explain how they had that information. But now..."

"You mean like working on her house," said Fitz. "They would certainly know about Mr. Cooper's death and that Mrs. Cooper was living alone."

"All of that is true, of course," said Barclay. "And if this were a single murder, I'd be more excited about this development. But a construction worker as a methodical serial killer of suburban grandmothers?" Barclay dipped a fry in his ketchup and shook his head. "I just don't see it."

Drummond said, "You think a day laborer is above multiple murders? Do you know how many serial killers have turned out to be blue-collar workers? Truck drivers?"

"My opinion is based more on our victim demographic rather than the killer's occupation."

"I think I see what you're saying, Boss," said Fitz. He ran his straw up and down through the lid. "Besides, a crazed construction worker knocking off homeowners where he's doing work doesn't seem too subtle." Drummond gave a shrug that said, *Maybe*. "Well, if it is one of those workers, good luck finding so much as a name from twenty-something years ago. The contractor probably paid his workers in cash and off the books."

"Now that I definitely agree with," said Drummond.

To Drummond, Barclay said, "Can you call Beck and have her try to run down the building permit for that job? And since she is looking into the financials, see if she can find a payment to a contractor within a few months of Mrs. Bates' death."

Drummond nodded as he stood to refill his tea.

"You have the other six locations mapped out for us?" Barclay asked Fitz.

"Yeah, Boss. Let's hope these next visits are as productive as our first."

————

THE SECOND HOUSE they visited was the one nearest to where they ate lunch. It was the scene of the fifth homicide: Sofia Graham. Located in a cul-de-sac, this house was similar in size and style to the Bates' home. Fitz drove slowly in front of the house, following the curve of the road before stopping on the opposite side of the street, giving them a wider view of the property.

The driveway was empty, and since there was no garage, they assumed no one was home. On the off chance there was, Barclay and Drummond went to the front door while Fitz began photographing the property as he had done previously at the Bates' property.

Drummond said to Barclay, "You go knock on the door, and I will make that call about the permits."

No one answered the door, and Barclay took out a business card and withdrew a pen from his inside coat pocket. He crossed out his name and wrote Winston Fitzsimmons, crossed out District Attorney, wrote Investigator, and left the card wedged in the jamb just above the doorknob. He was the first back to the car, followed by Drummond and Fitz a few minutes later, with his Nikon DSLR hanging around his neck.

Back in the car, Drummond said, "Beck's going to run down the building permit. As for the financial information, finding out where these victims did their banking is proving tougher than expected. She told me she's almost done with the human trafficking case and will be on this one full-time then."

Barclay said, "Call Shirley Bates. Ask where her parents did their banking and get that info to Beck."

"How about I just put Beck in touch with the Bates directly? Especially since she'll be working on the building permit."

"Good idea. But go ahead and call Shirley to let her know to expect the phone call." To Fitz: "You see anything walking around the house?"

"Nothing that stood out. I got a few pictures. Photograph the rest of the sites, and maybe collectively, they'll tell us something."

———

THERE WAS no one home at either of the next two houses they visited, so they were relegated to Fitz photographing the exteriors along with the surrounding landscape. They also left business cards in the doorjambs. They planned to visit all five of the remaining crime scenes that afternoon; however, after what happened at the next house they visited, it would be their last for the day.

TWENTY-FOUR

The fifth house of the afternoon was the scene of the last murder of the previous set: Claire Albritton. The two-story craftsman was located in a cul-de-sac at the rear of one of Towne's oldest neighborhoods—the same neighborhood of Barclay's best friend Duncan Pheiffer, who was also murdered in his home more than two years ago—and was now owned by a young couple: Jason and Tara Melton. The lawn was about a week past needing to be mowed, and the flower beds had been neglected, but the house was in excellent condition given its age. The HardiePlank was light blue with white squared-off and tapered columns, and an Alabama state flag was hanging from the column to the left of the front door.

Barclay rang the doorbell, and after about a minute, the door jerked open, and they were greeted with a "What?" from a frazzled-looking woman in a white terrycloth bathrobe.

She was short, maybe five feet tall, with angry brown eyes and dark brown hair pulled into a loose ponytail, stray hairs framing her forehead. She cinched the top of her robe tight. A crying baby could be heard inside.

Barclay showed his badge and introduced himself, Fitz, and Drummond. After learning they were there to speak with her, she asked the three men to wait outside while she put on some clothes and slammed the door.

Fitz said, "We must've woken up the baby. Not a great way to start."

A few minutes later, they were in the living room and learned why they were able to catch Tara Melton at home in the middle of the day. She was on maternity leave, having given birth to a baby boy just twelve days ago. The place smelled of baby powder, Lysol, and old formula.

Mrs. Melton was woefully unprepared for what the next hour had in store.

Barclay began by trying to make small talk, hoping to relax the new mother by discussing parenthood, but she wasn't having any of it. Whether due to sleep deprivation, postpartum hormonal swings, or the fact that ringing the doorbell woke her sleeping baby, Barclay genuinely believed he was about to be the second homicide victim inside this house when he realized—too late as it turned out—that she had no idea she occupied a murder house.

She yelled, she screamed, and she threatened before bursting into tears and falling into Fitz's arms, the look on his face like a man who just sat on a warm toilet seat in a public restroom. He looked as comfortable consoling this stranger as a man does, looking his doctor in the eye when he's asked to cough. It took a few minutes, but Barclay finally coaxed her husband's cell number from the new mother; he stepped outside to make the phone call.

Barclay introduced himself and barely got the words out that he was at the man's house with his wife when Jason Melton said, "I'm on my way," and hung up.

Eight minutes later, Tara stopped crying and was holding the baby. All five of them sat quietly in the den when the front door burst open, and Mr. Melton stormed in. He strode past his wife, who was getting to her feet, and turned to go down the hallway.

"Jason, honey, come back here," she yelled to his back before following him with the baby in her arms.

Left alone in the den, Drummond said, "Look, man, make it quick, and let's get the hell out of here. They aren't going to know anything."

Barclay was about to speak when Jason blew back into the den with a cardboard box, followed by his wife and baby. He set the box on the floor and, through tears, said, "Here, take it. That's all there is. I swear."

Like a switch, everything went quiet. Barclay, Fitz, and Drummond stared first at the disheveled man before them, then at one another, then slowly at the open Amazon box. After a few seconds, Fitz slowly squatted down and pulled out a sixteen-ounce Gatorade bottle. He looked at it and then back down into the box. From his crouch, he looked up at Barclay and said, "There are eight bottles in here."

By this point, Barclay's mind was running a hundred miles an hour, so he didn't comprehend what he was seeing. Drummond, though, understood immediately.

The detective said, "Is that meth?" Then to Jason: "Are you fucking making meth." Then in as loud a voice as Barclay had ever heard from him: "With a fucking baby in this house?" He lunged at Jason—a wisp of a man compared to Drummond—who jumped back before Barclay intercepted the charging bull.

Once again, there was silence, but only for about three seconds before the room exploded in noise. Tara began screaming, the baby began wailing, and Drummond began yelling and jabbing his finger at Jason, who was crying and looked as steady as a Weeble.

Fitz put the Gatorade bottle back in the box, stood up with it, and carried it out the open front door. Determined to do something, Barclay grabbed the shaky homeowner by the upper arm and dragged him out the back door, which took him a moment to locate. Drummond made to follow them, but Barclay put his palm out in a *stop* gesture and shook his head.

In the backyard, Barclay gave Jason a slight shove as he released his grip. "Alright, Mr. Melton, tell me...what the hell is going on?"

The man walked a few steps toward the back of the yard, stopped, looked skyward, then turned to face Barclay. He croaked, "I have no idea."

"What? We found—"

"Meth, yes, I was making meth. But that's not what I mean. I...I have no idea how I got here."

Barclay kept quiet and allowed him to explain in his own time. Jason Melton worked for the local Edward Jones affiliate but had also taken to day trading. Mildly successful at first, he began taking larger positions, but then his good fortune took a turn. He began losing and losing big. A guy he met at an Edward Jones conference in Philadelphia offered him the drug as a way to stay up and push through to trade in the overnight markets.

He got addicted but still managed to hold it together enough to hide it from his family. One night, he had a wild hair that he wanted to try and make the stuff himself. He mixed it up in the Gatorade bottles and stored them in the home's air vents. He began to get nervous when his wife complained about an odd smell throughout the house for the last two weeks. When Barclay called him, he assumed she'd found it and called the cops. He swore he had no intention of selling it. He was just making it for himself.

After hearing the story, it was Barclay's turn to take a lap around the small yard, thinking. He made it back to Jason, who was sitting in the grass, arms hugging his knees to his chest, head resting between his knees.

Barclay's voice pulled his head up. "Alright, here's what we're going to do. My investigator will dispose of those bottles, and you have to agree to get some help."

Jason sprang to his feet. "Am I going to jail?"

Barclay waited a moment before saying, "I am going to talk to your wife and let her know that you've agreed to seek treatment for your addiction. Assuming she doesn't leave your sorry ass, I'm going to tell her to contact me personally if she suspects anything, and I do mean *anything*, that suggests you're still using, you understand?" A weary nod. "I've got you on possession and manufacturing. Manufacturing alone gets you life. You got me."

"Oh, God," he moaned, and Barclay made to catch him, but the man managed to keep his feet.

"Yeah, and then there's child endangerment, too. Hell, you could've blown your house up."

He put his face in his hands and began shaking his head. Barclay let him think about all of this.

After almost two minutes, Barclay said, "Look, you're not going to jail today. You won't ever go to jail if you handle this properly, okay?" Jason snapped up to look at Barclay, his eyes red and puffy with damp eyelashes. "You are receiving an incredible opportunity. You have a beautiful home, a beautiful wife, and a beautiful baby—do not fuck this up. If you do this shit again after what I am going to do for you, then that would embarrass me, and I will make it my life's mission to see that you spend the rest of your life in prison. You understand me?"

He began to nod his head vigorously. "Oh yes, sir. Absolutely, sir."

Barclay was just now feeling the adrenaline spike begin to ebb. He took another circuit around the yard to calm down. There was a decent-sized outbuilding at the rear of the property, and when he got to it, he peered in through a window. A workbench sat against the far wall, covered with a pegboard and a few tools hanging from it. Two bicycles leaned against another wall, along with a wheelbarrow and a collection of shovels, rakes, and bags of mulch and dirt. In the middle of the space was a simple wood desk with a large computer monitor and some papers stacked in neat piles. There was a well-worn desk chair behind it turned askew.

Barclay stepped back and took in the building. He was familiar enough with the neighborhood to know this was not original to the home. The houses around here were sixty-plus years old, and none he'd seen had anything more substantial than a metal storage shed.

He yelled over his shoulder, "Mr. Melton, what can you tell me about this structure?"

A confused look crossed the man's face. He began walking toward Barclay. "Huh? What?"

"This building," Barclay said when the man was beside him. "Did you have this built?"

"No. It was here when we bought the place. It's quite unusual for a home in this neighborhood. It's heated and cooled, a nice space. We use it for general storage, and my wife uses it as her home office. Going to come in handy with the baby now; a place she can get away to when she needs some peace and quiet to work."

"May I?" Barclay asked, gesturing to the door.

"Sure. It's unlocked."

Barclay walked in, followed by Jason. It was even nicer once inside, the walls lined with pine boards matching the floors. "This is a fantastic space. Any idea when it was built or who built it?"

"No idea about either. The previous homeowner was a cabinet maker. He used this space as his workshop."

Barclay nodded as he looked around the room, taking in the custom cabinets and other details. "I wish I could do this kind of work. Always wanted to learn."

"You'd have loved this space, then. When we bought the place, it came with all his equipment and machinery."

"Given how empty the space is now, I'm guessing you're not into woodworking."

"Me? Goodness, no."

Looking confused, Barclay said, "Then why buy the equipment in the first place?"

"It was included with the house. The owner died, and the attorney working with the estate sold it, sold everything in it—lock, stock, and barrel. They had some kind of estate sale before we bought the house, which took care of most of the furniture inside the house, but, for some reason, a lot of the woodworking equipment remained. After we moved in, I sold it all to a guy."

———

EVERYONE WAS BACK in the house now. Fitz had whispered to Barclay that the box was in the truck. When Barclay told Tara Melton about Jason agreeing to treatment for his drug addiction, her mouth fell open, and Jason shot her a look, then Barclay.

Shit, Barclay thought. *Of course, she doesn't know.*

"Ah, jeez," he said. "I'm sorry. Look, I'll let you two talk and call you tomorrow to discuss further." Tara was about to say something when Barclay held up both hands and said, "You two talk. I will call you tomorrow."

With a move of his head, he signaled Drummond and Fitz they were leaving.

"But what about—"

Barclay interrupted Drummond with: "Later. Let's get out of here."

Drummond cursed under his breath and followed Fitz out the door.

Barclay was right behind them when Jason spoke. "Hey, I never did ask why you were here. What this was actually about."

Barclay flashed a look at Tara, who was holding the baby. She put her face into her free hand and began to cry. He said slowly, "I'm going to let your wife tell you."

———

AT THE ECHO of the car doors closing, Drummond said, "Alright, what the hell was that about? We just gonna act like we didn't find a clandestine meth lab in that house?"

"I talked with the guy. Made a judgment call."

"I don't believe this shit."

"Look, I don't believe this guy should be jammed up on something that is over and won't be happening again. He was a user— not selling. It was his personal stash." Seeing the skepticism, he said, "Just showing a little grace, Detective."

"How can you be so certain he's done with the stuff? How many people you know just up and decide to quit meth and do so?"

A shrug. "I can't be certain about Mr. Melton. But I do believe it."

Drummond still wasn't convinced, and Barclay knew he was thinking about the baby in that house. Barclay was, too, and he prayed he hadn't misread the situation and wouldn't be wrong in his decision.

"Besides, we may have another lead."

TWENTY-FIVE

On the drive back to the DA's office, the decision was made to forgo visiting the last crime scene. They all agreed some time was needed to decompress after what had just occurred. However, the rest of the afternoon would not be wasted as Barclay informed them what he had learned from Jason Melton.

"The workshop in the backyard was not original to the house," he told Fitz and Drummond. "So, by my count, that's two for two site visits where we learned that the home of a murder victim had undergone a renovation of some sort."

Drummond said, "It's interesting for sure, but that seems pretty tenuous. I mean, houses undergo renovations all the time—especially houses as old as the ones we just visited. We don't even know when the workshop was built. Could have been years before or after the murder, which, in either case, wouldn't be relevant to the crime."

"I agree with everything you're saying," said Barclay. "The first thing we need to do is try to find out when the workshop was built and who built it. Go ahead and ask Beck to look into any building permits for the Melton property since she's already doing the same thing for the Bates property."

Drummond nodded, took out his phone, and texted his partner the property's address and what they needed her to research.

———

ONCE AT THE OFFICE, Drummond grabbed his car and headed for the PD to work on the most recent homicide—Freida Nelson.

Fitz went to work dumping the photographs he'd taken onto his laptop, wanting to get them emailed to Barclay and Drummond by the end of the day. After that, he planned to scan the case files of the seven previous homicides and email them to Barclay, who had taken to reading such documents on his iPad. Barclay liked that he could have all his cases in an accessible, portable format, mark them up, add notes, and share them when needed.

Barclay returned to find a phone message from Rebecca Kirby, the crime reporter for the Towne Tribune, taped to his office door. He thought all the local media members had his cell number but couldn't remember ever speaking with Kirby. There was a bond revocation hearing just beginning that involved one of their more frequent flyers, so he grabbed the pink phone message and headed to courtroom four.

On his way down the hall, Barclay punched the number Kirby had left into his cell phone. When he hit *send,* the name Anna Livingston popped up on his screen. Barclay made a face as he stared at the screen and heard a tinny voice coming from the phone—he hadn't even heard it ring. The voice spoke again before Barclay put the phone to his ear.

He said, "Hello?"

"Hello?" replied a female voice.

"Hey, I'm looking for Rebecca Kirby."

"Speaking."

"Oh...hey. This is Barclay Griffith. I got a message you called."

"Oh, hey there," she said in a rush. Barclay could hear papers being handled in the background. "One second."

"I don't guess we've spoken on the phone."

"Huh? What?" She was distracted.

"I said I don't believe we've ever spoken on the phone. Otherwise, you'd have my cell number and called or texted. That's what most reporters around here do."

She was slightly out of breath. "Oh, yeah, well, I do have your number, actually. This is Anna Livingston's old work phone."

Ah, thought Barclay.

"Since I replaced her, I got her old—and I do mean old—phone, which has your number in it. Just wasn't sure you liked being bothered on your cell."

"That's why I have it, so feel free to call anytime. If I don't answer, I will call you back."

"Cool, cool."

"So what can I do for you?"

"What can you tell me about a serial killer in Towne?"

Shit. Barclay was descending the stairs and stopped. "Give me a second to get somewhere I can talk." He got to the first floor and dipped into the first courtroom he came to, but the normally vacant room had a hearing of some sort going on.

The judge stopped mid-sentence, looked at the door, and Barclay with the phone to his ear. Barclay apologized and dipped out. He got to the next courtroom and, looking through the glass insert, confirmed the courtroom was empty before entering. As soon as he was in, he said, "Who said anything about a serial killer in Towne?" Barclay's interaction with Rebecca Kirby had been limited, but it was enough to know she was pretty sharp. He felt a bit stupid playing it like this, but he needed time to think.

She said, "I can't tell you where I got the information—"

"No, of course not," he interrupted.

"So, you going to answer my question?"

"Boy. Right to it, huh." A beat, then, "Can you give me some time?"

"How much time?" Skepticism dripped from her question.

"How much can you give me?"

"Not much." She was playing hardball. She was new and possessed a big nugget of information, so she pressed it.

Barclay, however, was no novice at handling the media. "Well, if you need something right now, I won't be able to discuss it with you. Or anything else for that matter...if you're hearing me."

"That's too bad. A 'No comment' from the DA on such a story will be all the confirmation my readers will need, and I doubt they'll be real happy to read that a potential serial killer is loose in their community and the police didn't tell them about it."

"Okay, you see, now you've overplayed your hand. I'm not refusing to comment on anything. I'm simply asking for a little bit of time." She began to speak, and he said, "No, you need to listen. Ask any of your colleagues, and they'll tell you that I will gladly speak to the media and answer any question I can and probably a few that I shouldn't. Like it or not, you don't need me on your bad side, and this is not how you avoid that, especially as we are just getting to know one another. I can be a lot more open with you if I know I can trust you, and how you play this will go a long way toward establishing that trust."

"But this is a big story. My biggest yet." She was almost whining.

"This story isn't worth jack squat without someone going on record, and I'm guessing without me, you don't have that." She didn't respond. "Look, I get it. Cop sees you hanging around, thinks you're cute, and figures the best way to get you talking to him is to give you a juicy scoop." She made a noise that told Barclay his theory wasn't far from the truth. He continued, "Well, it may be a big story. Or maybe you don't realize just how much of the story you *don't* have, and it's not near the story you think it is. Either way, are you willing to trade a single story, no matter how big it may be, for no access at all as long as you're with the *Trib*? Which, incidentally, won't be very long once your boss realizes you don't have the access you need to write good stories."

He gave her a few seconds, and he could hear her turning all of this over in her head.

"Listen, Rebecca, I don't know you very well, but from what little I've seen, you have the chops for this job. Not everyone does. Not everyone gets it, but it seems to me you do. I want to help you; honestly, I do. But I need some time, and if that's not good enough and you run with what you have now, I guarantee you Mr. Manning will not be happy because it will be a half-ass article with zero corroboration." Lou Manning was the owner of the *Towne Tribune*.

"Fine. How much time do you need?" Barclay was thinking when she said, "I swear, Mr. Griffith, if I get scooped on this..."

"Look, you're not going to get scooped, okay? I promise you that. And call me Barclay."

"Whatever. How can you guarantee no one else will get the story."

"Oh, someone else may get it, but they'll be in the same boat you are. They'll need someone on the record, and no one, and I do mean no one with the PD who is leaking anything to the media will go on the record."

"You think?"

"Why'd you call me instead of the police?"

She thought about the question. "Because I was told the chief doesn't like to talk to the press."

"More like he refuses to, except at press conferences, but yes, that's why you called me. Because I'm the only one willing to go on record, and I will, but give me the time I need. I'd like to say it will be this evening, but I'm not going to say that because I can't be sure I can get back to you by then. But I will do my best to do so."

"I don't know."

"This is off the record, okay?"

"Okay," she said, drawing the word out.

"I mean it. You burn me on this, and you will be done here, that I promise. I won't ever tell you what you can and can't print regarding anything I say on the record, but I will destroy you if you dishonor any agreement you make regarding not being on record, am I clear?"

"Yes."

Barclay waited for more, but nothing came, so he said, "We're off the record?"

"I guess." He didn't respond. Finally, she said, "Yes, we're off the record."

"Don't act so sad. You've got a long career ahead of you. You need to relax a little."

"Whatever. I just don't understand why you need so much time."

"Do you want the families of these victims reading in the newspaper that their loved ones were the victims of a serial killer?"

Silence. Then, "Holy shit, you mean the families don't even know?" He heard her typing on a keyboard.

"Remember, off the record."

"Dammit," she hissed.

"There is a lot going on here, Rebecca, and almost all of it pre-dates me by a while, and I'm just learning a lot of this as well. We also want to be careful what the killer knows about what we know."

"Oh. Cool, cool. That makes sense."

"Good. I'm glad you understand." Barclay chuckled. "Oh

man, Wendy Wade is going to have a come apart when you break this story."

She groaned. "I didn't even think about her getting this story."

"Don't worry about it. Remember what I said about needing someone on the record? She'll call me if she gets even a whiff of anything. I will put her off."

"And if you can't?"

"I can." He paused. "But *if* I can't, I will let you know and give you as much of a head start as possible. Go ahead and write up what you have, just in case you need to run something in a hurry. It won't come to that, but I don't want you to get beat on this because you're trying to do the right thing."

"Cool, cool. Thanks."

"I'll call you later. If you haven't heard from me by the end of the day, shoot me a text."

Barclay hung with the reporter and dialed another number. The call was answered after the first ring.

"Hey, Chief. We have a problem."

TWENTY-SIX

"Dammit!" Chief Greenhaw pounded his fist on his paper-strewn desk. He stood up, sending the worn cloth desk chair rolling into the bookcase behind his desk, causing a heavy plaque to fall off the shelf and crash to the floor. He ignored it as he walked from behind the desk to the window.

Barclay had been vague about his conversation with Rebecca Kirby in his call to the chief. He'd simply told him that a reporter was asking questions about the homicides, and they needed to meet to discuss ASAP.

In the chief's office, now, Barclay had just laid out the details to the chief and Captain Tony Jones.

Barclay had asked for Jones to be present because he had a good idea of what the chief's reaction would be, and he needed TJ present to be the cooler head.

TJ said, "Now, Chief, we knew it was only a matter of time—"

Greenhaw turned from the window and cut him off. He held up two fingers and said, "We couldn't even keep it quiet two days...two *fuckin'* days!" He turned back to the window and crossed his arms. Barclay and TJ exchanged a look.

"Chief," Barclay began before Greenhaw spun around again and pointed at TJ.

Greenhaw said, "Find out who's running their mouth. I'm sick of this shit. We've got too many cops who want to tell everybody and their mother everything they know. It's got to stop." He paused, then said, "Make an example of one or two of 'em, and that shit'll stop."

Sensing the chief was done...for now, Barclay said, "All due respect, Chief, but we can worry about that later. Right now, we need to discuss how to handle this."

Barclay looked at TJ, who said, "The DA is right. Let's deal with this newspaper reporter, and then we'll work on figuring out who talked."

Chief Greenhaw was back at the window with his arms crossed. He shook his head, made a noise, and walked back behind his desk. He groaned as he stooped to pick up the fallen plaque using the corner of the desk for support. He laid it flat on his desk rather than placing it back on the shelf from where it fell. He sat in his chair and rolled up to the desk.

"Okay," he said. "Let's talk through this. Barclay, you talked to her. Is there any way to hold her off on doing the story?"

Barclay shook his head. "No way. All she has right now is some off-the-record information, which is why she needs you or me to go on record and confirm what she's been told. Without that statement, it would be tough to put together anything of any depth, but this girl is smart. I have no doubt she could figure out a way to shoehorn something into the paper vague enough to cover her ass but with enough info to have you and me answering some tough questions tomorrow. She doesn't know exactly what she has, but she's smart enough to understand the gravity of her information. She sees this story as a big opportunity for her, and she's probably right."

The chief looked sick. "So, she's running with it regardless of what we say."

"Not necessarily," said Barclay.

TJ said, "Do you think it's all or nothing with her? Is she amenable to working with us on this?"

"That's my thought, Cap. We need to go ahead and face the fact that we're on borrowed time, and it will become public sooner rather than later. At least this way, we can maybe control the narrative a bit. I made it very clear to her that the benefits of working with us far outweighed the ramifications of her steamrolling us on this."

"Chief, I'm with Barclay. We've got to consider the long game here. Ignore her or try and shut her down, and we risk her printing God knows what. We can either let her print innuendo and supposition or give her enough for her story while not hurting the investigation. Plus," TJ shrugged, "we give her something, and maybe we get an ally in the media."

Barclay nodded at TJ. "My thought exactly."

TJ: "And maybe a news story shakes the right branch, and some useful information falls out."

Barclay: "Didn't think of that. Good point."

Greenhaw leaned back and rubbed a hand over his face and down his throat. He patted his chest and said, "Where'd y'all leave it?"

"She agreed to give me some time to get back to her with a response."

The chief perked up and leaned forward. "So we *do* have time."

"I told her I'd do everything I could to get back to her this evening." Barclay looked at his watch. "It's almost five o'clock.

We've got maybe another four hours before they go to print. I'd like to get back to her by eight."

"Tell her you did everything you could and you couldn't get back to her tonight." Chief Greenhaw shrugged and looked between the DA and the captain. "Sounds perfectly reasonable to me. Gives us an extra day before the story breaks."

Barclay began to slowly shake his head. "I don't think that's how we need to play this, Chief. She was ready to run this, and I talked her down. Like it or not, she's doing us a favor by giving us the time we asked for, and I don't want her to see that that trust was misplaced by screwing with her."

"There's also Wendy Wade," said TJ.

"Christ," said Greenhaw.

"That's another concern Kirby has. Not getting scooped by Wendy," added Barclay.

TJ laughed, "Oh man, Wendy is gonna be some kinda pissed."

That drew a small laugh from the sullen police chief, who looked at TJ and then Barclay. "Hell, that's reason enough to help this young lady out. So, what do you suggest we do?" Barclay was about to speak when the chief held up a hand and said, "We are going to maintain our policy of not commenting on open investigations, clear? That's non-negotiable."

"I don't see that being a problem," said Barclay. "I think we confirm there are some older, unsolved homicides that may be connected, and those cases are getting a fresh look in light of new evidence. As for the current case, unless you object, I think we take the same approach. Tell her there may be a connection between this most recent homicide and some older, unsolved cases. We don't give anything specific with regard to that possible connection for the sake of the integrity of the investigation."

"She'll be good with that?" TJ asked.

"I don't give two shits what she's good with," said Greenhaw.

"This little greenhorn isn't going to waltz in here thinking she's Woodward and Bernstein making a bunch of demands."

Barclay said, "I already made it clear to her that there were things we weren't going to be able to discuss, and I impressed upon her why there were also certain sensitive pieces of information that, if made public, would hamper the investigation and she was fine with all that."

"You think she'll attempt to identify the specific cases?" TJ asked.

"I do. You remember that article she wrote about the cold case grant where she listed all the open, unsolved cases? Well, those are public record now, so I expect she will tie those cases together."

"Wonderful," said Greenhaw.

"Which brings me to our biggest issue," said Barclay, and Greenhaw gave a look that said, *What now?* "We need to speak to these families before the newspaper prints an article saying their loved ones were the victims of a serial killer."

"Oh, Jesus," croaked Greenhaw, putting both hands over his face.

TWENTY-SEVEN

I t was a few minutes before 7:00 AM the following morning, and Barclay was transitioning from his last round of wall balls to his thousand-meter row cash out when his Apple Watch buzzed. He assumed it was letting him know he had reached a fitness benchmark, so he ignored it as he strapped his feet into his rower. Then it buzzed again, then again. He checked his watch on his first pull and saw it was Wendy Wade calling him. *The article.*

He ignored it and kept rowing. His watch buzzed again. She was calling him back. He cursed to himself both because sweat was stinging his eyes, and Wendy Wade wouldn't leave him alone for four more minutes.

His watch buzzed yet again, this time with a text from the reporter. He didn't take the time to read it, choosing to concentrate on his burning legs and shoulders and increasing heart rate.

Three minutes and forty seconds after beginning his row, he reached a thousand meters, loosened his foot straps, and rolled off the machine onto the floor, exhausted. As he lay on his back, he checked his watch and read Wendy's text.

Call me. ASAP

After about a minute, he got up off the floor and began putting away his equipment, noting the sweat angel he had left on the dark gray floor.

He was in his car leaving the gym when he returned the reporter's phone call.

"What the fuck, Barclay?"

"Well, good morning to you too, Wendy."

"Cut the crap, Barclay. I mean, seriously, what the hell? You gave that to her instead of me?"

"You think I wanted this out there? She put it all together and called me late yesterday afternoon about it."

"So you had plenty of time to give me a head's up, is what you're saying."

"Oh, come on now, Wendy. You know I couldn't do that to her any more than I would do that to you."

"So what can you tell me?" Just like that, she went from angry to reporter mode. Barclay respected her passion and professionalism.

"I can give you what I gave her." She made to interrupt, but he cut her off. "It's an ongoing investigation, and you know better than anyone what that means."

"Off the record?"

"Come on, Wendy, you're killing me here."

She made a sound that was something between a purr and...a something. Wendy Wade did not beg for information. She just made this noise that told you she *really* wanted more. Barclay had no doubt this throaty sound melted lesser men keen on withholding precious knowledge of a criminal investigation and caused many a cop to loosen their tongues.

Barclay almost always gave her more information than could be reported, not because of her feminine wiles but because he knew the value of their mutually beneficial relationship, and she had never violated his trust with information before. As frustrated as she made so many others with her timely reporting, she was the consummate news professional.

"Alright. I didn't give the newspaper the connection between the cases." He paused for dramatic effect. He needed her to understand the gravity of the information he was giving her. She'd want more—she always wanted more—so he had to make even the smallest disclosure seem exceedingly valuable. "He leaves a calling card at the scene, and this most recent killing bore the same hallmark."

"Which was?"

"I can't tell you."

"Ugh. You're driving me crazy, you know that? Just spill it. You know I won't say a word."

"I know you won't, Wendy. I just can't. This is a major piece of information in this investigation, and it cannot, under any circumstances, be made public."

"But Barclay—"

"I can't. You know I would if I could, but I can't."

She exhaled. "I know. I know you can't." She paused, then: "Can I guess."

Barclay laughed. "You can do whatever you want, but I'm not going to comment on anything you say."

"Does he take trophies?"

"You watch too much television."

"I thought you weren't going to comment," she said with a smile in her voice.

"Yeah, well, your reporter Jedi mind trick made me do it." She began to speak, and he said, "Sorry, Wendy, gotta go; I'm pulling up to my house now. I need to get cleaned up and into the office. You want me to send you the statement I sent the *Trib* reporter?"

"Sure," she grumbled.

―――――

BARCLAY HAD BARELY SAT down at his desk when his cell phone, email, and office phone began blowing up with reporters reacting to the story in the *Towne Tribune* intimating a possible serial killer on the loose. The serial murder angle expanded the interest in the case from local to statewide. *People Magazine, USA Today*, and the Associated Press even contacted him. His response to each one was the same: he either emailed, texted, or repeated the statement verbatim that he had given Rebecca Kirby. A few reporters merely asked if the statement in the *Trib* was his statement and asked him to affirm the statement so they could use it.

The media barrage finally subsided just after 10:00, and Barclay was able to focus on actual work. While he'd been fielding phone calls, he'd had to turn away four attorneys in his office who needed to speak with him, and he was just now taking those meetings. He was currently talking with Stacy Steen about one of the more heinous murder cases to occur in Towne in recent memory.

Antonio Raile was a small-time hood with a habit of attempting to defraud banks—sometimes successful, sometimes not. He started his "career" by stealing checks from mailboxes, washing the payee names off the paper, and inserting an alias for which he had opened a checking account. He would deposit the check via a mobile app on his phone, and then before the check would clear, he'd go to the bank and cash the check while also withdrawing the money from the account. He took a total of three banks for more than eight thousand dollars before finally getting caught.

He pleaded guilty to three counts of theft and criminal possession of a forged instrument and received an eight-year suspended sentence to go along with five years of probation. A month after he was sentenced, he had a new scheme. He and a friend would drive to

Atlanta, less than two hours away via interstate, and recruit a home-less person to ride back to Towne with them to pass bad checks at banks. These checks were printed on a cheap laser jet printer using account and routing numbers from fast food restaurants, general contractors, and any other business he had friends working at that would give him the relevant information off their paychecks.

He would then send the homeless person into the bank with the promise of a percentage of the proceeds. This scheme worked more times than it didn't. When it didn't, the person arrested was the homeless person because they were the person in the bank actively attempting to pass the forged check. The police were aware of the scheme, but none of the homeless arrested gave up Raile, either because they didn't know his real name or because they were terrified of him or both. They just took their charge, pleaded guilty, received probation, and went back to being homeless.

On one particular occasion, the homeless man was more than willing to cooperate with the police. He gave the detective a phys-ical description and the name he overheard one of them use: Stank. The police knew Stank to be Antonio Raile. The homeless man picked Raile out of a paper lineup, and Raile was subse-quently charged and had his probation revoked.

At Raile's preliminary hearing, the defendant's attorney, Daryl Blaine, asked the case agent to reveal the witness who identified Raile as the person behind the scheme. In the days after his arrest, the police had listened to jail calls where Raile was putting the word out to find the snitch and handle him.

No witness, no case.

It wasn't quite that straightforward, but the police knew what they were hearing. Because of that, after the preliminary hearing, the detective told the homeless man to get back to Atlanta, where he'd be safe, and the police or prosecutor would be in touch if he were needed for trial. They did not tell the homeless man about the threats.

Maybe because he decided he liked Towne or more probably because he lacked the ability to get back to Atlanta, he never left, and three days after the prelim, a 911 call came in about a fire. When the fire department reported to the scene, they found a person duct taped to a sidewalk bench engulfed in flames. On the opposite end of the bench was the word *Snitch* in white spray paint. The burn victim was the homeless man from the Raile case. He had survived the initial fire but succumbed to his injuries twenty-seven hours after he was rescued.

It took a couple of weeks, but a female in her early twenties met with a detective late one night to tell what she saw. She knew the man who had set the witness on fire and gave the police his name. He was a known associate and frequent partner in crime of Antonio Raile. There were also numerous calls between the two since Raile's probation was revoked. Both the man identified by the witness and Raile were charged and subsequently indicted for capital murder.

Stacy was in Barclay's office because, with the trial three months away, their lone witness to the murder was now causing problems. She was now recanting her statement that had been turned over in discovery to Raile and his co-defendant. Raile's attorney, who secured the witness's recanting of the statement in his office, under oath, and before a court reporter, was now in Stacy's office with the transcript demanding the case be dismissed immediately.

Barclay asked Stacy what she wanted to do, and she stated she wanted to move forward. She wanted time to work on the witness, undeterred by the defense attorney's tactics. She could not prove coercion or tampering without the witness's cooperation, but she knew it had occurred.

Barclay agreed with her position.

"Still," she said, "will you talk to this jackass? I've given Fiddlesticks his answer, and he refuses to leave my office. I was only able to slip out because I told him I needed to discuss it with you."

"Let's go." Barclay got up, and Stacy followed him down the hall to her office.

Daryl Blaine was a doughy man of average height with heavily gelled hair and a part that showed his scalp just above his left ear. He wore an electric blue suit and a poorly tied bright yellow tie. He had once worked in the DA's office but lasted less than a year before striking out on his own. In his first jury trial as a prosecutor, he referred to the defendant's actions as "shenanigans," which earned him the unflattering moniker "Fiddlesticks," and it had stuck.

He heard Barclay approaching and stood as they entered. He said, "Barclay."

"Look, Fiddlesticks—"

"It's Daryl," the man said through clenched teeth.

"Stacy gave you her response," the DA said. "She and I discussed it, and I agree with how she is handling the case. Now, you need to leave."

The bulb of fat spilling out above his shirt collar began to jiggle, then shake as he shook his head. "Look," he said, waving around what Barclay presumed to be the transcript of the witness's recantation. "Your witness said she was mistaken. She didn't get a good look at the person who did this. You can't possibly prove my client is guilty without her. You're ethically obligated to dismiss this case."

Barclay took a single step into the shallow office and was nose-to-nose with the shorter Blaine. "Don't you lecture me about ethics, you hear me. You threatened this girl into this statement, and I'll be damned if I'm going to let your client benefit from this bullshit."

"How dare you. I did no such thing—"

"Just get out of my office," Barclay yelled and stepped aside, pointing to the exit.

"I wanted to try and work something out before filing a motion to dismiss. Co-defendant's counsel will be doing the same."

Barclay closed back onto the defense lawyer. "Good. No, really, that's good." He was speaking in an even, measured tone. "I'm going to open an investigation into witness tampering, and the judge *will* go along with it. She knows what your client did, and she isn't going to want that piece of shit out, either. That should delay the trial a few months.

Meanwhile, your guy gets to sit back there and rot. Better yet, he'll get sent to DOC while we sort this out." Barclay let that hang, then said, "You know he should have been in DOC already because his probation was revoked, but I was all set to allow him to stay here in the county until his trial. Keep him near his family. And it's a hell of a lot less savage here. But it appears you've left me no choice. I'll tell the sheriff he can go ahead and put him on the next bus to Atmore."

Blaine's eyes went wide. "You can't do that."

"Watch me." Then Barclay called for Fitz. The yelling had already drawn the investigator out of his office, so Fitz was at the doorway almost instantly.

"Yeah, Boss?"

"Get this guy out of here." Barclay left Stacy's office and was walking back to his own when his cell phone rang. He checked his watch and, seeing who was calling, hustled back to his office to answer his phone.

Fitz said from the hallway, "Come on, Fiddlesticks. Let's not make a scene."

Again, through clenched teeth, Blaine said, "It's Daryl."

"Yeah, yeah. You need to leave."

———

BARCLAY GRABBED the phone from the windowsill where it sat charging. "Hey, Chief."

"Hey, Barclay. It looks like you're handling all the media calls. This damn thing has absolutely blown up."

"Yes. I've been giving them all the statement we agreed to last night. Nothing more."

"Okay, good. I've been no commenting."

"That all you needed?"

"I wish, but no. The attorney general called me a few minutes ago to tell me he's heading up here to meet with me about this case. He said he'd be here at 2:30. I didn't get the impression he would be calling you, so I am. I'd like for you to be here at the meeting."

Barclay silently cursed. "The son of a bitch is coming to take this case."

"He said he just wanted to offer the help of his office, and he wanted to hear what all we had so he could best decide how he could assist us."

"Bullshit. He sees the publicity this case is generating and wants it. We need to be very, very careful what we tell him unless we want him holding his own news conference telling the world everything we have."

"You really think he'd do that?"

"Oh, hell yeah. He wants to be the next governor and can't wait to tell everyone how involved he is in this case. What better way to get the point across than to give some inside info to the general public? He doesn't give a damn about the outcome of the case. By the time we solve it—if we solve it—go to the grand jury and then to trial, it could be two years or more down the road. He'll be in the governor's mansion by then if he has it his way.

He's a politician, not a prosecutor. He doesn't care about the victims or justice."

There was a silence as Barclay awaited the chief's response. Finally, the chief said, "But he's the AG. Can we really not tell him everything?"

"Of course. He has no authority here." Barclay went silent as he thought. Maybe ten seconds later, he said, "Call him back and tell him this afternoon doesn't work for you."

"What do I tell him I'm doing?"

"Tell him whatever you want. Make something up. Or better yet, don't tell him anything at all. It's none of his business what you're busy with and he shouldn't automatically assume that you'll be available whenever he up and decides he needs to chat on a whim."

"I guess," said Chief Greenhaw, but he didn't sound convinced.

"Look, I'll take the heat. Besides, it's me he'll ultimately have to deal with on this if and when we ever make an arrest and have an actual case to prosecute. He doesn't want the investigation because his office is nowhere near equipped enough for a full-scale criminal investigation. Without a guaranteed arrest, he won't come within a million miles of it."

When the chief didn't respond, Barclay said, "I have a lunch meeting to get to. Call the AG back and tell him you can't guarantee you'll be able to see him today—he won't want to waste a trip up. Whatever you do, do not meet with him today. I promise you, we will all regret it if we do. I'll swing by after lunch, and we can discuss it further."

TWENTY-EIGHT

Barclay was passing through his office lobby a minute before noon when he heard his name called. He turned to locate the source and saw a gangly dark-haired man in glasses and dressed in a well-fitted suit. "Yes."

The man closed the distance in two strides, holding out his hand. "It's Franklin Masterson. We met a few months ago at the Crafty Lefty. I was with Stacy Steen."

Barclay shook his head. "Right...Franklin. Yes, sorry." He extended a hand, and they shook. "It's just been one of those days. A few days, actually."

"Yes, I've seen the news," said Masterson, sticking his hands in his pockets. "Something about a serial killer?"

"Something like that. We're still evaluating everything. You know how it is."

"I don't actually. Know how it is, I mean." He removed his hands from his pockets and held them out beside him in a casual shrug. "I do tax and estate law, remember?"

"Right. Well, we all have our issues regardless of the area of law we practice." Barclay had angled his body toward the exit, hoping Masterson would read his body language and allow him to leave.

"But nothing like you, right?"

"What do you mean?"

"I mean, you deal with death and murder. Serious stuff. Nothing like the mundane, boring stuff I handle every day."

"Screw up someone's tax shelter or their loved one's will, and I bet it's not too mundane," Barclay said with a polite laugh that Masterson didn't return.

Masterson said, "Making any progress?"

A shrug. "We'll get there."

Stacy Steen came through the inner door into the lobby. Barclay made the connection, pointed between the two, and said, "Ah, you're here to see her."

Masterson had made his way back to his original spot and picked up a briefcase Barclay had not noticed before. "Had to bring something to the clerk's office, so I figured I'd treat Stacy to lunch."

"Nice," Barclay said. "If you'll excuse me, I have to grab something myself."

"You're welcome to join us," said Stacy.

"Oh, no, thank you. I have a meeting at one, so I have to make it quick."

Barclay was at the door when Masterson said, "Nice seeing you again."

———

BARCLAY AND CAPTAIN JONES sat in front of Greenhaw's desk in the chief's office. The chief had just told them that the AG agreed not to come by today with minimal false truths needed. After going through that, he asked Barclay, "You believe that'll be the last we hear from him on this?"

"Not likely. We have some time because, like I said, it's just an investigation at this point. But I thought about it during lunch, and he'll regroup and come up with some compelling reason to get involved in the investigation somehow. He won't want to lead it, but he'll want his office involved. That'll get him the requisite media face time he's after, and, as I said earlier, he'll tell it all."

Greenhaw absently played with a ball of rubber bands, looked at Captain Jones, and said, "What are you thinking, TJ?"

"That we'd better solve these cases. And quick."

———

WHEN HE WAS DONE with the meeting at the police station, Barclay saw he had a missed call from Fitz. He returned the call when he was in his Tahoe on the way back to the DA's office. The call went unanswered, and he hung up without leaving a message.

Back at his office, he went looking for Fitz. Seeing his office empty, Barclay went to see his assistant and asked if she knew where the chief investigator was.

"He said someone you went to see yesterday called, and he was going to meet with them. I guess you know what he's talking about?" Barclay nodded and headed to his office.

Barclay was back in his office replaying the meeting with Chief Greenhaw and wondered how long he would hang tough with the Attorney General. He was worried another call from the AG would crumble his already shakey resolve.

He was in his desk chair staring out the window when Fitz walked in with two quick knocks on the open office door. He said, "Hey, Boss, I heard back from the owner of Loraine Mount's home—victim number four. Hers was one of the houses we stopped by yesterday and left a card."

Barclay swung his legs off the window sill and spun around to face the dapper detective. "Anything good?"

Fitz shook his head. "Nothing. I don't know how many times that house has changed hands since the murder, but the current owners didn't buy it from the Mount family, nor did they know the Mounts. They're not even from the area; they moved here a couple of years ago for the wife's job. The realtor told them about the history of the house before they bought the property, but beyond that, they weren't able to provide any useful information."

Barclay sat forward and leaned his elbows on his desk. He steepled his fingers at his lips and let out a breath.

"I called Beck and asked her to see if there were any construction permits associated with the property," Fitz said. "I know it's a long shot, Boss, but at this point, she's already doing the same for the Bates and Albritton properties. Surely, it's worth a look. If she doesn't find anything, we can cross that off the list as a potential connection."

"No, Fitz, you're right. It's a good thought."

"In the meantime, I'm going to see what I can find out about the previous owners and reach out to them."

Barclay told Fitz about the chief's phone call from the AG. They talked through it, and ultimately, Fitz's opinion mimicked that of Captain Jones. He said, "We'd better solve these cases... quick."

TWENTY-NINE

The killer had not had a productive day at work. That morning, after reading the Towne Tribune article online about the potential link between his murder of Freida Nelson and the killings from two decades ago, as well as the strong possibility of a serial killer operating in Towne, Alabama, he went on to read similar articles from various state news outlets and even a few national ones. The *Trib's* article was the most informative, with nothing new revealed by the other news outlets. By the end of the day, he could recite the DA's statement by rote, given the number of times he'd read the same words over and over in each story.

It had worked, at least so far. He had initially believed that the key to getting away with murder was killing someone you had zero ties to, leaving the police with no way to connect the victim back to their executioner, and had followed that guideline in the Jed Burlington killing; however, he had violated that rule in the Nelson slaying. He debated that issue with himself for days, going back and forth on whether or not to move forward with the murder. Ultimately, though, he opted to take the risk for two reasons. First, because his knowledge of Ms. Nelson and her living situation would aid in the commission of the act, and second, it's how the original killer operated—each victim had a connection to her tormentor.

He had followed the original killer's methods, and so far, so good. He understood times had changed, and the proliferation of technology and forensics made murder a much more difficult crime to get away with. Still, he had rationalized that should the police knock on his door, he would merely acknowledge that, yes, he knew Ms. Nelson, and he was devastated to hear of her violent passing.

The killer settled into bed shortly after midnight, mentally running through the article written by Rebecca Kirby. She was a smart one, he decided. She saw the serial killer angle where no one else had. It broke sooner than he'd expected, but that was of no bother to him.

He also continued replaying the DA's statement in his head, trying hard to shut his mind down for some much-needed rest but failing. Instead, he embraced the thoughts.

Knowing what he knew about *all* the murders—his and the previous killer's—he was confident from the statement that the police had made the connection. He didn't need them to admit as much publicly for him to be certain of that.

Now, laying under the covers—the darkness pierced only by the red dot of light of the wall-mounted television—unable to fall asleep and buoyed by the apparent success of this latest homicide, he began planning his next kill.

THIRTY

B eck Lawson and Tina Crump stayed at the police department until almost 3:00 in the morning, finishing up with the child pornography and human trafficking cases for the bond hearing. Tina emailed the completed reports to the prosecutor handling the hearing before going home and getting a few hours of sleep. Beck emailed Chief Greenhaw and Drummond, letting them know she was now clear to focus exclusively on the Freida Nelson case as well as the associated homicides.

Beck was awakened from a deep, dreamless sleep by her ringing cell phone. She first knocked it off her nightstand and then sightlessly fished for it under her bed. She answered, not bothering to check the caller ID, voice thick with sleep.

"Wake up, kid, it's time to get to work," came the overly enthusiastic voice of Wayne Drummond. After a beat of reciprocal silence, he said, "Come on now, rise and shine. We got a murder to solve." The jubilant voice was muted a bit by the fact that her long hair was pressed between her iPhone and her left ear.

"What...what time is it?" Beck asked, rolling over onto her back.

"It's 9:30. Now get up. I'll be by your place in fifteen to pick you up."

"Wait, what are we going to do?" Hearing nothing, she said, "Hello..." She pulled the phone away from her ear and looked at the screen. Drummond had hung up. "Ugh."

Drummond pulled the beleaguered Dodge Charger into her driveway as she closed and locked the front door behind her. She deposited her computer bag and sweater in the front passenger floorboard before dropping into the passenger seat, hot coffee sloshing out of her travel mug onto her right hand. "Shit," she said, taking the tall silver cup with her left hand and releasing it into the cup holder, sloshing more out.

Drummond smiled and said, "Trying to impress the boss with three AM emails is bad karma. No one likes a suck-up."

She was in no mood and asked if Drummond had a phone charger in the car. He reached over and pointed to a spot below the radio where an adapter was plugged into the car's lighter socket.

Beck nodded and reached for the long silver braided cord, her arm moving as if reaching into a jar of honey. She slid her hand up the cord until she reached the end and plugged in her phone. "I guess I was so exhausted when I got home this morning I forgot to plug it in."

"You know," Drummond began, "you still have sleep marks on your face."

She clasped a ponytail holder in her teeth as she scraped her hair into a ponytail, sliding the elastic band into place and wrapping it around a few times until it was secure.

She leaned back into her seat with a huff, then said, "I've spent the last two days looking at some of the most vile images you can imagine. I finally managed to get those images out of my head long enough to fall asleep when you called." He gave her a sideways glance but didn't comment. "So please excuse the sleep marks."

He didn't know what else to say, so he went with, "Sorry."

She waived it off and took a swig of her coffee. "I'm just glad to be onto something else. Where're we headed now?"

The car bounced and glided down the road the way only a police interceptor did. He said, "We started visiting the scenes of the old murder cases yesterday and got to all but one of them. We are headed to the place we missed. Site of the first homicide: Cindy Stover."

"Gonna be just us?"

"Yep. Barclay is tied up, and Fitz is doing computer work on the case this morning. We'll check it out and let them know if we find anything." They rode in silence for another couple of minutes when Drummond said, "I don't suppose you've had a chance to look into any of the financials or building permit stuff."

He felt more than saw the stare she gave him in response to his question.

"Hey, I was just asking."

———

THEY ARRIVED at the address a few minutes past 10:00 and parked in front of the house—there were two cars in the driveway. Unlike the other houses they had visited, this one was not in one of Towne's older, more established neighborhoods. By the looks of the lack of mature trees and repeated home designs, Drummond surmised this was a development favored back in the nineties.

Clear-cut a large acreage of land, give prospective buyers three or four elevations and floor plans to choose from, and build them as quickly and cheaply as possible. Over the years, the place had gone to seed, with lots of peeling paint and yards that were more dirt and weeds than grass.

Beck rolled up the sleeves on her pink and white striped Brooks Brothers oxford as she exited the car and finished tucking in her shirttail as they walked up the cracked driveway and followed the buckled concrete walkway to the faded and peeling blue front door. Beck was making one last run around the waistband of her navy blue chinos when she nudged Drummond with her elbow. When he looked at her, she motioned her head ever so slightly, first at the corner of the roof line they were approaching, then at the corner of the roof line at the opposite end of the house.

Drummond casually followed her directions and saw what she wanted him to see. He gave her a quick look that communicated everything. At the door, Beck noticed the video doorbell and again glanced at her partner. She pushed the button and stepped back. Drummond was off her right hip approximately three feet. They heard the bell sound inside the home but received no response. After a minute, she moved to press the doorbell again when Drummond said, "Bang on it."

Beck angled her body and banged on the door three times with the side of her left fist, her right hand resting on the butt of her gun. They heard movement inside. She looked back at Drummond, who nodded. She lifted her fist to bang again when a voice came through the video doorbell.

"Yes?" It was a woman's voice—older but not old.

Not taking her eye off the door, Beck said, "Ma'am, we are with the Towne Police Department, and we'd like to ask you some questions."

A pause, then, "You got a warrant?"

Beck subconsciously bladed her body to the door, making herself a smaller target while not taking her eyes off the door. She heard the slight scrape of Drummond unseating his weapon from the stiff leather holster. She could tell from the sound that he hadn't removed it entirely; he'd merely gotten it into position for a quick draw. She also felt him move back slightly, creating a better sight angle for the door.

Beck said, "No, ma'am. We only want to ask you a couple of questions. Won't take long."

"What about?"

"It's about a previous homeowner."

Another long pause, then, "Go ahead. I can hear you just fine."

"Ma'am, we need to do this face-to-face. If you could please open the door."

"But you done said you ain't got no warrant."

"We don't want to search the place. Just ask you some questions about the previous owners." Not receiving a response, Beck continued, "Look, I have a doorbell just like this one on my house. The video and audio are recorded. You have us on record stating we don't have a warrant, so we have zero authority to search your home. You also have us on video stating our purpose for being here, so if we do anything more than ask you questions, we can be fired and maybe even charged with a crime for lying to you."

Beck thought she'd blown it until she heard a series of locks disengaging and the door opening slowly. In the doorway stood a woman who looked to be in her mid-fifties and a leftover from Woodstock. She had wild gray hair, fingers covered in rings, and bracelets halfway to her elbows. She wore an ankle-length multi-colored caftan, and she was barefoot.

"Thank you," Beck said, walking through the open door, not giving the woman a chance to protest.

The woman said, "Hey," as Beck brushed past her. She made a half-hearted attempt to close the door on Drummond, which failed because he closed the distance on his partner, quickly following her inside. The woman stood with her left hand, grasping the edge of the door, while her right hand held a smoldering cigarette. She said, "You two need to leave. Now."

Beck made the short trek from the doorway to the living area and was met immediately with the overwhelming smell of incense. She turned around as Drummond moved past her in a practiced movement. She was free to focus on the woman while Drummond watched the rest of the small house.

The interior of the house mirrored the exterior in its state of disrepair. The wallpaper was separating at the seams, Drummond could see at least one ragged hole in the wall, and the entryway was bare concrete covered in dried glue from where the linoleum flooring had been pulled up.

"Like I said, Ms..."

"It's missus, and the name's Harriet."

"Okay, Mrs. Harriet—"

"No," the woman interrupted. "My first name is Harriet." She took a drag on the cigarette.

Beck waited to see if she'd get more. When she saw she wasn't, she said, "Okay, Harriet. As I already told you, we have a couple of questions."

"Then will you get the fuck out?"

"Of course."

Drummond: "Do you own this house?"

"What the fuck kind of question is that?"

Beck: "Ma'am—"

"I told you it's Harriet."

"Harriet, we're just trying to—"

"You don't look like no cop," Harriet said, eyeing Beck up and down. "Now him," she waved the 100's cigarette in Drummond's direction, "he *looks* like a cop."

Beck said, "Yeah. It's unfortunate, I know. I've been on him about that mustache."

"Wait a minute," Drummond said in mock protest.

"Show me some ID," the woman wheezed.

They each produced a badge wallet and held up their badges long enough to get a nod from Harriet.

"What's all this about," boomed a voice from down the hall that startled both Beck and Drummond, who still had not re-seated his sidearm. He backed further into the living room, keeping space between himself and the man walking down the hall. He was shirtless with a paunch and a single nipple ring. He, too, had wild gray hair, but his hair ringed the side of his head as he was bald on top. His stone-colored cargo shorts were ripped in a couple of places, and he was also barefooted.

Beck kept watch on the woman while Drummond dealt with the man.

"Sir, what's your name," Drummond demanded.

Harriet yelled, "They're cops." Then, back to a conversational tone, said, "That's my husband, Harold."

Beck said, "Harold and Harriet. That's sweet."

"Cut the shit, Missy. Just ask your goddamn questions and leave."

"Why don't we go sit down in the den so we can all look at one another," suggested Beck as she backed into the den.

When Harold saw Beck, he said, "You're hot for a cop. Anyone ever tell you that?"

Beck snorted, tilted her head toward Drummond, and said, "This guy's my partner. What do you think?"

Harold let out a cackle, showing at least one missing tooth.

Drummond said, "Let's all just have a seat, and we can ask our questions and get out of your hair." He instinctively looked at Harold's wild mane. "No offense."

Harold gave him a confused look, then said, "Ah, fuck it. I gotta take a shit," and walked back down the hall from where he came.

Neither detective saw where Harold went from where they

were standing, but they heard a door close and a lock click into place. Make that two locks. Beck and Drummond shared another quick glance.

"Questions, questions," said Harriet, making a *hurry-up* motion with her ashy cigarette.

"Right," said Beck. "How long have you and Harold lived here."

"Since 1996. That it? Will you go now?"

Ignoring the question, the detective pressed on. "I don't suppose you bought the house from a Cindy Stover."

Harriet squinted her eyes as if trying to figure a complicated math problem. "I think that was her name. Old broad was murdered here?"

That surprised Beck. "Yeah. You know about that?"

"Of course I do. We bought the house, didn't we?"

"Pardon me for saying so, but most people wouldn't be too interested in buying a home where a violent death occurred."

Harriet raised the cigarette to her mouth, the ash falling to the floor. She took a drag, and smoke poured out of her mouth and nose as she spoke. "The fuck do I care about that? Got a helluva deal on account of that *violent death,* as you call it."

"I don't suppose you—"

"Where the fuck you going there, Magnum?" Harriet said, causing Beck to look back, taking her eyes off the old woman. She saw Drummond clear his gun of his holster and blazer as he edged down the hallway. She saw him take no more than three deliberate steps when she heard Harriet yell, "He's coming your way, Harold!"

What happened next, Beck would later say, unfolded in slow motion.

THIRTY-ONE

Detective Beck Lawson swung her gaze back to the hippie woman in time to see her flick her lit cigarette, hitting the detective in the hollow of her throat, sparks flying as the butt fell to the floor. She didn't realize it then, but the cigarette caused a circular burn to her skin.

As Beck drew her duty weapon, she heard locks disengaging down the hall and then heard Drummond yell, "Show me your hands!" followed by a single gunshot.

Acting on instinct, Beck charged Harriet and drove her out the still-open front door, slamming it shut and throwing the dead-bolt. She spun and made the corner of the hallway where she crouched, peeked down the hall, and saw a large body lying on its left side and struggling to sit up. *Drummond!*

She crossed the narrow opening of the hallway and, still in a crouch position, leaned against the wall on the right side. "Drummond," she half whispered. "Talk to me. What happened?"

"Ahhhh," Drummond groaned, struggling to get into a seated position. "Fucker shot me."

"What?" More groans from Drummond as his upper body toppled back down to the floor, his head toward Beck. "He's holed up in there." He pointed a bloody hand at the only door on the left side of the hall.

"I'm coming up behind you." Beck stood and, back square against the wall, made her way down the hall, crossing one foot over the other, gun pointed at the closed white door.

She made it to him and went to a knee by his head. "Where are you hit?"

"Gutshot," Drummond said through gritted teeth. "Sonofabitch was quick. Poked his head out, then up popped a gun."

"We need to get you out of this hallway." She looked up and saw an open door past Drummond's feet, thought *bedroom*, and tried to sit him up. He let out a pained cry, and she laid him back down. She was now aware of banging on the front door, which drew her gaze back up the hallway. "I'm going to try and drag you to the living room."

"Okay," he groaned, sweat beading on his forehead.

Beck told Drummond she needed both hands and asked if he could still handle his gun. When he said that he could, she asked him to cover the door just in case. She then reluctantly holstered her gun and grabbed his blazer by the shoulders. She squatted down and leaned backward, trying to drag him, but the only thing she could move was his jacket. She tried a second time with no success.

She stood, re-evaluated, and this time grabbed him under his armpits. Slowly, she was able to inch him down the hall and into the living room. When she finally got him clear of the door, she fell backward onto the musty carpet, sweat running into her eyes and gasping for breath. She pulled out her phone and dialed 911, telling dispatch they had an officer down and gave them the address. She also told them about Harriet standing outside. She described the old lady and told them to make sure they took her into custody.

She assessed Drummond's wound, seeing a Rorschach pattern of blood on the white dress shirt, then rolled him on his side and felt for an exit wound, finding none. Then came more banging on the front door, accompanied by yelling this time. She could hear enough to make out it was Harriet screeching but nothing more.

"Okay, Wayne, you've got a gunshot to the stomach with no exit wound, not seeing a lot of blood. I've called it in."

"Jesus, it hurts. Burns."

She positioned herself on a knee so she could see his face. "Tell me what happened. What did you see?"

He took a couple of deep breaths, forcing out his words. "Cameras. Outside." Beck nodded. More deep breaths. "I saw the television." Beck looked up, trying to locate the TV. She saw it and knew exactly what had happened.

"Surveillance," she said.

He made a noise between a laugh and a grunt. "Only one reason for a dump like this to have cameras."

Again, Beck nodded, "Dealers."

On the television were crystal-clear feeds from six external cameras arranged in two rows of three. She noticed the first two feeds were from the cameras she spotted on the front of the house. The third feed on the top row was from a camera mounted above the front door they hadn't noticed, and she saw the top of Harriet's squirrel's nest of a hairstyle.

"Saw the images on the TV." He let out a breath, then inhaled and spoke again. "Heard him throw the locks." Another exhale followed by a big inhale. "That's when I knew for sure..."

Beck nodded and looked back down the hall. Hearing more pounding on the front door, she looked back toward it and noticed four heavy-duty locks. Her mind went back to the sounds of all the locks being flipped before the woman opened the door. She knew she and Drummond had been on the same page with their suspicions.

She said, "You good if I go deal with Harold?"

He blinked sweat from his eyes. "Kill the sonofabitch," he said, his voice strained, spittle flying. She mopped his brow with her forearm sleeve, patted him on the shoulder, and went down the hall.

Just up from the door, back to the wall as before, and gun raised, she yelled, "Harold! Can you hear me?" Nothing. "Harold, I'm not going to bullshit you. You shot a cop, so you know it's bad. I need you to come on out before it gets any worse, okay?"

Was he crying?

"Harold, I need you to slowly open the door and toss the gun out." After a beat of silence: "I need you to acknowledge me."

Nothing.

"Harold, if you don't give yourself up, it's going to go real bad for you. I need you to go ahead and come on out."

"How is he? The cop?" Harold's muffled voice filtered through the wall.

"He's fine for now. Help is on the way. You still have a chance to walk away from this."

"They're gonna shoot me...You're gonna shoot me. I just know it."

Beck closed her eyes. She opened them and said, "Look motherfucker, you don't toss that gun out here and give yourself up, I *will* shoot you...through the fucking wall...right fucking now! You understand me?"

She began to hear sirens in the distance. After several seconds, she heard a lock click and then another. She saw the doorknob turn slowly and the door open inwardly. A small silver pistol was tossed out the door and landed across the narrow hallway at the threshold of the open bedroom door she had spotted earlier.

"Good, Harold. Now, I need you to exit the room slowly, walking backward with your hands up."

The sirens grew louder as Harold emerged from the doorway exactly as instructed.

"That's it, Harold. Nice and easy. You so much as fart, and you'll get all seventeen rounds. Am I clear?"

"Goddamn, woman," said Harold as he emerged from the room, hands up and walking backward toward her.

"Stop! Get facedown on the ground and interlace your fingers behind your head." He did as he was told.

When he was on the floor with his hands behind his head, Beck approached, gun still out, and pointed at the prone figure in a two-handed grip. She said, "Spread 'em," and kicked his legs apart. The sirens were at their loudest; the police and ambulance were here. She walked up between Harold's legs and dropped to a knee on the middle of his back, summoning a grunt from the old man.

Beck holstered her gun and withdrew handcuffs, ratcheting a cuff first around the right wrist and then the left, two clicks tighter than necessary. She stood up and observed the man face down on the filthy, matted carpet, her breathing coming under control.

Without really thinking about it, she drew back her right leg and let loose a kick. The toe of her leather Frye ankle boot made square contact between Harold's legs, eliciting a satisfying howl.

Harold recoiled into a ball and rolled over, facing up at the detective. "What the fuck, lady!" he yelled, then went into a violent gagging fit.

There was banging and shouting at the door.

Beck moved to let in the police and the paramedics when Harold managed to squeak out, "Oh, thank God...the ambulance is here."

She stopped and looked back down at the pathetic man and said, "That ambulance is not for you, you piece of shit."

Tears began to flow, and Harold rolled over onto his side and said, "Please, lady, I'm sorry." He gulped a breath and whimpered, "Just call me an ambulance, will you? Just call me an ambulance."

Beck sucked her teeth and said, "Alright, you're an ambulance," and fired another kick to the man's groin before going and unlocking the door.

THIRTY-TWO

Beck was walking alongside the gurney being wheeled out to the ambulance, holding Drummond's hands in hers, resting them on his chest. The paramedics pronounced him stable and said the wound did not appear life-threatening. As he was about to be placed into the ambulance, Barclay Griffith came running up.

He put a hand on the gurney and said breathlessly, "Got here as fast I could." To Beck: "How is he?"

"I'm fine," said Drummond through an oxygen mask.

Beck said, "Gutshot by a piece of shit .22. Breechloader—probably last used in the Civil War. It took four detectives to figure out how to open the damn thing. Hoping they can retrieve the bullet. Should be fine." She looked down at Drummond and said, "That about cover it?"

Drummond responded with a laconic half-nod and a thumbs-up.

To Beck, Barclay said, "Greenhaw said they have a grow operation inside." Then to Drummond: "Meth lab yesterday, marijuana grow today. That has to be a record."

"Make sure you arrest this one, huh," said Drummond.

"We gotta get him outta here," said a paramedic.

He began to push the gurney into the ambulance when Drummond reached out and grabbed Beck's wrist. The paramedic paused. "Great work, Detective." He winced as he spoke through labored breathing. "You saw those cameras...put us on notice... could have been a whole lot worse."

She nodded and wiped away a tear.

Drummond waived her in close so he could speak into her ear. He said, "And whatever you did to that motherfucker to cause him to scream like that...thanks." He coughed.

Beck laughed and sniffed as she stood. "Get him out of here."

She and Barclay backed away, watching the gurney being pushed into the ambulance, followed by the paramedic.

Barclay said, "What did he say?"

Beck smiled and wiped her eyes. "He commended me on the peaceful surrender of the shooter."

As the ambulance pulled away in full lights and sirens, she and Barclay were about to speak when Sheriff Ramos called from the front stoop: "Detective. Join us inside?" It was an order formed as a request.

———

THE KITCHEN WAS the only room in the house not being processed for evidence. Since it was not teeming with investigators and crime scene techs, that is where Beck Lawson, Sally Ramos, Chief Adam Greenhaw, and Barclay Griffith stood discussing what had taken place inside the house.

Since the victim was a TPD detective, Sheriff Ramos was now taking over the investigation from TPD. However, this case promised to be a lot less complicated than the Hunter Stanton murder.

"Walk us through it," said Ramos.

Beck began by explaining why they had gone to the house in the first place and then took them through every step after arriving as she could remember it. Given the traumatic events that unfolded, some details were missing, but she more or less got it right.

"This place is wired pretty good, so a lot of this should be recorded somewhere," said Beck. "We were recorded arriving, and my interaction with the female should be documented on the doorbell's video and audio. Make sure you grab that."

When Beck was through laying it all out, Sheriff Ramos said, "Just so we're all on the same page, there was a pretty significant marijuana growing operation going on in that room. Probably why all this damn incense is being used; cover up the odor of weed."

"Yeah, well," said Greenhaw, "knowing what we know now, you can definitely smell the weed. The hint of it, at least."

Ramos said, "The grow room will give you a sure 'nough contact high. Hell of a setup in there. Lights, irrigation."

Barclay said, "But why shoot a cop over weed? Have they not gotten the memo that no one seems to care about that anymore?"

"Good question," said Ramos. "Ol' Harold is damn sure in the shit now, though."

Evidence Technician Angie Presley walked into the kitchen wearing blue latex gloves and holding a gallon-sized Ziplock bag filled to capacity.

"What've you got, Angie?" asked Ramos.

"I'm guessing it's heroin. There are bricks of this stuff lining the closet in the grow room."

Chief Greenhaw said, "Guess the weed wasn't what these two hippies were concerned about protecting." He immediately unclipped his phone from his hip and dialed a number. "Hey, TJ... yeah, we're still here...Drummond's going to be fine...Okay, I will.

Listen, get with narcotics, and see if they have any intel on this address...Thanks."

Beck got a look on her face. She turned to Barclay and said, "What was that you said to Drummond about a meth lab yesterday?"

"Meth lab?" parroted the police chief.

"Oh, uh...nothing," said Barclay. He shrugged. "Inside joke. Just trying to boost his spirits."

"But he said something about arresting *this* one," said Beck.

"I didn't hear that. Huh. You sure you heard that correctly? Maybe the pain meds were kicking in."

Beck was about to speak when Barclay's hard-set jaw and penetrating gaze stopped her. Everyone was looking at her. "Must've misheard," she said. "You need anything else from me, Sheriff?"

Ramos said they were done for the time being, but she asked the detective to report to the sheriff's office to make a formal statement.

Beck was walking off when she turned back. "What about Harriet? I assume she was taken into custody?"

Ramos said, "Yes. The first officer on the scene subdued her. Of course, it took a couple of rides on the Taser, but he got her handled."

"She resisted?" asked Barclay.

Ramos smirked and said, "According to the officer, she stated she was giving up, but with an officer down inside and what with that big ass muumuu she was wearing, who knows what she had hidden underneath. I'm pretty sure she made a furtive movement."

"Gold star to the officer," said Barclay, smiling. "Sounds like he may have saved some lives with his quick thinking."

The meeting broke up, and Barclay walked out with Beck. He said, "Let's not lose sight of your initial reason for being here,

Detective. We need to see if there's a connection with the Stover homicide and the others."

She said, "I asked Harriet about the house before all hell broke loose. She and her husband bought it from Ms. Stover...after the murder, obviously."

"That all she said?"

"That's as far as we got. That's when Drummond started down the hall and..." Her voice trailed off.

"Well, that's something, I suppose. Maybe we can ask her more about it later. I'm going to do a walk around the house, then conduct a walkthrough when crime scene is done—see if anything jumps out. We'll regroup in a day or two. Just let me know when you're up to it." She nodded. "And about the meth lab comment," he said. "I'll explain later."

Beck began to walk to her car when Barclay called after her. He said, "Excellent work today, Lawson. From start to finish. A helluva job."

THIRTY-THREE

"I paid our friends another visit this morning...still not talking," Sheriff Ramos told the others seated around the table in her conference room. Greenhaw, Barclay, and Beck Lawson were all present to get an update on the shooting of Detective Drummond as well as planning a path forward in the Freida Nelson murder case.

Barclay asked, "Have they asked for a lawyer?"

"Not yet. Both of them just sit and stare at me when I try to question them. Doesn't matter, though, because we've got them dead to rights on attempted murder and the dope charges. The geniuses had a camera in the grow room. You can hear Harriet yell something that lines up with what Detective Lawson said about her shouting a warning at her husband that Detective Drummond was coming. It's faint, but you can hear it." She reviewed her notes. "Then you see him grab that little pistol on a table, lean into the hall, and fire despite Drummond's ordering him to show his hands."

"Do you hear what Drummond is saying on the video?" Barclay asked.

Ramos nodded. "Yes. With the door open, the cameras picked up the audio pretty clearly. Lucky for us, it was an expensive camera setup. Everything was captured in high definition."

"There was video inside the house?" Beck asked, her thoughts going to kicking Harold in the balls.

"Just in the grow room," said Ramos. "Guessing they were only interested in keeping watch over their stash. I did reach out to our narcotics guys as well as the feds, but the Reynolds were not on anyone's radar. According to their network of informants, however, the Reynolds are most definitely players in the heroin market. Not exactly earth-shattering news, considering they had more than eighteen pounds of the stuff in that closet."

"What do you think about me going in there to ask them about the old cases? You think they'd talk if they weren't asked about the drugs or the shooting?" asked Beck.

"I doubt it, but even if they would, they almost certainly won't talk to you," said Ramos. "The *only* thing the man or the woman said had to do with you specifically. They each called you a word that begins with a *C* and rhymes with *Bunt*."

Beck reeled back. "Oh my."

"Yeah, I can't even bring myself to repeat it."

Barclay said, "Until they ask for a lawyer or invoke their rights, we can continue trying to question them—"

"Absolutely not. To hell with both of them," interrupted Chief Greenhaw. "They're cooked, and I'm through begging them to talk to us. As far as the Stover murder is concerned, we'll just have to work around them."

"I will add Ms. Stover to the list with the others I'm researching and see what I can dig up," said Beck.

"Which brings me to something else we need to discuss," said Greenhaw. "Beck, I'm assigning you as case agent of the Nelson case, which also puts you in charge of the old murders."

She nodded and was about to speak when Greenhaw said,

"Good. And just so you know, before I could even bring it up with Drummond, he brought it up to me, so don't think you're stepping on his toes. He'll be down for a while, so it's up to you to keep this thing moving." To the group, he said, "Drummond can't contribute physically, but he's got the grey matter to be an asset on the case. He said whatever we needed from him, he'd do. Utilize him. Probably be good for his mental health, too. I was shot in ninety-nine—" Seeing the looks he received, he said, "I was shot in the hand. Not a big deal, but it messes with you. I can't imagine getting a scare like Drummond received. He'll have a lot of time on his hands, and he will replay what happened a million times, wondering what he did wrong...what he could have done differently. Some work to occupy his mind will be good for him."

To Barclay, Ramos said, "If you're good with where we are with the Reynolds, I'd like to get focused back on the Nelson case." Then to the police chief, "Assuming you're also good with that, Adam."

"Of course," said the chief.

Barclay agreed. "Like you said, we've got them nailed on the shooting and the heroin. Your investigator can clean everything up while we get on Nelson. I will get to work on getting Bonnie and Clyde no-bonded. With two cop shootings in the last seven months, we need to send a very strong message that this will not be tolerated. If someone wants to shoot the police, Towne isn't the place to do it." That got nods around the table. "In the meantime, I'll assign Fitz to this team until further notice, and Freida Nelson's case will get his full attention."

Ramos asked Greenhaw to give a medical update on Drummond.

"The surgeon said they were able to retrieve the bullet, which has been sent off to forensics. There was no significant internal damage due to the small caliber of the bullet. His intestine was nicked, and they are keeping an eye out for sepsis, but that's the extent of it. I told Drummond last night in recovery that he was lucky there was still enough muscle in his midsection to keep the bullet from tumbling around too much." That drew a laugh.

"Did he respond to that?" asked Barclay.

"He said something about Naomi at the diner taking care of him." Seeing the looks at the table, he shrugged. "Beats me. Guess the anesthesia still had him a little loopy."

Beck asked about his long-term prognosis.

"It's good. He'll be in the hospital for the next day or two, depending. After that, he'll be out for six weeks at a minimum. The doc doesn't want him moving around as his internal injuries heal. After that, we'll just have to see. I expect he'll try and come back sooner than any of us thinks he should. That's just who he is. I'd give him a few days; let him get home. Then get him involved as needed."

Plans were made to visit Drummond in the hospital, and the meeting broke up. Since she had been busy with the human trafficking case, Beck asked to be brought up to speed, so she and Barclay stayed behind to discuss the status of the Nelson investigation, which didn't take long.

Barclay then began explaining the possible connection to the six unsolved homicides from the late nineties. He was recounting their work on the older cases and the houses they had visited when she told Barclay that Drummond had mentioned visiting the Inez Cooper and Claire Albritton murder scenes in the car on the way to the Reynolds house.

"He didn't get into any detail," she said. "Only that y'all spoke to the current owners."

"Beck...about the Albritton house," Barclay said. "That's what Drummond meant yesterday with the meth lab comment. When he told me to make sure I arrested this one?" Then he explained everything.

"Oh my."

THIRTY-FOUR

Fitz sent Beck a secure link to download all of the old case files, complete with the photographs he had taken. Emotionally drained, Beck grabbed a Chasing Rainbows IPA from her refrigerator and poured the contents into a pint glass, which she carried into the den of her downtown loft.

Her third-floor balcony door was open, letting the unseasonably cool night breeze in, along with the hum of sporadic rainfall, which filled the room with a pleasant, earthy smell. She set the glass on a side table, dropped cross-legged into a modern-looking yellow armchair, and began clicking through files on her computer.

Having made quick work of the Nelson file, given the paucity of information at this point, she set out to see how she could fit the old cases with the new. She began by making a list of all seven homicide victims—the original six plus Freida Nelson.

Typing the header "Original Six" in her spreadsheet made her think of her late father. He grew up in Winnetka, Illinois, with Rocky Wirtz, the current owner of the Chicago Blackhawks of the National Hockey League—a team he lived and died with eighty-plus times per year. He always boasted that the "Hawks," as he called them, were one of the NHL's "Original Six," and when any team other than one of the "Original Six" won the Stanley Cup, he referred to them as a *Johnny-come-lately*. She smiled at the memory and made a mental note to call her mother later.

The list she made included the names of the victims, along with their age, race, sex, marital status, and the date they were murdered. The list was sorted by date of death.

Original Six:

V1: Cindy Stover—86 years old—White—Female—Widow—February 3, 1996

V2: Inez Cooper—72 years old—White—Female—Widow—October 23, 1996

V3: Gayle White—63 years old—White—Female—Divorced—January 26, 1997

V4: Loraine Mount—81 years old—White—Female—Widow—August 30, 1997

V5: Sofia Graham—79 years old—White—Female—Widow—December 2, 1998

V6: Claire Albritton—42 years old—White—Female—Married—July 19, 1999

New:

V7: Freida Nelson—74 years old—White—Female—Widow—September 15, 2024

A cursory view of the spreadsheet revealed the killer had a very definite type, with the exception of victim number six: Claire Albritton. Not only was she two decades younger than the youngest of the other victims, but she was the only victim married at the time of her murder. Although statistical anomalies were very definite things in serial homicide investigations, Beck knew that a victim profile so far outside those of other victims was something that demanded a closer look.

The little bit she knew of the killer that operated back in the late nineties showed him to be a calculated individual. He preyed on older women—less likely to be a threat and more easily controlled. He preyed on single women—much easier to kill when you don't have the threat of someone walking in on you doing the deed.

She had the photographs Fitz had sent her documenting the outside of some of the houses. Wanting a clearer idea of where these houses were located, she found each address on the maps app on her computer. She discovered there was nothing at all secluded or hidden about the houses where these women lived—murder was something one typically wanted privacy for. Not spur-of-the-moment or heat-of-passion homicides, of course, but these were, more likely than not, pre-planned, which made his choice of killing inside a house in the middle of a neighborhood a poor strategic decision on its face.

The exception to each of these choices was again Claire Albritton. If not for sharing the killer's calling card with the previous five victims, she would never have been included as even possibly being connected to those homicides.

Beck closed her laptop and leaned back in her chair blindly but carefully, reaching for her beer and taking a long drink. She noted the neglected brew was not as cold as she'd have liked, but almost immediately, she felt the alcohol begin to unknot her mind.

On top of being a statistical outlier, Claire Albritton was also the last kill for more than twenty-five years. Was it significant that the outlier was the final victim of the original six?

She took another drink and registered why this was currently her favorite beer. In that moment, she also determined that, among the old homicides, Albritton's murder was the one that would get her attention first.

She reached for her cell phone and saw it was almost 10:00 in the evening. She paused, considering. After a beat, she found Fitz's number in her contacts and dialed.

"Let me guess," said Fitz, answering on the second ring, "you've been reading the case files."

"Is that too pathetic?"

"Why would a single person sitting at home alone on a Friday night reading thirty-year-old murder files be pathetic?" Beck made a noise Fitz interpreted to be a laugh. "Besides, it can't be pathetic because that would make me pathetic."

"Doing the same thing, huh?" she said.

"Yep."

"We're both pathetic," Beck said with a groan.

It was Fitz's turn to laugh. Then he said, "I don't suppose you've found anything."

"I'm not sure. Maybe."

"Well, that's more than I can say. What do you have?"

She explained the anomalies in the Albritton case compared to the other six homicides, and he agreed that they were strange. Like her, he felt one anomaly could be explained, but likely not all of them.

They talked through it, and he told her he was less enamored by the fact that the Albritton home was more private than the others. He couldn't articulate why exactly; he just didn't view it as significant as she had. As for age and marital status, he did agree with her that those were compelling deviations.

"Had that been his first kill, then I could see it. She fought back; maybe her husband interrupted; he learned as he went, that type of thing."

"But not his last kill," she said.

"Definitely not his last kill. Especially considering that after he decided to kill again after all these years, and the latest victim matches the first five to a T."

"So you agree that's the case we should look into first?"

"Hundred percent," said Fitz.

"My latest coffee-of-the-month shipment arrived in the mail today...it's a bold dark roast...I could put on a pot."

"Yeah, buddy. I'm on the way."

——————

Twenty minutes later, Beck and Fitz sat at her kitchen table, each with a tall steaming cup of coffee. Fitz had the Albritton paper case file open in front of him while she viewed the same thing on her computer.

She said, "Let's start by walking through what we know about the case, which unfortunately isn't much." Fitz nodded and took a sip of coffee. "Claire Albritton was found by her husband..." She scrolled through the case narrative. "Her husband Sam. He found her at approximately 9:30 in the evening. Have you listened to the 911 call?"

"I have not," said Fitz.

"Me neither." She opened up the notes app on her MacBook, began a case to-do list, and added *Listen to 911 Call from Husband*. As she typed, she said, "He admitted that 9:30 was late for him getting home and that he was typically home by 6:00. He told police he was late that night because he was installing kitchen cabinets and the homeowner had him on a deadline to finish the job because they were hosting some kind of party that weekend. The police checked with the homeowner, and they confirmed he was installing their cabinets, and they also confirmed they made it clear to him the job needed to get done." She paused here, taking her first drink of the strong brew.

She continued: "She was found in her bed, throat slit, and the letter *A* written above her on the wooden headboard, much in the same way as the five that preceded her."

Fitz sifted through the photographs, producing the shot encompassing the body and the headboard. He then fished into his shoulder bag and plucked out a manila folder that contained six similar photographs—those of the other murder victims, including the most recent victim, Freida Nelson—and laid them out in an array on the table.

"I went ahead and brought these so we could compare them," he said.

Both investigator and detective sipped coffee and scanned the images as if the thing they'd been missing this whole time was in the pictures somewhere.

Fitz said, "The killer was nothing if not consistent and meticulous in staging the bodies."

Beck stood up from her chair and leaned over the table. After several seconds, she pointed to the Nelson scene. "No blood spray. Here, look."

Fitz stood, his bulk looming over the cluster of photos. "I see what you mean." He leafed through each photograph, picking them up for a close but brief inspection. Still flipping through the pictures, he said, "Are you keeping notes, or should I?"

"I've got it," said Beck, typing into the notes app. "You were at the Nelson scene. Anything else stand out versus the original six homicide scenes?"

"I haven't reviewed the old scenes that closely, but the chief said something about this case being more disorganized."

She said, "We can check on that later." More typing notes. Done with that, she went back to the Albritton case file and scrolled until she found the report from the medical examiner. "Albritton's body was still somewhat warm, and rigor had begun to set in. The best the ME could do on time of death was three to eight hours before the police arrived."

"So she was killed between..." Fitz began running the numbers in his head. "...roughly 1:30 and 6:30 pm."

Beck said, "According to the homeowner Sam Albritton was working for, Sam, arrived that morning at 7:30, was still working when they got home around 5:30 that evening, and completed the cabinet install somewhere around 9:00 that night." More scrolling from Beck. "Says here in the statement from Troy Gaithers, the homeowner, that given the late hour, they all agreed that Sam would come back the following morning for a final inspection of the cabinets, so when he was done, he left. Looks like he even left some tools behind."

Fitz said, "Yeah, the police asked him about that. He said that since he was coming back in the morning, he hadn't bothered packing everything up. Mr. Albritton said he was exhausted and just wanted to get home, get some dinner, and go to bed."

Beck was scrolling through the case file. "In the original detective's notes, he posited that the husband killed his wife using the previous murders as cover. Figured the police would assume his wife to be yet another victim of this unknown serial killer."

"But he couldn't have known about the previous killings... could he? The way I understand it, no one outside of the police knew about the possibility of a serial killer at work, and even within the police, it was only a select few."

Leaning into her screen, she said, "That's where the detective ran into a roadblock with his theory. That was the same thought the police chief had at the time. That and the fact that Sam Albritton had an alibi effectively excluded him."

"But Sam was alone all day, right? Didn't you just say that Gaithers left him in the morning and didn't return until the evening?"

She scrolled back up. "Yes. Both Gaithers and his wife left for work sometime before 8:00 and got home around 5:30."

"Not much of an alibi. Certainly not enough to exclude him on that basis alone."

"I agree," Beck said somewhat absently as she scrolled through the report. After about a minute, she said, "This detective was thorough."

Fitz leaned forward. "What did you find?"

"He asked Gaithers to approximate the progress the cabinet install was in at the beginning of the day, then had a contractor review the work done. According to the contractor, the work done was commensurate with the thirteen hours or so Sam said he worked that day. The contractor did say that an experienced cabinet man working quickly could shave off an hour or two. He said that would be difficult if he were working alone, but certainly not impossible."

"Was he working alone?" asked Fitz.

"I haven't seen anything to suggest otherwise. An assistant would have been an additional alibi for Mr. Albritton, so there would be a name in the file if that were the case."

"So he could have killed her, but it doesn't seem likely."

Beck considered this. "That seems to have been the consensus of the PD back then. I'm not convinced the detective wanted him excluded, but what else could he do? It seems he was given orders and moved on. I've seen it before."

"Sounds like you'd like to take a closer look at Sam Albritton?"

"I don't believe we have enough to ignore him for his wife's case. As we've already discussed, that murder does not fit the others. Perhaps the original detective was onto something, and Mr. Albritton used the subterfuge of an active serial killer to murder his wife."

Fitz weighed this and slowly shook his head. "I agree his alibi isn't super solid, but how do you reconcile his knowledge of the previous murders? He'd have to know some pretty intimate details."

"You don't think in a town this size he knew someone. Someone who let slip about a person who killed women and painted their last initial above the bed in the victim's blood?"

"You say it like that, and I tend to agree it's possible, but if that were the case, would all of it really have been concealed this entire time? I mean, we're talking multiple decades."

"So," Beck began, "we keep him on the list for his wife's murder, but he's not the serial killer, and he couldn't have reasonably known the details about the previous killings in order to act as a copycat. That about sum it up?"

"I think you nailed it."

"My coffee's cold," she said abruptly and stood. "My brain needs a break...and I could use another cup."

Fitz drained the last of his. "Me, too."

THIRTY-FIVE

The next morning—a Saturday—Beck and Fitz met for a coffee at The Knockbox—the scent of coffee beans and cinnamon rolls met them as they entered. Fitz was dressed casually in jeans and a golf shirt with the DA's office logo on his left chest. Beck was also wearing jeans of the dark indigo toothpick variety and a peach-colored Lululemon pullover. The cool front that rode in on the overnight rain lingered in the area.

The pair had worked until well after midnight examining photographs, talking through theories of connections and possible motives, and adding items to the to-do list she created. They drank a pot of coffee between them and felt better about where they were now versus when they started the day. If nothing else, their collaboration had produced even more avenues of investigation. Movement was everything in a criminal investigation. Like a shark, as long as the case maintained motion, no matter how slight, the case stayed alive.

Despite finishing a whole pot of the high-octane coffee, both investigators reached the point of diminishing returns. Awake and alert were two different things, and while the coffee had kept them awake, neither was as alert and productive as they needed to be, so the meeting was halted with an agreement to meet at the local coffeehouse in a few hours.

Their plan for the day was to visit the last two scenes of the original six murders. Barclay, Fitz, and Drummond had visited both houses three days ago, but no one answered at either location. Their previous visit was on a weekday, so Beck suggested they ride by on the weekend. Fitz agreed it was a good idea.

Fitz offered to drive, and she retrieved her computer bag from her personal vehicle. Their first stop would be the former home of Gayle White, victim number three.

The ride was mostly silent as Fitz sipped his coffee and Beck her Americano—jazz played softly in the background. They arrived at their destination, and from the road, Fitz could see the white business card from Wednesday still stuck in the door. He pulled into the driveway and shifted into park.

"I guess they haven't been home since we were here," he said, looking at the front door.

"I bet there's a door under the carport," she said, jutting her chin in that direction. "Unless they get a visitor, they probably never even go to the front door."

"Good point," Fitz said, eyeing the empty carport. He unbuckled his seatbelt and said, "I'm going to go leave a card in that door." He opened his console, retrieved a pen, and exited the vehicle. As he walked, he removed a business card and wrote his cell number on the back. He wedged the card into the doorjamb beside the handle.

Beck had the maps app open on her iPad when he got back to the SUV. "Would you mind riding by the other crime scenes while we're out? I've seen the pictures and examined them all on Google Maps, but I'd like to see them in person. We don't have to get out, just cruise by—let me get a feel for them."

"May as well." He fastened his seatbelt and then pointed at her iPad. "Those pins represent the scene locations?"

She nodded. "Plotted them last night." She consulted her notes and said, "I only need to see Cooper, Mount, Albritton, and Nelson." She examined the map and, after a few seconds, said, "We'll go Cooper first, then Nelson...probably visit Sofia Graham's house after that...then Mount. We'll hit Albritton last."

"Map us out a route." He put the car into gear, backed out of the driveway, and drove toward the neighborhood exit.

THIRTY-SIX

On the way to the house where Inez Cooper was murdered, Beck reviewed her notes and realized this was the family she was supposed to contact about bank information as well as a possible building permit. Fitz cruised by slowly, then turned around and rode by once more. Fitz told her about their visit and pointed out the addition to the house as the reason for the permit search. Beck made notes as Fitz went on to explain the conclusion he and Drummond arrived at concerning the killer knowing the women.

"Did Drummond discuss any of this with you?"

"No. We never got around to discussing any specifics."

Fitz told her that both of the houses they visited on Wednesday, where they were able to speak with someone, had undergone some type of construction project. "Inez Cooper's place was actually under construction at the time of the murder."

"And you want to know if there is a connection with the construction projects?"

"Pretty much."

"That seems like a bit of a long shot."

"I don't disagree with you, and I'm not sure Barclay would disagree with you, either. But if all it costs is some time and research..."

"Noted."

Approximately five minutes later, they were cruising by the location of Freida Nelson's murder. Riding by, they observed two vehicles parked in front of the house at the curb, and a mid-size U-Haul trailer hitched to a late model black GMC pickup truck backed into the driveway. Two people exited the front door carrying what looked like a dresser on a furniture dolly.

They discussed the Nelson case only briefly as they made their way to Sofia Graham's old house, the only one other than Gayle White with whom no one had spoken.

Fitz pulled up to the curb, and they took in the surroundings before getting out. The house was a brick split level with beige trim. Two vehicles occupied the driveway—a silver Ford Explorer with stick figures on the rear window of a man, a woman, a little girl, and four dogs. The other car was a yellow VW Bug with a light blue *30A* sticker in the lower left corner of the rear window, which referred to a popular beach destination in Florida. Fitz also noticed the card was gone from the front door, so he was hopeful someone was home.

He grabbed his camera bag from the back seat and followed Beck to the door. Before she could ring the doorbell, barking dogs erupted inside; it sounded like a kennel. Beck laughed and pointed to a round wooden sign hanging on the door. It said *No need to knock. We know you are here.* along with four dog faces with what they assumed were the dogs' names painted under each dog. Maybe ten seconds later, the door was cracked open by a woman doing her level best to keep the dogs from leaping out the door and onto their guests.

"Yes," the woman said, using her leg to close the gap in the door. Two light-colored muzzles probed underneath and above the woman's bent knee.

Beck smiled, showed her badge, and introduced herself and Fitz.

Hearing Fitz's name, the woman looked at him and said, "Did you leave us a card?"

"Yes, ma'am, I did. On Wednesday."

She nodded. "Can you give me one second?" Without waiting for an answer, she closed the door. Amid the cacophony of barking, the two investigators could hear the woman yelling at the dogs inside. "Come on. Time to go outside. Let's go. Mason, Daisy, Chef, Mrs. Potts, out."

Fitz looked at Beck: "Mrs. Potts?" She pointed at the door hanger. The names matched.

The door was opened again, and the woman was out of breath. "Come in, please." She appeared to be in her early forties. Her dark brown hair was held back by a pair of glasses perched atop her head. She wore a white T-shirt with "Plant Mom" in hot pink script over dark green yoga pants.

The house was clean, and if they hadn't heard or seen the dogs, they'd have never known dogs lived there. The home had a masculine scent owed to two burning candles visible on the kitchen island through the open floor plan. And there were plants —a lot of plants.

"Please, sit down," the woman said, regaining her composure and wiping down her pant legs. With an embarrassed grin, she said, "Sorry about that." Then, she held her arm out to a couch where Beck and Fitz sat while she took a cloth armchair. Everyone seated, she said, "I'm sorry I never called you Mr. Fitzsimmons. My husband and I were out of town for work, and my daughter was here by herself. She called us after she found your card in the door when she got home from school. We just got home ourselves last night, and I was going to wait until Monday to call you."

Fitz waived it off. "That's quite alright. I hope it didn't cause you or your daughter any stress finding a card from the DA's office like that."

"Honestly, I was too busy to give it any thought."

"May we ask your name?" said Beck.

"Oh, I'm so sorry, it's Juli Katzenberger.

Fitz said, "A dog lover named Katzenberger."

Juli shrugged, laughed, and said, "And I hate cats. Go figure."

Beck said, "May I ask what you and your husband do, Mrs. Katzenberger?"

"Call me Juli, please. We own a software company." Seeing the looks on her visitor's faces, she said, "It's not that glamorous, I assure you. Our company processes online payments for fraternities and sororities: dues, formals fees, that sort of thing. As you can imagine fall is our busiest time of the year. We added a dozen new universities to our client list this year and have been visiting them to ensure the implementation goes smoothly. We're a very small company. My husband and I do it all ourselves."

"Where is your husband now?" Beck asked.

She sat forward in her chair, alarm playing across her face. "He's out playing golf. Does he need to be here?"

"Oh no," the detective said quickly. "I was just asking. And to put you at ease, we aren't here about anything bad. Well, nothing concerning you anyway." Seeing the look of concern, she continued, "Were you aware a woman by the name of Sofia Graham was murdered in this house in 1998?"

Juli sat back in her chair. "Yes. Our realtor mentioned something about that." She thought for a moment and said, "We are the second owners since that happened, so to be honest, it didn't really bother us. The couple we bought the house from—the Crances—did a pretty extensive renovation, so it was practically new inside. And we aren't exactly the superstitious type, so..." She chuckled nervously.

"The Crances did the renovations?" Fitz asked.

"Yes. Is that important?"

Beck said, "When was this house built? Do you know?"

Juli cocked her head and glanced upward, thinking. "Mid-seventies? 1974, I believe."

Fitz said, "Any idea how long after Ms. Graham's murder the Crances bought the house?"

Juli made a face and said, "Wow, I don't know." She gave it some thought. "Can I go get the closing documents? It may be in there?"

"Of course," said Beck.

Juli left the room toward the rear of the house. A few minutes later, she was back with a brown Pendaflex file pocket. She unstrapped the thin elastic cord that held it closed and flipped the top back. Her fingers crawled along the tops of the section separators, pulling various sheaves of documents, reviewing them, and putting them back.

About two-thirds toward the back, she found what she was looking for: "It says here that Bob and Barbara Crance purchased the house from the estate of Sofia Graham on September 15, 2003." She held the documents out for Fitz or Beck to review.

Beck held up a hand. "We don't need to see that." Juli nodded, slid the papers back into its slot, and wrapped the strap around the bulky file.

Beck thought about what to ask next. She looked at Fitz, who was scratching his chin, also thinking.

"Does that help?" Juli asked.

"Not really," said Beck.

"Do you mind if I ask what this is about? Maybe if I knew what you were looking for..."

"We're looking into Ms. Graham's death. We look into old unsolved cases from time to time."

"Do you think the people we bought the house from had anything to do with it?"

"Oh, no. Nothing like that. We're just turning over rocks. Maybe we see something the original investigators didn't. That sort of thing."

"That makes sense, I guess."

Fitz said, "I don't suppose you know if there was any other work done on the house before the Crances bought it."

Juli laughed and said, "Not hardly. When the Crances bought the house, it was all wood paneling, shag carpet, and avocado kitchen appliances, toilets, tubs, and sinks. At the closing, the Crances gave us a photo album of the transformation process. Would you like to see what the house looked like before being renovated? The change was quite remarkable."

In part to be polite, in part because she couldn't think of anything else to ask, and if she was being honest, out of just plain curiosity, Beck said, "Sure."

Juli stood from the chair and took the Pendaflex back the way she came. After hearing a door open and close, she was back with an off-white photo album about two inches thick. She placed the album on the coffee table in front of the two detectives and said, "Take your time."

Beck reached for the picture album and slid it closer to the edge of the polished mahogany table. Both she and Fitz scooted to the edge of the couch and leaned forward to view the pictures.

The first ones were of the kitchen and bathrooms.

Fitz said, "Whoa." He laughed. "This brings back some memories." In one of the pictures, he placed his finger on a kitchen table with a white round top with a flower design and yellow metal legs. It was surrounded by four matching chairs. "I can picture a fondue pot perched right there in the middle of that table. In fact, I'm pretty sure my momma had that exact table."

"I told you," Juli said. She got up and moved onto the couch beside Fitz, putting him in the middle so she could also view the pictures. "It was as if the place had been preserved in a time capsule."

Fitz pointed to a photograph of the guest bathroom. "My grandmother had those same toilet seat covers. So thick you had to hold the seat up, or it'd fall right back down while you were doing your business."

Beck slowly flipped through the first few pages, with Fitz and Juli making comments and sharing childhood memories. Beck was a nineties kid, so she just listened. Her mother had been into scrapbooking when she was growing up, which made her more interested in the work that had been done cropping, labeling, and securing the pictures into the album.

The first pictures of the living area where they were now sitting showed the Crances—smiling arm in arm—in a gutted room. Beck looked around the room to get her bearings. She thought the camera had probably stood about where they were sitting.

The pictures showed swaths of wallpaper torn off the walls, a bare concrete floor where the carpet had been removed, and a short stack of drywall. Fitz and Juli were laughing about a story from Juli's childhood when Beck picked up the book and placed it on her lap.

That got Fitz's attention. "You find something?"

"Look at the date," said Beck, pointing at the yellow starburst next to a photograph of the Crances standing in the gutted living room. The caption said, *Day 1—8/21/2003*. She placed the album back on the coffee table in front of Fitz.

He slid the album closer and said, "What about it?"

Juli said, "That's the date they closed on the house."

Fitz still didn't understand. He looked at Beck and studied her face.

Beck said, "That's an awful lot of work for day one of a project. And as you can see, it's still daylight outside. So, what, they close on the house, then go home and peel wallpaper, remove all the carpet, and buy some drywall? All in the course of a few hours?"

"Hmm," was Fitz's reply. All three stared at the photograph, willing it to tell them something. Finally, he said, "Maybe they had a crew."

"Even so," said Beck, unconvinced.

"There's more pictures," Juli pointed out.

Beck slid the photo album in front of her and flipped pages. The next several pictures were of the same room from different angles. The room where they now sat was nothing more than a shell in the photographs. One of the photos showed a wall with new drywall—taped and mudded. Based on the sequence of photos, it appeared as if the renovation removed a wall between the living room and kitchen and rebuilt it to create a more open space.

Beck said, "So not only did they demo the living room, but they also had time to build a wall, hang the drywall, tape, and mud?" She gave a sly smile. "You still think all this was done on August 21, 2003?"

Fitz shook his head and shrugged. "Maybe they started before the twenty-first? I'm guessing the place was empty. Maybe they got the Graham family's permission to start before the closing date."

Beck's resolve faltered just a touch before she said, "What about here." She flipped back to the first picture in the series that caught her attention. She pointed at the caption and said, "It says *Day 1,* and it's dated the twenty-first."

"Maybe that just means it's their first day as homeowners."

"You could be right." Beck flipped through a few more pages

before flipping back to that first picture and pulling her cell phone from her back pocket. She hovered the iPhone over the photograph and snapped a picture with a loud *snick*. She then pulled up the photo on her phone and zoomed in with her fingers. She examined the picture on her phone for a few seconds before quickly flipping to other pages and snapping additional photos. Done taking pictures, she pulled up each one and zoomed in, examining it closely just as she had done with the first one. Juli and Fitz watched her do this with keen interest, not having any idea what she was after.

Finally, she nodded with a satisfied look on her face and swiped back to the first picture on her phone. She zoomed in and passed the phone to Fitz. "Look," she said, pointing to the screen. "Cobwebs." Fitz brought the phone closer, squinting, then moved it away at arm's length, still squinting.

"Here," said Juli, grabbing the readers from the top of her head and handing them to Fitz.

"You sure? I've got a big head."

Juli waved a hand at him. "I get them at the Dollar Tree. They're all over the house."

He put on the pink cats-eye-shaped readers, cutting a look to Beck that said, *Not a word*. She smiled.

He examined the photo again. Then swiped and looked at the others. "I don't know. All zoomed in like this...maybe it's just blurry. You know, with the pixels and stuff?"

Frustrated, Beck leaned forward to see around Fitz and asked Juli, "I don't suppose you have a magnifying glass around here, do you?"

Juli thought about it. "Maybe. Let me check."

It took her a few minutes, and Fitz and Lawson passed the time by flipping through the rest of the photo album.

"Found one in the garage," Juli said, handing a contraption

down to Beck. It had a metal base with a metal coil off to the right, two metal arms with an alligator clip at the end of each one, and a magnifying glass attached to a flexible metal arm looming over all of it.

"What's this?" Beck asked as she held it.

"It's a soldering stand. My husband uses it to make computer motherboards and stuff. He also likes to make Halloween decorations with LED lights. Uses it for that, too."

She flipped back to the first photo and positioned the magnifying glass over it. She leaned in for a second, then placed the soldering stand on the open album, pushed it all over to Fitz, and made a sweep of her hand.

Fitz picked up the readers from the table, put them on, and then positioned the magnifying glass over the photograph as Beck had done. He examined it briefly before flipping to other pictures in the album and doing the same thing.

After looking at a half-dozen photographs, he pushed the book away and handed the glasses back to Juli.

He said, "Okay. I agree. Cobwebs."

Beck waited for him to continue, but when she saw he wasn't going to say anything else, she said, "The building materials have cobwebs. The drywall, that stack of two-by-fours, the upper corners where the walls intersect. There hadn't been any work done in that room in quite a while."

"So what does all this mean," Juli asked quietly.

Fitz said, "It would appear that work was begun well before the Crances became involved with the house."

"And?"

"And," Beck said, "that means Ms. Graham undertook the renovation herself...before she died."

Juli was confused as to why that was important, but she did not comment.

"Perhaps her family began the project to try and make the house easier to sell after her death," said Fitz.

"And just abandon the project? Put the house on the market with the house in that condition?"

"Touché," said Fitz.

THIRTY-SEVEN

Before leaving Juli Katzenberger's home, Fitz took some exterior photographs. Given the renovations to the home's interior, the photos were more perfunctory than anything.

Beck had noted the Crances' full names so she could look up their contact information. For good measure, Juli had retrieved the names and phone numbers of the Crances' realtor and the attorney who had done the closing in case they needed assistance locating them.

As Fitz drove back to the office, he asked, "You still think this construction connection is a long shot?"

"We've confirmed, what, three out of four of our victims had a construction project completed or ongoing before the murder?"

"Three out of five. At least for now. I met with the owners of the Loraine Mount house, and they didn't know anything about anything. It was one of the locations I was going to ask you to research."

"Still," Beck began, "even three out of five is something."

"That would be quite a coincidence."

"You know what cops say about coincidences."

Fitz glanced at Beck. "What's that?"

Beck thought about it and said, "I don't know, but I'm sure some cop somewhere said something witty about them."

"I knew a detective with Mobile PD who said coincidences in an investigation made his balls itch."

"See."

They pulled up to the traffic light at the neighborhood's exit.

"Which way do I need to go?" Fitz asked.

"To get back to my car?"

"Don't you want to ride by the remaining murder scenes?"

"Yes, sorry." She searched her bag for her iPad and plotted a route to the next location.

———

FITZ DROVE by the home where Loraine Mount was killed much the same as he had done with the others, making a couple of slow passes, allowing Beck to see whatever it was she was interested in seeing.

Their final drive-by for the day was the former home of Claire Albritton. On the way, Beck reviewed the case file on her iPad, swiping through scanned statements, reports, and photographs.

As Fitz made his way to the rear of the neighborhood where the Albritton house was located, Beck muttered, "I'm so stupid."

"How's that?" Fitz asked, not taking his eyes off the residential street teeming with children and families outside enjoying the cool weather. He even had to stop once for a group of kids playing football in the street.

"Sam Albritton," she said, looking at Fitz.

His brow furrowed. "Claire Albritton's husband?" He could see her nod from his periphery as she swiped intently on her iPad.

"He's the connection."

"How do you mean?"

She put her iPad down and looked at Fitz. "It's been in front of us the entire time."

"It has?"

She nodded and said, "Follow me here. You and I believe the Albritton case deviates from the other cases seemingly without explanation, right?"

Fitz answered affirmatively in a tone that asked where she was going.

"We also agree that that's the case that could be the key to all of this, right?"

Same response from Fitz.

"And Barclay believes we may be looking for a builder, handyman type. Is that fair?"

"That's fair."

"Well, what was Sam Albritton's alibi?" She didn't wait for an answer. "He was installing cabinets in a kitchen renovation." When Fitz didn't immediately respond, she said, "He's a contractor, Fitz. You told me the Albritton house has a full workshop on-site. It fits." She swiped to the notes she'd made the night before when they'd met over a pot of coffee. "When the Meltons bought the house, that outbuilding was full of power tools and woodworking equipment. Far more than what you'd expect from a weekend warrior or a hobbyist. He's our guy. I know it."

THIRTY-EIGHT

S am Albritton was dead. He died almost five years ago.

That was the bad news. The good news, however, was that Beck believed she had found the connection between the original six homicides.

The previous day, Beck Lawson called on Tina Crump for her help. They spent the day doing what Tina does best: working the computer. Being a Sunday with no government offices open, she was limited to Google searches and law enforcement databases. Still, despite the perceived limitations, she was able to confirm the fate of Sam Albritton fairly quickly.

When Beck finally took a breath, Chief Greenhaw said, "You just threw a lot at us, and this meeting isn't even"—he checked his watch—"four minutes old. Now start back from the beginning and slower this time."

It was a few minutes past 9:00 on Monday morning, and a half-dozen bodies sat around the chief's conference table. The meeting was hastily put together at Beck's request. She had told the chief about her work with Fitz and Tina over the weekend and that she believed an update was needed.

She stood behind her chair, both hands on top of it. "Fitz and I got together to try and make contact with the two homeowners we hadn't spoken to yet: the homes of Gayle White and Sofia Graham. I also wanted to ride by the other four homicide scenes to familiarize myself with them."

This was more than the chief wanted to know, but he'd asked her to start from the beginning, so he supposed he had asked for this.

Beck continued, and after explaining that the homeowners at the Gayle White scene weren't home, she moved on to Juli Katzenberger at the Graham house. She explained the roundabout way she had come to the idea that the victims were all beginning a renovation, had recently completed a renovation, or were in the midst of a renovation project when they were killed.

As for Sam Albritton becoming her primary suspect, she explained how, at least anecdotally, Sam appeared to be a builder. Probably not on the scale of someone who would build a house, but definitely someone who could do anything from light construction to something as complex as a renovation or an add-on. She recounted the workshop built on the Melton's property, which had belonged to the Albrittons.

"Just so I understand, Detective, you believe Sam Albritton is a serial killer because he had some power tools at his house."

Beck's jaw clenched in frustration. Not trusting herself to speak, she didn't. She was formulating a response when the chief turned in his chair to find Fitz at the table. He said, "What's your take on this, Fitz? You believe Sam Albritton is our guy?"

The large investigator leaned up on his elbows and cleared his throat. He didn't quite share his partner's assuredness about Albritton, but the last thing he wanted to do was undermine her to her boss. He said, "The idea isn't without its merits." In his periphery, he could tell Beck wasn't thrilled by his tepid response.

"Well, there's a ringing endorsement," said Greenhaw.

Barclay broke in. "Actually, Chief, I floated the idea to Fitz and Drummond of the connection being the commonality of the construction projects." He handed it off to Fitz with a nod.

"That's correct. And I conveyed that idea to Detective Lawson to get her up to speed on the investigation."

The chief said, "But, as you've avoided answering my question directly, am I to take it you don't share Detective Lawson's opinion on Sam Albritton?"

Fitz: "As I said, I believe her inference is not without merit." The chief opened his mouth to speak, but Fitz plowed on. "First of all, Claire Albritton's murder is an outlier from the other five in every aspect except for how the body was found and the killer's signature found at the scene.

"We also know at least three of the six victims lived in homes that had in the past or were currently undergoing a renovation of some kind." The chief began to speak again, and again Fitz pressed on, holding up a hand this time. "Of course, there are three other cases we have not established as having such a connection, but we also haven't ruled them out.

"And I believe, given the time to work this theory, Beck will either confirm we're on the right track or be able to rule Sam Albritton out entirely through bank records and any other evidence we're waiting on."

"Where are we on the other three cases as far as tying them to Albritton?" asked Greenhaw.

Beck said, "I will get with Sheriff Ramos. See if she'll ask Harold and Harriet Reynolds if they're aware of any work being done on the house before they bought it. I'll also get with her crime scene folks and see if they came across any paperwork from the house that may shed some light."

Fitz said, "Now that I have something concrete to ask about, I'll go back to the owners of the Loraine Mount house and ask them about that issue specifically. I will also stay on top of the Gayle White property. Hopefully, I will hear back soon."

Beck sat back down in her chair. "Even if I'm right—we're right—it still doesn't get us to who killed Freida Nelson."

"Where are we on the Nelson case? Or have you been too focused on the old cases that Ms. Nelson's murder has been ignored?" Greenhaw asked.

Captain Tony Jones spoke for the first time. "Chief, I had discussed it with Drummond—before he was shot—and asked him to see what he could find in the way of a connection to the old cases. Without much to go on in the Nelson case, I chose to work the case from both ends and assigned Detective Whitaker to Nelson while Drummond looked into the older cases. Seeing where we are now, I'll get Whitaker to forward Beck what he's done up to this point, which isn't much because there isn't much. He will continue to assist on Nelson, as needed, with Beck taking the lead."

Beck nodded.

Everyone was looking at one another around the table. Chief Greenhaw finally broke the silence. "Alright, it sounds like we at least have an idea of where to go from here. Please keep me posted with updates."

———

WITH RENEWED ENERGY, Beck and Fitz spoke in the corner of the conference room and dashed off a quick plan. Beck's first act was to call Shirley Bates. With everything going on over the past week, she had not had an opportunity to pursue any records related to the murders, but that was going to change in earnest.

She placed the call as soon as she got back to her desk. Shirley Bates answered the phone, and Beck introduced herself.

"Oh, yes, Officer. One of your colleagues, a man named

Drummond, if I remember correctly, was here last week. He called to let me know someone would contact us about my parents' banking information."

"That's right, Mrs. Bates. I am following up on that request. I don't suppose you have that information for me?"

"I sure do. My parents were meticulous record keepers, and when they passed, we moved everything to a storage unit my husband maintains for all of his business files. He's a retired lawyer, so he had loads of client files he couldn't throw away. Anyway, after I spoke with Detective Drummond..." Shirley Bates' voice trailed off.

Thinking the call was disconnected, Beck said, "Mrs. Bates? Are you there?"

"I'm here," she said after a few more seconds. "Was that...was Detective Drummond the police officer I read about in the newspaper...the one who was shot recently?"

"Yes, ma'am, it was."

"Oh my. Please tell me he's okay."

"Yes, ma'am. He's going to be okay. He'll be out for some time, but he's going to be fine."

"That is so wonderful to hear." The relief in Mrs. Bates' voice was obvious and genuine. "You people don't get paid enough, I tell you."

"Thank you, Mrs. Bates. I will be sure to pass along your concerns to Detective Drummond. I know it will boost his spirits."

More silence when Beck said, "Mrs. Bates...the bank information?"

"Yes, yes. I'm sorry, dear. That just has me shaken a bit. After all, he was just in our home. Hang on one moment, and I will get you that information." Beck could hear the telephone receiver being set down on a hard surface and then heard sounds in the background: walking, shuffling paper. "Here we are. Do you have something to write with?"

Beck said she did, and Shirley Bates gave her the bank's name and account numbers. She wrote down the information and read it back to Mrs. Bates to confirm that she had recorded everything correctly.

Beck was about to end the call when Mrs. Bates said, "Do you still want the name of the contractor that worked on this house?"

"You have the name of the contractor?"

"Of course. I told you, my parents were meticulous record keepers. It took us a while, but my husband and I found the contract for the carport enclosure."

Beck was stunned. She was getting the bank information to see if they could find the contractor that way. She never imagined the Bates would give her a name.

"Yes, Mrs. Bates. If you have a name, that'd be great."

"His name is Sam Albritton. Do you want a copy of this paperwork?"

THIRTY-NINE

C hief Greenhaw and Captain Jones were in the chief's office drinking coffee from styrofoam cups and discussing their budget submission to the city council for the upcoming fiscal year when Beck walked in and sat in the empty chair next to TJ. The two men looked at her, and she held up a piece of paper.

She didn't wait to be invited to speak. "Sam Albritton was the contractor on the house where Inez Cooper was murdered."

Captain Jones leaned up, held out his hand, and said, "May I?"

Beck gave him the document Shirley Bates had photographed with her phone and texted to her. She had asked Mrs. Bates to send her a pic of the contract, telling her she would be by later to pick up the original. The older lady sounded offended when Beck asked her if she knew how to take a picture and text it.

TJ quickly scanned the single page and handed it across to the chief, who snapped his front-connecting CliC readers and examined the picture more closely.

The chief unsnapped his readers and let them hang around his neck. "You have my attention, Detective. Is it too much to ask for the other five cases to be this easy to connect to Mr. Albritton?"

Beck said, "I don't expect the rest to be anywhere near this easy. We're just fortunate the Coopers were meticulous record keepers and that the Bates didn't toss it all in the trash. Keep in mind, too, that Mrs. Bates was Inez Cooper's daughter and lives in the same house. That likely won't be the case with the other five victims. We'll get there, though. Either we'll prove he's our guy, or we'll definitively rule him out."

———

ON THE WAY to her office at the PD, Beck stuck her head into the office of Dell Whitaker, the detective assisting her on the Freida Nelson murder investigation. The gray-haired detective was the longest-tenured member of the Towne Police Division. He was within a few months of maxing out his retirement and wouldn't work a single day after hitting that milestone. He had seen it all and done more; however, the closer he got to retirement, the less he liked to actually get out and do.

The veteran detective was leaned in on his computer monitor when Beck rapped on the door frame. He looked at her over the top of his computer monitor, keeping his hand on his mouse.

"Hey, Dell, got a second?"

"Yeah, but first, let me ask you a question. What do you know about fishing boats? Anything?"

"Sorry, Dell. I'm not a fisherman. And outside of a cruise ship, I don't have much boat experience."

"Well, you're not any help."

"Again, sorry. You buying a boat?"

"Oh, I don't know. The wife has already signaled that I need to find something to keep myself busy in retirement, preferably out of the house."

"Well, I hope you find what you're looking for." He answered her with an absent nod and focused back on his computer screen as he scrolled using his mouse. "Say, Dell," she said.

"Yeah," he said, not taking his eyes off the screen.

"I've got a name, and I'd like to see if there is any connection to Freida Nelson."

He reached for a reporter's notebook, grabbed a pen from his shirt pocket, looked at Beck, and said, "Shoot."

"Name is Sam Albritton." She rattled off his date of birth and social security number.

As he wrote, Dell said, "What's his relation to the decedent?"

"That's what I need you to look into." She gave him the Cliffs-Notes version of Albritton and his possible connection to the older homicide cases.

Detective Whitaker was Patrolman Whitaker when the unknown killer claimed his first victims. "So you think this cock-sucker could be that Alphabet asshole?"

"That's where we're focusing our efforts right now."

"Do you know where this Albritton fella is now?"

"If he's our guy, hopefully rotting in hell."

Whitaker, not one to miss much, said, "Oh, he's dead?"

"Yep."

Whitaker tossed his notepad onto his desk and his pen on top of the notepad. "Wait a minute. He *just* died, or he's been dead?"

"Been dead. He's not the doer on Nelson, but the crimes are so similar that if he *is* the original killer, then maybe he can lead us to who did Ms. Nelson."

Whitaker appeared to weigh that, nodded once, and went back to scrolling on his computer.

FORTY

From her office computer, Beck logged in to her account with TLO, a skip-tracing service. She input the name Bob Crance and received a few hundred hits. She refined her search to Alabama, which cut that number down to just eighteen; however, none were the people who had purchased Sofia Graham's house.

She began a new search, using the name Robert Crance and preemptively limiting her search to Alabama. This rendered twenty-one results. She began clicking through the list, looking at each person's residential history. The Robert Crance she was looking for was twelfth on the list.

Sofia Graham's address was associated with this name, and Barbara Crance was associated with the name as a possible family member. According to TLO, he now resided in Martin, Tennessee. The most recent number associated with this Robert Crance had a 731 area code, and when Beck looked it up, she found that it was the area code for Martin.

She grabbed her desk phone and dialed the number, which rang several times before an automated voice answered and said,

"I'm sorry, but the person you called has a voicemail box that has not been set up yet. Goodbye."

She slammed the receiver into the cradle. "Damn." *Idiots*, she thought to herself.

With no way to leave a message, she doubted he would call her back. Guessing this was a cell phone, she grabbed her phone out of a desk drawer and was in the process of drafting a text message to the number when the switchboard operator's voice came through her desk phone's speaker via the all-call intercom system: "If you called Bob Crance, he is on line two."

She set down her cell phone and grabbed the desk phone, punching line two. "Hello, Mr. Crance?"

"Yes, this is Bob Crance."

"Hi, Mr. Crance. This is Detective Beck Lawson with the Towne County Police Department. Thank you for calling me back."

"Is anything wrong, Detective?"

"Everything's fine. I just had some questions for you regarding a house you used to own here in Towne."

A nervous laugh from the other end of the line. "Oh. I didn't answer your call because I didn't recognize the number, and you didn't leave a voicemail, but seeing the call was from Towne, I figured I'd better see if it was something important. Guess I was right."

"I tried leaving a voicemail, but I got a message saying your voicemail hadn't been set up and the call was terminated."

"Not set up? What's to set up? You mean it doesn't come that way?"

"I think you just have to go into your voicemail settings and set it up. I'm surprised your cell phone carrier didn't set it up for you when you bought your phone."

"Well, they didn't," Bob said, a little indignant.

The last thing she wanted to do was go down this rabbit hole, so she said, "Mind if I ask you a couple of questions?"

"I don't mind. You said this was about our old house there? The one on Wareingwood Drive?"

"Yessir, that's the one."

"We haven't lived there in almost twenty years. What would you like to know?"

"There was a woman murdered there—"

"Sofia Graham."

"Yes, Sofia Graham. When you and your wife bought the house from her estate, had she begun having work done inside the home?"

"Actually, yes. How in the world do you know about that?"

"We spoke with Juli Katzenberger, and she showed us some photographs you left of the house that showed some construction going on."

"Okay," he said skeptically.

"The first thing I wanted to verify was that Ms. Graham had begun the renovation as opposed to you and Mrs. Crance or anyone else."

"That's right. It was pretty dated, and if I remember correctly, she was gifting the house to her daughter and son-in-law and was updating it for them. Seems like she was preparing to move into an apartment in a retirement community. Waverly something or other."

"Waverly Manor?" Beck asked, knowing it was Towne's only retirement apartment complex.

"Could be. Maybe. Anyway, after her death, the daughter couldn't bear moving in—couldn't even carry out the renovation. The house had sat on the market for quite a while by the time we looked at it. My wife liked the idea of a renovation project, and we got a really good deal owing to"—he cleared his throat—"Ms.

Graham's death, so we bought it, but we didn't get to enjoy it for very long after everything was done."

"Why's that, if you don't mind my asking."

"My son took a job up here at the university—head football coach—and since my wife and I were about to retire anyway, we sold the house and bought a small farm nearby to be close to him."

"Wait, your son is the head coach at UT-Martin?"

"Sure is." She detected a great deal of pride in his voice. "You know the school?"

"I once dated a guy who did some professional rodeoing, and one of his best friends on the circuit was on the rodeo team at UT-Martin."

"Well, how about that? Small world."

"Indeed it is. Say, Mr. Crance, you wouldn't by any chance have the name of the contractor who did the work on your house, would you?"

Where Bob Crance once sounded skeptical of the phone call, he now sounded eager to help.

"Oh goodness, I don't know. That's been a long time. The only thing I remember is that it was just a couple of men. I remember one was the owner, the main guy who mostly did the work himself, but some days he would bring someone else in to help hang drywall and other things he couldn't do by himself."

"But you don't have a name." It was said as a statement.

"Not off the top of my head, sorry. I can check with my wife, though. She's good at remembering things like that."

"That would be great. And any paperwork you might have related to the construction could be helpful."

"I'm sure we tossed all of that out long ago. Is something wrong with the house?"

"Not that I know of. We're just looking into a few things, that's all."

"Not gonna tell me, huh?"

"As you may or may not know, Ms. Graham's murder was never solved, and we're looking into it."

"Oh, a cold case. My wife loves those kinds of shows. Wait until I tell her about our conversation. I can tell her, right?"

"Of course. If she has any idea the name of your contractor, please let me know." She gave him her direct line and said, "If I can find a picture of someone for you and your wife to look at, can I email it to you?"

"Absolutely." She took down his email and ended the call.

———

AFTER THE PHONE CALL, Beck typed up a supplement to the case file memorializing the phone call with Bob Crance. That done, she began a supplement documenting her conversation with Shirley Bates earlier that morning. She was completing her narrative when she felt more than heard someone walk into her office. She looked up as Detective Dell Whitaker set a piece of paper on her desk. He dropped the paper and was turning to walk out.

"Hold on, Dell," she said, picking up the paper from her desk. "What is this?"

"What does it look like? You asked me to find a connection between Sam Albritton and your homicide victim. I found it."

Beck Lawson still had not looked up at Dell. She was busy scanning the piece of paper. She recognized it as a photograph from Freida Nelson's kitchen. "What am I supposed to be looking at?"

Dell exhaled a frustrated breath. "Pull up the crime scene pictures on the J drive." The J drive was the local server where the department's case files were stored digitally.

She clicked open the Finder window on her MacBook, found the folder containing the Freida Nelson case file, clicked on the folder labeled *Crime Scene,* and then clicked on the folder labeled *Photos.*

"Alright, which file?"

"Hold on," he said and left her office. He returned with his reporter's notebook and read off the file name. She clicked on it, bringing up the photograph on her computer screen.

"Now what?" she asked.

He pointed to a spot on the kitchen wall near the telephone that was missing the receiver. "Zoom in on that."

She looked at where he was pointing and zoomed in. She leaned in closer to the screen as the image enlarged.

"Holy shit."

"I don't know about all that, but there you are," said Dell.

He turned to leave when Beck, eyes still on her computer screen, said, "How the hell did you find that?"

"Been doing this job longer than a coon's age, sweetheart."

"Amazing," she said, still not taking her eyes off the screen. She was looking at a business card pinned to a small corkboard on the wall beside the butter-yellow telephone.

The business card was taupe with black lettering. Centered on the top line of the card was the name *Sam Albritton.* Centered underneath it were the words *Residential Contractor.*

FORTY-ONE

The revelation of the business card at Fredia Nelson's house initially raised more questions than answers for the case agent. As Beck stared at the photograph, specifically the business card, she wondered why the card was there. The man had been dead for nearly five years, so why was the card still pinned to the corkboard? Had he done work for Ms. Nelson at some point in the past? She made a note to see what she could find regarding any possible work that had been done to the Nelson house. In her mind's eye, she did a quick mental walkthrough of the house, and it was pretty dated, so nothing jumped out as having been remodeled—at least not on any meaningful scale.

The detective scanned the other items pinned to the small corkboard: various restaurant coupons, a square card for a food delivery company listing its website and phone number, another printed card with the name and number of a veterinarian, and a picture of a smallish fluffy white dog.

She couldn't tell from the photo when the coupons expired. She also couldn't recall the case file mentioning the presence of a dog, so she made a note to call the vet to find out. She wanted to know if the contents of the corkboard were kept up-to-date or if something got pinned to the board and forgotten about. If it was the former, then the presence of the card could be more significant than if it were the latter. Had the card been there for a while, or was it recently placed there? If recently placed, why? Why was the business card of a long-deceased man a new addition to the other items pinned to the board? The board looked too organized to have something as innocuous as an old contractor's business card pinned to it.

Beck also made a note to call the food delivery company to determine how frequently Fredia Nelson used their services. If she used it often and used her landline to order food—she'd also ask the delivery company about the number they had on file for her—then she was at that corkboard fairly regularly, and it wasn't so crowded that the business card would be missed if it shouldn't have been there.

The more she thought about it, the more she came to the decision that the card had either been there for years or it was placed there by the killer. No other explanation really made sense.

She opened up the spreadsheet she had created with the list of the murder victims and added a column at the end that she labeled *Sam Albritton Connection*. In that column and in the row for Inez Cooper, she wrote *Confirmed*. She did the same for Claire Albritton and Freida Nelson.

Beck then looked up and downloaded Sam Albritton's driver's license photo. She actually downloaded his last three photos because the computer system didn't have DL photos any further back than that. She studied them for a few minutes. An older white man with short gray hair, thin on top, brown eyes, and a mouth set in something between a smile and no expression at all was set against a blue background. Was this the face of a serial killer? He looked like someone's grandfather.

The detective could not make the images she was looking at

jibe with a killer, a monster. She knew better than to allow her mind to be swayed merely on appearance alone, but she found it hard to separate. She emailed all three photos to Bob Crance.

———

BECK MET Fitz at a food truck set up across the street from Towne's newest open-air retail development. She asked him to meet her for a late lunch to update him on everything she'd found.

They each ordered a double fried onion burger from the Local Burger Joint food truck. Fitz added fries and water, while Beck added chili cheese fries and a Dr. Pepper. They found a wood and wrought iron picnic table under a large umbrella in an outdoor food court.

"So," Fitz began, "we have Sam Albritton connected to three of our seven cases, including the most recent homicide. That's quite the coincidence." Beck nodded, her mouth full of burger. "My balls are itching."

Beck began to laugh, then coughed. She grabbed her can of Dr. Pepper and took a long drink. She said, "You can't do that to me when I have a mouth full of food."

"Sorry," he said as he chewed.

She took another drink, coughed again, wiped her mouth, and said, "But yeah, I agree, no such thing as a coincidence. Not here." Fitz bobbed his head up and down as he ate some fries. "I emailed some photos to Bob Crance hoping he or his wife can identify Albritton as the guy who worked on their house."

"When we leave here, I'll drive out to Loraine Mount's house —have another conversation with them," said Fitz. "Still nothing from the folks at the Gayle White house. If I don't hear from them in the next day or two, I may be inclined to look for a cell number or try to call a relative. We've got a little more urgency now than when we started this thing."

The two of them ate in silence for a couple of minutes. Beck finished off her burger, grabbed a fork, and started on her fries.

"How do you eat all that and stay in shape?" Fitz asked.

Beck shrugged as she chewed. Fitz shook his head as he drank some water.

She took another drink of Dr. Pepper, wiped her mouth with a napkin, and said, "When I get back to the office, I'm going to get with the sheriff on the Reynolds house. See if her folks found anything pointing to Sam Albritton knowing Cindy Stover." She also told Fitz she would contact the vet and the food delivery company to try and get some context for the business card at Freida Nelson's house.

"You brought the photos with you?"

She nodded and reached into her work bag on the ground at her feet. She handed across two pages, and Fitz wiped his hands on a napkin before taking them from her. One of the pages was the original picture, while the second was an enlargement of the corkboard.

Fitz studied the first picture, then the second. After a minute or so, he was still looking at the picture when he said, "I'm siding with the idea that the killer left that there. To your point, this little board by the phone is not a collection of detritus. Everything here has a purpose. None of it looks old, either." He put the photo down and looked across at Beck. "I don't suppose the crime scene folks collected this, did they?"

She shook her head after chewing. "I checked on that." She stabbed her gooey fries and looked up. "You know, I bet it's still there. We're not even two weeks removed from the murder, and I'm not aware of any relative or anyone else requesting access to the house."

"Want me to swing by and check it out?" Fitz asked. "Gonna be out anyway. It's sort of on the way to the Mount house. I can collect it and bring it to you."

She considered it. "Sure." She pulled out her cell phone. "I'll text Whitaker. Get him to get the house key to a patrol officer. Have them meet you at the house."

Fitz drank the last of his water and said, "Just have Whitaker collect it." She gave him a look that asked if he was being serious. He said, "Good point."

"Fitz, I'd rather we not mention any of this until we've run down these last few items. The next report I make, I want to present as complete a picture as possible. I don't get the feeling Greenhaw is fully in on the Albritton connection."

Fitz nodded as he swiped the last of his fries through ketchup. He wiped his hands together and began to gather his trash. As he did so, he said, "How about this? While I'm at Nelson's, I'll do a walkthrough. See if anything jumps out that looks like it could have been renovated or worked on. See if anything stands out that can explain that card."

Beck held her chili-covered fork of fries in front of her mouth. "Do that. I actually considered that same thing and took another pass through the crime scene photos. The kitchen and the master bedroom were the only rooms that were photographed, and they clearly haven't been updated any time in the last three decades." She ate the fries.

"Even so, I still can't make it work why that card would still be there."

She finished chewing and pointed the empty fork at Fitz. "Unless the killer put it there."

"Unless that."

FORTY-TWO

The two investigators parted ways just after 1:30 in the afternoon. Beck returned to the office while Fitz drove to the Nelson crime scene. There was a black-and-white TPD patrol vehicle waiting for him at the curb. Fitz parked in the driveway and walked to the small SUV, where the officer handed him a key through the open window.

Inside, Fitz went directly to the kitchen and took the entire corkboard off the wall. He then did a quick survey of the inside of the house and then did the same outside, circling the premises. He didn't see anything that said *renovation* or *addition*. He gave the key back to the patrolman, thanked him for driving it out to him, and twenty minutes after he arrived, he was on his way to the Loraine Mount property.

The Mount house was the largest of all the victims. It was located in a smaller neighborhood; Fitz surmised there couldn't have been more than fifty houses in the subdivision. The house at 334 Whetstone Drive was on a corner lot and looked like it was plucked from the beach and dropped where it now sat. The three-story coastal was white with light gray accents, a slate roof, and a wraparound porch. The middle bay of the three-car garage was open, as was the tailgate of the large dark-colored SUV occupying the space. Fitz observed two suitcases inside.

He ascended the porch steps and knocked on the glass door. He could see shadows of movement in the house and was about to ring the doorbell when a slender black man wearing a white linen dress shirt—cuffs rolled above the elbow—linen pants, and tan leather huarache sandals answered the door.

"Yes," said the man in the slightest accent. "May I help you?"

Fitz displayed his credentials. "My name is Winston Fitzsimmons. I'm the chief investigator with the district attorney's office. Are you Dr. Higgins?"

The man took a step back, opening the door a little wider. "I'm Dr. Higgins, yes. Is there something wrong?"

"No, nothing is wrong. I just thought...I came by here last week and spoke with your wife. I thought maybe she had mentioned it to you."

Dr. Higgins looked skyward, thinking. He said, "Yes. Yes, she did, as a matter of fact." He laughed a nervous laugh. "I forgot about that. Something about a woman being murdered here?"

"That's right. May I come in?"

"Of course," said the doctor, stepping back and opening the door further. "And please, call me Lloyd."

Inside the house was an open floorplan, all light colors and hard surfaces—the fragrance of eucalyptus strong in the air. Fitz felt like he was at a spa. He noticed two more suitcases and three pillows by a door to his left that he assumed opened into the garage.

Fitz raised an eyebrow and said, "I'm sorry. It looks like you're either headed off somewhere or just getting back..."

"You're very perceptive," said Dr. Higgins with a big smile, the accent a little more pronounced. "We are leaving for Jamaica this evening. We are preparing to go to Atlanta to catch a flight."

"Ah, very nice. Me, I've never been, but I imagine it's a beautiful place."

"It is very beautiful, Mr. Fitzsimmons. It is also my home country."

"So you're going to visit family?"

"Visiting family and taking one final vacation before the girls have to go back to school."

As if on cue, two teenage girls, one clearly older than the other, banged down the stairs arguing about something when they looked up and saw a stranger in the house.

"It is okay, girls," Dr. Higgins said again with his bright smile. "This is Mr. Fitzsimmons. He is with the police." Seeing their expressions, he said, "Nothing is the matter. He is following up on an investigation from long ago." Then, to Fitz, he said, "Is that correct, Mr. Fitzsimmons?"

He nodded. "Yes. A very old case." As quickly as the girls appeared, they were gone toward the rear of the house, their worries seemingly abated.

"So, Mr. Fitzsimmons, what can I do for you...perhaps I should get my wife?"

"Please, Lloyd, call me Winston. I just have a couple of questions I'm hoping you can help me with." Dr. Higgins nodded, and Fitz continued, "When I spoke with your wife last week, it was more of what you'd call a fishing expedition. The investigation was in the very early stages, and I was hoping that perhaps I'd find something, anything, that could help. But, as I'm sure she told you, she didn't have anything to offer of value, which, quite frankly, is what I'd expected. You all are just too far removed from the homicide."

"Yes, Nina said it was a short conversation. She felt bad she couldn't have been more helpful."

A female voice came from the back of the house. "Lloyd, darling, did you pack your Kindle and your allergy pills?" Nina

Higgins appeared from the hallway and stopped short. "Mr. Fitzsimmons." She walked towards them. "What brings you back here? You solved your case, I hope."

"No, ma'am." He looked between Dr. And Mrs. Higgins. "We have had a potential development, which is what brings me back here. This is going to sound a little bizarre, but are you aware of any renovations or small construction projects that had been done to your house prior to your moving in?"

Nina sidled up to Lloyd, interlacing her arm with his. They looked quizzically at one another. Lloyd said, "I'm not sure I understand."

Fitz thought for a minute. "Maybe an outbuilding was added after construction, a deck out back? Perhaps the kitchen was reno-vated...or the master suite. Maybe a home theater was added. Anything like that. Something not original to the house."

Lloyd said, "Yours is indeed a strange question, Winston. Let me think."

Nina said, "What about the upstairs den? The playhouse and built-ins?"

"I did not think of that. You could be right." Dr. Higgins asked Fitz to follow him to a room on the third floor. Nina said she was going to finish packing and left the men as they made their way up the stairs.

Lloyd spoke as they walked. "The den up here has a large princess playhouse that I'm certain was not built with the home. It does not seem like something that would have been a part of the original construction. Perhaps that is the type of thing you are referring to?"

"Could be."

Lloyd led Fitz into a room with a sofa, two recliners, a beanbag chair, and a flatscreen television on the wall. YouTube was pulled up, and several video thumbnails about make-up application tech-niques were on the screen.

Lloyd saw Fitz looking at the screen, smiled, and said, "Teenage girls."

Fitz laughed. "Oh, man. I wouldn't even know where to begin with daughters."

"Oh, do you have boys?"

"No. No children. Maybe one day."

Lloyd nodded. He extended his arm, presenting the room. "Here we are."

The walls were a very pale pink with a mint green scalloped crown molding. There were lavender built-in bookcases and the wooden playhouse matched in every way. Fitz wasn't terribly handy with tools, but he recognized craftsmanship when he saw it.

"This space is fantastic. I imagine your girls love it."

"We couldn't get them out of here after we moved in. That was many years ago, of course, and now they feel like they are too old for such things. They want to remove the playhouse and paint the room something more in line with their tastes now, but my wife isn't having it." Lloyd laughed. "I try telling her they aren't our little girls anymore, but do you know what she says?"

"What's that?"

"She says, 'Lloyd, my dear, they will always be our little girls.'" Fitz smiled along with Lloyd.

Fitz inspected the playhouse, unsure what he was looking for. He asked, "Do you mind if I take some photos?"

"Feel free," the doctor said, extending an arm. "Can you tell me what you're looking for, or is that like top secret?"

Fitz pulled out his iPhone and began snapping pictures. "Just looking for evidence of who may have killed Loraine Mount. I wish I could tell you more, but then I'd have to get into some things we aren't too sure about and, well..."

"Say no more," Lloyd said with a wave of his hand.

Pictures taken, Lloyd was leading the pair down the stairs

when Fitz asked, "Did you and Nina buy the house from the Mount estate?"

"No. I don't remember the names of the previous owners, but it wasn't any Mounts. I got the impression it hadn't been lived in for a while when we bought it. The place was empty when the Realtor showed it to us."

"Any chance you know who the previous owners bought it from?"

"No, I'm sorry."

"Eh, it was worth a shot." They exited the stairs and walked through the open kitchen and toward the front door. Fitz stopped and said, "I don't suppose the name Sam Albritton means anything to you. Maybe you've seen some paperwork with that name on it? Anything like that that may have been left here?"

"Like I said, Winston, the house was empty. There was some stuff in the garage—" Lloyd stopped and was silent for a few seconds.

Finally, Fitz said, "The garage, Lloyd?"

"Wait, you said Albritton?"

"That's right."

"Come with me," Lloyd said with a wave of his hand for Fitz to follow.

They walked past the luggage and pillows and through the door into the garage. A late-model red Volvo wagon was in the bay immediately adjacent to the door they had just walked through. They walked in front of the Volvo, the SUV, and a black Honda CRV in the last bay to a tall metal cabinet in the corner. Lloyd opened the cabinet, pulled out a toolbox, and set it on the countertop.

The doctor flipped the latches on the toolbox and said, "When we moved in, I found several things in the garage left by the previous owner. Mostly junk they left behind rather than throwing it away. Scraps of wood, some rope, old paint cans, that

sort of thing." He lifted out the top tray of the royal blue Rubber-
maid toolbox and produced a bright orange tape measure. "They
left this, which is the only thing I kept." He pointed to the top of
the tape measure. "There."

Fitz took the tape. Written in black permanent marker in all
capital letters, the width of the plastic tape housing, traversing
from front to back, was the name ALBRITTON.

FORTY-THREE

"What's this?" Detective Beck Lawson asked, picking up the orange tape measure from her desk. Fitz had walked in unannounced and set it on top of the casefile she was reading.

"It's Albritton's tape measure. Picked it up at Loraine Mount's house." He explained how he came to possess it. He told her about the playhouse and the other built-ins in the Higgins' upstairs den. "I'm guessing he left it behind when he was doing work there. I called a buddy of mine who is an electrician, and he said he's left tools behind on jobs before."

Beck set down the tape and moved her computer mouse, stopping the screensaver, and typed into her spreadsheet. She said, "We now have confirmation of Sam Albritton being connected to five of the seven victims—four of the original six and Freida Nelson."

Fitz snapped his fingers. "That reminds me, I've got the corkboard in my truck. I'll be right back." He turned to leave and stopped. "Wait, you just said five confirmations out of the seven. I thought Mount was number four."

"Bob Crance emailed me back. He ID'd Albritton as the guy

who did the work for them. He said when they bought the house, they were given the name of the contractor who began the project, so they just stuck with him and made a few changes before construction got too far down the line. Said he was a super nice guy. Very talented."

"This is great and all, but the Freida Nelson thing is just weird. I mean, the guy's dead. How in the hell could he be involved here?"

Beck leaned back in her chair, hands behind her head. "Beats the hell out of me." A pause, then, "I'd like to shore up Cindy Stover and Gayle White before going back to the chief. I don't want to give them any wiggle room on this." She deepened her voice to mimic Chief Greenhaw: "So three of our victims had the same handyman. Hell, you can't even tie him to the first murder, and you want us to think he did all of them?" Then back to her voice: "It'll just piss me off."

Fitz said, "You work Stover, and I'll continue to work Gayle White."

Beck rocked forward in her chair and nodded.

Fitz left to retrieve the corkboard, and then he would go to his office. He was tired of waiting for the owners of Gayle White's house to get back to him.

———

INPUTTING the address into his skip-tracing search engine, he discovered the property owners were Barney and Mary Grace Cook. Through TLO, he found a cell phone number linked to Barney Cook with a 94% probability.

He dialed the number and, after four rings and growing impatience, the phone was answered: "Hello?"

"Hello, Mr. Cook?" said Fitz.

"Yes. May I ask who's calling?" Fitz introduced himself. There was a lot of commotion in the background, and Barney Cook asked Fitz to repeat himself, which he did. "We are in the Atlanta airport," Barney said in a raised voice. "Just landed. Can I call you back when we are on the road home?"

"Sure, that's fine. I will text you the number to the main switchboard so you will know I am who I say I am."

"Okay. Give me about half an hour."

Almost forty minutes later, Fitz's office phone buzzed. The receptionist told him there was a Barney Cook on the line, and he asked her to put the call through.

"Hello, Mr. Cook. Thank you for calling me back."

"I apologize for the delay getting back to you. The line to exit airport parking was crazy. Then, when we got to the kiosk to pay for parking, the arm wouldn't go up. Just a mess." Fitz could tell from the background that the phone was on speaker.

"That's quite alright. And just to let you know, I left a couple of business cards on your door, so you can disregard those when you get home."

"You went to our home?" Then, to someone in the car—Fitz guessed it was his wife—Barney said, "He went by our house." Then, to Fitz, he asked, "Is everything okay?"

"Everything is fine, Mr. Cook. Are you aware of a previous owner of your home dying at the property?" Fitz was careful not to tell them someone was murdered there in case they weren't aware of its history. He could hear the Cooks discussing something.

"Yes, Mr. Fitzsimmons, we know about the lady that passed away inside the house."

Passed away, Fitz thought. Had they not known the true nature of what happened there? One thing was for sure: he wasn't going to tell them. He had already experienced one freak out in this case from an owner learning they lived in a murder house, and that was something he did not want to deal with again. He thought about how to approach this.

"Hello? You still there?" Barney Cook asked.

"I'm still here. Are you aware of any construction or renovation projects that may have been undertaken in the house before you and Mrs. Cook bought it?" Fitz hoped he could avoid mentioning anything about an investigation, not wanting to get into the details of what happened to Gayle White in that house.

"Renovation?" Barney asked, confused. Fitz heard him ask his wife the same question. Almost a minute passed, and the only sound was the white noise of the outside rushing by.

Then Fitz heard Mrs. Cook say something. All he could make out clearly was, "Bathroom."

"That's right," Barney said to Fitz. "When we moved in, there was one of those walk-in bathtub showers in the master bathroom. You know, like for older people who have trouble stepping over the wall of a regular bathtub?"

"I've seen them advertised on television," said Fitz, nodding.

"Before we moved in, we had the master shower redone to go to a more traditional tub and shower. It turned out the walk-in was a fiberglass insert, and when it was removed, our plumber found that there was tile behind it. Really nice tile, in fact. In great condition.

"He figured the walk-in tub was after-market. He told us it's pretty rare to see one of those tubs original to the construction."

Fitz thought about this. "But you don't know when it was added."

"I don't. The people we bought it from were, oh, I don't know, in their fifties, maybe. They seemed far from infirm the few times we were around them. I can't imagine they put it in."

"Any idea how many times the home was sold from when the lady passed away to when y'all bought it?"

"Not a clue, Mr. Fitzsimmons."

He asked Barney who the listing agent was when they purchased the house, but neither Barney nor Mary Grace could remember anything more than the company that listed it. Barney told Fitz they might be able to find that information for him when they got home, but Fitz told them that the name of the real estate company should be enough; however, if it weren't, he would be in touch.

Believing he had gotten all he would get from the Cooks, he thanked them for their time and ended the call.

———

IT WAS NEARING 7:00 in the evening when Fitz dialed Beck's cell phone. She answered on the second ring with, "You still at the office, too?"

"I am," he said. "You?"

"Yep. You got something good for me?" He told her about his conversation with Barney Cook.

"After the call with the Cooks, I called the real estate company. It took a few minutes, but they gave me the name of the listing agent. She told me the walk-in tub was added by the original homeowner—which would be Gayle White—but nothing more than that. I was hoping you could reach out to the various banks in town. Try to find out where Ms. White did her banking and see what you can find in the way of payment for the work done."

"I can do that. I will also see what I can find concerning building permits. I'm working both of those angles with the Stover house. I'll email all my banking contacts again and add Gayle White to Cindy Stover looking for closed accounts."

There was a pause as Beck added to her case to-do notes on her computer. When she was done typing, she said, "I spoke with the CSI folks at the sheriff's office about their search of the Reynolds' place, and they didn't have anything for me. The entire place is a dump, so if any work *had* been done, there's really no way to tell."

"I don't suppose Ramos had any luck with the Reynolds?"

"Nope. They got a lawyer, or rather two lawyers—the Morrison brothers."

"Good God, they'll have Harold and Harriet in the death chamber before the week is out." Beck laughed.

Everyone in the Towne County criminal justice system was well aware of the ineptitude of the Morrison attorneys. They were the very embodiment of why ineffective assistance of counsel appellate claims existed.

Beck said, "Ramos reached out to one of the lawyers—she didn't know if it was Carl or Curtis—and told him what she wanted to know regarding possible work done on the house. He started hinting loudly at a trade. He would get them to answer her question if she would work with them on the criminal charges."

"For attempted murder of a cop? Them boys got balls, I'll say that. What'd she say?"

"Ramos told him to go fuck himself."

FORTY-FOUR

Late the following afternoon, Beck Lawson addressed the group sitting around the table in the conference room at the PD. She walked them through everything she and Fitz had done since they were all last in this same room the morning before.

She began by going in reverse order that the murders occurred, starting with the most recent homicide, Frieda Nelson. She was allowed to speak uninterrupted.

"Dell"—Beck motioned to the old detective—"found the business card belonging to Sam Albritton pinned to the cork board next to Freida Nelson's phone. It doesn't make any sense for it to be there. Albritton has been dead for a few years now, and neither Fitz nor I believe it was placed there years ago and forgotten about."

She then spoke briefly about Claire Albritton, addressing how she was different from the other victims by being the youngest in age by between twenty-six and forty-four years—not insignificant —and she was also the only married victim.

She then moved on to Sofia Graham and the interior renovations, followed by the Crances' positive photo ID of Sam Albritton. Next, she discussed Loraine Mount. She summarized the
work Fitz had done, including speaking with the current homeowners—Dr. and Mrs. Higgins—and finding Albritton's
measuring tape at the home.

The next victim she spoke about was Gayle White. She began
by explaining how Fitz tracked down the current homeowners and
the master bath renovation they did, which led to the discovery of
the bathtub replacement.

"I contacted every bank doing business here," said Beck, "and
I was able to locate a closed account at East Alabama Credit
Union. Based on what we know regarding the timing of the work
being done at the Cooper and Graham houses and their deaths, I
got the credit union to review all checks written on Gayle White's
account in the six months prior to her death. They were able to
locate a $9,500 check written to Sam Albritton Construction in
November of 1996. She was murdered in January 1997."

Beck told the group about Inez Cooper's daughter, Shirley
Bates, locating the paperwork for the carport enclosure her parents
had done. The paperwork listed Sam Albritton as the contractor
on the project.

Lastly, she spoke about Cindy Stover. "None of the local
banks could find any evidence that Ms. Stover ever had an account
with them. Could be she did her banking with a bank that wasn't
local, could be they just hadn't located her account for one reason
or another.

"Regardless, I went back to the house myself this morning and
saw what the sheriff's office crime scene folks saw: that the place
was a real shit hole. If that house ever had any work done on the
interior, there just is no way of knowing by looking at it. There
was a deck out back, though. It was in pretty rough shape in line
with the rest of the property, but it was attached to the house,

which would have required a permit. After going a few rounds with the city's Inspection Services department, I found it. Sam Albritton Construction obtained a permit for an attached wooden deck in October 1995. Cindy Stover was killed in February 1996."

Beck could have walked into the meeting and merely stated what she'd found connecting Albritton to each victim. While discussing the meeting with Fitz beforehand, though, he agreed with her that it needed to be thorough and detailed. Make sure the chief knew the lengths they went to verify all of this in an attempt to squelch any pushback ahead of time.

There was silence around the table when she had stopped speaking.

"So," Chief Greenhaw said, breaking the long silence, "Sam Albritton is a common denominator, it would appear."

"*A* common denominator?" Beck said. "I believe we can safely say that he is *the* common denominator, Chief. The odds that he worked for all six women within just a few months of their murders is a little more than a coincidence...Sir."

Greenhaw surveyed the group around the table before finally resting his eyes on Beck Lawson. "Until we get some actual evidence of his involvement in the murders, I'm not inclined to move past the coincidence stage just yet."

She flashed an exasperated look at Fitz, who caught her gaze, cleared his throat, and gave the slightest shake of his head.

"My balls itch, sir," Beck exclaimed.

Fitz began coughing to cover his laugh.

Barclay Griffith said, "What?" with a burst of a laugh.

Greenhaw shot a look at Fitz, then to Beck, and said, "What was that, Detective?"

"It's not a coincidence, sir. Not a chance. He's our guy...has to be. No other way to explain it."

Chief Greenhaw's face began to heat up, the color in his

cheeks creeping toward his forehead. "Then how do you *explain* his name showing up at Freida Nelson's house...Detective? Because, as you told us yesterday, he's been dead going on five years now. Or do you believe he returned from the dead to finish the job?"

"I don't have an answer for that yet, Chief," she answered.

"Well, find one because as of right now, even if you're right, all that gets us is a connection, and we don't close murder cases because we find a connection; we close murder cases because we find the killer. A killer whose culpability we can prove."

Beck threw another look to Fitz, who said, "We're open to suggestions here. We know that solving these cases goes through Sam Albritton. To ignore that is to ignore the evidence. So, let's talk through this."

Fitz didn't work for the police chief, so he could be more direct than Beck. Few bureaucratic and political hierarchies were as resolute as a law enforcement agency, and its members had to be mindful of what they said and, more importantly, how they said it. Fitz had no such restraints, and he didn't want her intensity to put her in a bad spot with the chief. They were getting close, and the last thing this investigation needed was to lose her as its case agent and lead detective.

Captain Jones said, "We need to take this one step at a time. Focus on one investigation at a time, and by that, I mean keeping separate the original six homicides from the murder of this Nelson woman, at least for the time being. I agree with Detective Lawson that Albritton is the common thread running through all seven murders. Now, did Albritton commit the original six murders? If he did, then there is a copycat at work because the one undeniable aspect of either of these cases is that Albritton did not murder Nelson. If we have a copycat, then we have a copycat who knows a hell of a lot about murders that they ostensibly should not know anything about. Even if Albritton did not commit the first six murders, then we could still have a copycat. Or is the original killer the same person who killed Freida Nelson?" TJ looked around the table. "Am I missing anything? Any other possibilities?"

Everyone at the table seemed to be running through what Captain Jones had just laid out.

Barclay was the first to speak. "Honestly, the idea that Sam Albritton is completely innocent seems a bit of a stretch. Seven people are dead, and his name is in the middle of all of it. Are we really to believe that he was framed by at least one person and maybe even two people who are quite possibly independent of one another?"

Beck said, "If he wasn't our original killer, I don't believe we can go so far as to say he was framed for those murders. We had to work our asses off establishing those connections. Surely, if he were being framed or even being used to scapegoat those crimes, his connection would have been more obvious. Especially to the original investigators."

"Good point," Barclay said.

"Even as far as the Nelson case is concerned," Beck continued, "the killer has to know Sam is dead, so no real frame up there either, which begs the question of *why*? Why even drag his name into it?"

"Why indeed," the chief chipped in, much to the annoyance of Beck.

"How about this?" said TJ, ever the diplomat. "Now that we have a name, let's go back through the old cases with Sam Albritton in mind. Maybe something in the case file looks different now; takes on a new meaning. Also, we know the connection between Albritton and the old cases, so we need to find the connection between Albritton and Freida Nelson. Why did she have his business card in her house?" To Beck, he said, "Nice work getting us here." She nodded back.

Chief Greenhaw said, "Alright. It looks like we have our way forward. In the meantime, Detective," he was looking at Beck now, "you might want to see a doctor about your"—he waved his hand around as if searching for the right words—"itchy balls."

FORTY-FIVE

The killer was frustrated.

It had been eight days since the murder of Freida Nelson. Although there was a flurry of news stories in the two days that followed, there had been nothing since. No updates on the investigation, no follow-up with which cases were possibly connected to Nelson. Nothing.

The articles themselves were somewhat nebulous when it came to connecting the old murders to the newest one—a lot of maybes and possibilities. The reporter from the *Trib* intimated there was a serial killer at play, but, the killer figured, without some sort of confirmation, she wouldn't come right out and say it. You didn't print in the newspaper that a serial killer was running around before you were damned sure of it.

Still, there should have been a bigger reaction, the killer thought.

The DA's statement was as bland as it was expected, but it told him they'd made the connection. Connecting Freida Nelson to the old cases was the easy part. Putting them on Sam Albritton was another story. He had left the business card behind, but would they notice it? And if they did notice it, would they understand its significance? The killer knew he had to be careful. He couldn't make it too obvious. The police needed to find the card and the name organically through the natural course of the investigation. Otherwise, they may see it for what it actually was: a false flag. He was enjoying the game even though it was just beginning.

Killing was a thrill in itself, yet he found the sensation abated with the adrenaline. Connecting his murders to those from years ago shielded him from scrutiny and suspicion while also making the murder event last by maintaining a connection with the case. For his secret to have power, the power he gained through this intimate knowledge, the media needed to do its part by keeping the murders in the public eye, which was not happening.

Perhaps the media could use a nudge, the killer thought.

Another reason he wanted more press was so he would know where the police were on the investigation. Were they pulling the thread that was Sam Albritton? When they did pull that thread, they would learn soon enough that he was dead, which he hoped would stymie them further. If and when they began closing in, he had a plan for that, too.

The police needed to take Sam Albritton seriously. If they hadn't yet, they soon would. The killer would make sure of it.

He was ready to kill again.

FORTY-SIX

I had arranged this meeting before I killed Freida Nelson. I did so because I had a feeling it may be needed, and scheduling a meeting with my second victim so close in time after the death of my first would look suspicious to even the greenest cop. This way, any potential link could be chalked up to happenstance.

I had been here before in the same capacity I was here right now, but those visits had been during the day. As unusual as after-hours house calls were in my business, they weren't a cause for alarm.

I was right on time for our 7:00 PM meeting.

Before knocking on the door, I observed a standard doorbell. As popular as video doorbells were becoming, they still had yet to catch on consistently among the boomer generation, another plus with my chosen victims.

The door was answered by Elise Hightower, a petite lady in her sixties who was all sharp angles with straight gray hair that brushed the tops of her shoulders. Her build and athleisure told of a woman who was still active.

She was expecting me, so she opened the door and invited me in, saying, "I have everything set up at the kitchen table like you asked. Would you like some water or coffee?"

"Water would be nice."

A southern lady could not invite you into their home without offering refreshments. I preferred water to coffee because people generally made the coffee too weak and rarely had the raw sugar and heavy cream I preferred, not to mention that easily accessible hot liquids made for a surprisingly effective self-defense device.

The house was cozy and modern, with the smell of fresh-cut citrus hanging in the air. A golden retriever lay curled up on the light-colored deep-pile carpet, following me with his eyes as his head lay on his paws. A TV mounted above a faux-rock gas fireplace was paused on a baking show.

She was a nice lady, and I almost hated what I had planned for her, but over time, I had developed emotional callouses to such feelings. As for *why her*, she checked the appropriate boxes: single (not so recently divorced), her closest family members were her three children, and she was separated from them by at least two states in three separate directions, and she is much smaller and presumably less aggressive than my first victim, the battle-tested Freida Nelson.

After Freida's murder, I went over what had gone wrong. I took her age to mean she was weak and vulnerable—I was misguided on both. When I flashed my knife, not only was Freida not scared, but it made her rather angry. I had chosen the large blade for utilitarian reasons. It was functional in its use as both a tool of intimidation and compliance as well as killing. Ms. Nelson, however, didn't get the memo that she was supposed to be intimidated and compliant.

That had resulted in a fight that could have proved disastrous. Fighting with a blade, even when you have the only blade in the assault, is fraught with peril—cutting yourself and leaving DNA being chief among them. Losing the weapon and having it used on you was also a potentially dangerous outcome.

I was determined not to make the same mistake this time. I still planned on using the knife because a gun was far louder and far more dangerous should Ms. Hightower gain control of it.

Atop the round kitchen table was a black plastic file box with the lid open, stacks of papers of varying heights, and a white coffee mug, evidence of a tea bag inside. I set my briefcase down and sat on the side of the table with my back to the window, hoping Elise would sit across from me rather than beside me, which would put her back to the kitchen's entrance.

She came to the table with a glass of water, and from the brief look on her face, I knew I had taken her seat. Her manners, though, forbid her from doing anything other than sitting somewhere else. She sat where I hoped she would and pulled the mug toward her.

I took a long drink from the glass and asked if I could use her restroom.

"Sure," she said, turning in her chair to point past the den and down the hallway behind her. "Second door on the left."

I nodded and excused myself from the table. I did go to the bathroom, careful not to touch any hard surfaces lest I leave fingerprints behind. I wore a long-sleeved green check shirt untucked over jeans and cheap white Walmart sneakers. As I entered the den and approached Ms. Hightower from behind, I reached behind with my right hand—my dominant hand—slid it under the tail of my shirt, and removed the 8 3/4 inch Bowie knife from its leather sheath. I angled my body, keeping the knife down by my right leg out of view.

Elise rested her elbows on the table with both hands wrapped around the coffee mug, sipping from it as she stared at the mass of papers in front of her. I closed to within eight feet or so of her and brought the knife around when a phone rang.

I turned toward the sound, which had come from behind me, and saw the offending device on a small table beside a cloth wing-back chair.

A cell phone.

I stared in stunned disbelief.

When I looked back toward the kitchen, I saw Elise staring at me—at the knife—mouth open, coffee mug raised chin level. Her mouth began to work, but no sound emerged. We stood that way for what felt like minutes, but it could not have been for more than two or three seconds, and then I pounced.

FORTY-SEVEN

Elise dropped her mug and stood, her chair falling backward to the green tile floor. Instead of moving to her left, to the interior of the kitchen, toward safety, she moved right—her panicked mind scrambled—and she was trapped.

I closed the distance to the table's edge, getting my feet slightly tangled in the legs of the table chair lying on its back, and she edged around the table, keeping distance between us. We now stood staring at one another, the table separating us, her chest rising and falling with every breath. She showed a measure of fear tinged with determination, and I could feel sweat forming at my hairline.

My only thought at that moment went to the previous murders, and I wondered how the hell the killer had managed to control the scene so well. Those scenes were pristine outside of the bedroom, and now I was zero for two in that department. Freida Nelson's kitchen had been left a bloody wreck, and all signs were pointing to the same here in Elise Hightower's home.

"Fuck," I said, low but loud enough for her to hear, and hung my hands by my side, and that was when she made her second mistake.

Her first mistake was one born out of panic. In attempting to get away from me, she put herself in a spot without escape. Behind her was a window, and I would easily cut her off if she tried to run left or right.

Her second mistake was taking my posture as a sign of defeat, and she relaxed...just enough.

In an instant, I grabbed the edge of the blonde wood table and lifted it, advancing towards her. I aimed to pin her against the window, but the table was much lighter than I anticipated, causing it to flip instead of moving forward. She swiftly dropped to the floor, ending up beneath the table, which now leaned against the window.

The plastic file box crashed to the floor, and the stacks of paper scattered. My forward momentum caused my foot to catch on the table as it landed, and I tripped, crashing onto the table's underside, banging my right cheek and also sending a jolt of pain to my ribs.

This woman, petite in size but large in fight, was scrambling underneath the upturned tabletop. I spotted a foot to my left as she was scurrying to escape, and I grabbed for it, making contact but missing before finally grasping the heel of her shoe. She continued to writhe, and her foot slid out of the running shoe as she squirted out from under the table to my right.

She scrambled to her feet and slipped down when she pushed off with her now shoeless sock foot on the tile flooring. I was flailing on the table, trying to get up, when the table slipped and slid down the window, coming to rest on the window ledge just above the floor. Elise pushed herself up, slipped again but stayed up this time. I, too, finally managed to stand up and found myself standing in the middle of the table's underside.

She was making for the front door, and I was right behind her.

She was running, reaching for the doorknob, when I dove at her and pushed her with two hands in the back. My force added to her momentum, and she slammed into the solid wood front door with a sound like a gunshot.

She was dazed but didn't go down. She drunkenly reached for the doorknob, unable to grab hold. I picked myself up off the floor just as she managed to wrench the door open, and as she angled her body through the narrow exit, I kicked the door closed with as much force as I could muster. The way her body was angled, the right side of her face took the brunt of the violence as it was slammed between the door and the jamb. She dropped in the door's opening.

I was gulping air as I staggered to the crumpled figure. I reached down and grabbed her by the hood and jerked her back inside, closing and then locking the door. It was only when she groaned that I knew she was still alive.

I surveyed the damage, and it was bad. Blood was all over the door. I looked down, and my right hand was slick with it. I returned to the kitchen, exhausted from the fight and the adrenalin dump. I rinsed my hand under the kitchen faucet—it burned, and I winced.

All four of my fingers were sliced open just below the first knuckle. I looked back to the upside-down table, spotting my knife; I noticed blood on the blade and on the table. I looked back at my hand and flexed my fingers, guessing that as I fought with the table, my hand slid down the knife's polished wood handle and over the blade.

I didn't straighten up Freida Nelson's kitchen because I was eager to finish the job and leave, and I was confident I had left no traces of physical evidence. This kitchen, however, was a CSI's wet dream.

I wrapped a dish towel tightly around my fingers and made a fist to grip the towel closed. I walked over to the bloody table and said, "Fuck me," as I took in the sight of my DNA littering the scene. Spilling blood in the kitchen was a blessing and a curse. In any other room, it may not look so bad nor spread nearly as much, but the kitchen was all hard surfaces, so a little blood went a long way. On the other hand, hard surfaces made for easy cleanup—no carpet to soak up and trap irretrievable blood.

The first thing I did—after making sure Elise was securely restrained—was hunt for bandages, which I found under the sink in a bathroom. I ran my fingers under more cold water in the bathroom sink, poured peroxide over the cuts, and then wrapped more gauze than I needed to around my right hand. Satisfied all of my blood was washed down the sink and none could escape the thick bandage, I went back to begin the kitchen cleanup. As I passed the front door, I noticed a streaked bloody handprint on the door that would have to be cleaned.

I collected all the papers that were previously on the table and found the overturned plastic file box. I threw the papers indiscriminately inside, closed the lid, and flipped the clasp, locking it shut. I decided to take the file box with me because some of the papers had my blood on them. Besides, I didn't know where the box went, and if it were out of place and the police looked inside, its contents could give them a clue to her night visitor. I didn't see that as a good possibility, but possible it was, so I took it with a plan to dispose of the documents before going home.

I placed the file box at the front door so I wouldn't forget to take it. Then I bent down to check on Elise, and she was still out but breathing.

Back at the table, I began spraying and wiping with Clorox cleaner and paper towels I found under the kitchen sink. The underside of the table was varnished enough that the blood cleaned up easily. As I was cleaning, I was struck with the thought that perhaps the reason the old murder scenes were so immaculate was that the killer had cleaned up afterward. I'm not sure why that thought didn't hit me until that moment, but it made much more sense now.

I went over the table and that area of the kitchen numerous times, spotting a missed drip here and a blood droplet there until I was satisfied I'd gotten all of it. Sure, Luminol would react to the iron in the hemoglobin of cleaned-up blood, but I doubted they would spray the underside of the kitchen table or anywhere in this area after I was done cleaning. So long as the pungent odor of disinfectant dissipated by the time police arrived, there wouldn't be anything in here signaling them to look.

After cleaning for nearly an hour, stopping four times to check on Elise, I turned my focus to her—killing her and staging the scene.

I scooped her up and laid her in bed as I had done with Freida. I made sure my knife was clean, not wanting to introduce my blood into the scene, just waiting on a savvy forensic biologist to find interloping DNA. I inserted the curved tip of the blade into the right side of her neck and pulled the blade across to the opposite side, opening the skin and creating a smooth, toothless smile.

Her eyelids fluttered as I dragged the blade across her neck. She made wet, strangled noises and moved her head side to side in slow motion, so I placed my left hand on her forehead to make her still. Blood spurted when the blade was first inserted but slowed to a thick gush as the gap in her neck expanded, and out it ran over her shoulders, down the sides of her throat, and soaked the bed.

I dipped my gloved fingers into the gaping wound and drew an *S* on the natural wood headboard. I stood back like an artist assessing their work, satisfied that everything was as it should be. I then took off the bloody glove inside out and placed it in the Ziploc bag I had removed from my jeans pocket.

I withdrew a second Ziploc bag from my rear jeans pocket and removed the Sam Albritton business card inside with my gloved left hand. Holding the card between my thumb and forefinger, I used the last three fingers on my left hand to open the drawer in the bedside table, which was only moderately full. I dropped the card in, making sure it mixed with the other contents, and pushed the drawer closed.

Back in the kitchen, I removed a Polaroid camera from my briefcase and returned to the bedroom. I resisted photographing my crimes because that was a wonderful way to get caught.

My predecessor took photos, which is how I learned about the crimes and got the idea for what I was doing.

As time passed after my first murders, the vivid memories of the killings faded from my mind's eye, and I was able to indulge in the details less and less. I further resisted taking photos of Ms. Nelson because, again, I did not want to get caught by something as sloppy and avoidable as photographs.

But I soon understood precisely why serial killers take souvenirs despite knowing it could very well be the thing that sees them die in prison: the fear of forgetting outweighs the fear of capture.

I pointed the 1980s-era instant camera at the bed, framing it just so. I pressed the red button, and after the click and the whir, a blank piece of film emerged. I grasped the film at the bottom edge and allowed it to develop.

Perfect.

I slid the now-developed film into the breast pocket of my shirt as I went to the kitchen for a last once-over before leaving. I had my briefcase in one hand and the file box in the other as I crossed the street to the side with no sidewalk and thus no street-lights, and I walked to my car, which was parked well away from the scene.

FORTY-EIGHT

V ivian Bates, a retired school administrator, was at the Towne County Boys and Girls Club, where she spent every weekday afternoon tutoring at-risk youth in the community. These were children, mainly middle school students with a few high school sophomores, who took advantage of the fun, safe, and constructive after-school environment rather than spending idle time in their less-than-ideal home lives. There were days when she believed her post-retirement volunteer work was more rewarding than her career had been.

Mrs. Bates volunteered her time as repayment to those in her life at the Boys and Girls Club in Detroit who encouraged her and developed in her the desire to go to college in an area where very few did. Her time at the Club also fostered a love for learning and led to her getting her bachelor's degree in Education at the University of Memphis. Spurred on by the goal of teaching at the university level, she attended Auburn University and received her master's degree in Administration of Higher Education.

After earning her master's degree, she stayed at Auburn and got her doctorate in Administration of Elementary and Secondary

Education. She had wanted to teach and did teach for a number of years, but she believed she could impact a school full of children rather than one class at a time if she were an administrator. So, she served as a middle school principal and then principal at the local high school for seventeen years.

She was saying her goodbyes at the end of the day when a young black girl in glasses came running up to her. The young girl had a cupcake in her hand.

"Don't forget one of my birthday cupcakes, Mrs. Bates. For dessert," the girl said with a laugh.

"Dessert?" Vivian said. "Girl, this won't make it home." That got a laugh not just from the girl but from a number of the children within earshot. "Happy Birthday, Tiana." The girl hugged Vivian, who hugged her back, holding the cupcake away from the girl's back.

Vivian made her way to her red Mercedes C-Class, unlocking the trunk with her key fob. She placed her work bag inside and closed the lid. She dropped into the driver's seat and was looking for somewhere to set the cupcake when her phone rang.

"Hold on, Pamela," she said to her caller. Pamela Campbell was Elise Hightower's daughter and one of Vivian's former students. Elise was Vivian's longtime administrative assistant, and they had a standing lunch date once a week.

She pressed the start button, cranking up the car, and waited a few more seconds as the vehicle's Bluetooth connected to her phone. Hearing the call coming through the car's speakers, she said, "You still there, honey?"

"Yes, ma'am."

"Okay. Sorry about that. I was getting in my car when you called. Now, how are you? It's been a while."

"I'm fine. The family's good. Same old, same old."

"That's good to hear. How's Bloomington?"

"Bloomington is good. Getting a little crazy up here with Ohio State coming in this weekend."

"I have a feeling the Hoosiers may surprise some folks this year with that transfer quarterback y'all got."

"Your mouth to God's ear. The restaurant business is a hell of a lot better when we're winning, that's for sure. Losing's good for drinking, but winning's good for drinking *and* eating. Tips are a lot bigger, too," she said.

"I'm supposed to have lunch with your mom tomorrow. I can't wait to tell her you called." Three kids walked out of the Boys and Girls Club with the person Vivian recognized as their mother. They waved at her, and she smiled and waved back.

"She's actually why I'm calling."

She detected the tone in Pamela's voice and said, "What's the matter?" as she concentrated on the car's LCD screen, which showed the name Pamela Campbell and that they'd been talking for two minutes and twelve seconds.

"Well, Mrs. Bates, I talked to Mom yesterday morning and haven't spoken to her since. I called her last night, and she didn't answer. I called back later, and it went straight to voicemail. I've called her four times today, and each time, it's straight to voicemail."

"Hmmm. Sounds like her cellphone is dead. That's unlike her."

"Very unlike her. Especially since she got rid of the landline."

"Want me to go by and check on her," Vivian asked.

"Oh, would you? That's why I was calling. You live so close. I hope it's not an inconvenience."

"Pamela, honey, your momma took excellent care of me for sixteen years. I've made it my duty to take care of her now. I will head there right away. I've got a key and everything. Probably take me about twenty minutes with traffic. I'll call you back."

It was only now that she realized she was still holding the

cupcake. She looked around for a place to set it before peeling the paper and eating it as she drove.

———

VIVIAN ARRIVED at Elise Hightower's house and pulled into the driveway behind her friend's car. She turned her car off and surveyed the area, seeing nothing out of place. She knocked on the front door, rang the doorbell, and then called out, "Elise? Elise, are you home? It's me, Vivian."

She had called her friend on the way to her home, but the call went directly to voicemail—she left a quick message just in case. But now, being here, she was worried. She dialed Pamela's number and told her Elise's car was in the driveway and that she didn't see anything unusual from the outside. "I've rung the doorbell and knocked, announcing myself without getting a response. I'm going inside if you're okay with that."

"Yes, please." Vivian could hear the distress in Pamela's voice.

She had her keys in her hand and found the one to Elise's house. She put the phone on speaker, then unlocked the door and opened it, knocking as she pushed inside. She announced herself again without receiving a response. The place was eerily quiet.

She took a few tentative steps into the house, scanning for anything that looked out of place when it hit her—the smell.

Her career in education didn't leave her in a position to immediately identify the odor, but she had watched enough television to get a decidedly uneasy feeling. She crept through the den and poked her head into the kitchen, scanning the area and seeing nothing unusual. She made her way back to the house.

"See anything?" Pamela asked.

Vivian shook her head, then caught herself. She raised the phone and answered, "No. Everything looks okay inside. I've checked the den and the kitchen. I'm going back to her bedroom."

Vivian heard Pamela begin to pray quietly but fervently. The odor was strengthening. She hesitated at the open bedroom door before walking in.

A strangled squeal came from Vivian's mouth, and she dropped the phone. "No, no, no."

Pamela's voice was coming from the phone, lying face up on the floor, but Vivian couldn't hear it. She brought two shaking hands up to her mouth, took two exceedingly tentative steps toward the bed, and leaned closer. She began to shake her head, and the tears came. She turned to run, then, remembering her phone—looked around wildly for it before spotting it on the floor. She scooped it up and ran out of the house, bursting into a full wail before reaching the door.

FORTY-NINE

Minutes after the 911 call, the first patrol car arrived at the house. The officer parked at the curb and got out. An older black woman with long braids came running at him from the yard. She held up both arms, waving them around.

"She's dead, she's dead, Lord Jesus, my friend is dead," she was screaming.

"Ma'am, ma'am. I'm going to need you to calm down."

"Here." Vivian thrust the phone at the officer. "I've got her daughter on the phone. Talk to her."

The officer nodded and took the telephone. He said, "Hello?"

"Hello?" said Pamela in a raw voice. "Who's this?"

"I'm Officer Shane Willet from Towne PD. I just got here."

"Is it true? Is she dead?"

"Who am I speaking with?"

"Pamela Campbell. I'm Elsie Hightower's daughter. Is she dead?"

"Ms. Campell," he said in a calming manner. "I just got here and have not been inside. I'm going to give the phone back to the person... whose phone is this?"

"Uh, uh," the stress of the moment was affecting her ability to think, "Uh, Vivian...Vivian Bates. She's a friend of my mother's."

"Alright, Ms. Campbell, I'm going to hand the phone back to Ms. Bates," he signaled Vivian over, "and go check on your mom?"

"Thank you," she said through a sob.

Officer Willet handed the phone to Vivian and said, "Where is she?"

"In her bedroom. Go inside and go to the left." He nodded and took off at a jog.

He reached down to his holster, pressed a button on the side, and pulled the gun slightly out, freeing it from the locking mechanism. He bladed through the front door and crept down the hall; the stench faint but unmistakable.

He made it to the bedroom and stepped inside.

He walked back to the den and called in what he'd found into his shoulder mic. He went outside and shook his head. He held out his hand, and when Vivian gave him the phone, he told Pamela what he'd found and that a detective would be in touch soon, and he handed the phone back to Vivian.

"That your car?" he said, motioning with his head toward the red Mercedes.

She nodded. "Yes."

"You got another way to get home?" He began walking down the slight slope of the front yard toward his car, Vivian following behind him.

"What? Another way home? Why?"

He pulled out a large roll of yellow crime scene tape from his trunk. "Because I'm about to tape off the scene, and your car's going to be inside it. You won't have access to it until we're done here. Could be hours."

"But I didn't do anything. I just got here."

"I'm sorry, ma'am. It was a part of the scene when I arrived. Nothing gets moved." He was walking to the front left corner of the property, looking for a place to secure the tape. He opted for a river birch that may have been on the neighboring property.

By the time he had made it around the house and back to the tree to tie off the completed scene, the first detective car arrived. He didn't realize it until he was headed back to his car to stash the roll of tape in his trunk: It wasn't a detective. It was the police chief.

———

WHEN OFFICER WILLET saw Captain TJ Jones exit the chief's vehicle, he knew this was bigger than some random home invasion murder. Along with the chief and the captain of detectives was Detective Lawson, whom he knew only a little.

She nodded at him, and he returned the nod. He put the tape in his trunk and closed the lid as a second vehicle came roaring up to the scene. It was District Attorney Barclay Griffith and his chief investigator, Winston Fitzsimmons.

There is definitely something up, Willet thought to himself. He approached the chief and filled him in on what awaited them inside. The patrol officer also pointed out Vivian Bates, who was standing at the base of the driveway outside the scene, and all five pairs of eyes landed on her. She looked anxiously at the group, trying to hear what was being said but getting nothing. She continued to watch them as they spoke for another minute or so before they moved as a pack toward the house, Officer Willet leading the way.

Additional law enforcement personnel—detectives, crime scene investigators, and patrol units—began steadily arriving.

At the door, Beck told Willet, "I'm putting you in charge of crime scene access. Start a log of folks entering and exiting, noting the times of each."

Willet nodded, slightly annoyed, before heading back to the tape.

The chief led the way inside, followed by TJ and Beck. Barclay motioned for Fitz to go in ahead of him. He would hang back at the front of the house and give the investigators space. As the other four went down the hall toward the body, Barclay took a moment to scan the den.

Murder scenes had a definite feel. The air was different—still, yet disrupted. A pall of sadness hung in the air as you stood amid someone's life interrupted. Unlike the vast majority of domestic homicide scenes he'd visited, this place was immaculate. No empty soft drink bottles tossed haphazardly, no piles of laundry on the furniture, and no pet hair covering everything.

He eased through the den and into the kitchen, where he did another quick scan before heading back to the bedroom to view the body. He almost collided with the head of the crime scene unit, Angie Presley, as she moved, head down, with purpose, from the front door to the bedroom. Again, he motioned for her to go ahead.

Barclay stepped into the bedroom, and though he knew what to expect, he was still jarred by the stark image of the body, the blood, and the killer's calling card on the headboard.

FIFTY

Barclay had been outside for several minutes, making small talk with some of the officers, when Chief Greenhaw and Captain Jones exited the home. He ended his conversation and approached the two men.

"What do you think?" Barclay asked.

"It's our guy," said TJ. "Gotta be."

"If that's the case, there'll be a Sam Albritton business card in there."

TJ nodded. "I told them to look for that."

"Let's go have a chat with the witness," said Chief Greenhaw.

As they approached Vivian Bates, she ended the phone call she was on and adopted an anxious look. Chief Greenhaw introduced himself and the others and asked her to repeat for them everything about how she came to be there and found the body.

The chief peppered her with a few questions. "When was the last time you spoke to Ms. Hightower?"

"I *spoke* to her probably five or six days ago, but we text fairly regularly. My last communication with her was, oh, two days ago, I'd say."

"Did you get the impression she feared for her life?"

Vivian seemed mortified at the question. "Of course not."

"Do you know anyone who would want to hurt her?"

She shook her head, chin quivering. "She was a retired administrative assistant from the high school. Why would *anyone* want to hurt her? I'm not aware of any enemies if that's what you're asking." Tears began to flow, belying the resolve on her face. "What I saw in that house...why would anyone do something like that?"

Captain Jones said, "The *why* isn't always easy to answer. It's the *who* we're most interested in right now. So let us get to work and see if we can't answer both of those questions." Vivian nodded blankly.

The chief's attention was drawn down the street as a white Ford Escape with the familiar red and blue stripe bisecting the hood neared the crime scene.

"Christ," he said.

TJ and Barclay turned to see Wendy Wade pulling to the curb across the street.

TJ yelled at a patrol officer, "Get her to move her car. Establish a perimeter a quarter mile or so in each direction. Block it off and tell her she has to stay behind that." The officer nodded and went to speak with the reporter.

"Let's go back inside," said the chief.

They were standing in the den when Maude Lazenby sauntered in with a burning cigarillo.

"The fuck, Maude?" exclaimed the chief. "Put that thing out. You know you can't smoke inside a crime scene."

In a voice dragged low and rough by decades as a smoker, she said, "Ah come on, Chief, you know I ain't good with that body smell."

"Then why the hell are you with the coroner's office?"

She took a drag and exhaled. "Pays the bills, Chief."

"Whatever, just put that thing out." She was looking around the room for a place to extinguish her cigarillo when the chief said, "For Christ's sake, Maude, take it outside." She turned to leave, and he yelled, "And by outside, I mean outside the tape."

To the room, he said, "Who the hell even let her in? She needs to stay outside until we need her." Growing more flustered: "And who called Wendy Wade? TJ, I need to know who's calling the coroner before we need them and who's calling the media at all. This is ridiculous."

TJ said, "The assistant coroner has a scanner, and I'm sure he's the one calling Wade."

He was about to say something derogatory about the assistant coroner when Angie Presley entered the den.

She said, "Hey, Chief, can you come back here?"

They followed her to the bedroom, and Beck motioned for the chief to join her at the bedside table, where a drawer was open. Angie Presley stood off to the side with her Nikon around her neck.

Beck nodded to the open drawer, and Chief Greenhaw looked inside. Sitting on top of an LL Bean catalog was a Sam Albritton business card.

"Has this been photographed?" he asked.

"It has," said Angie.

"Anyone have gloves?" Greenhaw asked, holding his hand out but not looking away from the inside of the drawer. Angie pulled a wad of blue latex gloves from her back pocket and dropped a pair into his palm. He put one on and put the other in his pocket. With his gloved hand, he lifted the card and studied it as he turned it over and then back. He held it up for TJ and Barclay to see, then handed it to Beck, who dropped it into an evidence bag. "Let's go out and talk."

They were filing out of the room when a toilet flushed.

Everyone stopped. The hallway bathroom door opened, and Maude came out with a lit cigarillo.

Greenhaw's eyes went wide as he looked between Maude and the open bathroom. He sniffed, then yelled, "Are...are you shitting in my crime scene?"

"I had to go," said Maude without the faintest trace of embarrassment.

Greenhaw's face was growing red from the neck up.

TJ stepped around him and grabbed Maude lightly around her upper arm, so skinny that TJ's fingers overlapped. He said, "Come on, Maude. We're not ready for you yet," and escorted her from the house.

After taking a few minutes for the chief to calm down, Beck suggested another conversation with Vivian Bates. She had a few questions for the witness.

They began to walk outside when Barclay grabbed Chief Greenhaw. "Are you going to make a statement?"

Greenhaw shook his head slowly and looked as if he were about to speak when Barclay said, "Look, Chief, I get it. Someone's talking out of turn, and it pisses you off. Me, too. But we now have two murders linked to six other murders. We don't tell the public what's going on, and more people die...I don't know, Chief, but I think we have to say...something."

Greenhaw thought about it and said, "My first priority is this investigation." Barclay was about to speak when the chief continued, "Tell you what, if I go out there right now, I'll just get mad and say something I don't need to. You deal with Wendy Wade better than I do. Go talk to her. Get a feel for what she wants, and then you and I will talk and figure out what we need to say."

Barclay and Greenhaw exited the house and walked down the porch steps. Barclay kept walking past Beck, Fitz, and TJ, who were all waiting on the chief, before speaking with Vivian Bates.

Beck suggested they not all go talk to the witness. "She's overwhelmed right now, and I don't think the four of us crowding around asking questions will be very helpful."

"What do you suggest?" Greenhaw asked.

"You've already questioned her," she answered, "so I believe it should be you and one of the three of us."

"Well, you said you have some questions for her, and a female presence probably wouldn't hurt, so we'll talk to her."

Chief Greenhaw explained to TJ that they would make a statement to the press at some point. He told him what Barclay had said, and TJ agreed that it was the smart thing to do. Greenhaw asked his captain to think about what they needed to say, and they would discuss it after Barclay spoke with Wendy.

Vivian Bates was talking with a neighbor from across the street when she looked over her shoulder and saw the police chief and the detective—she couldn't remember either of their names—walking toward her. She excused herself from the conversation and met them in the middle of the road.

"Ms. Bates, Detective Lawson and I have a couple more questions before we cut you loose."

She nodded.

Beck nodded her head toward the man Vivian had been speaking to. "Do you know him?"

Vivian looked back at the man and then back to Beck and shook her head. "No. He was asking me what was going on. I told him I didn't think I could say and that he needed to ask the police."

Beck nodded and made a mental note to have an officer speak with all the neighbors to find out if anyone had seen anything.

Beck said, "Do you remember if the door was locked or unlocked when you arrived?"

Vivian opened her mouth to speak, closed it, and looked up thoughtfully. "I used my key," she said, still looking skyward. She closed her eyes now, concentrating. She began to shake her head.

"I guess I can't say for certain that it was locked." She opened her eyes and looked at Beck. "I didn't try the knob before I used my key, but I didn't register it being unlocked, if that makes sense." Beck nodded. "To be honest with you, I wasn't paying any attention to that. I was just focused on getting inside and checking on Elise."

"Since you used your key without first trying the door, can I take that to mean that Elise typically locks her doors?"

"Oh, yes. Her son is a probation officer in Oklahoma, and he has a thousand stories of homes being broken into because the door was unlocked. Even when she was home, the door was locked."

"Do you know if she kept a spare key outside?"

Vivian shook her head and said, "I don't."

"What about letting people inside her home?"

"How do you mean?" Vivian asked.

Beck thought about it. "Like, if a stranger knocked on her door, say a person selling something or handing out religious tracts, would she allow them inside or invite them into her home."

"Hmmm," Vivian began, "I suppose if someone was in trouble or needed help, then maybe. But other than something like that, I don't believe she would, no."

Beck looked at Chief Greenhaw and asked if he had any questions, and he shook his head, *No.*

She then told Vivian she was free to go, but they may have more questions for her as the investigation progressed.

"I gave my number to Officer Willet. I will be happy to help in any way I can."

"We appreciate that," said Beck

"Um, I don't mean to sound callous, but when will I be able to get my car?"

Chief Greenhaw said, "Where's your car?"

Vivian pointed at her red Mercedes in the driveway. "Right there."

Greenhaw looked at Beck, who said to Vivian, "Can you give us a little more time? Maybe an hour or so? Our crime scene folks are inside right now, and I don't want to pull them off. We need to check around your car and under it as you leave in case the killer parked in that same spot."

Vivian nodded. "I can do that. I may call a friend and go get a coffee. I'm not sure I can stand out here much longer, knowing what's just on the other side of that door."

FIFTY-ONE

While Greenhaw and Lawson were speaking with Vivian Bates, Barclay had made it to Wendy Wade, who was now joined by the *Towne Tribune's* Rebecca Kirby. Wendy had set up her video camera on a tripod and was holding her cellphone in landscape mode as she broadcasted on Facebook Live. Rebecca was standing a few feet away, taking photographs of the scene.

He approached Rebecca because Wendy was in full Facebook Live mode, and he didn't dare approach her lest he wanted to be the focus of the broadcast.

"Hey, Rebecca."

She aimed the camera at him, focused the lens, and snapped a picture. She pulled the camera from her eye and smiled. He returned it.

She motioned with her head toward the television reporter and said, "You don't want to be *Live with Wendy Wade*?" She said the last part in a mock news anchor voice that wasn't meant to be complimentary.

"Stop it," he said lightly. Wendy worked hard and was

unapologetic about it. This did not endear her to her fellow journalists.

She leaned against her car and said, "So, does this have anything to do with those other killings?"

"Ever the reporter. We'll be making a comment in a bit."

"Oh, come on. Give me the scoop. I helped you out once, remember? Just a few days ago, in fact."

"You did," he said as he slid his hands into his pockets. "And I really appreciated that. But you also got your scoop if memory serves, so I'd say we're even." She shrugged as if she weren't ready to concede the point.

The young reporter grew serious and said, "I need to ask you about something."

"What about?"

She flicked her eyes at Wendy Wade, then back to Barclay. She leaned in and spoke quietly, "Is the killer leaving a signature? Something about a bloody letter on the wall?"

The back of Barclay's neck grew warm. "Who said that?"

She looked back at Wendy again. Barclay furrowed his brow and glanced at Wendy, who was so engrossed in her broadcast that she hadn't noticed him. Focused on Rebecca, he said, "What does she know?"

She shrugged a hesitant, unconfident shrug.

"Bullshit. What did she tell you?"

Barclay's reaction was stronger than Rebecca expected. "Nothing."

Barclay made a face that said, *Don't lie to me.*

She said, "I swear. She didn't *tell* me anything."

Barclay caught the emphasis. He looked back at Wendy to think, buy time. To Rebecca, he said, "This is off the record, clear?"

"Don't start with that again, Barclay." She had quickly shaken the nervous, unsure bearing and replaced it with something like cheek.

"I told you we're making a statement later."

"Yeah, to both of us, which may as well mean just to her with her following compared to mine and the *Trib's*. That last story was great for me because I broke it; my editor almost likes me now. But I need something different—something more than what she will have."

"I did exactly what I said I would do last time, right? I didn't give Wendy a heads-up, and I gave you the green light to publish. I could have gone to her as soon as your story went live online, but I didn't. I made her call me, and that was not a fun conversation, let me tell you. So, whatever we discuss right now is off the record. Afterward, depending, I may go on the record about some of it."

"Really?" she said, bouncing off the car.

He held up his hands. "No guarantees."

She weighed that, realized it was the best she could do, and said, "I walked up to speak with Wendy when I got here, and she was texting with someone. Her eyesight must be terrible because her font is *huge* on her phone. I didn't know the font could be that big. Anyway, I glanced over her shoulder...and...well, I caught something. At least, I think I did."

She bit her lip and looked up at Barclay, a little sheepish, which he could not determine if it was genuine contrition or an act. He suspected the latter. She was slick, which would serve her well in her chosen profession.

"What did you see?"

"Well—" she drew out, "I saw a message that mentioned a bloody letter on the wall."

"And?"

"And...that's it."

Barclay was shaking his head. "I don't think so, Rebecca. You used the term *signature*. Where did you get that from?"

"So it *is* a signature."

"Don't get cute."

"Okay, I saw the word *signature*. And that's it. I promise. She looked up about the time I read it, and I thought she busted me reading her message, but if she suspected as much, she didn't say anything about it."

He was about to say something when he had another thought. "I don't suppose you saw who sent the message?"

"Nope. I'm holding that."

"Rebecca..."

She was shaking her head. "Nope. No way. A girl's gotta keep something to trade later. Besides, don't you know we can't reveal sources?"

"First of all, *you're* the source. You saw the message—no one gave you that information. And secondly, the source is technically hers since the message was sent to her. You were just being nosey."

"Fair enough, but I'm still not saying. Not yet."

Barclay looked back at Wendy, who was still prattling on saying hello to her most loyal followers, as she saw their name pop up, showing they were watching the live video.

"Rebecca, what I'm about to say is absolutely off the record." She opened her mouth to speak, and Barclay held up a finger. "I'm dead serious. This could cripple the investigation if this information is made public." A pause, then: "We clear?"

"Clear."

He nodded and said, "These cases, the old ones, along with Freida Nelson and now Elise Hightower, are all connected."

"Elise Hightower?" Rebecca repeated as she pulled her reporter's notebook out of her back pocket and wrote in it.

"You can't print her name until we've spoken to her family."

"Since when? That won't hurt the investigation."

"Come on, Rebecca, that's just common decency."

"Fair," she mumbled.

"They're all connected, and yes, the killer leaves a signature, and that signature is the first letter of the victim's last name written in blood above the bed. Sometimes on the wall and sometimes on the headboard."

"Holy crap." She went to write, then stopped and looked at Barclay.

"Go ahead. But do *not* print a word of it. In fact, don't tell your editor or show him your notes. He will pressure you to put it all out there."

"He wouldn't if he knew it was off the record."

"If he knew you had confirmation that a serial killer was active and you had the killer's signature, there's no way in hell he would allow you to sit on it. He doesn't care if he burns you. Not for a story like this."

She looked a little disillusioned at that thought, but he could tell she knew he was telling the truth.

She quickly recovered and asked, "Is it the same person doing all the killings?"

"We don't think so."

"But they're linked?"

"We're about ninety-eight percent sure they are."

"How?"

"Can't tell you that."

"Why don't you believe the killings were done by the same killer?"

"Can't tell you that either."

She was steadily writing in her notebook. "This is good stuff." Then, "Is there anything else you can tell me?"

Barclay thought about it. "I don't think so. We haven't discussed what we're going to say at the press conference yet. It's possible we could give more information then."

She was about to ask another question when Wendy Wade said, "Barclay Griffith. Do you want to come speak to our viewers?

Tell them what's going on out here?"

He turned around and found her iPhone aimed at him. "No, Wendy. We aren't where I can comment at this point, but expect a press conference soon."

Back to her phone, Wendy said, "There you have it, folks. Direct from the DA himself. There will be an official press conference shortly. I need to get prepared for that, so until then, I will see y'all later. Bye-bye, now." She winked at the camera and ended the live broadcast.

"Alright, Barclay," said Wendy, "you and I need to talk."

FIFTY-TWO

"You can't put the information out there, Wendy."

"So you're confirming these murders are connected, and his signature is writing their initials on the wall in blood?" asked the eager reporter.

"I'm not confirming anything. I'm simply telling you that what you just asked me about can't be made public," Barclay explained.

Rebecca Kirby was edging closer to the conversation when Wendy cut her a look that stopped Kirby in her tracks.

"Barclay, *you* may not go on the record confirming it, but I have a source that already has. People are dying—make that being murdered by a lunatic serial killer—and the people have a right to know."

"You're not broadcasting, Wendy. No need to be dramatic."

"Fuck you, Barclay. Are you going to give me something or not?"

"Look, alerting the public to a possible serial killer is one thing, but putting his signature on blast is something else entirely and wholly unnecessary."

"Letter in blood on the wall is this killer's signature. Got it."

"Damnit, Wendy, I didn't say that. Look, I already told you we're having a press conference later. You'll get more then. I need you to understand how critical it is at this stage of the investigation to keep certain things back from the public, specifically details of the crime. I'm just asking you to sit on this information for the time being."

Wendy crossed her arms and gave Barclay a hard stare. "I want an exclusive."

Barclay saw Rebecca stiffen out of the corner of his eye, but he didn't dare look over at her.

"I mean it," she pressed. "When it's time, I want it. Little miss perky tits over there got it last time, but I will not get beat again."

"Wendy—"

"Don't *Wendy* me, Barclay. Yes or no?"

Barclay closed his eyes, opened them, and said, "Deal." Out of the corner of his eye, he saw Rebecca Kirby storm off.

"There," said the smug and satisfied reporter. "That wasn't so hard." She reached out and squeezed his arm.

He wanted to go talk to Rebecca but he didn't have time for all of this. She was a big girl and would have to toughen up in a hurry if she were going to compete with the likes of Wendy Wade. Besides, he had work to do.

———

A HALF-HOUR LATER, Barclay and the police chief were standing in front of Wendy Wade's news camera and iPhone, and Rebecca Kirby was holding her iPhone out to record the audio of the press conference. If looks could kill, Barclay would be struck dead right now, and Greenhaw would have to arrest Rebecca for the homicide.

The public information officer for the Towne Police Department had sent out a notice announcing the press conference, and Wade and Kirby had been joined by another television station and the owner of the weekly paper *The City Observer,* who also served as its reporter, editor, and publisher.

It was now dark outside, so the setup was moved to beneath a streetlight. The lights from the two news cameras weren't large, but they were bright enough.

Chief Greenhaw began the press conference: "An officer conducted a welfare check this afternoon and discovered a deceased female inside. While we will have to wait for the medical examiner to conduct her investigation to determine the cause of death, the manner of death has been ruled homicide. The victim's name is Elise Hightower, and she lives on Walton Road in the Woodhaven neighborhood. If anyone out there has any information, no matter how insignificant they think it may be, please call the police non-emergency number or the secret witness hotline." He then gave the numbers for each.

As discussed, he announced the possible connection of this homicide to six older homicide cases and the most recent murder of Freida Nelson. He rattled off the names of the six older homicide victims and again made a plea for information.

He said, "I want to reiterate...we have not found any definitive proof these cases are related, but we do believe a connection is a strong possibility. In order to maintain the integrity of the investigation, we are unable to share any details of the crimes at this time. I am making this announcement so that our citizens are aware of what's going on for purposes of their own safety. Please understand we are doing absolutely everything we can to find the person or persons responsible for these heinous acts. With that, I will take questions."

The four reporters raised their hands, and Barclay held his breath as the chief called on Rebecca Kirby. Barclay suggested this, and he hoped giving her the first question would make up for her not asking about the killer's signature.

She said, "Chief, you stated you believed they were connected. Do you believe these crimes were all committed by the same person?"

Chief Greenhaw: "We do not. I can't get into the reason we believe that, but we do believe this is a separate actor. That belief and the basis for that belief also plays into our thought process on whether or not these homicides are connected."

"I'll be blunt, Chief," said Kirby. "Do we have a serial killer active in Towne?"

"We're going to hold off on such proclamations for now."

Before Kirby could ask another question, Greenhaw quickly called on the representative of the weekly paper, who asked, "What would you like to say to the families of the victims of these murders?"

The chief talked about how they were working hard to bring justice for their loved ones. Yes, these cases are old, but they have never stopped investigating them. "Unfortunately, some cases just take longer than others to resolve," he said. "But they are all receiving the exclusive attention of multiple detectives, and we are making progress."

The chief called on Wendy Wade, who was about to speak when Rebecca said, "One more question, Chief."

"Yes," he said, frustrated with the lack of adherence to protocol.

Barclay groaned inwardly. *Here it comes.*

The young newspaper reporter stared at Barclay, knowing full well what she was doing. He chanced a glance at Wendy—she was pissed. Kirby said, "Did you know the six older cases were connected back when these murders originally occurred?"

"We considered that possibility at the time just as we do today, but, again, we didn't have any evidence we would label as definitive then, just as now. You see—"

"That's not exactly true, now is it, Chief?" Wendy Wade asked.

Barclay fixed back on Wendy and was inwardly saying, *Don't do it. Don't do it.*

"What do you mean, Ms. Wade?"

It was at this exact moment that Barclay wished he had told the police chief what Wendy knew. He didn't say anything because he didn't want the chief to lose it, which he would have. The press conference would have been a train wreck, which appeared to be precisely where it was headed.

"I mean, the killer leaves a signature, doesn't he, Chief?"

"A signature?" Greenhaw was buying time, but it didn't matter. Barclay saw the chief's ears redden and thought it was like seeing an impending car crash and not being able to do a damn thing to stop it.

"The killer places the victim in the bed and scrawls their last initial in blood on the wall above the body, and has done so in each of these eight cases. Wouldn't that qualify as a signature?"

Barclay glanced at Rebecca, who was standing with her mouth agape.

Greenhaw said, "As I stated previously, we aren't going to discuss any details of the case, and we certainly aren't going to engage in conjecture or rumor."

Barclay cringed inwardly at that response. The answer began fine with refusing to discuss details and evidence, but his emotion got the better of him, and he tried to zing her with the *conjecture* and *rumor* comment. She knew the truth, and she would not allow herself to be made to look like some rookie cub reporter. Barclay knew she would respond. *In for a penny, in for a pound,* he thought.

Wendy pressed on. "So, you're denying any such signature exists? Over the beds where the victims are found?"

"Ms. Wade," the chief began, "I already told you we aren't getting into any details of these cases. We don't talk about such things because it could hamstring an investigation; it could help the bad guy get away."

Wendy made to respond, but Greenhaw held up a finger and kept talking. "Now, I know you have your little following on the internet, and you think it's all about you, but we have real victims here. Someone's daughter, mother, grandmother, real dead people. And it's up to us to find out who did it and up to the DA here"—he motioned to Barclay without taking his eyes off Wendy —"to make sure they get convicted. We have a tough enough job without you coming in here trying to look like you know everything.

"What's your station's little slogan? *On your side*? Isn't that it? Well, I gotta tell you, you're not. When you run your mouth about things you don't know anything about, you can hurt people. But hey, whatever's good for ratings, right?

"I don't know where you're getting your information, *Ms. Wade*, but I know it's not from us. And by 'us,' I mean the police department. So you need to be careful about putting stuff like that out there. I'm told you have a lot of followers. I don't know because I don't fool with social media. You have an opportunity to do some public good in your job, but you can also be very, very dangerous." He paused briefly as he surveyed the small gathering before saying, "This press conference is over."

There were a couple of shouted questions, but the chief turned and stalked off toward Elise Hightower's house.

Rebecca Kirby marched up to Barclay and said, "What the hell, man? You said you would handle it. She wouldn't bring it up. That's what you said."

"Rebecca...I—"

"Oh, did I spoil something?" Wendy Wade asked in feigned nonchalance as she sauntered up to them. Before either could answer, she said, "What? You think I don't see what was going on? You think I didn't know you two had some kind of agreement on that last story you shut me out of, Barclay? And now you're not returning my calls. Come on, I'm not dumb, sweetheart." She winked at Rebecca.

Rebecca was about to respond when Wendy leaned in and said in a growl, "Next time, keep your eyes on your own paper, you bitch. I catch you reading over my shoulder again, and I will claw your fucking eyes out."

Rebecca looked ready to cry.

Barclay turned on Wendy. "That's enough," he yelled. "You don't get it, do you? We keep details private for a reason, Wendy. This is going to make things much tougher on us, tougher to find the killer and get justice for these families. Hell, you just made it easier for some copycat to murder someone and throw it off on this other killer. And for what? What the hell did announcing that crap about the signature accomplish? Did the public *really* need to know about that? Is that information being made public going to make Towne safer as a result?

"It's not. Not at all, and you know that. But what it will do is make this case even more difficult to solve, and you know what *that* will do? Make our community decidedly less safe. Congratulations, Wendy. This is the part where I'm supposed to say, 'I hope you're proud of yourself.' But I'm not because I know you are. In your own perverse little mind, you're glad you blew things up for reasons I will never know, nor do I care to.

"It's all I can do to get law enforcement around here to trust the media, and stunts like that are the exact reason they can't stand you. Enjoy your little Facebook fiefdom for now because it's about to get a hell of a lot harder without access."

Barclay took a few steps before turning around. "And I know

who your source is." Wendy eyed him coolly. "When the chief told you it wasn't one of his folks, you didn't say a word. If there's one thing I know about Wendy Wade, it's that she wouldn't have let that go if it weren't true. Someone sent you that information, and it wasn't a cop, so I'm guessing it's Curtis Hammond since he's your source on everything else." He studied her, looking for some manner of confirmation that he was right, but the veteran reporter gave nothing away.

He glanced at Rebecca, who gave him nothing in the way of feedback. He jabbed a finger at Wendy. "You tell that mother-fucker he pulls some shit like that again, and I'll bury his two-ax-handle-wide ass myself."

FIFTY-THREE

As Barclay walked back to the crime scene, he saw Vivian Bates' red Mercedes backing out of the driveway. A uniformed patrol officer was holding the tape up so she could go under it.

The slow walk cooled his anger, and by the time he dipped under the tape to re-enter the scene, he was back focused on the immediate concern, which was figuring out who was killing these women.

He was about to ask for an update when Greenhaw said, "What the fuck was all that about back there? How the hell did she know about the killer's signature?"

This caught the others by surprise. TJ said, "She knew about that?"

"Asked me about it live on camera, damnit."

Barclay decided telling the police chief that he was aware of her knowledge before the press conference wouldn't help matters, so he kept that to himself. He said, "I know her source."

"Who?" Greenhaw asked eagerly.

Barclay gave him a look that said, *Who do you think?*

"Hammond?" Greenhaw said.

"Yep."

The chief cursed under his breath and walked off a few steps, then back to the loose huddle. "I swear—"

"Chief, we can worry about that later. We've got to focus now." It was TJ who spoke. He was the best at diffusing situations and the man the chief trusted above all others. "Beck, why don't you recap for the group what you and the chief learned from Ms. Bates."

The detective nodded and said, "There are no signs of forced entry, and Ms. Bates was adamant that our victim kept her doors locked even during the day when she was home. She also wasn't the type to let strangers into her house. It would seem that either she knew her attacker or someone talked their way inside."

Greenhaw said, "Bates was unsure about an outside house key, so we'll need to ask her children about it. Fitz, can you see about getting in touch with her? You're good at running down phone numbers. Her son is a probation officer in Oklahoma, so maybe start there."

Fitz nodded and typed the son's name into the notes app on his phone.

Barclay said, "What if the killer attacked her immediately? She opens the door, and the killer's on her forcing himself inside?"

Beck said, "At first glance, the entryway looked awfully clean for there to have been a struggle there. But she isn't a big lady, so it wouldn't have taken much to subdue her." She thought for a moment, then said, "Probably need to keep that possibility open for the time being. All that said, everything in the house is telling me she let the person inside, so I'm thinking she knew this person."

TJ said, "I'll get Detective Whitaker to look into our victim. Where she goes to church, what clubs or charities she's involved in, phone records—anything to tell us who she may know that could possibly have done this."

"You know," said Beck, pointing at TJ, "what you just said about who our victim may know. The first six victims were all connected by the fact that they had some personal involvement with Sam Albritton. What if the connection between Nelson and Hightower isn't Albritton but something else...or some*one* else?"

After a beat, while they all considered this, Fitz said, "We know Albritton isn't the killer, and I don't believe we're going to find any connection between him and either of these two ladies other than the presence of his business card. Assuming we have a copycat, then these two women will be connected to their killer the same as the previous six victims were connected to their killer."

"Their killer?" Barclay said. "Are we going ahead and putting down Sam Albritton as the original killer of those six women?"

Greenhaw said, "He's the only one that makes sense."

Beck was on her phone typing, scrolling, and touching the screen as she said, "I think we need to hold off on those old cases for now and focus on these most recent homicides. Those older cases will be there, and if Albritton is our guy, he's not doing any more killing, so we need to get the one who's active right now." They all agreed. She said, "I pulled up the investigative file on Nelson, and I'm looking at the photos from the scene. We don't have any pictures of the entryway." Looking up at the group, she said, "Anyone remember what condition it was in?"

They thought about it and agreed that nothing stood out one way or the other.

"What are you thinking?" Fitz asked.

"If the front door to the Nelson house had been kicked in or otherwise looked tampered with, someone would have noticed and photographed it, right?" Nods around. "Since there are no photographs, and I don't recall seeing anything in Drummond's narrative about it, that tells me there was nothing unusual there."

She paused, seemingly for effect. "What if our killer knew both of these women, and that's why there weren't signs of a break-in? What if he knows them, so they invite him in? Our new killer is following the pattern of the old killer, going so far as posing the bodies on the bed and writing the letter in their blood. He even leaves a nod to Sam Albritton behind.

"If he is taking it all to heart, then our new killer has a connection to his victims, same as Albritton. It's also the same conclusion Fitz and Drummond came to in the old cases: these crimes couldn't be random. The killer knew these women were home and home alone. No husband, no visiting friends or family, totally and completely alone."

They were discussing Beck's theory when evidence tech Angie Presley approached, holding two clear plastic sleeves, each one containing a single piece of paper.

She said, "I thought you'd want to see this," and handed Beck the sleeves.

She looked them over one at a time and passed them on until everyone had seen them.

"Where did you find these?" the detective asked.

"There's a laundry alcove set into the wall adjacent to the kitchen table. It's just wide enough and deep enough for a washer and dryer; the space is covered by louvered bifold doors. You told us to open every door, and when we opened those doors, we noticed these pieces of paper peeking out from under the dryer. Just seemed odd and out of place. Then, when I saw what the papers were, they *really* didn't belong there."

Beck held one of the sleeves in her left hand and one in her right. Holding up the one in her left hand, she said, "We have a deed to this property and"—holding up the sleeve in her right hand—"a summary of a retirement account in Elise Hightower's name from Rankin Wealth Management Group." She dropped the sleeves by her side. "Any ideas?"

A uniformed officer tapped Barclay on the shoulder and said, "Mr. Griffith?" When Barclay turned, the officer said, "There's a reporter at the tape that said she needs to speak with you."

He rolled his eyes and said, "What now?" as he turned, expecting to see Wendy Wade. His face registered surprise when he saw it was Rebecca Kirby. He walked over to see her.

"Hey Rebecca, what's up?" She held out a torn piece of paper, which Barclay took.

"It's Wendy's source," she said with a grin.

Barclay looked back at the paper and then back to Rebecca. "But it's a phone number."

She shrugged. "I guess she doesn't have the sender's number programmed into her phone."

"But how..."

She adopted a mischievous expression from her mouth to her eyes. "I'm good."

"What happened to holding out for a trade?"

Another shrug. "I heard what you said to Wendy. Don't get me wrong, she has a job to do the same as me, but...I don't know. I guess I got to thinking about that poor lady's family and...well, I don't know. Potentially messing up your case...it just didn't seem right. I'm new, and I'm young, and I need you to be able to trust me. You gave me your word before, and you kept it. That meant a lot to me. Just consider this a thank you."

"Thank you, Rebecca. I do appreciate this."

"Don't get used to it," she said with a playful punch to the arm.

———

BARCLAY WALKED BACK to the group, and seeing the look on his face, Fitz said, "What did that girl say?"

Barclay held up the slip of paper, and Chief Greenhaw said, "What's that?"

"It's the phone number of Wendy's source."

"But—," began Greenhaw.

Barclay nodded, anticipating the chief's question, and said, "I thought it was Curtis Hammond, but his name would be in Wendy's phone. All that was on the screen was a number. No, her source is someone else. Someone with intimate knowledge of this investigation. Someone who knows the details about the old killings and the new." All eyes were locked on Barclay's. "Could be a cop. But I think it's our killer."

FIFTY-FOUR

The killer heard his phone signal a notification that Wendy Wade was live on Facebook. It was the third such notification since the most recent murder, with the first two being false alarms—one was the scene of a car crash, and the other was a building fire out in the county—so he wasn't in any hurry to check it. About fifteen minutes later, he was at a stopping point with work when he thumbed open the app and tuned in.

This time, it *was* about the murder.

He watched attentively for the next half hour when he began to lose interest as the reporter stared into the camera, flipping her long, loose black curls and droning on and on, repeating herself. She clearly was not getting any information about the investigation, which was what he was after. He was about to turn it off when he heard Wendy Wade say, "Barclay Griffith. Do you want to come speak to our viewers? Tell them what's going on out here?"

He gripped his iPhone with both hands, knuckles going white.

"No, Wendy. We aren't where I can comment at this point, but expect a press conference soon," Barclay said on the screen.

Wendy shifted the camera back to her *because, of course, she did*, he thought, and she said, "There you have it, folks. Direct from the DA himself. There will be an official press conference shortly. I need to get prepared for that, so until then, I will see y'all later. Bye-bye, now." She winked at the camera, the killer rolled his eyes, and the live broadcast was over.

The killer checked his phone's battery—less than fifty percent —plugged it in, and laid it on his desk, where he would see and hear when she went live again.

Disappointment began to set in as he replayed what he had just watched. Dissatisfied with the sanitized reporting on the murders to this point, the killer set out to see if he could jump-start things himself. He had sent her a text message earlier in the day that he was certain would get her journalistic juices flowing, but not only had she not mentioned it, she didn't appear as someone sitting on a sensational nugget of information not known outside the walls of the police station.

Finding Wendy Wade's cell number was easy. On all of her social media platforms, she listed a tip line for news stories encour-aging people to text rather than call. So that's what he did. He bought a TracFone for cash at a Dollar General across the border in Georgia—he wore a baseball cap and kept his head down to avoid the surveillance cameras. On the way home, he pulled to the shoulder of the interstate just short of an overpass and used the phone exactly once to send the text. He then pulled off the battery, removed the SIM card, and broke the flip phone in half at the hinge. He walked onto the bridge and tossed the battery and SIM card into the reedy swamp below. He got back into his car and, a few miles down the road, tossed half of the phone out of the moving car, then a few miles later, tossed the other half. A few miles after that, he released his hat into the wind to blow and dance off the blacktop, never to be seen again.

Had she texted him back to try to verify the information? Perhaps she had reached out and, not hearing anything more from him, decided the information wasn't reliable enough to publish. He was so intent on destroying the phone, what with all the advances in tracking cellular devices, that he never considered she may need to confirm she was dealing with someone with legitimate knowledge versus some nut job who liked to rub one out to the beautiful Wendy Wade. He suspected she got her fair share of weirdos contacting her.

He cursed himself. Then he cursed her. He had been counting on her vanity to run with the information about the killer's signature; he didn't peg her as having a deep font of journalistic integrity. Had he misjudged her? He didn't believe so...but...the report she had just broadcast was the perfect opportunity to tell the world that a serial killer was on the loose, and she didn't take it.

Perhaps another nudge was in order. Perhaps he would need to nudge someone else. The queen of local Facebook news had had her shot. Maybe there was someone else—another person who would take him seriously.

That's when he thought of the newspaper lady—Kirby something. He remembered her name from the article about the Nelson murder. She was the first to suggest a possible connection to other cases, and then there was the article she had written about the DA's cold case unit that started him down this path.

He was formulating a plan for safely contacting her when his phone pinged. It was another notification that Wendy Wade was going live on Facebook.

When the broadcast was over, he tossed the phone on his desk. Now, the public was aware of the existence of the secret that only he and the police had known. He finally felt the satisfaction he'd been chasing. He leaned back and allowed himself a small smile.

FIFTY-FIVE

"Alright, let's go through what we've got," said the weary police chief. After Barclay had dropped the bombshell of the phone number, the decision was made to regroup back at the police station to talk through everything.

Beck said, "We can all agree Elise Hightower was killed by the same person who did Freida Nelson, right?" Everyone nodded, and someone said, "Yep." She said, "They are still going through the house looking for any connection between Albritton and Hightower and Nelson and Hightower. We have the deed and the page from Hightower's investment account. And we've got a phone number which"—she looked at Barclay—"you believe is from our killer. I'm curious why you don't think it's a cop."

Barclay cleared his throat. "A couple of reasons. The first is that during the presser, when the chief told Wendy that she couldn't have gotten the information from a cop, she didn't respond to that...at all. She wouldn't burn a source, but I don't believe she would have let it go, not with the way Chief was ripping her up. He made the point that no information about the investigation should be trusted if it's not from law enforcement.

That damaged her information at least a little bit. I doubled down on that after you left, Chief, and she didn't so much as hint that her source was solid."

"But would she have?" asked Greenhaw. "Like you said, she wouldn't burn a source, and admitting it was a police officer would be tantamount to doing just that with the circle of people being so small."

"And that's another reason I don't believe her information came from law enforcement. Who knows the full extent of these cases? Like everything. Outside of this room, who knows all of that about the old cases and painting the letter?"

Everyone in the room looked at one another. TJ said, "I don't believe anyone outside this room..."

Beck said, "I think Dell Whitaker knows. When I first spoke with him about the Nelson murder, he mentioned the Alphabet killer. I don't know to what extent, but he at least thinks there was a possible serial at work back then. It wouldn't be a stretch to believe he knew about the letters on the wall."

The implication hung thick in the air.

TJ said, "No way. I know Dell. He's a cop's cop. He'd never talk about something like that to a reporter, and he's damn sure too old to have his head turned by Wendy Wade."

There was silence around the table.

After a moment, TJ said, "Wait a minute. Do you think Dell Whitaker is the killer? You've got to be kidding me." His voice was booming now, which belied his typically unflappable personality.

Chief Greenhaw said, "TJ, I don't think anyone here believes either of those things about Dell."

TJ looked around the room, challenging anyone to say otherwise.

Barclay said, "Like I said, I don't think it's a cop. If it were, it would most likely be someone in this room."

"Or Drummond," Beck said. "Let's not forget about him."

"For fuck's sake, can we not?" said TJ.

Greenhaw said, "Beck, have Tina Crump run down the phone number. Fitz, you call on the wealth management company and see what they have to say. Maybe Freida Nelson was also a client. Also, ask them why Ms. Hightower would have had her deed out with her retirement account paperwork. Maybe they can make some sense of it. It's late, so let's meet here tomorrow after lunch. That should give everyone enough time to run these things down. It's been a long day. Go home and get some rest while you can."

FIFTY-SIX

Just after 8:00 the following morning, Fitz was on the phone with the Rankin Wealth Management group receptionist. He introduced himself and, when asked why he was calling, only said that it was a matter involving a client, and he wasn't able to give her a name. He would need to speak directly with the managing partner, which he was told was Durham Rankin. The receptionist informed him that Mr. Rankin had not made it in, but he could come by the office around 9:00, and he should be available—there was nothing on his calendar until 10:30.

Promptly at 9:00, Fitz stepped off the elevator and into a well-appointed lobby that was all dark wood and glass and bright abstract paintings on the wall. He approached the substantial L-shaped reception desk and said, "Mrs. Burns? I'm Winston Fitzsimmons. We spoke on the phone this morning." He had his badge wallet open, and she leaned in slightly, lifting the reading glasses that hung around her neck on a beaded chain but not putting them on. She examined the badge.

She dropped her glasses, leaned back, and smiled, "Yes, Mr.

Fitzsimmons. After we spoke, I called Mr. Rankin and told him that you wanted to see him. He asked me to let him know the moment you arrived. If you want to have a seat"—she made a hand motion to a seating area to her left—"I'll let him know you're here."

Fitz nodded and returned her smile. He chose a comfortable chair in the corner and picked up a magazine. The kind-faced receptionist said, "Mr. Rankin will be with you in a few minutes. May I offer you anything? Coffee, tea, water?"

"No, thank you."

Fitz found himself reading an article from Sports Illustrated about a former Austrian snow skier who crashed during an Olympic qualifying event, paralyzing her from the waist down. She was now preparing for the upcoming Paralympic Winter Games. He was so engrossed in the article that he didn't hear his name when it was initially called.

"Mr. Fitzsimmons," said a male voice a little louder this time, which got the investigator's attention. He looked up to see a man he guessed to be in his mid-to-late fifties with a hardscrabble face. He wasn't tall, but he looked sturdy.

"I'm Durham Rankin. You wanted to see me?"

"Yes, Mr. Rankin, thank you." Fitz stood and held up the magazine. "I was just reading an incredible story—"

"The alpine Olympic skier?" Rankin said with a smile.

"That's the one. Quite remarkable."

"Remarkable, indeed. I wrestled in college and tore my labrum going into my junior year. It was enough to make me quit and concentrate on school." Rankin pointed at the magazine in Fitz's hand. "What that young lady is doing? I'm not sure I would have had the courage or the discipline to do that."

"You and me both," said Fitz. He tossed the magazine on the coffee table with the others and followed Rankin through the glass door leading from the reception area into the offices. He said, "I played football in college and knew a few wrestlers. You guys were the toughest S-O-Bs on campus."

Rankin laughed. "As George Costanza once said, 'I'd disagree if I could.'" That drew a laugh from Fitz.

They entered a spacious office, and Rankin sat at a round table, inviting Fitz to do the same. "Now, what can I help you with?"

"I'm not sure if you heard about the homicide yesterday, but I believe she may be a client of yours, and I had some questions."

The man leaned forward and adopted a concerned look. "I didn't hear about that. My goodness. Who was the victim?"

"Elise Hightower."

Rankin sat back in shock. "Elise? Oh, no, that's awful. She was a client, yes. Not mine, personally, though. She worked with my partner, Alexis Washington. May I call her into this meeting?"

"Sure, that would be great."

He walked to his desk, picked up the receiver, and punched three numbers. He asked the person on the other line if they were busy, then asked them to come to his office with the Elise Hightower file.

A few seconds later, the door opened, and a light-skinned black woman entered. She was wearing a gray pencil dress that hugged her athletic frame. Rankin introduced her to Fitz, but her smile lacked the humor of her partner. She sat at the table, and Rankin told her about Elise.

Alexis put a hand to her chest. "Oh my God. I just spoke with her not two weeks ago. She was such a lovely person."

Fitz nodded, opened his black leather folio, and produced the clear evidence sleeve containing the document from the crime scene. He laid it on the table. "Ms. Washington, we found this at the scene. Nothing terribly unusual about it except where we found it. I'm out of my depths in this world and hope you can be of some help."

"I'm happy to help however I can."

"And I appreciate that. Honestly, it's likely this doesn't have anything to do with anything, but we're following up on a lot of information. Mr. Rankin has confirmed that Ms. Hightower is a client here, so my only real question is why that piece of paper"— Fitz tapped his finger on it—"would have been out? The deed to her house was also found near it. Any ideas?"

Alexis exchanged a look with Durham, then she moved to pick up the document, stopped, and said, "May I?"

"Of course."

She picked it up and read it. "Well, as it states on the page here, it's a retirement account statement. I can tell you that it's not the first page of the statement and...just a guess here, but I'd say it's probably page two."

"Is that significant?" Fitz asked.

A shrug. "Not really. But it is odd that this was the only page you found. There isn't much information here, so I don't know why she would have this particular page out as opposed to the first or even the last page. This seems quite random."

"Is there any significance to the fact that her deed was nearby?"

She sat back and appeared to weigh the question. "Not really," she said slowly as if still considering the question as she answered it. She seemed to be about to say more before shaking her head. "I don't know."

"If you had to hazard a guess, why would a person have their retirement financials and property deed out together?"

She and Durham again looked at one another. He spoke this time. "Maybe she was getting her affairs in order for one reason or another. It's not uncommon when dealing with older individuals, especially older women, when there isn't a spouse in the picture."

"Why would it be less unusual for a woman to do this than a man?" Fitz asked.

Alexis said, "Because women worry about these things more

than men. Men don't like to admit they don't have everything together. Women don't mind asking for help."

Fitz nodded slowly. "But wouldn't she come to you about this? Getting her affairs in order as you said?"

Durham said, "Maybe...if it were just related to her finances. But that wouldn't explain the deed."

"It would if she were dealing with a will or a trust," said Alexis.

"How do you mean?" asked Fitz.

"I don't know all of the legalese, but I've assisted estate lawyers in the past when they've worked with one of our clients. The lawyers set up the trust or whatever, and I handle the money side of things."

"So a lawyer would be interested in her deed and finances."

"I really don't know, Mr. Fitzsimmons. Perhaps."

Fitz was quiet for a long moment as he thought about any additional questions to ask.

"One last question," he said. "Does the name Freida Nelson ring a bell? Maybe she's a client?"

"Doesn't mean anything to me," said Durham.

"Me neither," said Alexis.

Durham got up, sat at his desk, and began typing on the computer. He tapped a few keys and made a couple of mouse clicks. He shook his head as he looked at his computer screen. "She's not a client of ours."

FIFTY-SEVEN

After lunch, Tina Crump joined Chief Greenhaw, Captain Jones, Fitz, Beck Lawson, and Barclay Griffith in the conference room for updates.

Tina went first.

"The phone number that texted Wendy Wade came back to a burner," Tina began. "It was attached to the T-Mobile network. I have a couple of connections there, so I was able to expedite the records. The phone had only been used once. It was used to send a text message at 10:24 the morning after the murder to a number we know belongs to Ms. Wade. The cell tower data showed the phone had connected to a tower near Interstate 85 in Georgia, approximately sixteen miles from the Alabama state line."

She explained that there was no further tower information after that text was sent, which likely meant the phone had been powered down. Tina surmised, "The phone was probably purchased for the sole purpose of sending that one text, and then the user most likely destroyed the phone afterward."

In her career analyzing digital forensics, she had seen disposable cell phones used in similar ways: buy it, use it, toss it. That, she told them, indicated a more intelligent criminal. However, there was little else to be gleaned from an evidentiary standpoint without the phone itself.

When she had finished, Chief Greenhaw said, "What's your takeaway from all that?"

"I'd say it confirms our killer sent the text," said Tina

"How so?" he asked.

"For one thing, I don't believe a police officer would go through the trouble or expense of buying a prepaid cell phone to send a single text message to Wendy Wade about a case. Secondly, and most significantly, was the time the text was sent. The text was sent before anyone except the killer knew Elise Hightower was dead in that house. Only the killer knew about the bloody letter on the headboard."

TJ said, "We don't know if the text message referenced Elise Hightower. All we know is that it referenced the killer's signature. It could still be a cop. If he knew about the old cases and Nelson, it still fits."

"True," she said. "But consider the timing—"

Barclay said, "You know what?" and fished his cell phone from inside his coat. He thumbed it open and accessed his call log. "Yep." He eyed Tina. "When did you say the text was sent to Wade?"

"10:24 AM."

He nodded and held up his phone. "She called me yesterday morning at 10:26. I was in court and didn't answer, so she texted me right after asking me to call her. I had forgotten about it by the time I got out of court. I bet she was calling me to ask about the text she received."

Tina said, "Again, if a cop had sent it, why would she call you? I believe she got a message from someone she didn't know and needed you to confirm the information. Back to what I was saying before, consider the timing. The text message just happens to be sent after Hightower is killed and before her body is discovered? That would be a hell of a coincidence."

The chief considered this information and looked at Fitz, who said, "My balls itch a little, sir."

Greenhaw said, "What the hell is all this talk about itchy balls?"

Tina Crump looked confused while Beck dipped her head and bit her lip.

The chief shook his head and said, "But why would the killer do that? He's taking a hell of a chance communicating with Wade."

"Not really, sir," said Tina. "The burner is essentially untraceable. As for the why, this is my first case involving a serial killer, but what little I know is that they often crave attention. We've been pretty tight-lipped about the case, and that may have frustrated him because he wasn't getting the press he felt he deserved. He's definitely got that now."

The chief said, "Tell me about it. After that stunt Wade pulled yesterday, I've got media requests coming out of my ass." Satisfied they'd discussed the phone number long enough, he said to Fitz, "What about you? Get anything good?"

Fitz's report was similar to Tina's in that it was informative but only mildly helpful. He told them about his meeting with Durham Rankin and Alexis Washington and confirmed that Elise Hightower was a client and that Freida Nelson was not. He gave them Alexis' thoughts about why the deed and the financials may have been out. He also mentioned that he spoke with two of Elise's three children, and both agreed that she did not keep a key outside.

"One thing I thought about on my way over here," said Fitz. "We need to check that house again to see if there are any other important papers there. What Ms. Washington said about the paper we found being page two of her financial report has been bugging me. She made it clear that there really wouldn't be any reason for bringing out that single piece of paper."

Greenhaw said, "But it was out, which tells us she got it out."

"Maybe. But think about where it was found. Inside that little laundry area underneath the dryer. How does paper even get down there?"

"And the deed is a pretty important piece of paper to be sitting under the dryer," Beck interjected.

"What are you thinking?" TJ asked.

"I don't know," said Fitz. "Just...doesn't seem right. It's like we're missing something staring us in the face.

FIFTY-EIGHT

"Nine-one-one. What's your emergency?"

"It's my wife!" the panicked voice on the phone said. "My God, you have to help her!" the voice cracked.

"Sir, sir, I'm going to need you to slow down. What's your name?" said the temperate dispatcher as she typed on her computer terminal, dispatching police and an ambulance to the address on her screen.

"What? My name? It's...my name is Alan. Alan Kramer."

"Okay, Alan. What's the matter with your wife?"

"I think she's dead!"

"Okay, sir, where is she?"

"She's, she's...I found her in our bedroom. There's blood everywhere...please you have to help her!"

"Police and an ambulance are on the way. Can you tell me what happened?"

"I...I...no...I don't know. I just came home and found her like this." The man's cadence was slowing, but he had begun to cry.

"Help's coming, honey. Help is on the way." Alan's voice sounded far away, as if he had pulled the phone from his mouth.

"Is anyone there with you right now?"

"Huh? What?"

"Is there anyone else in the house? Any children?"

"N..No. We don't have kids."

"Alright, sir. The police should be there shortly. Please stay on the line with me."

He didn't speak, but she could hear his sobs through the phone.

"Sir, I'm showing the police are less than a minute out. I need you to go out front and wait for them."

"Why?" the man croaked. She was about to respond that it would help the police identify the location faster when he said, "Why did he have to do this? Why *her*? Why her?"

The dispatcher leaned forward slightly in her chair. "Sir, do you know who did this?" When she didn't get an answer, she said, "Sir, do you know who is responsible?"

"Huh? Oh...what?"

"You just said, 'Why did he have to do this?' Do you know who did this to your wife?"

"He's been in the news...that killer," he said, his broken voice barely above a whisper.

"Sir?" she said, pressing her headset closer to her ear.

"That goddamn serial killer!" he roared.

———

OFFICER JIMMY PULLMAN thundered through the neighborhood, sirens blaring. It was late afternoon on a Monday, and the neighborhood was largely deserted, with most residents not yet home from work. He saw the sign indicating Brookstone Drive ahead on his left and tapped the brakes before stomping on the accelerator and rocketing through the turn. With so few cars in driveways, he could see the full length of the street without obstruction. He spotted a man walking out of his house, maybe ten houses ahead on the right; he was there in a blink. He slammed the gearshift into park and shot out of his seat as the car rocked forward, then back.

"Are you Alan Kramer?" Pullman asked

"Yes. She's in here." Pullman followed him into the house.

Alan reached the bedroom door and stepped aside, not going in. He pointed with his phone and mumbled, "In there."

Officer Pullman hitched up his belt and stepped across the threshold, taking in the grisly scene before him. He caught up short at the site before continuing up the left side of the bed to the prone figure covered in blood amid blood-soaked sheets. He was so focused on the carnage on the bed that it wasn't until he stepped back to call it in that his eyes drifted upwards.

On the wall, above the blood-spattered white headboard, was the letter *C* scrawled in blood.

The officer stared at the letter, keying up his shoulder mic, and called dispatch. When his call was answered, he said, "Yeah, Sally, this is Pullman. I'm at 1175 Brookstone. Listen, it's bad. Get a detective out here, crime scene...and you can call off that ambulance."

He released the transmit button on the mic and received an affirmative response. He turned to leave and stopped. "Hey Sally," he said into the mic, "you'll want to send the chief out here. There's something he needs to see."

FIFTY-NINE

Half an hour later, 1175 Brookstone Drive has all the earmarks of a crime scene: yellow tape, marked and unmarked police units, uniformed officers and detectives, the crime scene van, citizens milling about in the street hoping for a glimpse of something, and Wendy Wade there to document it all.

"Something about this seems off," said Beck, standing at the foot of the bed, taking in the scene as the body was photographed from every angle.

Greenhaw asked, "How so?"

"I need to go back and look at pictures of the other scenes, but something just isn't right."

A detective poked his head in the room and said, "Chief, if you're good with it, I'm going to go ahead and take Mr. Kramer to the station—take his statement."

Beck said, "I'd like to take the statement if that's alright."

Greenhaw looked at her, then nodded to the detective. "Set him up in the conference room and keep him comfortable. Beck will move him to an interrogation room when she gets there."

"You got it," the detective said, then he knocked once on the doorframe and left.

"Hey, Waters!" Beck yelled.

The detective stuck his head back in the bedroom. "Yeah?"

"Ask him for his cell phone and his passcode. Also, ask him for his wife's passcode."

"You got it," he said again and was gone.

"I'm going to go grab my computer and look at a few things," she said to Greenhaw.

"Yeah, sure," he said distractedly as he studied the scene.

Twenty minutes later, Greenhaw walked down the hall toward the kitchen, where Beck was set up with her laptop. Barclay walked in, and he told the DA where to find the body. Barclay went to the bedroom while Greenhaw headed to the kitchen. There, he saw Fitz had joined Beck, and they were both staring at the screen.

"Still no sign of a Sam Albritton business card," the chief said as he entered the kitchen.

"I don't believe they're going to find a business card—or any connection to Sam Albritton, for that matter," Beck said, not taking her eyes off the computer's screen.

Greenhaw made a face. "Why not?" He pulled out a chair opposite the two investigators. "What've you found?"

"I've just given this a cursory glance, but some things are different with this one than the rest."

"Such as?" Greenhaw asked.

She closed her laptop. "Timing for one. Every other murder was committed after dark...which makes sense. The killer would be looking for as much cover as possible. Going into someone's house during the day is far too risky, and it breaks his pattern. It may not be a waste of time to speak with a profiler. Find out just how common it is for a serial killer to change how they operate. I'd guess not common at all, but it would only be a guess."

"But the timing does work when you consider the time between kills. The last two were right at a week apart."

"Eight days," said Beck.

"Eight days," the chief repeated. "And here we are, what, six days since the last one? Maybe he's escalating—seeing his crimes in the media has spurned him on."

"Hold that thought," she said. "Our victim here is twenty-seven, which makes her too young by several decades from our killer's preferred victim demographic. And she's married. Only one other victim was married, and it was Albritton's wife."

"Maybe," the chief said, turning it over in his mind.

"Remember standing outside Elise Hightower's house when we discussed the killer's method of entry?"

Fitz answered, "There was no evidence of forced entry, and we figured he knew the victims or got himself invited in. How does that play here?"

Greenhaw said, "The backdoor," and Beck knew he understood.

Fitz furrowed his brow. When he arrived, he had entered through the front door and joined Beck at the table without bothering to walk the crime scene. He got up now to go look for himself.

What he found was a door that had been kicked in. There was a large dent just under and to the right of the doorknob, with at least a partial shoe print inside the dent. The deadbolt was extended but bent, the strike plate was on the floor, and the doorjamb was splintered.

He came back to the table and found Barclay standing behind the seated police chief.

Fitz said, "This is damn interesting, Boss."

Beck flipped open her laptop and spun the computer so they could see it. The picture displayed was Elise Hightower's headboard with the letter *S* on it.

She said, "The killer left the letter *C* down the hall, right?"

"Yeah," said the chief, staring at the image on the screen.

"And it was on the wall...*above* the headboard."

"That's right," he said, now looking at Beck.

"Look at each of these." She scrolled through eight photographs, each showing the bloody letter from all the previous murders.

When she was done, she said, "Did you notice anything?"

None of them did.

She continued, "Our killer has put his mark—the bloody letter—on either the wall or on the headboard. To be exact, he put the letter on the headboard five times and on the wall three times. Of the three times he used the wall, one victim had no headboard, one had a cloth-covered headboard, and one had a wrought iron headboard. The only times the killer didn't leave his mark on the headboard was because he was unable to. You can't paint on a headboard that isn't there, you can't paint on the bars of a wrought iron headboard, and you can't really paint on a stuffed, cloth-covered headboard. Well, you could, but it wouldn't have the same effect."

She pulled out her phone, pulled up a photograph, and held it out to the group.

The picture was of the bloody letter over Laura Kramer's body down the hall. It had been applied to the wall above a white headboard. It took a few seconds for the implication to land.

"Huh," said Barclay at the same time Fitz said, "Well, I'll be damned."

"Ah, shit," said Greenhaw. "So if this isn't our guy, we've got a new lunatic on the loose."

Beck said, "I don't think we totally flush the idea it could be our guy, but, yeah, I don't think it's our guy." She stood up and began to move inside the small space. "The first thing we need to do is make sure there isn't a Sam Albritton business card here.

We've found one pretty easily at the first two, so the fact we haven't found one yet is compelling, but we need to make absolutely sure there isn't one."

"That fuckin' Wendy Wade!" yelled Barclay, startling everyone within earshot.

"What's up, Boss?" said Fitz.

"Detective, can you go back and view the Hightower press conference from last week on her Facebook page?"

"Sure," Beck said and began to work on her phone.

"When you find it, cue it up to the part where she asks Chief about the signature." Beck nodded, staring at her phone.

Fitz gave Barclay a questioning look. Barclay said, "We'll see if I'm right."

"Got it," Beck said. She turned up the volume and laid the phone on the table.

Wendy Wade's tinny voice played through the phone's speaker:

"I mean, the killer leaves a signature, doesn't he, Chief?"

"A signature?"

"The killer places the victim in the bed and scrawls the victim's initial in blood on the wall above the body. And has done so in each of these eight cases. Wouldn't that qualify as a signature, Chief?"

"You can stop it there," said Barclay. "When she asked her question, she said, 'The killer places the victim in the bed and scrawls the victim's initial in blood *on the wall above the body.*' She said, 'the wall.'" He pointed toward the bedroom where the body currently lay. "You heard Beck. Our killer would have used the headboard—no question."

After a few seconds, Beck said, "I think whoever killed Laura Kramer wants us to believe she was the victim of our serial killer."

SIXTY

Beck opened the door to the conference room, where Alan Kramer sat slump-shouldered, staring at the polished table; two empty paper coffee cups and an unopened granola bar sat in front of him.

She said, "Hey, Alan. Sorry it's taken so long. I'm Detective Beck Lawson, and I'll be handling your wife's case. Would you mind coming with me?"

"Why? Where are we going? I need to see my wife."

"We just need to get a statement from you, that's all. Shouldn't take too long, then we can get you out of here and to your wife."

He sat forward in his chair. "A statement? But I don't know anything. I came home and found her...like that."

Beck nodded. "We have to get all of that on the record. When we catch who did this, we're going to need it for court. You may not remember all the details two years from now when we have the trial, so it's best to get your statement now while it's fresh in your mind."

"I don't think I'll ever forget what I saw tonight," he said, eyes going back to the table.

"I'm sorry, Mr. Kramer, but we need to do this. The sooner we start, the sooner it'll be over, and we can get you on your way."

He shook his head, then slowly rolled his chair away from the table and stood. Beck said, "You can take that granola bar with you. It's probably been a while since you've eaten."

Alan Kramer looked down at the metallic green-wrapped block and stared at it as if perplexed by a complex math problem. Finally, he grabbed it and followed the detective out of the conference room and through a series of turns into an interview room.

He stood in the small, stark space and looked around, taking in the pale yellow walls, the small patch of threadbare industrial carpet, the metal table and chairs, and the general smell of body odor tinged with marijuana. "Is this in an interrogation room? Why did you bring me in here? Isn't this for, like, suspects and stuff?"

Beck looked around. "It's where we conduct all of our interviews, Mr. Kramer. It's wired for video and sound. This is where we interview suspects, of course, but we also interview victims and witnesses here. Certainly nothing to be concerned about." She extended an arm to an empty chair. "Please have a seat, and we'll get started."

He hesitated before sitting down. Beck did the same with a chair perpendicular to where Kramer sat.

She set her laptop in front of her with a manila folder about an inch thick laid on top. "Before we start, Mr. Kramer, can I get you anything? Water, coffee?"

He shook his head.

Beck scooted her chair up to the table and opened the folder. She pulled out a single sheet of paper: an Explanation of Rights Form. She pulled a pen from her pants pocket, clicked it, and wrote the date and time in the designated spaces in the top right corner of the document, as well as the location of the interview: TPD.

"What's that?" Kramer asked, pointing with his chin.

"It's an Explanation of Rights Form," she said, eyes on the form, her pen poised and ready to write. "Now, what is your full name?"

The man hesitated, staring at the paper.

After a few seconds, she looked up and said, "Your full name, Mr. Kramer?"

"Uh, it's, uh, Alan Bryan Kramer."

She nodded and began to write before looking up. "Your initials are ABC," she said with a slight smile.

He shrugged and returned a forced half-smile. She went back to filling in the form—the noise of the pen on the paper on the metal table was the only sound in the room.

"How old are you, Mr. Kramer?"

"Twenty-Nine."

More writing from the detective. She filled out his home address from memory and then asked how far he had gotten in school.

"Bachelor's degree."

Beck nodded and wrote some more. Kramer leaned forward and angled his body, trying to read what was on the paper.

"Is this really all necessary, Detective? I thought I was just giving a statement, telling you how I found her like that and everything."

"That's right," she said. "This is all standard stuff when we interview someone." She leaned in conspiratorially. "Paperwork. The bane of a cop's existence, but the brass loves it."

Even though it didn't address his concerns, he nodded as if it had.

"Alright, Mr. Kramer. I'm going to read you your rights, then have you read them back to me, okay?"

"My rights?" His melancholy attitude turned to indignation. "You think I killed my wife?" He stood, tipping his chair backward. It would have clattered to the floor if the room were a foot larger. As it was, the chair came to rest against the wall at a scuffed and paintless strip from where the chair had undoubtedly been pushed against the wall countless times before.

"Mr. Kramer, I already told you this is standard. We do this with every witness we interview. I don't do it, and it's my ass." She was staring up at him, and he down at her. After almost a minute, she said, "Please sit down, Mr. Kramer. It's late, and we've had a long day. I imagine we both want nothing more than to be home in our beds, right?"

It took a moment, but he reached back for the chair and sat.

"This is just to make sure that you can read and understand what it says. If you don't understand, now is the time to ask any questions, okay?"

Kramer nodded.

"I need you to answer out loud, Mr. Kramer."

"Yes," he croaked.

Beck spun the form around where he could see it. "Alright, now I am reading from this form." She traced the lines with her pen as she read: "I have been advised that I must understand my rights before I answer questions..." She went on to read the rest of the paragraph, which was the standard Miranda warning explaining Kramer's right to remain silent, right to a lawyer even if he cannot afford one, and that by agreeing to answer questions without a lawyer, he can stop at any time and speak with an attorney. "Do you understand everything I just read?"

"No."

She looked up. "What part don't you understand?"

He shook his head, frustrated. "No, I understand what you read, it's just...I don't understand...any of this. Why I'm in this room? Why...I didn't hurt my wife!" He emphasized his last statement with a fist to the metal table, creating a loud, hollow boom in the small, hard room.

"First of all, Mr. Kramer, I need you to calm down." He opened his mouth to speak, and she held up a hand. "I know this is a difficult time for you. Believe me, I do. And I don't want to do this any more than you do because I know how it looks from your perspective, but I have no say in the matter. The chief says this is how we do things, so this is how we do things." She fixed Kramer with a warm, caring look before continuing in a softer tone. "I assure you this is only for the benefit of this investigation. No one is accusing you of anything. Your statement very well could lead us to the person who did this to your wife."

He shook his head in irritation. "Whatever. Let's just get this over with."

"Thank you, Mr. Kramer. Now, I need you to read it back to me." Alan Kramer did so quickly and in a clipped tone.

Taking the page back, Beck asked if he had any questions, and Kramer said, "I guess not."

"Please ask me anything, Mr. Kramer."

"No, it's fine."

She nodded and said, "Now, the next portion—and then we will be done with this and ready to talk—is the waiver of your right to remain silent. It says, 'The above rights have been read to me and by me. I understand what my rights are. I am willing to answer questions and make a statement. I do not want a lawyer at this time. I understand and know what I am doing. No promises or threats have been made to me, and no pressure of any kind has been used against me.' Do you understand what I just read to you?"

Kramer nodded and said, "Yes."

"Can you now please read it out loud?"

He snatched the paper and did so before tossing it back on the table.

"Mr. Kramer, are you willing to speak with me today? If so, I need you to sign right here." She pointed her pen to a line below the last paragraph on the page and laid the pen down on the paper.

Alan Kramer picked up the pen, hesitated, moved to sign it twice before finally doing so.

Beck then took the page back, signed in the space marked *witnessed,* and listed the date and time of the signing.

She set the pen aside and said, "The time is"—she looked at the underside of her wrist and checked her watch—"10:47 pm on the night of Monday, September twenty-ninth."

She crossed her legs and laid an arm on the table as she locked eyes with the man before her.

"Now, Mr. Kramer, let's talk about what you did to your wife."

SIXTY-ONE

L aura Kramer was not the third victim of the serial killer they were hunting; that much became clear.

In the few hours between Alan Kramer being taken to the police station and Beck Lawson leaving the scene to question him, the house was turned upside down. Nothing was found indicating a connection to Sam Albritton, which confirmed what they had already come to believe.

The task, now, was finding out who killed Laura Kramer.

Most homicides were solved in the first few hours of the case. Real life wasn't the movies and there was rarely a criminal mastermind behind the killing. It was typically someone the victim knew, and oftentimes, it was someone they knew well.

Alan Kramer was the first and easiest person to check because he was both the husband and the person to find the body.

Beck set aside thoughts of her forthcoming interrogation of the husband and focused on the crime itself.

She had noticed the couple's Ring doorbell on the house and texted Detective Billy Waters as he was transporting Kramer to the

PD to have him ask Kramer about accessing their Ring doorbell account so they could view the video activity.

Waters texted back immediately that he got Kramer's phone and passcode along with his wife's passcode. He said he would ask him about the doorbell.

The police had Mrs. Kramer's phone at the house, so Beck texted back, asking for the passcode. She also asked him to call Tina Crump and gave Waters her cell number.

Using the passcode, she opened Laura's iPhone and looked through text messages, emails, internet history, and photographs, not finding anything of note. She set the phone aside and texted Waters again.

Beck: *I need Tina to analyze our victim's phone, too.*

Waters responded with a *thumbs-up* emoji.

Beck: *Have her bring her gear and Alan Kramer's phone to the scene. She can analyze both phones here.*

Waters: *You got it.*

A forensic analysis would uncover anything on the phone that had been deleted. Her husband knew her passcode, so it wasn't a stretch that if he did kill his wife, he would have gone in and deleted anything incriminating.

She was talking to a group of five patrol officers when she got another text from Waters: *I asked him about the Ring doorbell. He said it isn't working. Said he didn't know how long it had been out.*

That was certainly an interesting development, the detective thought.

She sent patrol units up and down the street, interviewing neighbors and checking whether any other houses had a video doorbell or other external cameras that could have captured anything of value. As word trickled back in, there was nothing of significance to report. By all measures, according to those who lived around them, they were a nice, quiet couple.

Fitz called Laura's mother. He knew she was on the road

making the four-hour trip down from Huntsville, so he first asked her if she was driving. When she told him that a friend from church was driving her, he felt better about what he needed to discuss.

He apologized for having to do it this way, but time was of the essence. He inquired about the couple's relationship. An already tricky conversation was rendered even more so when she grew hysterical at the question, demanding to know if Alan Kramer had killed her daughter.

Fitz assured her the investigation was ongoing, and they had not yet identified a suspect. Everyone in the police department and district attorney's office was working on it, and they had even gotten assistance from the sheriff's department. They were casting a wide net and covering all avenues.

According to Laura's mother, she wasn't aware of any problems with the marriage.

"As far as I know, their finances were fine," the woman had said. "They had even begun discussing having children." Her voice broke in the middle of the last sentence. The grief-stricken woman could not see any way her son-in-law was involved in such a horrible thing.

There were no paper bank statements at the house, but Angie Presley did find a life insurance policy along with some other personal papers in a desk drawer in their home office.

Barclay knew the agent personally from the Rotary Club, and he called to inquire about it. He learned that they had a $750,000 policy on one another.

"That seems like a lot for a young couple with no children," he said to the agent.

"It's on the high side for sure, particularly with them not having any children to care for, but Alan does own his own business, so I recommended a little more coverage because of that."

"So the life insurance was your idea?"

"The life insurance, no. The amount, yes."

"Did you get an impression of the couple when you dealt with them? Like, were they both on board with the insurance?"

"I guess so, yeah. I mean, nothing stood out otherwise."

Barclay thanked the insurance agent and ended the call. Another dead end.

Computer forensic expert Tina Crump eventually arrived, and Beck filled her in on the investigation.

She said, "We haven't found anything to suggest he's involved. The phones are our last avenue to check, so if there's nothing on the phones, then we can probably cross him off the list."

"Let's see what we can find out," said Crump, who set up at the kitchen table, opening her laptop, unfurling cables, and unpacking the hardware she used for cell phone extractions.

Officer Jimmy Pullman found Beck and Chief Greenhaw talking in the dining room. He said, "Detective, I think I found something."

He led them out the busted back door into the unfenced back-yard. He held up his tactical light and clicked the rubber power button on the end of the flashlight with his thumb. A blinding white LED light illuminated the rear of the house that shared a backyard with the Kramers. He pointed the bright light first at the right corner of the house's roofline, then swung it around to the opposite corner.

Security cameras.

"Hell of a find, Jimmy," said the police chief.

"Thank you, sir."

Beck had been so focused on cameras filming the front of the house that she hadn't even considered the back side. Pullman volunteered to speak with the homeowner and left.

While waiting to hear back from Pullman, Beck entered the kitchen where Tina had begun work on Alan Kramer's cell phone. Sitting there with nothing to do except wait for others to report back, she opened Laura's cell phone and scrolled through it on the off chance she missed something.

She went back through text messages and emails, going a little slower this time but still not finding anything of significance. She went through the call log and wrote down any phone numbers that didn't have a name assigned to them. When Laura's mother arrived, she'd have her look at the call log and identify any of the named individuals she could.

With nothing left to view in the regular locations, she decided to swipe through the phone, looking at the apps to see if anything stood out. She found nothing she hadn't expected to see until the next to last screen.

It was a calculator app.

She scrolled back to the first screen on the phone and examined it. She then moved to the second screen, and that's where she saw it: the calculator app that comes installed on the iPhone.

To verify this, she opened her own iPhone and compared the two icons—identical. They were also both labeled *Calculator*. She then scrolled to the second calculator app on Laura's phone, which was labeled *Calculator #*.

"Why do you have two calculator apps?" she said out loud but to herself.

"Did you say something?" Tina asked, looking at the detective over the top of her computer.

Beck stared at the phone and decided to open the app. A calculator keypad appeared, and she entered some calculations.

"It's a calculator," she said again to herself.

Then it hit her.

"Well, looky here."

Tina came around behind Beck and leaned over her shoulder to look at the screen. "What is it?"

"I think this is a photo vault."

"Oh, yeah. Kids use them to hide stuff from their parents.

Looks like a calculator, works like a calculator, but punch in the right numbers, and it opens up to whatever you have stored behind the wall."

Beck opened the App Store on her phone, searched *Calculator Photo Vault*, and scrolled through the results until she saw the icon that matched the one on Laura's phone. "You sneaky, sneaky girl."

She did a quick internet search and found out she would need a four-digit PIN number to access the hidden contents, which she relayed to Tina.

"Any idea what it could be?" Tina asked.

"Not a clue."

Beck located Fitz and told him what she found. "Would you mind calling her mother back and asking her if she has any ideas for a four-digit number her daughter would use for a PIN?"

"I'll do it right now." He dialed her number and put the phone on speaker. "Hello, Mrs. Dumas? This is Investigator Fitzsimmons again. Would you happen to know what numbers your daughter might use for a four-digit PIN?"

She thought about it and said, "Her birthday is May twenty-fifth. Maybe try that?"

Beck typed in 0-5-2-5. Nothing happened, and he shook her head.

"That didn't work. Any other ideas?"

"Her anniversary, maybe? December 17."

Beck typed in 1-2-1-7—same result.

"Not that one either," said Fitz.

"Well, I just don't know. Can you tell me what it's for? Maybe that will help."

He looked at Beck, who nodded her head. Into the phone, Fitz said, "We found an app on her phone that we believe she may have used to store photographs or other items she didn't want anyone to find."

"Why would she...Wait. Try one, nine, five, seven. Nineteen Fifty-Seven."

It worked.

"That's it, Mrs. Dumas!"

"What's in there? What is she hiding?" Mrs. Dumas asked excitedly.

"Let us go through it, and we'll discuss it when you get here."

"Oh, dear. Okay. Waze is saying we'll be there in about forty minutes."

"Good, Mrs. Dumas. Be careful on the road, and we'll see you soon...say—," Fitz said quickly, hoping he had caught her before she hung up.

After a beat and him believing she had disconnected, she answered back and he asked, "Mind if I ask the significance of that number?"

"That was her father's PIN number. 1957 is the year Auburn won their first national championship in football." She laughed for the first time since he had begun speaking to her. "The poor fool loved to tell everybody his PIN number was Auburn's first national championship. It's a wonder our bank account was never cleaned out."

When the PIN was accepted, the screen changed from a calculator to an array of icons indicating a place to store photos, videos, audio files, documents, and a myriad of other things. It took less than a minute to know the investigation had most assuredly changed. Any doubts about who their killer was evaporated.

SIXTY-TWO

"What do you mean 'What I did to my wife?'" Alan Kramer asked Detective Lawson.

"I meant just what I said, Mr. Kramer."

He began shaking his head. "I don't know what you're talking about. I...I came home," his voice began to quake, "and I...I found her there. In the bed. All covered in blood." He put his face in his hands.

The detective waited him out. It took about thirty seconds to lift his head and face her. His eyes were red, but tears were conspicuously absent. She'd seen this tactic used all too often.

"Tell me about your relationship with your wife, Mr. Kramer?"

He threw his hands up in the air. "Fine. It was fine. Our relationship was fine."

Beck nodded thoughtfully. "Did you ever hit your wife, Mr. Kramer?"

"Wha...What? Hit my...come one, Detective, that's disgusting."

"You didn't answer my question."

He fixed her with a steely-eyed stare. "No. I did not hit my wife."

"Then who did?"

He suddenly had that look. That look that Beck had seen on many a face of a suspect when they saw the circle closing in on them.

"I don't know what you're talking about," he said with an almost eerie calm.

She went into the manila folder, produced seven photographs printed on 8 1/2 by 11 paper, and laid them out across the table without comment. The pictures were a three-hundred-sixty-degree documentation of a woman's bruised and battered torso.

She stared at the photos, then stared at Alan Kramer. He stared back at her, not so much as glancing down at the array.

When it became clear he wasn't going to speak, she said, "Someone took those photos of her, Mr. Kramer. I don't think it will take us very long to find out who did. I expect when news of her death hits the media, the person who took these pictures will call *us*." She paused before saying, "Now, who did this to your wife?"

"Oh, please, Detective, that doesn't prove anything."

"No, you're right, Mr. Kramer, it doesn't." She removed another document and laid it out in front of him. "This is a document she typed up that goes into great detail about the abuse you subjected her to with dates, locations, and reasons." She paused again, allowing him to take this in. "Reasons! She actually typed out the *reason* you beat her." She shook her head at the man in front of her. "I can't imagine the humiliation of doing such a thing."

He was unmoved and unmotivated to say anything. He couldn't even be bothered to look at the pictures or the document she had set before him. She knew that he didn't have to. He'd seen his damage firsthand whenever she was undressed in front of him.

She continued, "We also have a video she recorded of herself laying these things out. I guess she just wanted to make sure she had everything documented...just in case."

A smirk formed on his lips. "I believe everything you've just mentioned—the pictures, this note you say she wrote, this video —is what is commonly referred to as hearsay. Right, Detective?"

Beck looked down and began to nod. Slowly, as if defeated. "You're exactly right. It is hearsay." She lifted her gaze to him and said, "It's not every day we get someone in this room—in that chair—who knows the rules of evidence. Who knows what is and isn't hearsay. But you do. Better than some lawyers I know." She reached back into the folder and flipped past several pages before pulling out the one she had been looking for and slamming it on the table.

Curiosity got the better of him, and he glanced down at the paper.

"Your phone's internet search history." She could have sworn she heard him swallow—so loud, she thought, it echoed around the tight space. "Why would you google *Hearsay*, Mr. Kramer? And in the last two days at that." He didn't answer; she didn't expect him to. "You know what I think? She has a friend. Probably someone she spends a great deal of time with, especially since it means less time with you, and you figure they talk. Laura probably confided in her....or him. You needed to know if what Laura told her could be used against you. Of course, I'm just guessing here. Care to tell me why you were reading about hearsay online?"

Silence.

She flipped for and found another piece of paper and laid it on the table. "This, Mr. Kramer, is downright strange when you consider the timing of everything." Again, he cast his gaze down to the paper, only he kept it down this time.

"Why were you searching..."—she picked up the paper to make sure she quoted the search terms correctly—"*Towne serial killer, Wendy Wade serial killer, Elise Hightower murder, Elise Hightower serial killer*? That's just weird. Damn weird if you ask me, Mr. Kramer. And weirder still is that you deleted your search history just this morning." She laid the page back down. His eyes remained downcast.

"And we know you watched Wendy Wade's Facebook broadcast of the press conference last week at the Elise Hightower murder scene twenty-three times. What, were you trying to glean as much information as you could to stage your wife's murder so we would think some serial killer did it?"

After nearly a minute, he raised his head and, absent much of the bravado from before, said, "It doesn't mean I killed my wife. I didn't kill my wife."

She lifted the screen on her MacBook Pro and used her fingerprint to log in. What she wanted was already pulled up and ready.

"You may be right, Mr. Kramer. I don't think you are, but you may be. Ultimately, though, it will be up for a jury to decide." She turned her computer so he could see the screen. "Maybe those pictures of your handiwork will come in at trial, or maybe not. Perhaps the document she created detailing your abuse of her or the video of the same isn't admitted into evidence because it is, indeed, hearsay evidence. And maybe the jury will just chalk up those internet searches and twenty-three video views as idle, if not somewhat morbid curiosity, and, who knows, I bet a good lawyer could spin your Ring doorbell not working when your wife was killed as just a brutal twist of fate given that it just might reveal the true killer in vivid high definition.

"Sure, the jury could...possibly...buy all of that, *but*...I don't think a jury will view any of that in your favor when they see this."

She pressed the space bar, and the footage from the security cameras mounted to the rear of the house behind the Kramer home began to play. The video was crystal clear, and it showed Alan Kramer approaching the rear door of his house, raising his right leg, and kicking at the door, eventually crashing it in. The cameras also picked up the sound of the kicks and the door splintering. It was faint but there.

"One thing you learn in the police academy is that kicking in a door isn't nearly as easy as Hollywood makes it look. Oh, and you left a fantastic boot print on the door. Once we knew you were our killer, we went into your closet and found the Danner boots that you were wearing when you kicked in that door." She fished out three final photographs: the first was of the boots, the second of the sole of the right boot, and the third was of the print on the door.

"And, to put your legal mind at ease, Mr. Kramer, we got a search warrant before we looked for your boots."

Kramer said, "I want a lawyer."

SIXTY-THREE

Back at the Kramer house, as the crime scene investigation was wrapping up, Barclay left to go down the street to where the media was posted up. He made a brief statement.

"Earlier today at just after 4:00 in the afternoon, police received a call via nine-one-one about a possible death. Police arrived to find a deceased female. Law enforcement is working tirelessly to determine what happened and who is responsible. If anyone has any information about this case, please call the police department or my office."

Not waiting to be called on, Wendy Wade shouted, "Is this related to the other eight homicides?"

Barclay closed his eyes, willing himself to remain calm. "I'm not going to discuss the findings of an ongoing investigation."

"I've received word that another bloody letter was found at the scene. Can you confirm this?"

"See previous answer."

"The public is scared, they're worried, can't you understand that? They want details."

"Ms. Wade, I won't jeopardize a criminal investigation to satisfy your vanity or your blood lust. That's all for now. Appreciate most of you being here."

As he was walking away, he heard that all-too-familiar voice screeching his name. He turned around, causing Wendy Wade to almost run into him.

"Careful, now," he said. "How can I help you, Ms. Wade?"

"Fuck you and your *blood lust* comment. That was bullshit, and you know it."

He stepped into her space. "Oh, I think that's *exactly* what this is."

"And that comment...," she spoke in an exaggerated voice, "*I appreciate* most *of you being here.* That was real fuckin' low, asshole."

Barclay gathered himself. "You know, Wendy, and this is off the record...yeah, I trust you enough to know you won't repeat this because God help you if you do...off the record, a young woman is dead in that house, stabbed all to hell and back because her husband wanted her dead. He watched your little Facebook Live video from last week a few dozen times and tried to make her death look like the other killer." Her face dropped, her mouth agape.

"That's right, Wendy. Thanks to you shouting about the bloody letter on the wall and all that other bullshit, he killed his wife and tried to make it look like this other guy killed her." He was breathing hard now. "I told you your actions would have consequences, and now a woman is dead because of your irresponsible behavior."

She opened her mouth to speak, but, for once, the wonderful Wendy Wade was without words.

"By the way, that comment about the bloody letter at the scene? Nice bluff. I tell you no, then later, when I don't answer regarding a detail at the crime scene, you can imply a yes. Very slick."

Her mouth worked, but no sound emerged.

"I like you, Wendy. You bust your ass at your job, and I respect that. I'm telling you, though, this time? You need to be very careful what you put out there and who you're communicating with?"

This got her words working again. "What? Do you know something?"

"Please be careful."

Barclay left her there in the dark street, out of range of the camera lights, wondering if he had been right about her causing Laura Kramer's death.

SIXTY-FOUR

The killer awoke the following day to a notification that Wendy Wade was broadcasting live on Facebook. He sat on the edge of the bed, thinking back to the night before of the first broadcast he watched of hers at the scene of a murder. He quickly grew bored and turned it off after only a few minutes. This notification, he noticed, occurred at 11:38, long after he had gone to bed.

He carried his phone into the bathroom, laid it on the counter, and opened the Facebook app. He went to Wendy's page and played the latest video. He watched with only slight interest as he brushed his teeth until he heard Wendy Wade say, "I've received word that another bloody letter was found at the scene. Can you confirm this?"

He spit out toothpaste and dropped his toothbrush into its holder, not bothering to rinse it. He wiped his mouth on a hand towel, his throat constricting. He stared at the phone screen—was this true? The DA didn't say one way or the other. Wendy had sources inside the police department. He knew this because all good reporters did. He leaned on the sink as he watched the last bit of the short press conference. When it was over, he used his finger to drag the video back to her question about the bloody letter and listened again.

What did this mean?

He stared at himself in the mirror, and whatever it was he was feeling at that point, he couldn't articulate; however, the emotions that grew out of it were anger...and rage. He knew those very well.

He'd be damned if someone was going to kill in his name. This secret would remain his and his alone.

Someone had to die at his hand, so he resolved to kill again. Despite knowing it wasn't quite time, the idea of it didn't even give him a moment's pause.

Time.

Whoever this copycat wannabe motherfucker was who killed last night had caused time to lose all meaning. His reflection stared back at him as moments passed. Then, he bared his teeth in a shark's smile as he had a thought. Maybe some folks needed a reminder of exactly who he was and what he was truly capable of doing.

SIXTY-FIVE

I am well aware this can't go on forever. If I continue to kill, odds are I will get caught. That's just how it is. I know this, and I have planned for such an eventuality. Despite my preparation and confidence in such a plan, I have no desire to implement it any sooner than absolutely necessary. That's why this next murder has me on edge.

But fuck Alan Kramer.

Seeing some amateur try and pin a half-assed murder on me made me furious. I was hit with a dose of irony, however. Wasn't that what I had been doing? Picking up where a serial killer left off to avoid getting caught? I did think about that for quite some time until...

I concluded I was no copycat.

I'm the real goddamn thing.

I also realized something else about myself: I have a killing problem.

———

I APPROACHED the house with a plan of sorts. With Nelson and Hightower, I had woefully underestimated their fight, their innate desire to live, to survive. I miscalculated—read: didn't calculate at all—the lizard brain.

The limbic cortex that exists in all of us, that primitive part of our brain that tells us to either fight like hell or get the hell out. Nelson had challenged me, whereas Hightower had chosen to try and run. Either of those things could have derailed my plans, and I had no intention of allowing that to happen again.

I knew my next victim. As I researched my predecessor, I determined that had been the key. That was my way in.

Dorothy Young was on the list.

When I realized I had stumbled on what I perceived to be a perfect plan—well, as perfect as such a thing can be because murder is never perfect. I studied my predecessor's kills as best as I could, which wasn't terribly exhaustive given my lack of information, but I believed I had learned enough to fill in the blanks. Anyway, Dorothy made the list even if she was further down than number three. The list wasn't numbered, per se, but I suppose there was some order to it; otherwise, I would have thought of her sooner than I had the four others in front of her. At least, I presupposed that's how the universe worked.

She was down the list, so why now? Her house was the most secluded of anyone else on the list. Since this was a plan I developed largely on the fly, I needed to minimize risk by seeking out the least densely populated area possible.

Sorry, Dorothy.

What I wasn't able to do with her was lay her death directly at the feet of another. When I started killing, I chose a killer the police already knew. If I ever felt I was close to being discovered, the police would find a killer they had never expected. That was, of course, what I believed to be the most ingenious part of my overarching scheme—pinning my crimes on another.

I had been able to lay that foundation with Nelson and High-tower, but I didn't have that luxury this time. I could only hope that with the first two so thoroughly linked to the "killer," the police would have no choice but to consider poor Mrs. Young, another victim of this vicious predator.

As with my previous kills, I parked some ways away and made my way to the house in the shadows. I knocked on the door, stood back, and fixed my face with a decidedly non-threatening smile.

"Who is it," said the voice of the seventy-something Dorothy Young as a shadow appeared over the door's peephole.

"It's your lawyer," I said in as friendly a voice as I could muster, widening my smile to the point it almost hurt.

"What? Hold on a moment." Then I heard a muffled, "My attorney's here," which struck me as odd.

This wasn't good, I thought. Then the lock clicked, and I moved closer to the door. I crouched just a bit, and as soon as the door began to open, I exploded into Dorothy Young, knocking her to the ground. I reared back and drove my fist into her face, opening a gash under her left eye and stunning the old woman. I climbed off her and stood over the prone figure when I heard, "Grandmother!"

I saw a woman in the doorway holding a small hammer at her side. Blonde, early twenties, quite pretty, not scared.

Shit.

I bolted toward her, and she ran, dropping the small hammer. I lost sight of her when she turned a corner, and then I heard her on the stairs. I took the stairs two at a time, banging my shoulder into the wall at the switchback on the first landing. I got to the top of the stairs and stopped, listened, and heard nothing. I took a step, leaning slightly, straining to hear. Still nothing.

I moved to the right, taking slow, tentative steps, the floor-boards of the old house creaking under my weight. I peeked into the first room I came to. It contained no furniture and had a large beige canvas drop cloth piled in the middle of the room along with several paint cans, the colors they contained showing in drips and smears on the outside of each. That's when I noticed the fresh paint smell of the house.

I had a decision to make. I assumed the woman had a cell phone, most likely on her, so calling the police was a definite possibility. I hadn't heard anything, so I was confident she had not done so yet. She was hiding and likely didn't want to risk discovery by talking on the phone.

But she could text.

Once again, I was faced with a chaotic situation that was less than ideal.

I went back down the stairs, stopping twice, craning my ear upwards, and listening for movement. Once downstairs, I walked to the open front door, looked out to make sure I had remained undetected, then closed and locked the door. I checked on Dorothy. Dead.

I was crouched over her body, breathing hard. I looked to the ceiling. *Think!*

The woman had seen me. The old lady had announced me as her attorney.

I had someone else to kill.

Standing there, I remembered the hammer and what I'd seen on the first landing of the staircase.

I was about to make a statement.

SIXTY-SIX

Lucy Young was helping her grandmother fix up the old house she had built with Lucy's grandfather in 1949. They had recently finished painting all the rooms on the second floor, and she was re-hanging all of the family photographs along the wall in the stairwell when she heard a knock at the door.

At first, she wasn't sure what she heard because she had been hammering a picture hanger into the wall. She stopped and listened, heard her grandmother say something about her attorney, then came a loud crash.

She ran down the stairs, and when she turned toward the living room, she saw her grandmother lying on the ground with blood under her eye. Her immediate thought was that her grandmother had fallen, but when she reached the doorway, she saw the man standing over the old woman, her floral print dressing gown riding up.

"Grandmother!" she said.

She locked eyes with the stranger, not comprehending but also growing angry. He shot towards her, and she turned and ran, her quick feet pistoning up the staircase. She grabbed the newel post with her right hand and used it to slingshot around the switchback.

She hit the second floor and bolted left. She dipped into the last room on the left and jumped into a closet, easing the door closed. Because of the stress and the running, but mainly the stress, her heart was hammering in her chest, and the blood rushing in her ears was so violent and so loud she was sure it would give her away. She also worked to control her breathing, which was heavy and, she felt, just as loud. It was then she realized she must have dropped the hammer she had been holding somewhere along the way.

She replayed what she had just seen in her mind and couldn't make it make sense. Why had that man been at this house? Who would do such a thing? Then, she thought there was the thing her grandmother had said about her attorney that made absolutely zero sense to her. She hoped the intruder would be scared off and leave. Surely, he wouldn't hang around; she wouldn't if it were her.

She knew he had run after her—the sound of him on the stairs fresh in her mind. But she also knew he stopped. She tried to be as quiet as possible and had gotten herself together. After what she could only assume had been several minutes, she began to relax and started the conversation in her head about whether or not she should leave the safety of her hiding place or continue to wait.

But what about her grandmother? She had only seen her for a few seconds, but it didn't look good. She slid down the wall facing the door and sat on something hard.

Her cellphone!

She leaned up just enough to remove the phone and silence it. The last thing she needed was for it to ring or ding with a call or a text message. She knew she needed to call the police, but what if he was still there? Would he hear her? Could he still be on the second floor, just waiting for the noise that would give her away? Could he be right outside of her closet?

She eventually dialed 911.

SIXTY-SEVEN

"Hello? Hello?" the woman in the closet said in a strangled whisper.

"Nine-one-one, what's your emergency," the male voice repeated in her ear.

"Hello? Yes, please help me. Some man broke into my grandmother's house, and I think he attacked her."

"What's your name?"

"Lucy. Young."

"Is he still there, Lucy? The man who broke in?"

"I don't know," she whispered. "I don't know."

The light in the room where she was holed up in the closet was off, but the hall light was on. A faint glow leaked into the room and crept, just barely, to the threshold of the closet. She was wide-eyed, watching the crack under the door, looking for any sign that the man was there. Though the house always seemed to have a chill about it, she was sweating, and the sweat clung to her eyelashes. She blinked and then blinked again, trying to squeeze out the sweat pouring in.

"Is your address 327 Lilly Pond Road?"

"Yes," she hissed. "Please, you have to hurry." She swiped her eyes with her shirt sleeve.

"I'm dispatching units now, ma'am. Did you get a look at this person?"

"Yes." Her breathing had calmed, but her heart still raced.

"What can you tell me about him?"

She closed her eyes, thinking. "I...uh...I don't know.

"Was he wearing a mask? Could you tell his race?"

"He wasn't wearing a mask. He was white."

"What about hair color?"

"He...he had dark hair...uh, and glasses. He wore glasses."

"How old do you think this man is?"

"I don't know," she said a bit too loud.

"Was he young or old?" asked the dispatcher.

"Wha...uh...Not young, but not old. Not too old, I guess."

"This is good, Lucy. You're doing great. Anything else?"

"What?"

"Do you remember anything else about this person? Anything else you can think of regarding a description?"

She closed her eyes again. *Come on, come on.* She willed herself. *You saw him. Give them something.*

The dispatcher said, "What about his glasses...or his clothing? Any tattoos or other marks you could see?"

His glasses, his glasses... "His glasses were retro-looking, I think, and he...he..." She squeezed her eyes shut, trying to grab it. *Oh, God, what was it...* "He had a ring," she blurted quietly. "A big ring. Like a college-type ring."

"What else? Did he say anything?"

Her eyes flashed open, and she blurted out: "He didn't, but my grandmother said he was her attorney." She squeezed her eyes shut again, banged her head against the wall, and silently cursed herself. Had she spoken too loudly? She prayed the man was gone.

"The police are on the way and should be there any minute."

Did I hear something?

"Lucy? Are you still with me?"

"Shhhh," she whispered as she gripped the phone in her sweaty hand. "I think—"

The closet door exploded open, and something slammed into her face, causing her to drop the phone.

"Lucy! What's happening?" asked the dispatcher.

The sounds of a struggle emanated through his earpiece for several seconds before silence took over.

SIXTY-EIGHT

"This sonofabitch is getting worse, if that's even possible," said Chief Greenhaw as he stood over Dorothy Young's corpse.

Standing beside him, Beck said, "He's angry about something."

The chief made a sound of disgust and left the room. He was in the living room when Barclay walked into the house. He locked eyes with Greenhaw, who nodded.

"We're sure?" Barclay asked.

The chief barked a laugh. "Oh yeah."

"You found a card?"

"Nailed to her fuckin' forehead."

"What?"

The chief walked back toward the bedroom and threw a crooked finger at the DA, signaling him to follow.

Angie Presley stepped back from taking pictures so the chief and the DA could get a look at the body.

"Jesus," said Barclay. He leaned in close to see the Sam Albritton business card affixed to the wrinkled forehead with a small gauge nail.

"There's more," the chief said, leaving the room with Barclay in tow.

They walked up the stairs to the last room on the left, where another CSI team was at work photographing, swabbing, and bagging evidence.

Barclay sucked in a breath at the gruesome sight before him. A body lay crumpled just outside the closet, the head a sticky, bloody mass of torn skin, bone, and brain matter. Had it not been attached to a torso, it may not have been recognized for what it was—a human head.

"Charlie," the chief said, and he made a lifting motion with his hand.

The crime scene tech held up a clear evidence bag holding a ten-ounce hammer covered in blood. Even from a distance, Barclay could see the strands of hair stuck to it.

Back downstairs, Greenhaw and Barclay joined Fitz and Beck, who were deep in conversation.

"Any thoughts on why our guy deviated with the business card?" Greenhaw asked.

"If I had to guess," Beck said, "I'd say he wanted to make damn sure we knew this one was his." Then something clicked for her. "If you were the killer, you'd be interested in the media coverage, right? I mean, these guys crave attention. What better way than to watch things as they unfold."

Greenhaw was about to ask what she was getting at when Barclay said, "Wendy Wade."

"Exactly," she said. "We know he's been in touch with her at least once, so it's not a leap to believe he's following her coverage. When you addressed the media last night on the Laura Kramer murder, Wendy asked you about a bloody letter being at the scene. What if he saw that? He would know it wasn't his, and if it were me, I might be kinda pissed at someone trying to steal my material, you know."

Fitz: "So he goes for a kill the next day to say, 'There's only one killer and I am him.'"

Barclay: "And makes the business card as conspicuous as absolutely possible."

They all considered that. Greenhaw finally said, "I think that plays."

"That could also explain this." She walked to the front door, and they followed. She pushed the open door almost closed with her gloved left hand and pointed at the ruined drywall with her right. "Looks like he had to bust his way in this time." She pointed to the drywall dust on the floor.

Barclay: "So why bust your way in tonight and not the other nights?"

Beck: "Like Fitz just said. He makes a kill to make a point. His hand was forced, at least in his mind, so he goes off the cuff. He didn't have time to plan as he normally does, which may entail a pre-planned meeting with his victims. That would explain the ease with which he gains access."

Barclay said, "So, what, he chose a stranger this time? That doesn't sound right with what we know."

A hint of a smile on Beck's face. "Nope. It was her attorney."

"What?" said Barclay.

"The deceased's granddaughter—the dead girl upstairs—called nine-one-one. She described the killer as having dark hair and retro eyeglasses and told the dispatcher that he was her grandmother's attorney."

"What?" he asked again.

"That's all we got," she said.

Greenhaw said, "What the hell are retro glasses?"

"Beats me," said Beck with a shrug. "There's no telling what retro means to a person her age. Last month is a long time ago when you're that young."

Fitz jumped in and said, "I thought the thing about it being her grandmother's attorney was odd, too, when I heard that. But then I got to thinking. Remember what Alexis Washington told me about the papers we found at Elise Hightower's house?" Getting no response, he said, "The lady I spoke with at the wealth management company."

"What about it?" Barclay asked.

"She said the deed and financial papers could have been out if she were meeting with a lawyer about her estate."

Beck: "That could be the connection we've been chasing. We'll get someone to start calling law offices in the morning to see who has Dorothy Young as a client. Then hope that the same lawyer represents Elise Hightower."

"Start with estate lawyers," said Barclay.

Beck nodded.

Fitz: "So knowing what we know, let's assume tonight was a last-second impromptu attack. He doesn't have time to schedule an appointment, so he shows up hoping that because he is familiar to his victim, she will let him in. But, for whatever reason, it doesn't go that way, and he has to force his way in."

Greenhaw was examining the door. "There isn't any damage to the door, so she opened it for him."

Beck: "Maybe she opens the door and sees something she doesn't like and tries to slam it on him. Whatever happened, it didn't go as smoothly as the others. Something else to consider is the presence of the body upstairs. He didn't take the time to make sure his victim was alone as he seemed to do with the others."

Greenhaw: "He got sloppy."

Beck: "He got emotional."

SIXTY-NINE

In a town this size, it didn't take them long to find Dorothy Young's attorney, who also happened to be the attorney for Elise Hightower and Freida Nelson. It was the fourth law firm they called.

The law firm of Brannon and Harris occupied a two-story building downtown, two blocks from the courthouse. Beck sat in the firm's lobby with Barclay. She was there because it was her case, while Barclay was there to not only walk the legal tightrope they were stepping out on but also to speak to the managing partner, one lawyer to another, which they hoped would put the man at ease. No other law enforcement was there because they didn't want to walk into a law firm looking like the Gestapo.

The interior was tasteful without being over the top. The walls were varying shades of gray, and the furniture was black. Splashes of color came from three artificial flower arrangements placed throughout the lobby. An automatic air freshener in an upper corner kept the lobby smelling of cinnamon apples, one electronic hiss at a time.

The solid wooden door set into the wall next to the reception desk opened, and a humorless middle-aged schoolmarm stepped through.

"Mr. Brannon will see you now."

She and Barclay got up and followed her through the door to Lawrence Brannon's office. They turned a corner, and Barclay heard someone call his name. He turned around and, not seeing anyone, walked back to the intersection with the hallway he had just passed. He looked to his left toward the office's interior and saw a tall, dark figure walking toward him.

"Barclay," the figure said again.

It took Barclay a beat before he said, "Franklin Masterson, how are you?"

"I'm fine," he said stiffly, and they shook hands.

"I didn't realize you worked here."

A shrug. "No reason you should, I guess."

"True enough. How are you and Stacey doing? Haven't seen you at the office since...since the last time I saw you there." Barclay smiled.

The smile was awkwardly returned. "We're fine. What brings you here? Professional or personal business?"

"For work."

"Oh," the young lawyer exclaimed. "You're not here about those terrible murders, are you?"

"Why would you think that?"

Masterson opened his mouth, closed it, smiled, and said, "No reason, I guess. I figure it's a big case, so what else would you be working on? But then you're the DA, and I'm sure you've got more going on than just the one case, right?"

Barclay jerked a thumb over his shoulder. "I need to catch up with Detective Lawson. Good seeing you, Franklin."

"Same."

Barclay turned to find Brannon's office. He made it maybe three steps when it hit him.

In that instant, something clicked, and Barclay knew this meeting would be a short one.

He also knew what Lucy Young meant when she had described the retro eyeglasses.

SEVENTY

Barclay followed the hallway around, making a large square, and found Brannon's office in the opposite corner from where they entered from the lobby. Whatever opulence was missing in the lobby was found here in the large corner office. The walls were lavishly covered in cobalt damask wallpaper, and the furniture was all dark mahogany. The room smelled of patchouli essential oil.

When Barclay walked in, Beck said, "We thought we lost you."

"Yeah, sorry. Saw someone I knew."

The jowly Lawrence Brannon had curly salt and pepper hair and wore a white dress shirt with a wine-colored patterned tie and matching braces. He stood and extended a hand across the desk. "Who do you know here?"

"Franklin Masterson. He's kinda, sorta seeing one of our ADAs, I guess you'd say."

That drew a good-natured laugh from the lawyer, which served to break the ice.

"We appreciate you seeing us on such short notice, Mr. Brannon. We know you're a very busy man," said Beck.

He waived off the comment. "Always happy to help law enforcement."

"We appreciate that. We're here because three of your clients have been murdered over the last couple of weeks."

Brannon adopted a grave expression. "So I was told. I must admit that was quite a coincidence. You don't believe my office is connected in some way, do you?"

Beck said, "Mr. Brannon, we know your office is connected—"

The beefy lawyer leaned forward and said, "Now wait a minute, if we need a lawyer—"

"Mr. Brannon," Barclay said, "slow down. When the detective here says your firm is connected to these homicides, she is merely speaking from the perspective that all three victims were clients of your fine firm. No one is saying that your firm has any bearing on these cases beyond that."

"Well...if that's all..."

"As you know, there aren't a lot of estate attorneys in our area, so the odds that all three victims all did business with the same law firm are pretty good," said Barclay

Brannon considered that and then began to nod slowly. "That is true. I don't suppose you can tell me anything about these cases. I mean...maybe knowing a little something would help me be of better assistance."

Barclay said, "I'm afraid we can't get into any details. I'm sorry." Brannon nodded as if he understood, but it was their loss. Barclay then signaled to Beck, who picked up where she had left off.

"Are your clients generally assigned to a specific attorney, or do they deal with several different lawyers?"

"Typically, attorneys secure their own clients; however, when a potential client comes in off the street, they would be assigned a primary attorney. That said, it would not be unusual for an attorney to request assistance from another lawyer in the office from time to time."

"And what about the three women we're here about: Freida Nelson, Elise Hightower, and Dorothy Young?"

"I'm afraid, Detective, that now it is I who must claim confidentiality. I'm sure you understand."

Barclay said, "Mr. Brannon, we're not seeking privileged information. Frankly, we have zero interest in the legal work you've done for any of your clients. We are simply trying to solve a murder...three murders, as you know."

"I've seen the news, yes. Just terrible." The lawyer's prominent jowls and throat quivered as he shook his head in concern.

Barclay leaned in, lowered his voice, and said, "Can we count on your discretion?"

The lawyer spread his hands and said, "I'm an attorney, Mr. Griffith. Discretion is what I do."

"Good. This cannot leave this office. We are asking that you keep in confidence anything we discuss today."

"Of course, you can count on my secrecy, sir," said Brannon, sounding slightly insulted.

Barclay nodded as if considering it further before saying, "We believe there is possibly a serial killer at work. I say that so you will understand the full gravity of what we're working under here."

Brannon placed two meaty hands on his glass-topped desk. "Oh my. A serial killer is afoot in our little hamlet? Just tell me what you need from me."

Beck said, "Who handled the work for Nelson, Hightower, and Young?"

Brannon spun in his chair to face a large flat-screen monitor. He swung a keyboard out from under the monitor and went to work typing, followed by a few mouse clicks.

He adopted a surprised expression, and then, without taking

his eyes off the screen, he said, "Tim Lansing represented all three women."

"Were they clients he brought in, or were they assigned to him?"

The big man leaned in toward the screen, the keyboard pressing into his midsection. "Nelson was assigned to him, and Hightower and Young were both brought on by Lansing."

Barclay said, "What can you tell me about Lansing?"

Lawrence swiveled around to face his guests and said, "Well, let's see, he's been here maybe five years. Good lawyer. Will probably be a partner here one day. Why?"

"Just curious," said Barclay. "I've never crossed paths with him." After a brief pause, he continued, "Franklin Masterson is a young lawyer, fairly new here?"

"He's been here two years or so, I think, but yes, he is one of our youngest attorneys," Brannon responded, leaning in and adopting a cautious look.

"And I suppose young lawyers typically work with or under more senior attorneys?"

Brannon's shiny bottom lip jutted out as he took in the DA with studious eyes. He finally said, "Yes," drawing out the word. "More or less."

"Did Franklin do legal work for the three dead women? Perhaps assisting Lansing?"

"I'm afraid that's verging on privileged information, Mr. Griffith. I'm sure you understand."

Beck sat up and said, "Mr. Brannon, once again, we are trying to catch—"

"A murderer. Yes, Detective, I heard you, and I understand that. But *you* must also understand *my* position."

Beck was about to push back when Barclay said, "Mr. Brannon, you've been a tremendous help." He rose from his chair, and Brannon followed suit, a look of surprise on his face. She remained

THE WOLF HE FEEDS 367

seated, looking up at Barclay, not hiding her frustration at the abrupt end to the interview.

Brannon said, "Are you sure? I don't know that I gave you anything...but if you say so."

"You did." Brannon came around the desk and shook Barclay's hand. "We would like to be able to reach out if we have any more questions."

"I hope you will." He held up a finger, walked behind his desk, and opened the middle drawer. He removed a business card and pulled a Montblanc pen from his shirt pocket. He twisted off the cap, wrote on the card, and handed it across the desk to Barclay. "Here is my direct line and my cell number."

"Thank you," Barclay said as he received the card.

Beck finally stood. Brannon offered his hand across the desk, and they shook.

They were no more than a step outside Lawrence Brannon's office when she turned on Barclay and said, "What the hell was that? I wasn't done asking questions."

"We'll discuss it outside."

———

BECK WAS the first out the door onto the sidewalk and immediately spun on Barclay, who grabbed her arm to turn her back around and said, "We'll discuss it in the car."

They got to Beck's police-issue Dodge Charger, and she stared at him across the roof.

He said, "Are you going to unlock the car?"

She shook her head and clicked her key fob, unlocking the doors, and they both got in. "Now, are you going to tell me what's going on?"

"Drive."

"Damnit, Barclay."

"I'll explain when we're on the road."

Beck angrily punched the start button, slammed the car in reverse, and stomped the gas pedal. She then slammed it into drive and stomped the gas pedal again, causing the tires to squeal briefly before catching and rocketing the car down the street.

Barclay pulled out his cell phone, and Beck said, "You can check Twitter later. Tell me what's going on. Why did you shut me down back there?"

Barclay ignored her until he found what he was looking for. In response to her question he held his phone up for her to see. When she glanced down, she slammed on the brakes, immediately stopping in the middle of the road. She grabbed his phone and said, "Holy shit."

She was staring at Franklin Masterson's photograph from the Brannon and Harris website.

"Retro glasses," she breathed.

"You caught it quicker than I did, but yes, I believe those would qualify as retro." Then Barclay said calmly, "You mind getting us out of the middle of the road?"

She was staring at the phone. "What?"

"The road?"

She looked up, then at her rearview mirror, hit the gas, and found a fast-food restaurant parking lot to pull into.

"Alright, explain."

"Remember when I said I saw someone I knew back there?" She nodded. "I've met the guy a couple of times. He's seeing Stacey Steen from my office."

"I know her."

"Well, after I got done chatting with Masterson, I turned to leave, and that's when I saw it. His glasses."

She tossed his phone at him. "You could have told me before we went through all of that."

"When? I couldn't say anything in front of Brannon."

"Oh, but you could tell him there's a serial in play?"

"I made a judgment call. He was going to be a hard case, so I threw him a bone as if we were letting him in on some big secret. It's not like it's any big mystery at this point, anyway. Not with Wendy Wade out there running her mouth. Besides, I believe we can trust him, and it got him to open up. Plus, if we need anything later, he'll cooperate."

SEVENTY-ONE

Beck had to will herself to keep her car reasonably close to the speed limit as she and Barclay traveled to the police station. Before leaving the restaurant's parking lot, she had called Chief Greenhaw, who said he would let TJ know. Barclay called Fitz and filled him in on the developments, asked him to run Masterson's criminal history, and then meet them at the PD.

Beck took charge of the meeting almost immediately upon entering the conference room. She secured the photograph she had printed from the firm's website with a magnet to the whiteboard. The picture was of a white male, twenty-nine years old, with dark wavy hair parted to the left and brown eyes behind a pair of eyeglasses. The upper portion of the eyeglass frames was black, while the lower portion holding the lenses in place was thin silver metal.

"Retro," said Greenhaw, staring at the photo. "I'll be damned. Lucy Young was right. My grandfather wore that exact same style."

Beck said, "This is who we're focusing on." She asked Fitz, "What did you find on his criminal history?"

"Outside of a speeding ticket when he was nineteen, he's clean. I also ran him through TLO and nothing stood out."

Beck closed her eyes for a moment, then said, "The nine-one-one caller said the killer wore a large ring—she described it as a class ring." To Barclay: "I don't guess you noticed if he wore a ring or not?"

Barclay shook his head. "I did not."

Fitz said, "I just found him on Facebook; it's a public profile." He was talking as he scrolled down the page. "Last post was ten months ago. He went skiing for Christmas. Looks like with his family." He scrolled some more. "Okay. Here we go." Fitz turned the computer so everyone could see the screen. It was a picture of him in a tuxedo as part of a wedding party. The groomsmen were posed with the bride in the middle, and they all held up beers in celebration. Fitz pointed to a zoomed-in portion of the photo. It was a little fuzzy, but you could make out a large ring on the ring finger of his right hand that was gripping a beer can.

"Good, good, this is real good," said Beck, talking quicker now. She was about to say something else when she stooped and said, "Fitz, go back to Wendy Wade's Facebook Live broadcasts covering each of the murders. I'm pretty sure it shows who watched and commented. See if Franklin Masterson shows up in any of those broadcasts. I'd check any broadcast she made related to the murders. Not just the ones the night of."

"Got it," he said and went to work.

Captain Jones said, "I think we need to put someone on this guy. If he is our killer, we need to be eyes on twenty-four/seven until we have enough for an arrest."

Greenhaw said, "Good call. Let's put a couple of detectives per shift on him. I'll approve any overtime necessary."

Captain Jones nodded and left the room.

Barclay held up his hands and said, "Everybody, just wait a minute. He's seeing one of my prosecutors. If he is our guy, we need to let her know. We also can't risk him doing something to her."

Beck said, "I know this is a tough spot, but if we tell her, what if she confronts him—"

"She won't," said Barclay.

"So," Beck pressed on, "you tell her, and then what? If she breaks things off with him on the heels of us going to his law office, he'll suspect something is up. If we ask her to stay with him so he doesn't get suspicious, it'll be weird, and he'll know something."

Fitz said, "Look, Boss, I get it, but Beck is right. Besides, this Masterson guy is going to be covered like stink on shit. I suspect he's already a little on edge after today's visit. He's got to know we're getting close. No way he risks doing anything to her."

After about thirty seconds, Barclay gave a big exhale and said, "Alright, but if something happens..."

Greenhaw said, "It won't. TJ won't let it."

Beck scanned the room before nodding, and then she ticked off what they knew. "This is what we have so far: our three victims were all represented by Tim Lansing, a senior attorney at the firm. The senior partner told us that it's common for young lawyers to work under senior attorneys. Now, we don't know for an absolute certainty that Masterson worked with these particular clients, but combined with everything else we know, it's as good of a lead as we can expect, so we're going to move accordingly."

She drank from a bottle of water before continuing: "Under our theory, Masterson would be familiar with these women and their personal lives. He knew they lived alone, and he presumably wouldn't appear to be a threat to any of his victims, so gaining access wouldn't be a problem."

"Except for Ms. Young," Barclay said.

"Yeah, that is a bit of a mystery, but we can set that aside for now. Lucy Young is the only person that we know of who saw our killer, and she described Franklin Masterson." She rapped a knuckle on the photograph on the whiteboard. "What are we missing?"

The room was silent for several seconds as everyone worked through everything.

Barclay said, "What's the connection to Sam Albritton? There has to be one, right?"

For the first time since leaving the law office, Beck deflated a little. "I didn't even think about that."

Barclay pulled his phone out of his inside jacket pocket. "Let me call Lawrence Brannon." He fished the business card out of his pants pocket and dialed his direct line. He put the phone on speaker, and they all stared at it.

"Hello, Lawrence Brannon."

"Hello, Mr. Brannon, this is Barclay Griffith."

"Yes, Barclay. Say, that was quick. Did you think of something else?"

"I did, actually. Sam Albritton. Was he a client of your firm?"

"Let me check." The sound of his office chair rolling across the plastic floor protector was followed by typing and more mouse clicks. "Yes, he was."

"Who was his attorney?"

"That's interesting. Tim Lansing was his lawyer."

That got silent fist pumps and celebrations around the table.

"Thank You, Lawrence."

Lawrence Brannon cleared his throat. "Mr. Griffith, I have a respected law firm with twenty-three employees. Is there something I should know?"

The man was smart, Barclay thought.

"Mr. Griffith, you there?"

"Yeah, I'm still here. There isn't anything I can share quite yet, but rest assured, if there is something we believe you need to know, we will tell you."

It was Lawrence's turn to be silent. He finally said, "I'm trusting you here, Mr. Griffith."

"Thank you, Lawrence. Your trust is not misplaced."

When Barclay ended the call, they all let out sounds of celebration.

SEVENTY-TWO

Lawrence Brannon set his cell phone on his expansive desk and thought of his call just now with the district attorney. "What am I missing?" the big lawyer said to the empty room.

He tugged on his bottom lip before spinning to face his computer. He pulled up the client files for the three dead women and Sam Albritton. After almost twenty minutes of scanning through the files, he had a thought: *Tim Lansing wasn't the only common denominator with those clients. Franklin Masterson's name was also sprinkled throughout.*

Lawrence Brannon began his career as so many lawyers had—as a prosecutor. His route was slightly different in that he was an Assistant United States Attorney for three years before heading to private practice rather than cutting his legal teeth in a local DA's office. He learned a lot about deductive reasoning and how police investigate crimes. How they view evidence, how they think.

He thought about Tim Lansing. Divorced, no children; married to the job; billed the most hours in the firm. In short, the man was always working. He didn't have time to kill.

The fact that he was even having this internal dialogue caused an involuntary shiver.

Then, he considered Franklin Masterson and the question the DA asked about young lawyers working with their senior counterparts. As he thought about things, he realized that neither the DA nor the detective seemed at all interested in Tim Lansing. Come to think of it, thought Brannon, the detective got quite upset with him for not revealing other lawyers who had worked with Freida Nelson, Elise Hightower, and Dorothy Young.

Could that mean...

After thinking it over for several minutes, he thought, *Damnit, I have an office and employees to worry about.*

He punched a number into the desk phone, and after two rings, it was answered: "Yes, Lawrence?"

"Come to my office, will you?"

Less than a minute later, Tim Lansing walked in. "Close the door, Tim." Lansing closed the door and sat across from his boss.

"You're close with Franklin, aren't you?"

Tim shrugged. "I suppose so, sure. I mean, it's not like we spend much time together outside the office, but we work pretty closely here."

"But you helped with his uncle's estate, didn't you? And you work with him a lot and he with you, right?"

"Yes. As I said, we work closely together. And yes, I helped him when his uncle died—helped with the sale of his house, anyway. He was new and didn't know anyone. Is there something wrong? Did I mess something up?"

"Oh no. Nothing like that. It's just...have you noticed anything about him lately?"

"What do you mean?"

Brannon was walking a tightrope of his own with his words and struggling. "Has he seemed...distracted or...I don't know...has he acted differently over the last few weeks?"

"I thought I saw the DA walk past my office earlier. Was he here asking about Franklin?"

The big man's eyes went wide, but he caught himself. "I'm afraid I've been sworn to secrecy about what was discussed."

"You know, Lawrence...never mind."

Lawrence leaned forward, the desktop pressing into his girth. "If you know something, just say it."

"No, it's nothing like that. I was just going to ask if you want me to keep an eye out for anything."

"Yes. Yes, that's good." Brannon reeled himself back in. "Let me know if anything, you know...seems...off with him.

———

TIM LANSING WENT BACK to his office and closed the door. He knew this was inevitable. Getting away with any crime, let alone murder, in this day and age was almost impossible, yet the truth was he *had* gotten away with it.

He didn't know what had brought the police to the offices of Brannon and Harris, but here they were. He always knew, or at least hoped, they would wind up here because that's where the evidence led. He made certain of that. It is, after all, where everything connected like a complicated knot.

Even before Frieda Nelson's murder, he had been planning for this eventuality, and now he had to trust the police would follow the trail he had created just like they had followed the evidence back to this law firm.

He would do as his boss asked. The irony was that Lawrence Brannon needn't have asked him to keep tabs on Franklin Masterson because from the moment he saw Barclay Griffith walking the halls of the law firm, Franklin Masterson became Tim Lansing's next project.

It was time to implement his exit strategy.

SEVENTY-THREE

Fitz informed the group that Franklin Masterson had not only viewed but also liked every Facebook live broadcast by Wendy Wade reporting on the murders.

Beck said, "That's got to be enough for a warrant, right?" She looked almost pleadingly at Barclay.

Barclay weighed the question he had already been going over in his mind. "I'd feel a whole lot better about a warrant if we had some manner of physical evidence tying him to the murders. Right now it's all circumstantial—" He held up his hand at the protest he knew Beck was about to lob. "You know I'm not scared of a circumstantial case. I've prosecuted and convicted on circumstantial evidence, you know that. But this is capital murder. The jury is going to want something beyond the fact that he was their lawyer and he liked some Facebook posts."

"But we have an ID," she pleaded.

"An ID from someone who can't take the stand. The identification most likely comes in via the nine-one-one call as a business record and possibly an excited utterance, but, again, this is a capital case—a death penalty case—and you never know what a judge is going to do in an effort to protect the defendant. If that ID goes away—and I agree it's pretty damn compelling—but if it goes away, what are we left with?"

Beck opened her mouth to speak, but she had nothing. She crossed her arms and stared at Barclay.

"We have him on lockdown, right, Chief?" said Barclay.

Greenhaw nodded. "He's not going anywhere without us knowing about it."

"Tell you what, I'll go to a judge for a search warrant. I believe we have more than enough for that. We'll grab his computers and cell phone, search his house, and see what we find. We find anything, and I mean anything of value, and I'll authorize an arrest warrant. We cannot afford to move too quickly or to get it wrong."

Beck reluctantly agreed. "How soon can we get a search warrant?"

"We need to make sure the warrant is airtight. You and Fitz have a handle on everything that ties Masterson to these murders. Put it all together, and I'll review it. We'll be pushing it to have it to a judge today, so maybe we should plan on a search early tomorrow morning."

"Tomorrow morning?" Beck shot back.

"We don't need to rush this. This warrant will take some time to put together, and we'll need a special master in place before we execute it. Since we're petitioning the court to search his work computer, that's a whole other issue due to privilege and client confidentiality. We have to be ready when we walk into that law office asking to take law firm property. We can't afford to get into a long, drawn-out legal battle with Brannon and his partners.

"We do this half-ass or go in unprepared, and we risk walking out without the property, which could be critical to our case. That happens, and then Masterson knows we're on to him. Who knows what happens then."

"He's right," said Greenhaw. "You've done incredible work on this case, Detective Lawson. Now is not the time to let your emotions get in the way. He's not going anywhere, and he's not going to hurt anyone else. Not while we're watching him."

Beck said, "What's our drop dead time today? When would you say we need the warrant signed and the special master in place to execute the warrants today?"

"I don't know. I'd say 4:30 this afternoon for sure. Depending on the judge, I may be able to get it done after hours, maybe as late as 9:00 or so, but we shouldn't count on that."

"Just don't give up on today," she said. "Not yet."

Greenhaw stood up and said, "I think now is a good time for a break. It's almost lunchtime, anyway. Detective, you and Fitz get to work on that warrant. Barclay, can you work on that special master you mentioned?" Barclay nodded. "Alright, I'll make sure we're getting eyes on our guy. It's coming together."

SEVENTY-FOUR

Franklin Masterson lived in a sprawling single-story house on three acres. He'd purchased it almost two years ago as a fixer-upper. It was his hobby turned passion project when he wasn't working, which he always seemed to be doing. His uncle, Sam Albritton, was a skilled craftsman, and Franklin always supposed his mother, Sam's sister, had passed him the woodworking gene. Franklin never knew his father growing up, so his uncle Sam had filled that role, and the work he was doing in this house was a kind of homage to the man. Hardly a day went by that he didn't wish he'd held onto all the tools his uncle had accumulated over the years. At the time, he couldn't bear the thought of keeping them, and now he was struggling, knowing he had gotten rid of them.

It was after 7:30 in the evening, and Franklin was reviewing documents in his study—well-appointed, masculine, and all his handiwork—when there was a knock at his door. Franklin picked his cell phone up off the desk and checked the time. He laid the phone back down and went to the door, where Tim Lansing stood on the porch.

Lansing was shorter than Franklin. He was thin but in a way that attested to a disciplined lifestyle. His longish blonde hair spilled out from under a black Brooks running cap, curling at his collar, and sinewy arms hung from the black Under Armour t-shirt he wore over black Vuori joggers. His fluorescent yellow running shoes gave him the appearance of an uncapped high-lighter.

Franklin took in his fellow attorney and said, "Tim, what's going on? We didn't have a meeting scheduled, did we?" Masterson was further confused as he looked past Lansing and didn't see a vehicle.

He was about to ask him about it when Tim said, "No. I just thought I would stop by. Lawrence talked to me about you today, and I thought you should know."

"Lawrence? What about?"

"Mind if I come in? Talk inside?"

"Yeah, sure, come on in." Franklin turned his back on Tim to lead the way to the den, and just as Tim had done to Dorothy Young, he was on Franklin in a flash. Unlike with Dorothy Young, however, Tim came prepared with more than a fist to subdue his quarry. He threw his arm around Franklin's neck and jammed a Taser into the man's lower back for the entire five-second cycle.

Franklin was weary and pliable but not out. Tim dropped him to the ground, went to the kitchen to grab a chair, and brought it back to where Franklin lay and Tim hit him with another five-second ride.

When Franklin was fully back, he was secured to a wooden chair with climbing rope wrapped around his chest. His hands were bound behind the chair back with a zip tie around his wrists cushioned by a kitchen towel—Tim did not want evidence of the restraints left behind. Each ankle was zip-tied to a chair leg—also cushioned by a towel.

"What the hell, Tim! What's going on?"

Tim sat in front of Franklin on the edge of the couch, an open backpack on the floor to his right. "You've done some very bad things, Frank. Very bad. And the police are going to find out about it."

"What? What are you talking about?" He began to rock his chair back and forth and struggled against his bindings.

"Save your strength, Frank."

"What the *fuck*, Tim!"

"Shhhhh. I'm going to tell you a story. Remember when your uncle Sam died, and you asked me to help with his estate? I understood you were a little emotional about things, and I was happy to help. I helped negotiate the sale of the house to that young couple. In his workshop, tucked in a back corner behind some equipment, was a safe.

"It wasn't large, maybe twelve by eight by eight, and I decided to take it before the sale of the house closed. I was curious about what was in it, so I looked up the model of the safe online and found that it took a six-digit combination. Interestingly, only four numbers on the keypad showed wear. I went through his personal details, and when I saw it, I knew immediately what the combination was—I got it on the first try. It was three, two, zero, four, two, zero—the last six digits of his social security number."

Tim reached into his backpack and pulled out a manila envelope. He undid the clasp at the top, opened it, and pulled out five polaroids. For the first time, Franklin noticed Tim wearing black latex gloves.

"What are those?"

Tim fanned them out like a deck of cards. They were facing Franklin, who leaned in and squinted. "I need my glasses."

"Oh," said Tim, looking around the floor. He picked them up and placed them on Franklin's face, who flipped his hair back to clear the curl that had flopped over his left eye.

Franklin could see more clearly but still leaned in. Then Tim saw it: recognition. Franklin made a horrified face and pulled back. "Wha...? What are those pictures?" He looked at Tim and said, "My aunt was killed like that."

"We'll get to that. For now, though, you need to know that I found these in your uncle's safe."

"His safe? I don't understand what you're saying." Franklin continued to shake his head in confusion. "Wait, are you saying my uncle killed those women? And those pictures are, what, souvenirs?" After a beat, his face clouded over. "My aunt was killed like that. Are you saying my uncle is this...killer? That he did all of...all of *that*?"

"The pictures are souvenirs, alright, but dear uncle Sam didn't kill these women." Confusion played across Franklin's face. "Your aunt Claire did."

Franklin threw his head back and stared at the ceiling before bringing it back down. "No way. She was a victim, too. How could she have been both the killer and the victim of the killer?"

Tim reached into the large envelope and pulled out a trifold letter on lined notebook paper. "This is a letter written by your uncle. I'll let you read it, but the long and short of it is that your uncle found these Polaroids tucked away in your aunt's underwear drawer. He immediately recognized these women as people he had done work for, and, as you can see, it's pretty clear they were murdered. He confronted Claire about it, and she admitted to murdering those women."

An uncomprehending look clouded Franklin's face. "Here, let me just let you read it," said Tim. He unfolded the letter and separated the pages. He held up the first page. "Let me know when you're done, and I'll put up the next page."

SEVENTY-FIVE
JULY 19, 1999

S am Albritton carried the old, open-topped wooden toolbox that had once belonged to his father to his and Claire's bedroom. The toolbox was worn smooth and shiny with age and held a small cadre of household tools: a hammer, wrenches, screwdrivers, a measuring tape, a boxcutter, and a scrap of sandpaper. He was home on his lunch break and wanted to surprise his wife by fixing the dresser drawer that had begun to stick—a handyman always neglected the things that needed fixing in his own home.

He set the toolbox on the carpet next to the antique dresser that had belonged to his grandmother and went to work. It took some effort to pull out the top drawer, which was what he was here to fix, and after shimmying the drawer out, he dumped its contents on the bed. He took the sandpaper and rubbed down the edges and the underside of the drawer. He sanded a little, tried the drawer, and sanded a little more. He continued this over the next few minutes until the drawer slid easily into place.

With the drawer no longer sticking, he began transferring his wife's underwear from the bed to the drawer. Upon carrying the second batch, something fell to the floor. He placed the underwear in the drawer and bent down to pick up what he believed to be a pair of pantyhose. Only when he picked them up did he discover something square and stiff inside. He reached inside the stockings and removed five Polaroid pictures.

At first, he didn't know what he was looking at. However, after flipping through them four times, he began feeling disgusted with what he saw. Then it hit him where he'd found the pictures.

"Why do you have these?" he said out loud as he numbly cycled through the pictures.

"They're my trophies."

Sam Albritton spun around, the photos slipping from his hands and falling to the floor in the process; his wife of twenty-two years stood in the doorway. All he could do was stare at her, uncomprehending anything of the last sixty seconds.

He slowly bent down and picked up each of the photographs. "I'm not sure I understand. Why do you have these awful pictures?"

She stepped into the room and said, "They're...souvenirs, I guess you could say."

Sam shook his head, uncomprehending. "Trophies? Souvenirs...for what? I don't...did you...?"

A beat passed, then: "Yes, Sam, I killed those women."

Standing there looking at her, he wasn't sure what bothered him more. That she killed these women or that she seemed to take some measure of joy in that fact. In that instant, he felt he was no longer looking at his wife but a monster.

"Sam, say something, will you? Please?"

There was a long pause before Sam was able to choke out, "Why?"

She looked past her husband to where the ceiling met the far wall before finally meeting his gaze and said, "I guess I kill for the same reason any serial killer does...I'm just wired wrong."

Sam absently tossed the pictures onto the bed and moved toward his wife as he said, "You're not...wired wrong. There's nothing *wrong* with you, Claire. I know you. You're not...this person you think you are."

For the first time, Sam believed he saw some hint of emotion —the slightest vestige of contrition or regret—as her eyes softened.

As he reached out to her, she said, "Just because I'm a woman doesn't mean I can't be evil." Then: "Please don't look at me like that, Sam. I have urges, and when I satisfy them, I feel good. I feel complete."

When he didn't respond, she said, "I've been at this for almost three years now and nothing. Nothing from the police, nothing on the news, not so much as the hint of suspicion whatsoever. It's as if I have been ordained to do this."

"Ordained?" Sam stared at his wife with a combination of pity, disappointment, and fear as he stood there, his hands gripping her limp upper arms. Everything he thought he knew about his wife had been shattered in an instant. He wanted to shake her but said, "Well, now you're going to stop, right?" A tear leaked from his left eye, running over the stubble on his jaw before turning under and running down his neck.

"Oh, Sam," she said, putting a hand on his damp cheek and using her thumb to cut the tear off under his eye. "I can't."

"I love you, Claire, but what about those women? People are dead because of you. Real people. Mothers, grandmothers, people that I knew and liked. People who helped us put food on our table. I'm concerned about how many others could die because of you. I need to know you're done. Now. Today. It's over. Tell me that, at least."

It was her turn to look at him with her own version of pity, and she said, "I don't know that I'll ever be *done*. I don't expect you to understand, but it's who I am. I love what we have together, but it just isn't enough. I do these things—"

"These things!" Sam shot back. "These things? By *these things*, you mean your murders, right? You kill to make yourself feel... alive?"

All he could feel was a deep sense of guilt and responsibility for her actions. This wasn't just someone else's problem—it was now his too. And he knew he had to do whatever it took to stop her, even if it meant turning her in and facing the consequences himself. He couldn't let her harm anyone else.

He needed to sit, and he found the side of the bed. He placed his head in his hands, elbows on his knees. He finally raised his head and said, "I can't let you do this to anyone else. You murder another person, and it's as if I did it myself."

"Don't be ridiculous, Sam. You didn't do anything. I'm the broken one, not you." But her words fell on deaf ears as Sam realized he couldn't live with the guilt and fear of knowing what she was capable of.

Sam Albritton wasn't aware of what he was doing until he had already done it. He sprung from the mattress, wrapped a hand around his wife's throat, and pushed her—hard—slamming her head into the door frame with a dull thud. She went limp but stayed up because he had her pinned with his hand around her neck.

He quickly pulled his hand away when he realized what he'd done, and she dropped where she stood, like a marionette with its strings cut. He stared at her piled upon herself, legs and neck askew. He bent down on a knee and examined her closer. He stroked her cheek and said, "My God, what have I done." The tears came. "I'm sorry. I'm so very sorry."

He eventually stood up and stared at the lifeless heap. Then he turned to the bed and the pictures that lay scattered across the floral duvet. His hands began to shake as he knew what he needed to do. He dropped down onto the side of the bed and reached for the ivory telephone. He picked it up off the cradle, triggering the dial tone. He turned the handset over, and the illuminated keypad stared back at him. He sat there so long that the dial tone was replaced with a loud, intermittent noise from the phone being off the hook.

He pressed the button on the handset, hanging the phone up, then released it, the dial tone coming through the earpiece once more. He pressed the nine with his thumb, holding it a beat longer than necessary. He then pressed the one. As his thumb hovered over the one, he glanced at the floor and the polaroids that were lying haphazardly in a small pile—three facing up and two facing down. He stared at them for several seconds before looking back at his thumb above the one on the keypad. He looked back at the photographs, then back at the phone.

He slowly moved the handset back to the base and hung up the phone. He then gathered up the photos and slid them into his pocket. He picked up his wife and then laid her on the bed. He removed a photograph and compared it to his wife lying there.

He put the picture back in his pocket and knelt beside his toolbox. He removed a few tools and set them on the carpet until he found what he was looking for. He thumbed open the boxcutter's blade and looked at it. Then he looked at his wife.

He stood and walked over to the bedside. His trembling hand held the blade over her neck, and he began to cry. He placed the blade to her neck, dimpling the flesh with the point, then pulled it back. More tears flowed as he put the blade back to her neck. He was unable to make his shaking hand work to do what needed to be done. He extended the blade further with his thumb.

Tears blurred his vision, and he wiped them with the sleeve of his left arm. He sniffed, said, "I'm sorry," and plunged the blade into her neck. A small spurt of blood escaped, then more of a flow of blood as he pulled the sharp blade across the neck, the skin parting like a plow being drug through damp earth.

He went to the backyard and began to rinse the boxcutter under the faucet mounted to the house. He was rubbing away the blood when he began to vomit until there was nothing left but a dry heave. He forced himself back to the running tap and finished washing the boxcutter. Next, he rinsed off his hands and then rinsed out his mouth.

He went back inside, back into the bedroom, and without looking at his wife's body or the large, bloody *A* on the headboard, he gathered his tools from the floor and placed them in the ancient toolbox.

He carried the toolbox through the house and stopped in the kitchen, placing it on the wood tabletop. He went to the kitchen drawer under the telephone hanging on the wall and pulled out a few pages of loose-leaf notebook paper. He grabbed a Bic pen from a worn paper Krystal cup tacked to the wall beside the telephone, sat at the table, and began to write.

He wrote down exactly what happened. He explained how he found the pictures and what they depicted. He wrote about confronting his wife and what she said she had done. He tried as best he could to write down everything she said just as she had said it. He confessed to killing her, not intentionally, then staging her body to make it appear as if she were a victim of the same killer who had taken the lives of at least five others.

He wrote that the purpose of the letter was so that if someone were to be accused of these murders after he died, he wanted to make sure the truth would be told. In the last line of the letter, he apologized for being a coward and not going to the police or letting the family of his wife's victims know the truth about what happened to them.

He folded the four-page letter three times and carried it to the workshop. After placing the toolbox on a shelf, he went to his safe and punched in the combination. He placed the polaroids and the letter inside and closed the door. He picked up the safe and tucked it behind his bandsaw.

In truth—he would later admit to himself— the reason he didn't go to the police or tell anyone about his wife, whom he still loved, was that, despite everything, he did not want her legacy to be as a murderer.

SEVENTY-SIX

PRESENT DAY

Franklin sat dazed, his tear-streaked face awash in confusion and heartbreak. His reading of the letter complete, he dropped his chin to his chest and sobbed.

Finally, he lifted his head, sniffed, and said, "What does all of that have to do with me? I read the damn letter. Just tell me why you're here."

"You're my exit plan, Frank. You have to die so that I can live." Seeing that his captive still didn't understand, Tim said, "The police figured out how all three of my victims were connected. They were all clients of the firm. More to the point, they were our clients. Yours and mine. Well, mine more than yours, but it's not going to matter."

"What?"

"I'm getting there. Anyway, I knew it was only a matter of time before they showed up there—it's a small town—and when I saw the DA this morning, I knew the time had come. I couldn't risk it another day."

Franklin was shaking his head. "Nothing that you're saying is making any sense."

"Don't you see? They made the connection. They were at the office today. If I just let things play out, they may eventually realize you didn't kill those women, and the false flags I planted would have been for naught. With their minds free to roam, who knows where they would take the investigation? I can't take that risk, so I need you to go."

"Wait, wait, wait. False flags?"

"That's right. The police need to believe you're their man so I laid for them a trail that will bring them right to you. Not too obvious, of course. You are an intelligent attorney who wouldn't be so careless.

"The first thing I did was put a meeting with Freida Nelson into your calendar for the night of the murder. Then, after the murder, I went back to the office and deleted it. No doubt they'll do a forensic analysis on your computer and see the deleted calendar entry. I did the same thing with Elise Hightower. I suspect they'll reach the proper conclusion that you scheduled an appointment with your victims as a guise to get inside their homes. Then, after you murdered them, you deleted the calendar entry, not realizing the police could recover that information."

"How did you access my computer? You know my password?"

Tim shook his head. "You taped your computer login credentials underneath your keyboard. I noticed it there ages ago for reasons I can't remember, but you made it way too easy."

"So that's it? You think they'll see those deleted appointments and assume I'm the killer?"

"Once you're dead, the evidence against you won't be questioned. Law enforcement shows up at your office asking questions about a string of murders—your clients no less—and that night, you take your own life. Just another distraught murderer taking the easy way out. They'll be all too happy to clear these cases."

"But it still seems weak." Franklin couldn't figure out how he was going to get out of this, so he tried talking with his captor. Drag it out as long as possible, and...who knows?

Tim smiled and held up a finger. "You see, I also had your Facebook login—you really shouldn't use the same password for everything—and watched and liked Facebook posts, news articles, and live broadcasts as you. It's nothing major, but still pretty good, I think. It's the subtlety of it all that makes it so clever. Just one more piece of the puzzle to justify their conclusions."

"But I rarely used Facebook, and, like you said, they'll analyze my electronics. They'll see I never logged into Facebook on that phone."

"Ah," said Tim, "but there won't be a phone for them to find." He reached into his backpack and retrieved an iPhone in a bulky gray Otterbox case. Franklin recognized it instantly as his phone. "While you were out, I hunted for it and found it on the desk in your home office."

"Won't they find my missing phone suspicious?"

A shrug. "Minor detail. But compared to everything else? They won't spend any time on it."

He then reached into his backpack and pulled out three Polaroids. He held them up for Franklin to see, and recognition bloomed on his face as he saw the three dead women Tim had killed and finally understood the significance. They *were* his clients. He had helped these women with tax and estate legal matters. Franklin squeezed his eyes shut as if trying to keep the images from imprinting themselves on his mind.

Tim said, "When police find these pictures in your house, that'll be it for the investigation. There is simply no way someone other than the killer would have these. Game. Set. Match."

"That easy?"

"That easy."

"So, what now? You kill me?" Franklin said somewhat facetiously.

Tim nodded. "Now I kill you." He stood and got to Franklin in a single stride, stuck the Taser into the man's ribs, and pulled the trigger.

SEVENTY-SEVEN

It was nearing 8:00 in the evening, and Beck was finishing her second revision of the search warrant. According to Barclay, they were almost there but not quite. As frustrated as she was about the rejections, she knew this was the prosecutor's realm, so she dutifully went back to work.

Barclay had secured a special master, a local civil defense attorney named Luke Jackson. He was a friend of Barclay's whose reputation was beyond reproach. He agreed to be available whenever he was needed.

Beck printed the revised search warrant and ran it into Barclay's office, where he was arranging his fantasy football lineup for the upcoming weekend slate of NFL games. He took the warrant, read through it, and pronounced it ready. He closed his laptop and called a judge on his cell. The judge agreed to see them, so he, Beck, and Fitz left the DA's office en route to the judge's home.

Two separate search teams had already been organized, and according to the SWAT commander, the teams "were sitting on G and waiting on O." When they had the signed search warrant,

Beck notified the chief, who relayed word to the search teams to set out. One group went to the law firm, and one set out for Franklin Masterson's home.

Barclay suggested hitting the residence first—it would be far cleaner than raiding a law firm.

The raid team's rally point was an empty office complex three miles from the Masterson residence. They went over the plan: who was going to breach the front and who was going to breach the rear; who was going in first in the front and who was going in first in the rear; what the warrant authorized them to search for, and where they were allowed to search.

When that was done, the fifteen-person team set out in four blacked-out SUVs.

A Google Maps satellite view of the property showed that approaching undetected could be problematic because the house was set so far off the road. Once the convoy got within a half mile of the property, they extinguished their headlights and moved quickly and nimbly up the long dirt road leading to the house using night vision. Two vehicles broke off in the front while two continued to the rear, bodies leaping from the SUVs before they reached a complete stop.

The SWAT team member designated first-in banged on the door with a gloved fist and announced, "Police, search warrant, open up!"

Getting no response, he signaled the breacher forward. A man wearing all black raced up the porch steps in a crouch and holding a battering ram. He pulled it back and slammed it into the door beside the doorknob, and the door and jamb splintered as they separated. The lead SWAT member kicked the partially open door, creating a gap wide enough for them all to pour in, yelling, "Police, search warrant," over and over.

The front breaching team met the team entering from the rear, and they began clearing the house. A voice from the back of the house yelled, "Stand down. Stand down. We have a body."

Someone from inside radioed outside, announcing the residence was secure. That was the cue to Beck, Fitz, and Barclay that it was safe for them to enter.

A group had gathered in Masterson's bedroom. There was a body in the bed slumped to the side, blood and brain matter up the headboard and wall where he had shot himself. The gun, a silver revolver, lay on the bed near where the body was bent at the waist.

The odor of cordite and blood hung in the air. Franklin Masterson had shot himself. Within an hour or so, they guessed.

Beck's first call was to Chief Greenhaw, and her second was to Angie Presley about dispatching a CSI team to the residence.

Barclay called Lawrence Brannon and told him what they had found in Masterson's home and that a team was posted outside his law firm awaiting entry to serve the search warrant. Barclay assured him they only needed Franklin's computer—for now—and Luke Jackson, who Lawrence knew well, had been appointed special master and would review the computer's files first, only passing along anything he deemed pertinent to the investigation. Lawrence was also assured that if Luke found something believed to be germane but bordered on privilege, he would withhold that from law enforcement and allow a judge to sort it out.

The room cleared of SWAT personnel, and Beck moved about, viewing the scene from various angles as she waited for the crime scene team to arrive.

———

ANGIE ENTERED the den wearing blue latex gloves, her DSLR hanging around her neck, and carrying clear evidence bags. She approached Beck, who was sitting in a recliner. "I thought you'd want these." The detective stood and took the evidence bags being offered.

There were three bags, and inside each was a Polaroid. Beck had seen them lying on the bed but had been unable to view them with any scrutiny because she didn't want to handle them before they could be photographed in situ.

She pressed the photographs against the plastic to get a clear view of what they depicted. Fitz and Barclay looked over her shoulder.

"It's Hightower, Young, and Nelson," she said as she shuffled through the bags. "Guessing he wanted to re-live the murders one last time before killing himself."

"Sick bastard," said Fitz.

"Fucking coward," said Barclay.

———

THE NEXT DAY Beck called Fitz, who put the phone on speaker for the benefit of Barclay, whose office he was sitting in. She said, "Computer analysis is back."

"And?" said Barclay when she didn't continue.

"And the only thing we've got are two deleted calendar appointments."

"How does that help us?"

"The appointments were for Nelson and Hightower both on the nights they were murdered. The entry for Nelson was deleted at 11:14 PM the night she was killed, and the entry for Hightower was deleted at 10:35 the night she was murdered."

Fitz said, "This confirms our theory on how he got into the house. Then he goes back and deletes the appointments, so if anyone comes around asking, there's nothing to find."

Barclay said, "Nothing about an appointment with Dorothy Young on the night she died?"

"Nope," said Beck. "That would explain the violent entry into the Young house; he didn't have an easy way in like he did with the first two. It also seems to confirm our theory that her murder was a last-second decision. She knew him enough to open the door for him, but he wasn't invited in for whatever reason."

After a beat, she said, "Oh, I can't believe I almost forgot this. We still have people at Masterson's going over the house and property. They found an envelope containing Sam Albritton business cards between the mattress and box spring. They're identical to those found at the other crime scenes."

"But we still don't know the connection with Albritton," said Fitz. "What is so significant about that man?"

They discussed this for a few minutes, with none of them having any plausible explanation.

As if to put a bow on the conversation, Beck said, "Gentlemen, I do believe we have our man."

EPILOGUE

The next seven months passed quietly without another murder—serial or otherwise—and the case against Franklin Masterson had been presented to a grand jury and exceptionally cleared with a no bill due to the death of the suspect.

Barclay entered the lobby of the district attorney's office, his head down, reading a forensic report he had just been given by a defense attorney who claimed it exonerated her client.

The receptionist said, "This came in the mail to you, Mr. Griffith."

He looked up and saw a large yellow padded envelope sitting on the corner of the desk. He grabbed it, looked it over, pressed on the lump toward the bottom, and carried it to his office.

Barclay laid the package on his desk before going into the restroom in his office.

He sat down at his desk and checked his voicemail. He had two messages, and he returned both calls.

He opened his laptop and noticed the envelope. He closed the computer, reached for the envelope, and ran a silver letter opener under the fold. He poured the contents of the envelope onto his desk blotter. The first item to drop out gave him pause, but the last item to tumble out froze his blood.

He yelled for Fitz to come to his office, and then he called Detective Beck Lawson.

———

BECK WAS SLIGHTLY out of breath when she crossed the threshold of Barclay's office. Barclay was seated behind his desk, where she noticed a number of clear evidence bags strewn across it. He was staring at his computer screen, and Fitz was leaning against the wall, staring at the floor.

They both looked up when she walked in.

She was about to speak when Barclay said, "Come look at this."

She stood beside Fitz as all three looked at the screen when Barclay hit the spacebar, causing the video on his screen to play.

The first thing you noticed when watching the video was the date—April 14, 2022—a date everyone in local law enforcement had burned in their collective minds. That was the date Towne County Sheriff's Deputy Hunter Stanton was gunned down in the parking lot of Walter's Gas and Grub.

According to the video's time stamp, he only had three more minutes to live.

They watched the video in stunned silence until the shots were fired against Deputy Stanton when Beck gasped. This was her first time seeing the video, and the shock she registered mirrored that of Barclay and Fitz upon their first viewing.

"Okay," Beck said, stepping back. "What the hell is that?" Seeing the looks from the DA and his investigator, she said, "I mean, I know what it is, but...what is it?"

Barclay said, "Grab a chair."

———

MONTHS HAD PASSED since the night I killed Franklin Masterson. Everything fell into place better than I could have expected. Before the week was out, they were standing in a room full of cameras and reporters proclaiming they had solved the recent spate of killings and the person responsible was dead by his own hand.

As with every case, the news cycle ran its course, although this one lasted a little longer than usual. Pretty soon, I began to fill an emptiness. In giving up Masterson, I destroyed my secret—my primary reason for killing.

However, my first kill awakened in me something I didn't realize I needed and now was having trouble living without.

I knew I couldn't kill—not right now—but I needed...something. The power of my secret was gone, taken away by the belief that another man, Franklin Masterson, was responsible for the murders—my murders.

I made a decision.

I knew it was a risk, but the emptiness needed to be filled.

———

"ALL OF THIS"—BARCLAY waved a hand over the evidence bags —"came to me in the mail today. The video you just watched was on a thumb drive from the envelope. I had Fitz burn the contents to a new drive before securing the original in evidence."

He picked up a bag containing a thick black plastic rectangle. "This, we believe, is going to be Hunter Stanton's body camera, the one that the shooter took off him. It even has blood on it. We'll get it sent off for DNA, but it'll be Stanton's."

Beck said, "I didn't see anything on the video on first look, but—"

Barclay shook his head and said, "Nope. We've watched it maybe a dozen times and even gone frame by frame. The only thing we know about the shooter is that they're white with dark hair."

"Dark hair?" said Beck. "But Ross Burlington was a blonde, like white blonde."

"Yep," said Fitz, "and daddy Jed was bald."

"So Ross didn't kill Stanton."

"And probably didn't kill his father either," added Fitz.

"That's not all," said Barclay. He leaned forward, picked up an evidence bag, and dropped it. He did this a couple of times until he found what he was looking for. He tossed two bags at Beck, one hitting the desk with a clunk. "Recognize those."

She picked up the two bags, turned them over, and said, "What...the fuck."

"Meet Franklin Masterson. Or at least who we were supposed to believe was Franklin Masterson."

Inside one of the bags was a pair of clubmaster-style eyeglasses identical to those worn by Masterson. In the other bag was a large gold collegiate class ring.

"But was Masterson wearing his glasses when he...when we found him."

Barclay nodded.

"Then what..."

"Copies," said Barclay

"Copies? The glasses do look identical, but what about the ring?" Beck asked, still turning over the bags in her hands.

"The glasses are identical, right down to the brand. We don't believe the ring is, though," said Fitz. "This ring is from Texas Tech, and we know Masterson graduated from Wake Forest."

Barclay said, "The eyeglasses had to be right, but the ring didn't need to match exactly. It was small enough that as long as it was generally the right size and color, anyone seeing it from a distance wouldn't know the difference."

"But why?" she asked.

"Fitz," said Barclay.

"The way we see it is that Masterson was set up. We don't know how or by whom, but he was set up by someone pretty damned meticulous. Masterson was going to be the patsy if it came down to it, and the real killer thought of everything all the way down to the possibility of being noticed by someone."

"Lucy Young saw exactly what the killer wanted her to see," said Beck absently.

"That's not all," said Barclay. He flipped two more bags to her.

"What's this?" she asked, picking them up. The first was obvious: a Sam Albritton business card. Holding up the second bag, she said, "And this?"

Barclay handed her some papers. "That bag contains a four-page letter written by Sam Albritton. Fitz photographed the pages before bagging the letter. He then printed them out. Go ahead and give it a read. It's a doozy."

"Dear God," she said when she was done. He tossed her the last of the evidence bags, and she picked them up—five bags containing five polaroids. She examined them. "Don't tell me."

———

I DIDN'T PARTICULARLY WANT to part with Claire Albritton's trophies, but I had parted with mine to sell Franklin Masterson as the killer, and I hadn't missed them like I thought I would. I had no further use for any of the other stuff and knew they could only cause me grave problems if they were found, so I threw all of it in an envelope, wearing gloves, of course, and drove to a small county post office in Georgia and dropped it in a roadside mailbox.

As I said before, it's only good to be the only one in on a secret if everyone knows the secret exists.

So, on the way back from mailing the envelope, I stopped at another Dollar General in a rural Georgia town and purchased a disposable cell phone. I texted Wendy Wade to alert her that Ross Burlington and Franklin Masterson weren't murderers, and the police knew it and had evidence proving as much. Then, just as I did the last time, I ditched the phone.

Without Masterson's Facebook account and no scapegoat needed—for now—I created a fake account. When Wendy Wade went live with the news that the killings of Deputy Hunter Stanton, Freida Nelson, Elise Hightower, and Dorothy Young were all now classified as open and unsolved, I'd be right there watching, feeling full, knowing I had my secret back once again.

THANK YOU FOR READING

I would greatly appreciate it if you would take a moment to leave a review on Amazon, Goodreads, or wherever you purchased this book.

Email me at brandon@brandonhughesbooks.com and visit BrandonHughesBooks.com. Sign up for updates regarding my next novel.

I look forward to hearing from you.

Leave a review on Amazon

Leave a review on Goodreads

ACKNOWLEDGMENTS

A heartfelt thank you to Steve and Liz McPhaul—your insightful edits and suggestions truly made this book better. And to Libba Harris, for your unwavering support and thoughtful feedback—I'm deeply grateful.

ABOUT THE AUTHOR

Brandon Hughes brings two decades of experience in the criminal justice system to craft authentic crime stories. He utilizes his real-world knowledge to expertly weave gripping crime narratives and skillfully invites readers into the intricate realm of criminal investigations with captivating authenticity. Criminal cases he has handled have been featured on numerous television programs. The Alabama Press Association awarded him Best Sports News In-Depth Coverage.

When he isn't writing, Brandon enjoys cooking and reading. He and his wife, Karen, live with their yellow lab, Poppy, in Auburn, Alabama.

Other novels by Brandon:
    The Hero Rule
    The 4th Prisoner
    The Red Room: A Dark Web Thriller

Visit Him Online:
BrandonHughesBooks.com

Printed in Great Britain
by Amazon

58883696R00243